Тари

JUDY CORBALIS

Tapu

SINCLAIR-STEVENSON

First published in Great Britain in 1996
by Sinclair-Stevenson
an imprint of Reed International Books Ltd
Michelin House, 81 Fulham Road, London sw3 6rb
and Auckland, Melbourne, Singapore and Toronto

A CIP catalogue record for this book
is available at the British Library
HARDBACK ISBN 1 85619 339 x
PAPERBACK ISBN 1 85619 6186

Typeset by CentraCet Ltd, Cambridge
Printed and bound in Great Britain
by Clays Ltd, St Ives plc

HE TOHU WHAKAWHETAI

He mihi whakawhetai ki a Tu Kemp,
he uri no Hongi Hika ma,
mo tona tautoko aroha i ahau.
Ka mihi hoki ki taku mokopuna,
ki a Tame,
mo tana atawhai pumau.

CONTENTS

AUTHOR'S NOTE

—————

In the early 1800s, Maori was a purely oral language. The name of the great Nga-Puhi chief was transliterated into a variety of forms: Shunghie, Shungie Ika, Chonghie and Chunghie were all used by Europeans. It was not until the language was written that it crystallised into Hongi Hika. Kendall, in his *Korao No New Zealand* (1818), made the first attempts to reduce Maori to a spelling system. As the methods of writing Maori improved, many Maori words were split into syllables; the system of syllabifying became prevalent between 1818 and 1830, and was further refined and used up to the 1890s. It was used by many eminent scholars of the nineteenth century for writing or translating Maori manuscripts and oral Maori histories. The deliberate use of hyphens between syllables and words in this novel has been strongly supported by Professor Pat Hohepa, my Maori consultant, not merely because it will assist readers unfamiliar with Maori, but also because it gives greater reality and authenticity to the main characters and the times in which they lived.

ACKNOWLEDGEMENTS

Tapu is a work of fiction. Although I have researched its historical background and used real people and events as starting points, the development of both the story and its characters is purely imaginary.

I am indebted to all those listed below but I wish to thank particularly the following four people for their generous help: Professor Pat Hohepa, Professor of Maori Language, University of Auckland, my Maori consultant, who is internationally recognized by both scholars and Maori elders as an expert in Maori matters, for his valued and continuing support, for his patience with my errors and his many personal kindnesses; Dr Judith Binney of the University of Auckland whose biography of Thomas Kendall, *The Legacy of Guilt*, with its invaluable footnotes, made my own research infinitely easier; Judge Ross Maitland Russell, formerly Resident Judge of the Maori Land Court of New Zealand for the Tairawhiti District, who has been unstinting in his help, has acted as my unofficial historical consultant, has provided me with otherwise unobtainable information and allowed me constant access to his extensive library of New Zealand books; and Penelope Hoare, my editor, whose support of her authors is deeply valued. Without her encouragement, *Tapu* would never have come to fruition.

I wish I could acknowledge everyone who has helped me but that is impossible. The following people, however, gave assistance in all sorts of ways and I am very grateful to them: the librarians of the Alexander Turnbull Public Library in Wellington, Ronda

Armitage, J. A. Barnett, former Director of the British Council in Japan, Terry Barringer of the Library of the Royal Commonwealth at Cambridge University, Paul and Olive Bush, Dorothy Butler, Roger Cazalet, Professor Mike Corballis, Jim Evans, Jillian Ewart, L. E. A. Fry, the staff of the Guildhall Library, London, Wesley Harry and the staff of the Royal Arsenal at Woolwich, Ted Homewood, the late James Joll, Professor John Keane, Rosemary Keen, former archivist of the Church Missionary Society, London, Phillip King, Lambeth Palace Library, the staff of the library of the Museum of London, Margaret Mahy, Robin Myers, honorary archivist to the Worshipful Company of Stationers and Newspaper Makers, Clare Naylor, James Nicholas, W. Noblett, Keeper of Public Records at the Library of the University of Cambridge, Margaret O'Dea, Nancy Pickmere, Rayma Ritchie, the Royal Greenwich Observatory, Pam Royds of André Deutsch Children's Books, Dorothy Russell, Anthony Sheil, Judge Andrew Spencer, Resident Judge of the Maori Land Court of New Zealand for the Tai Tokerau District, Stuart Strachan, Hocken Librarian at the University of Otago, Rose Tremain, the Photography Department of the University of Cambridge, the Warburg Institute, Barbara Watson.

And my thanks to the Authors' Foundation for their grant which enabled me to gain writing time in which to complete this book.

Tapu

---

tapu – sacred, set apart, forbidden

The sun burns down into the gully. In the widest part of it the river has formed a pool, sandy-bottomed, secluded.

'Here,' says the tattooed man, throwing off his flax shoulder mat. 'Swim, eh-Keni.'

Thomas Kendall, man of God, schoolmaster, virgin nudist, looks uneasily into the dense bush on either side of the river, takes off his jacket, wrenches off his sodden collar and shirt and, after another edgy glance, makes up his mind, removes his breeches and boots and wades out behind the wide brown back of the Maori chief.

From the bush at the north side comes a shouted comment and smothered laughter. Kendall ducks under the water.

'You understood?' The chief, Shunghie, is laughing, too.

Kendall shakes his head.

'Boys,' says the chief. 'All day they have been following you, waiting to see. And now this one is calling to the others, "Yes, it is true. He is white all over."'

He looks directly at Kendall's nudity, throws back his head and laughs again and Kendall finds himself, against his will, joining in.

JANE KENDALL.

WIFE.

BORN BROCKLESBY,

LINCOLNSHIRE,

1784.

DIED NEW SOUTH WALES,

1866.

Sometimes it comes to me to wonder what me life had been if I niver seen this place. Where might I be now? Milking cows mebbee in a Lincolnshire byre?

Me mither dead, me father gone, me sister, me brother, me cousin. And I, that niver saw them again, can cry for them still and see them clear as the day they stood on the shore waving and weeping us into the distance. I didna know, had no idea, how far.

'How far?' I remembers I cried every day, every night, through all that blistering vomiting stinking heat, waiting, waiting for the first sight of land which I thought, soft wench that I were, to be same as England, Lincolnshire mebbee, transported to the other side of God's world.

But I didna cry it aloud. Tom being in hopes of ordination in the Colony, I must comport meself as the wife of a man of God.

But when they buried the Baby Kelly, tipping her over the side into the maw of the sea, no gravestone niver to mark her place nor loss, and me daughter, Susannah, cried out for her Gamma and home, I held her to me with a fierce terror that she too might be suffered by God Almighty such a fate, and inwardly I wept as hard as she for all so far and gone that I held dear.

Be not the same to love your man and child as it be to love your parents and your home. I felt meself a plant taken from the soil by me roots, shaken, then set back to grow best as I might in alien soil. And still I know, old as I be now, I niver grewed again so strong, so straight, so tall, no matter how many roots I trailed out, how long I struggled for nourriture, turning me face hopefully to these foreign heavens.

Days I thinks: Supposing, just supposing, some miracle was to happen.

In at me window comes an angel, white as Lincoln snow, and says to me, 'Jane, I'm transporting ye home. To Lincolnshire. To Brocklesby.'

And clasps me to his feathered breast and rises up and flies with me away across that fearful ocean. And the land and all the people, black, white, yellow, brown. And all them gone lost years.

In at the window of me mither's cottage.

'Hullo, our Jane,' says me mither. 'Hold skein for me, wilt tha?'

And there I stands while she winds, with me arms out, blubbering like a soft wench, yet me mither doesna notice. And out in the yard, me da and me uncle chopping chaff and little Hannah singing in the corner, 'Baa, baa, a black sheep, come on, our Jane, sing with me, sing with me.'

'Mither,' I says, but quiet. 'Mither. Listen.'

'What be going with thee, our Jane?'

'Mither, I been on a vessel and there were a Quaker lady

and she had her some oranges, so many oranges. Stored-like in her cabin for all t' voyage.'

Already I'm speaking back in me native tongue.

'And oh, Mither, she sees me a-watching at her while she peels one and "Have thee an orange, lass," she says. But I, that would die for a taste of it, the smell making me to slobber already, says, "Nay, nay thank ye, ma'am. I canna take it."

'I wanted for her to say, "Tha must. Here. 'Tis thine." Stern she looks at me. Like Mr Wood in Marylebone. "Thou liest, girl," says she. "Thou wantest very much. And yet thou deniest thy desire. So thou shalt not have the orange. Nay, thou saidest and nay is thine answer. Look thou, be truthful. Let thy yea be yea and thy nay, nay. Understandest thou?"

'"Aye, ma'am," says I, miserable-like, and guilty too.

'"Thou'rt young," says she. "Remember this. Take that which is freely offered to thee in life and do not deny the truth of thine own heart."

'"Aye, ma'am," says I and goes to the cabin and weeps and weeps.

'And, Mither, the smell of that orange, it haunted and followed me like to a will-o'-the-wisp, till she did leave the ship at Rio.'

Me mither goes on winding. 'Well, so then,' she says, 'them were her oranges. Happen she can do as she like with 'em. Nowt to cry over.'

'Be not just them oranges, Mither.'

She winds some more.

'The men,' I says. 'All dark-skinned and prick-marked and nothing on their backsides. And clubs in their hands to strike me skull swift like a eggshell.'

'Our Jane,' says me mither, laughing. 'Allus telling stories. Happen mebbee the sun heated thy brain.'

'Mebbee it did,' I says. 'Happen mebbee it did.'

I be standing on the dyke. Frosty and white and the cold biting at me ears. Samuel, me brother, poaching with us cousin, Isaac. Me shivering while I waits. A bit with cold and a bit with fright. What if he comes, the gamekeeper? What if he be just now hiding in the dyke side waiting to catch us? Hanging's the poacher's penalty. John Tindall, him with the sister with the shrivelled leg and the old, old mither, cried cockles after the last Assizes, and all for a pheasant or two.

'Made his last mistake, I reckon,' said Sam. 'Forgot the poacher's only rule. Niver take twice in the same place.'

And us been here afore. Often. Me looking and scanning in the sharp moonlight. The mud have ice in little crusts over it. But no footprints nowhere. It be quiet. Dead quiet and silent. Mebbee the grave be cold like this. Have he felt it long, John Tindall, the hempen collar a-twisting his neck as the cart were drove away? Were it the gaping hole of Hell made him to scream and kick out as he swung? Pissed hisself, and more, said Isaac. Fear mebbee. Of what he seed afore his dying eyes. Mebbee ... it were even the Messenger of Darkness shewed to him.

And as I thinks this, I looks up and sees hanging silent above me a great white short-eared owl, still as the water in the dyke. Watching me. The Devil's familiar. Watching me.

I wants to scream and run but me legs and me throat is stricken. And just then I hears a leveret call.

'Eeuubb, eeuubb.'

And a answering call. Isaac! I sucks on the back of me hand with blue lips.

'Eeuubb, eeuubb.'

Podging along the dyke's edge, sliding and slipping through the mud, Isaac and Sam raises their hands to show me five brace of pheasant and the leveret. I looks up and the owl have flown away. No gamekeeper showing neither.

'To take a pheasant,' Isaac be saying to Sam, voice clear over the water, 'don't niver seem to me the same as taking sovereigns from a rich man's pocket.'

'Seems to me,' says Sam, 'pheasants be made by God for iveryone. And poor and rich should share 'em alike.'

'Git on home,' says I. 'Don't seem like that to the gamekeeper.'

*

6

Kitchen be hot and steaming. Wet goes running down the walls from the kettle. Fire crackles hot and orange-flamed. Me whole frame shivers to get warm. All winter I dreams of heat. Sunshine gold, water in the river pool warm and silky, the feel of the sun on me back, the steamy smell of the men working in the meadow, the sweat sliding in tracks down their chests making me nostrils to tingle. I shivers again.

'Here, Mither,' says Sam, tossing their bag on to the table.

Mither raises her head from chopping onions. 'Well now,' she says mildly, showing no emotion-like. 'Better than 'edge 'ogs any day, our Sam.'

'And our Isaac,' says Isaac, making to take off the pheasants.

'And our Isaac, o' course,' says me mither. 'Goes without saying.'

She chops the onions crossways from other side of the board.

'Young Tindall,' she says careful, 'him with the sister with the leg bewitched . . .'

'Not bewitched, Mither,' says Sam. 'There's foolish talk.'

'Perfect legs both, when she were born,' says me mither, setting her face. 'Mither Alsree, it were, delivered her. Perfect, she says, and within the year the left one twists and turns and hangs there useless. Witchcraft, that were, if iver I knewed it.'

'I'll have no talk of witchcraft here,' says Father, coming into the kitchen in a cloud of cold. 'Bitter outdoors, eh, Silas?'

Me uncle pulls the door close behind them.

'Witchcraft it were and stays,' says Mither, defiant.

'I'm telling ye,' says Father, 'that be talk of daft old crones. And dangerous talk, an' all. Hush thy mouth, Mither. I'll not have witchcraft talk under this roof.'

He sights the table through his finger-blowing and stamping. 'Eh now, Mither,' he says, 'there's good for ye.'

'Wonderful good,' says me mither, slamming pots now. 'Ye with a full belly and him with a long neck,' nodding at Sam. 'Like young Tindall after the Assizes.'

But when Isaac were taken, it weren't for him the long drop off the gallows but the transportation.

7

'Botany Bay,' says me Uncle Silas, near to weeping.

'Better than dead, Silas,' says me father, quiet-like. 'This way ye've hope.'

'Hope!' says me uncle. 'Oh, indeed. If he don't die on t' voyage or in Botany. Or mebbee come home after seven long years, crazed and calloused in t' head like daft Matthew Grewn down by t' river. Be well for you, Sam not being taken. Only me Isaac.'

'Hush, man,' says me father, near to weeping hisself. 'Would ye be wanting to be sitting under the three-legged mare, then? Waiting to fight over his body? I tell ye, man, he'll be back. A strong lad be Isaac.'

Me mither gives me uncle, so I notices, the largest bowl of broth.

'Boys,' she says, 'boys. Nowt but trouble, boys.'

The angel lifts me up again. Drifts like a cloud to the thicket by Rotherton, near to the huntsman's house. Me like the owl now, hanging in the air, watching. Watching me, meself. Just as I were. And Isaac. With his hands on me.

'Nay,' says I as me other-I floats there, spying. 'Nay, our Isaac.'

'Eh, Jane, not so cruel,' says Isaac, sliding his hands down in between me bodice and me skirts. 'Tha's skin like satin.'

'Thee! When hast tha felt satin, then, Isaac Quickfall? Very grand thou art, sudden.'

His hands be making shivers in me stomach, down me back. Seems like I can feel as well as see from in between the folds and feathers of me angel. Me nipples be hot. Nice. 'Stop it. I needs get back.'

'Ah,' coos Isaac in me neck. 'Tha wants me, Jane. Tha knows it.'

'Nay,' says I, meaning aye. 'I does not. Stop it now, our Isaac, or I tells Sam.'

His face is in me hair. 'Tha smells of Daisy.'

'Moooo,' I says, silly with how I feels. Like I wants him to go on but knows I shouldna.

Clatter of the flesh-cart clipping by. Us sinks down low and silent into the ditch. Isaac puts a hand across me mouth. Driver do dismount, clump so near to where us be, I trembles.

Then I hears the sound of a carcass being dragged, flung on to the cart, the cut of the whip, and us breathes again easy.

Isaac slides his hand from me mouth. Further down. Moves it forwards.

'Nay,' says I, pulling at it. 'Dinna.' Thinking: What if I were bleeding and he done that?

'Dinna,' I says again and something in me voice stops him.

'I loves thee,' he says, a bit rough.

'Tha'rt teasing me, Isaac.'

'Nay, Jane. Niver. I does. I wants thee.'

And I realises sudden that hard lump digging into me upper belly be his. Like the rams when they comes into the ewes' field to cover them. Ram rod. And the men laughing and me father saying to me uncle, 'Eh, Silas, they be lucky. All they wants, wheriver they wants. And no need even to take off their breeches afore they be inside.'

I snatches meself away from Isaac and runs and runs back to the dairy, towards me mither and home.

'Come back,' cries Isaac. 'Come back. Tha mustna leave me, Jane.'

But I be gone so fast that, as I stumbles back over the fields to safety, I runs right into Milady and her daughters a-carrying their sketchbooks and easels, and I trips and sprawls in front of them.

'There's a great tumble, to be sure,' says Milady. 'Raise her up, girls.'

And, one on each side, they does. I drops a curtsy as I mumbles me apology.

'No matter,' says Milady, 'but surely, miss, you should be in the dairy at this hour?'

'Aye, Milady,' says I, 'but I were a-taking the curds to Lower Dyke to the huntsman's house and be only now come back.'

'In fear of the bull chasing you, it seems,' says Milady. Her girls laughs. 'And is your mother recovered?'

'A little, Milady,' says I.

9

'Please to tell her we miss her at the Hall,' says Milady. 'Soan has not such a hand with the fine linen.'

'Aye, Milady,' says I, waiting to be dismissed.

'That will be all, girl,' says Milady.

'Thank you, Milady.'

'But remember,' she says,' if you really must run and tumble about the fields, be sure not to venture by the dykes. Lord Pelham and the keepers are just now setting man-traps there against the poachers. It would never do to have those fine black curls torn out in a trap.'

I puts me hand to me cap. 'Nay, Milady,' says I. 'But, Milady, I be no poacher meself.'

'No, indeed,' says her ladyship. 'I am sure not. The running deer, not the huntsman.'

Her round owl's eyes rests on me a second, unblinking. Me back stiffens. Do she mebbee know I been with Sam and Isaac all along the dykes? I feels a brush of fear and hears a far-off scream, the echo of a keening, a man snapped in the jaws of a man-trap, locked thrashing like a giant bird in the tangles of the keepers' net. The poacher poached.

I shakes it away out of me head.

'Aye, Milady,' says I. 'Thank you, Milady.'

'Off you go, then.'

So I curtsies and I goes. Back to the cool dairy, the warm white milk and the grunting chewing heavy-eyed cows. And red-hot thoughts of Isaac heaving in me head, tightening and hardening me hand so much I grips and pinches Daisy and she stamps and kicks at me, blowing her grievance over me in sour grass-stinking breath.

It falls out strange how the world do go. I, that has said farewell to Isaac for iver – it being that none of us shall nivermore see him after he be took away to Botany – has found, within a seven year, Tom and all us bairns and me, meself, five months gone with me sixth, bound for that same far-off land. On the transport ship *Earl Spencer*. Different vessel, same cargo.

Like to following Isaac. Be as if I be bound, whether I

would or nay, to come behind him where he were gone. Just as I done so often afore, trailing after while he were poaching all along the edges of the dykes.

Nowt of Tom's folk to say farewell but all of mine be down to London to see us on us way. And Sam on his own come early, afore the others, spoke to me special.

'It be Isaac, ye must know, I comes about.'

I knew it well.

'Ye must find where he be in Botany and send word. Nowt have Uncle Silas heard. Dying, he be, from the grief of it, our Jane. Thee must find Isaac, then send by some person on a ship to give word to us. Silas believes he be dead, belike of fever or the chain-gang labour.'

'And what if he do be dead?' says I. 'What then?'

'Find out his grave and send word of that at least. Better for Silas even that intelligence than nowt.'

'Sam,' says I, trembling. 'I canna do it.'

Sam looks at me, deep and cold. 'Why so?'

'It be Tom, Sam. He wants to be ordained in Botany. He must be, to do God's work. But if the Church knows he be related to a transport . . .'

'God loves Heathens but not convicts, did ye say, our Jane?'

'Nay, Sam. But it be hard for Tom, ye must understand.'

'It be hard for Uncle Silas. Dost *ye* understand?'

'Me meself, I does, ye knows that, Sam. I loves Isaac like to me own brother. But Tom . . .'

'I sees how much tha loves Isaac. Glad I am it be not me, thy true brother, in Botany, Jane. Long time I mebbee waiting for Christian charity from thee.'

And takes both cap and coat and leaves.

And me chasing after down the street. 'Stop. Tha must stop, Sam. Wait.'

By the corner he do stop. 'Nowt to say, Jane. Mebbee some day tha'll come back. Thee or Isaac. For Mither's sake, tomorrow I shall wave thee off. But not for thee.'

'Please, Sam,' says I, pleading-like, 'truce. Let me talk it more with Tom and come to thee this evening. Truce, our Sam. Please.'

'Talk with Tom Kendall!' he says, his face hard set. 'Great good would that do, lass. No truce, our Jane, no truce.'

And he do turn the corner and be gone from me. For iver.

I seen him on the morrow in the distance with the others on the dock, blurred by the wind and spray and me own salt tears. And as us stood by the rail, waving, waving, all I iver knewed or held dear in me life shrunk first to thimble size, then to little pinheads and finally were lost in the fog closing thick about us.

Us journey to Botany seemed to me then nearest I might iver come to Hell. Like sailing with the Damned, it were, that voyage, and niver could I bear again to suffer it. And Botany and Parramatta, them long-awaited shores, strange and alien to me with niver one face I knewed nor voice that sounded Home. But for Tom. And him taken up most days with fixing for us Mission to New Zealand with Reverend Marsden.

First off I hated him, Mr Marsden. Airs and graces. Fat, shiny face. Little eyes that put me so in mind of Nancy, me mither's prize saddleback. Ate like Nancy, too, anything that come his way and often. So no wonder how his neck hung low across his collar. Wanted to find me out in sin, did Mr Marsden. Many and many a day I feels him watching, waiting for me to confess some wickedness that he might prove his goodness by offering me his pardon.

He couldna abide that Tom might mebbee have his own thoughts and ideas and not always same as Mr Marsden's.

'Obedience, Mr Kendall, was the virtue of Christ's apostles,' I recalls him saying time after time when Tom were arguing the Scriptures and Marsden pressed to hold his temper with him. 'Obedience.'

And Tom struggling hard to bite his lip and keep it back, the thought that were bursting to break free.

I seen the first of the natives in New South Wales. In Parramatta. By the Marsdens' meadow out beyond the vegetable garden. Not the savages of the Colony, which was different, but the ones of New Zealand.

In all them times, when Tom have seen the Light, when he be talking about doing the Lord's work, being ordained and such, I knowed us would be in another place. But with folk which waited only for the Word to enter their lives and transform their Heathen spirits. And in me head, they was white folk, mebbee poor folk – even, it could be, evil – but folk who looked like Tom and me, lived in hovels mebbee, might sleep rough upon their streets, in some strange far-off country. And all the way upon that journey, Tom and me, us talked of them, of the great work us be going to do in the Lord's name, and us thought and prayed for them poor savages at the other side of the world waiting only for the Saviour to come to their open hearts.

Us was wrong. So wrong it do shake me still to remember.

Some of them Heathen be staying at Parramatta, at the Mission House. The sons of chiefs or chiefs theirselves, they was, but gone on some journey along the coast when us arrived, me daughters wobbling crooked on their legs on the dry land. And me, nearly nine months gone with yet another, aching for to be off that tossing crowded vessel. Natives was the last thing in me mind. Only a bed, a table, fields and land around me, trees, birdsong, the world staying still in the one place for a time.

Hot, it were, and wet, and the infant kicking and raging in me like the sea itself. Only Thomas Surfleet smiled and run steady in this new land. A good sailor, our Thomas. Loves the ocean with the passion of a native, but not from me, his mither. I has a fear of the sea. For months I has felt it waiting, heaving below us, ready to snatch and haul us down, changing its face from calm to waves to breakers as the ship crashed or slid or fluttered across its surface. Mither, unless that the angel brung me, I niver could face again that terrible journey.

First days at Parramatta all I did be sleep. Hot, it were, like I niver knew afore. Great belly on me so huge, no matter how I shifted, turned, composed meself, I took me sleep in short

13

uncomfortable draughts and half-dozed between times. All five bairns was put by Mrs Marsden in care of her nursery maid. A transport, she was, a trusty, but, for all that, a slattern such as I seen afore in Shoreditch, back to the wall, waiting to take a quick penny. I wouldna have such to mind me own children. Put them in Sannah's charge, I did, and nowt said to Mrs Marsden.

'But why not leave them with Mary?' she asks, next day.

I be up and awake, almost able to walk for five minutes together without that the earth rises below me, hurling and swelling like the sea.

'Nay, ma'am,' says I. 'Better them with me. Still strange, they be.'

'Take rest while you can, Mrs Kendall. Soon enough you'll have another.'

But I stays firm. Lets them play where I can see them, in the garden under the queer purple tree.

Two days more and I be well enough to eat at midday with her and the children, though not yet at supper with Tom and Reverend Marsden and her two eldest girls.

And the next day after, I heaves meself round Mrs Marsden's rose garden at her special request.

Mrs Marsden were partial to them roses. They amounted to a kind of currency in her mind and she told all us that was trapped at the Mission and anyone else minded to listen, over and over, how the old king had his roses, the Prince of Wales had his, Lady Wilkington of Ilminster, where she come from as a girl, had hers and she, Reverend Marsden's wife, had her little rose collection too. It did seem they made her elevated in her own mind, them few sorry bushes, struggling for water and the shade.

'The scent,' says she, inhaling from a dark-red bloom and sighing far down in her bosom. 'The glorious, glorious scent.' She closes her eyes a moment, then, 'Smell, Mrs Kendall,' she instructs me, 'the very whiff of England.'

I arcs forward over me huge lump and puts me nose to a wizened petal. Little, it be, more like to a nut flower than a rose, but the hard sun have made it to smell forty times its size. And suddenly I be blown like a summer cloud back into me mither's skirts, peeping from below her at the proud and pretty ladies clustered in the gardens of the Big Hall while she do carry clotted cream from the dairy for that night's pudding for them all. And Miss Pelham, seeing me, picks me a red rose, thrusts it into me baby-fat hand and, 'Take it, child,' she says. 'Smell.' But I, overcome, pricks me finger on the thorn on its stalk and wails and buries me head into the skirts while Mither do lift the rose from the ground and takes it back home and puts it into a dairy jar. Where it do make the room to smell for all of a week.

And what me heart cries out for now be Mither and Brocklesby and home. But Mrs Marsden, head on one side, watching, warbles, waits for me to praise.

'Be beautiful,' I mutters.

'Dear Lady Wilkington is quite taken with the pink variety but I incline to Queen Charlotte's tastes and favour the deeper reds.'

'Yes, ma'am,' says I.

'The watering,' says she, 'is much of a chore, but Stockwell has two transports just for the fetching and carrying and he assures me the roses will survive. Nay, flourish.'

'Stockwell, ma'am?'

'A trusty, Mrs Kendall. You will see him engaged in the garden work. He has a great understanding of the roses.'

I feels meself tiring. 'Belike,' I says, 'I may go inside, ma'am. This one be taking me strength from me.'

'It is the heat,' says she kindly. 'They tell that it is cooler in New Zealand. The winds blow more and the sun is softer.'

'You has been there, ma'am?'

'No, not I myself. Nor my husband either. He sails with you for his first visit. But the black fellows who come from there to the Mission tell us it is milder in their land.'

'There be North Cape black fellows here? At the Mission?'

'Indeed,' says she. 'Sons and daughters of the chiefs. But do not trouble yourself with that, Mrs Kendall. They come nowhere near this part of the house. They are here to learn of Christianity and the love of God.'

'But how be it they understands the Bible, ma'am, if they be black fellows?'

'Ah, now in that,' says Mrs Marsden, tossing her head for the wonder of it, 'they are remarkably quick to learn. Several of them speak already passing well in English, God's own tongue, as we tell them. And they are greatly desirous of learning of the love and salvation of their Saviour. Miss Marsden and Miss Charlotte have made it their most particular duty to show them, by precept and example, the generosity and loving-kindness of the true Christian nature. My daughters are much engaged upon the conversion of the Heathen Maori.'

She bends low over a rose, makes a clicking noise of her teeth and tongue. 'Worm,' says she. 'And see, here too. I must speak with Stockwell. Go in, Mrs Kendall, and take your rest.'

I bids her farewell till tea time and sets off to take in Basil and Joseph to rest with me and to put the others in care of Sannah. Mrs Marsden disappears to the orchard. And as I be nearing the purple-flowered tree, from out the bushes near to the vegetable garden comes a man.

'Jane,' he says to me, quiet-like, gentle, 'Jane Quickfall.'

I starts with shock. 'I niver afore set eyes on thee,' says I, 'so how dost know me name?'

I were aware of me belly, pushing out in front like some great house cow. Full, I were, to bursting with what I knew to be another Hannah, me dragging body clumbering in the heat.

He drops down his voice so I strains to hear him. 'Jane Quickfall, Mrs Kendall, I must speak with you alone.' An educated man. I hears it clear from his speech.

'Mither!' calls Sannah. 'Come here, Mither. Boys is fighting and Thomas Surfleet—'

'Hush,' cries I. 'Wait.' And low I says, 'But, sir . . .'

'Take care,' he says. 'Behind you comes Mrs Marsden. Speak of the roses. Quickly.'

'Them do smell most wonderful,' says I, very loud.

'Come tomorrow,' he whispers, 'to the vegetable garden.'

'Stockwell,' says Mrs Marsden, approaching, 'there is *worm* in the roses. And I fear it is taking hold. You must come and look now. Immediately.'

'Mrs Kendall,' he says, 'was kind enough, mistress, to commend their scent to me.'

'Ah,' says she, 'such scent I never knew.'

And she makes away with him to the roses whilst I collects and sorts me bairns with thumping heart. Who be he? What do he have to tell me? Long time it be till tomorrow, thinks I.

The more something be wanted, the more it do go away. The rest of that day dragged like I niver knew afore.

At four o'clock it seemed it were midnight. Five o'clock and Tom be coming from Reverend Marsden's daily sessions of instruction, stoked up and keen.

'Well, Jane?' says he. 'No change?' He places a soft hand on me belly.

'Nay,' says I, almost snapping at him, 'not yet. But this heat do try me, Tom. Tomorrow, I needs must walk a bit.'

'A walk?' says he. 'But, Janey, where will you walk here?'

'The garden,' says I. 'Where else be there in this frightful place?'

'It may be Mrs Marsden will not like you walking in her garden. Now. So close to your time.'

'It came to me,' I lies, 'that mebbe I might be looking to see what vegetables flourishes in this vile heat and dust. I needs know for the growing of such at New Zealand.'

He pats me head. 'Time enough, dear Jane, when you have little Hannah safely delivered.'

'Nay,' I says. 'I be fretting cooped up here, Tom. Do you to mind the bairns for me tomorrow morning? Just an hour. Please, Tom. Me heart be set on it.'

'But I must be at morning prayers, and sawyer's instructions after.'

'*Sawyer's* instructions? Why so? You be the schoolmaster in New Zealand.'

'No sawyer, no smithy, no cooper, no carter where we are going, Jane. At New Zealand, in Rangi-Houa, all must be done by us, ourselves.'

I stares at him. 'No carter?'

'The natives have no carts. They do not know the wheel. They travel on foot and by water.'

'On horseback?'

'No horses there either. So says Mr Marsden. And the horse that the chief, Tuai, took back last year perished at sea. Just as well, too, since they had neither hay nor grass to feed the poor creature.'

'If they had nowt of hay nor grass, why, then, have he took it? Or Mr Marsden give it?'

'To keep the chief in humour, he gave it. And for prestige and honour, so he says, it was demanded. The chief had a notion he would learn to ride on its back and terrify his enemies by appearing on it in battle.'

'What battle?' I feels cold for the first time since I has come here.

'A battle of no consequence. Some silly squabble amongst themselves. No fears. Nothing to do with us, Janey. We are their friends and brothers in Christ. Mr Marsden has assured me of it.'

'But Mrs Marsden says Mr Marsden niver were there. At New Zealand. So how do he know?'

'By the talk and demeanour of the Maoris here. I have been this very day, and yesterday too, in their company. Most awesome and inspiring I find them. Healthy, strong fellows and quick to learn. One of them is the son of the chief of the Northern parts. Nga-Puhi is his tribe. And he shows a talent for smithying that would be remarkable even in an Englishman.'

'But how may you talk with them?'

'Why, in our own tongue. They are some of them already conversant with English and sent here by their fathers to learn more. Their desire to come to God is an inspiration to us.'

'If Reverend Marsden were niver there, what have made them to come here?'

'Ships putting in at their coasts in need of supplies of food and water. Whale hunters and sealing men.'

'Tom Kendall,' says I, 'whaling and sealing men I seen

many and many a time in Grimsby. And niver no talk of God nor Jesus save in their oaths. The pox they brung, and the slinging hook, but Salvation, niver.'

Tom laughs. 'Nay, Janey. You are right. But the chiefs, says Mr Marsden, saw quickly it was to their own advantage to trade pig and fish and their sweet potato. And for that they need language, knowledge, translators. They came to Botany on the traders' ships and here they found, as well, the knowledge of the Lord. God moves in a mysterious way, Janey.'

'Oh aye,' says I. 'And what gets the blackfellows from the trading?'

'Axes. Which they prize. And nails, blankets, clothing. One of them sports, they say, a top hat and tail coat but no breeches or shoes. Rum, as well. And guns.' His face clouds over. 'Muskets they covet above all things.'

'They has powder?'

'Only what they can trade for. Or find in Botany. But it is a flogging offence to supply them. In their fighting they use their own native spears and jade clubs.'

'Mebbee,' says I, uneasy now, 'they will fight near to us.'

'No,' says Tom. 'We are safe in the power of the Lord.'

Tom be excited and fired up. Thoughts of God in his head. I knows it from afore. And always, in that mind, he comes hot for me. This one I begot in that red passion he brung home after the London Mission desired him. Now he pulls off his shoes, breeches, shirt, throws himself down beside me, runs his hand on me sweaty breasts, huge and ugly with blue knotted veins starting out from their sides.

'Not tomorrow; *now*, tonight,' he breathes. 'Hast room in there for me, Janey?'

'Nowt for a blade of grass, Tom Kendall,' says I. 'Not so much as a fine bone splinter could I fit in there. But tomorrow, if I walks, it mebbee Hannah unsticks herself from me and joins us. More trouble, this one, than all five others together.'

And as I says it, I feels how true it be, how this one I canna love, not like the others. This one be alien to me, a foreigner.

The others has all felt part of me, meself. This one be different. An intruder. She belongs to that great wild water which have flung us here at Botany and Parramatta.

'Tomorrow,' says Tom, 'I will go to prayers, then come back to gather the children and take them to the sawyer's yard. And you may have your walk.'

He clutches at me side, rubs his face across me skin, then slides his hand down to me hairy tufts. At which, Hannah do kick him hard in the belly, and us laughs so long me thoughts slides away on a swell of mirth just like in old times afore Tom were took by the Lord and Salvation.

Something in them, these godly folk, do stir and worry at me. Something not so good, not of angels but of devils. Like a watching, a reckoning, a coldness at the centre. A hard underbelly has these clericals, and I has yet to see a one of them that be elevated also to be poor.

'Be Christ-like,' says Mr Wood of Marylebone, who be hisself not a sawyer, nor do give none of his goods to the poor and who wears fine clothes and keeps a hearty table and a wife also dressed in best muslin and bonnets of fashion. And quick, so quick, each of them be to sit in judgement one on the other and his neighbour also.

I thinks of that first sight of Mrs Marsden by the river's edge at Parramatta. Seen from far off as the ship come drifting down the current, she were a black crow in skirts, but as I were lifted down on me chair into the little bum-boat she changed as her face come visible. Shivered, I did, afeared she might suddenly turn into a sparrer hawk, rise into the air and fly over the water to peck out the eyes of them she took against. Hooked set of lips, nose like a beak, and two eyes beading on either side of that nose. Black hair flattening round her face and scraggled into a knot at the back inside her bonnet.

And I knewed deep, deep inside meself, whativer Tom might believe, whativer God Hisself might believe, this were not Salvation nor nowt near the path to it, neither. I seen her face, a hawk waiting for rabbits, like I seen a hundred times afore at home and I knewed, and right well, this were no best place for me and mine. Whativer might be at New Zealand, I feared it less then than I feared Reverend Marsden and his wife, with faces that might destroy the hearts of all small fieldmice such as I.

Morning, I seeks out Mrs Marsden. She be giving instructions on dusting of the parlour to two of her transport servants. All that red earth so fine comes into the house over and over. Swab the floor at noon and by evening the dust be creeping and swirling gently back indoors again.

'I has a mind to walk in the garden, if you please, ma'am,' says I. 'It will mebbee bring me to me time.'

So engaged be she in her battle with the Parramatta soil, she barely heeds me. 'I cannot yet accompany you. Perhaps in half an hour . . .'

'Nay, ma'am,' says I, hasty. 'A fancy has I taken to smell again them roses. They do ease me sickness.'

She be gratified indeed. ''Tis true, Mrs Kendall, as Lady Wilkington so often observed at Home, that the scent of the rose is a very balm to the spirit and the body.'

'Aye, ma'am.'

'I shall search you out when I have completed my duties here.'

'Thank you, ma'am.'

And I escapes as fast as it be possible dragging such a cumbrous weight inside meself.

Out I sways, past the purple tree, past the roses, and turns to where lies the kitchen garden with vegetables in rows and four small lines of stunted, dried-up apple trees. At its far end I sees him, the convict, plying a hoe, boots and breeches' bottoms earth-red, sweat trickling down his shirt, which sticks already to his back though it be but early and the heat of day hardly risen up. I be unsure if I should come near to him or even if he have seen I be there. Then it comes to me: he be slowly advancing down the row towards me, a-flicking with his hoe at this weed, that dry leaf. I keeps me eyes fixed on the hoe, me heart jumping behind me swollen breasts. Hammering inside me head be the one question: I niver afore seed him, so how do he know me name?

Closer and closer comes the scritching of the hoe. Yet he dinna look once at me.

I canna stand it more. 'Good morning, Mr Stockwell,' says I.

'Good morning, ma'am.'

I waits uneasily. The heat be pressing at me, the soil below me boots burns up through their soles, and nowt of respite, neither.

He speaks so low, I barely hears his voice.

'Follow me. Observe what I do and say nothing. Not a word. Look only at my labours with the greatest attention you may command. Take regard of Mrs Marsden. If she should appear, speak not at all to me but to her only; convey your most urgent and fervent wish to learn the cultivation skills required for a garden such as this.'

'Thinks thee I knows not how to plant?'

'Hush. Indeed I do not. But here the soil is dry and water difficult to transport. Utilize this to your own ends that you may be permitted to come here to meet with me again.'

'But—'

'I urge you silence, ma'am. Listen well. The message I have for you is from your cousin. Isaac Quickfall.'

'*Isaac!*'

'He that was transported.' He regards me a moment with a look of pity.

'Quick, tell me! Be Isaac alive?'

'Alive, he is.' He moves along the row. 'Come, follow me. We should not speak at all but, if we are observed from the orchard or the house, we must seem to be engaged in discussion of planting matters. His body is strong though weakened by the chain-gang work. But his mind—'

'Chain gang! Why be thou here and Isaac on a chain gang?'

'Hush, Mrs Kendall. Keep yourself calm, your hands still. Stare at the earth, I beg you. No good will come to Isaac if you betray the subject of our discourse.'

'Where be he?'

22

'By night in the barracks. By day, working where he and the others are taken.'

'Why be he not here? At the Mission. Like thee.'

'Isaac, you are aware, has a hasty tongue, a quick and sudden temper.' He sighs. 'Life in Botany, Mrs Kendall, is a gamble.'

'Jane. Tha must call me Jane.'

'By no means can I, Mrs Kendall. It would be your undoing. And my own. Life here, depend on it, hangs upon favour, privilege. Offence to the wrong man, insubordination, imagined slights: all these grow out of proportion in such a place. The imagined becomes real, the lesser, greater, and—' He falls, of a sudden, to his knees to root out with his hands a withered stump. 'Mrs Marsden approaches.'

It were indeed that terrible lady, large and savage, moving towards us. 'You are there, Mrs Kendall,' cries she, a mastiff scenting an escaped prisoner. A little dribble hangs upon her lip. 'I feared you had fallen amongst the roses. It is surely too hot for a lady in such delicate condition to be out?'

The convict trusty pulls and tugs upon the stump. Of his mistress he gives niver a sign of recognition.

'It do indeed be hot, ma'am,' stammers I. 'Hotter than iver I knewed in Lincolnshire. But here I sees one engaged in growing vittals and I must learn the way of the soil of this New World.'

I hardly knows meself what I blethers but Mrs Marsden do seem content with it.

'Why,' she answers, civil, 'time enough for that, surely, when your infant has been delivered.'

'Ma'am,' I stumbles, and why, but that I knows somewhere in me heart I must find what more he have to say to me, this convict, Stockwell, with his speech of a gentleman, his talk of our Isaac, 'to bring a suckling out into air so torrid . . .'

'True,' she says. She pauses and her large drooped eyes grows wet upon the edges. 'Two have I already buried, safe in God's keeping, there in the churchyard. Boys, both. Not so strong a hold on life as girls.'

For a minute, I feels the hand of pity at me heart. 'Hard to lose a little one,' says I.

'God's will,' says she. 'The Lord giveth and the Lord taketh away. And six others, all strong and healthy, has the Reverend Marsden got upon me. The Lord is good.'

She falls quiet.

'I were thinking, Mrs Marsden,' says I, seizing me chance while part of me be marvelling at the thought of Mr Marsden occupied in such a business with his wife. 'At Brocklesby, the head cowman did say I were wondrous in me touch with the udders. And quick to learn, too, so he did tell me father. Mebbee I might watch this gentleman at his work and take some useful instruction for New Zealand.'

Mrs Marsden takes me arm, leads me to one side. She purses up her mouth, a drawstring bag. 'Ah, Mrs Kendall, such a country wench you are. Stockwell is a transport, a convict, albeit a trusty. He can no longer be considered to be a gentleman. By the charity of my husband, he is permitted to work here at the Mission. But Satan pulls us down, so often by our brightest gifts. I must warn you, he is a dangerous man. His crime is the spreading of sedition.'

I bends me face to the nature of her indignation though I knows not what she means.

'Oh, aye,' says I.

Stockwell be hoeing and pulling, tossing aside roots and weeds, hoeing again. Sweat do glimmer across his chest and the shirt be fast to his back. Of a sudden me thoughts springs away to Isaac under the Lincoln sun, back bent so, hard muscles shewing so, sinewed under his shirt.

Stockwell straightens, rubs at his back, lays down the hoe against a tree and clears his throat.

'Something troubles you, Stockwell?'

'It is the roses, ma'am. If you will observe the tiny holes, you will see that the worm appears to be a caterpillar.'

And as she be bent down over a bush, peering, he looks full at me, shapes his mouth and silent says, 'Tomorrow morning, here,' making with his hand a motion to the spot and nodding, then says aloud, 'If it is a caterpillar, we must search for and destroy any chrysalises we may find before it takes a hold and spreads itself.'

'Indeed, Stockwell, indeed. See to it as your priority task.'

'Reverend Marsden was most minded I should look to the vegetables as soon as may be, ma'am.'

'Fiddle the Reverend's wishes,' snaps she. 'It must be the caterpillar that is of first concern. Indeed, if it were to spread to all the vegetables, Reverend Marsden would be lamenting loud and long.'

'Then I shall begin here at the source of the problem tomorrow, whence to the vegetables and Mistress Kendall's instruction,' and he bows politely to me, 'and following, back to the roses.'

'And be sure to instruct Mrs Kendall also in the detection of the caterpillar. I should be distracted to think it might be carried to New Zealand.'

Mrs Marsden takes me arm and steers me great bulk away across the garden.

'Do you to go indoors and rest. Your complexion is quite ruddy with the heat.'

'I thanks thee,' says I, going in.

And now I canna take me thoughts of Isaac from me head. Up he do rise afore me: seems I be back with him in Brocklesby and all here have fallen away.

I be again far from the dairy where I has that morning set the curds, then been sent off with a heavy jar of skimmings for the puppies in the kennels yard. And after, sent by me father, head kennelman and prouder of them pups than iver he have been of any us when new-born infants, or so do say me mither, with a message to his lordship. That the other bitch have whelped but her runt be sickening and seeming very poorly.

And Milord being out upon the turnip fields with his overseer, I finds meself near Lower Dyke.

And it being that I needs must piss, I squats beside the thicket, none being by to see, then raises up and shakes me skirt about, the better to dry me fanny.

And starts with shock when out from the thicket do come a man. Our Isaac.

'Isaac! Tha frighted me.'

'I seen thee at the field. Followed behind thee, half a mile and more.'

'A-walking in the dyke?'

'Aye, the better to be not seen.'

'By me?'

'Nay. By his lordship.'

He comes towards me. 'None there be here but thee and I, Jane.'

I looks about. Me heart do beat and brush like owls' wings.

A silence falls between us. Something in the air do wait. Stir me. I feels in want of space, though all around be nowt but empty vastness.

'I be on me way back to the dairy.'

Times when us has ate cream, there being extra and Mither sent a stoneware jar of it by the dairyman with Milady's compliments, I feels how the cream do stick to me throat and cloak it as it slips down. Clots me voice for a long time after.

Isaac's voice be clotted now but no cream smears to his mouth. I has looked to see. And he, that catches me look, takes from it another meaning.

'Tha knows tha wants me, Jane.'

I canna deny it so I turns to go, the owl fluttering harder in me breast. But Isaac be too quick. He seizes me from behind, clasps his arms about me. His breath be hot on me neck, warm and sweet as hay as it billows round me. I be breathing his breath.

His left hand strokes me breast, kneading it like to bread, and he rubs his chin across me hair.

'I canna, Isaac.'

'Tha must.'

And I turns to him, sinks me face in his sweaty, salty chest. And then he have pulled me to the ground and the lump in his breeches hard as me mither's pestle as he grabs me hand and pushes it there for me to feel.

A hotness comes between me own legs, empty wet heat,

like I be the missing mortar, and me own chest pounding and heaving. And Isaac, fumbling with his breeches' fastening, swears, then hauls down the front of them. And puts me hand on his dangler, naked now and huge and slimy-wet, drops oozing from the little slit in its end.

Then he lies hisself atop me, kisses me mouth and eyes and whispers in creamy words how he loves me, how I be his wife, be his foriver.

It be harder than I thinks for him to get within me. Gets me skirt about me waist but slips pushing hisself inside and takes a hold on his dangler hisself and raises up, face red and panting, groaning his desire.

And I, half-dying for what he be doing, half-afeared, feels his great ram-rod push deep in and a pain like to tearing, then rawness, as he thrusts and thrusts and gives a final groan, then drops his head against me, shuddering and gasping.

I lays with his heavy weight upon me. Wet seeps out between me thighs. The sky above me be the same but I can niver now again be what I were afore.

I likes it more the next time, in safety, in the darkness of night in the grazing fields. And the time following.

And the time after, I surprises Isaac, slipping into bed beside him in the forenoon, one ear cocked for Mither from the Hall, when he be laid low with fever and a poultice to his chest.

Seems he be even hotter for me with a fever than without.

At Parramatta, mebbee half of four next morning, I wakes with a pain in me belly, dragging, tearing, low. I feels the lump that be Hannah stiffen and rise to a mountain peak, quiver with the swell of pain, then sink back to softness for a time, rise and harden again. Five has I delivered already. I knows what be doing with me. A kind of pleasure seizes me in the midst of the hurt, a great desire to be free, be mistress of me own body again, throw from me this other, this dead weight, fling out from me this thing that have caused me to turn into nowt but a great beast of burthen. I touches meself down there with me finger and blood shews. Today, then. A great wave of relief comes rising up in me. And then I remembers.

Today I must speak more with Stockwell, him that be known to Isaac. Had it in me head to shake Tom, asleep so deep beside me, but now I does not. With each shudder, each little mounding, I stays me cry, holds tighter to meself and wills meself be up and dressed, bonneted and in the garden. 'Wait now, Hannah,' says I silently, bent double of a sudden as she strikes me while I tries to tie me bodice. And she lies mute, ebbing and flowing as she will, like to that great sea on which she have travelled here.

Five o'clock now and hot already. Blowflies buzzing at the window, air thick with the promise of heat, the wind sluggish and falling, dying before it have blown anything of coolness to us inside. Thick stink in the air too. The flowers here smells too heavy, too much, so that the breeze do cloy with it.

Tom wakes as I puts on me bonnet. 'Where are you going, Janey?' Starts to toss off the cover and pull on his clothes.

'Nay, nay,' says I. 'Early still, it be. Go back to sleep.'

'But why . . .?'

'Out for air. Hard to breathe for me. Hannah have all me space. Just leave me walk in the garden a little and take a time from Sannah and Lizzie and me boys. Soon enough I be held captive by this new one. Belike I wants quiet and rest.'

'Lie down then, Janey. I will rub thy back.'

'Nay. It be air and breath I needs.'

And I slips through the window to the verandah and disappears to the garden before he can say me nay. Behind I hears Joseph's whine: 'Mumma, Mumma, Mummaaaa.' And Tom's voice rumbling low in answer.

Morning be the best time here. In Brocklesby, I loves the gloaming falling gently over the meadows, softening the voices of the lambs, silencing the hounds' bark, throwing a blanket on the human sounds from the grounds of the Hall. Believed in God, I did, in the early nights of Lincolnshire afore I knowed the sea.

It comes to me Stockwell be not here. Me heart goes down at this and I stares around me. Everything be different in the early morning, silent, waiting. Earth have another smell to it. Softer-like. I heaves meself towards the vegetable garden and spies him at the roses, cutting and pruning off dead heads and stalks. I thinks I makes no sound but he hears me behind him just the same. Turns. 'You are very early, Mrs Kendall. I was not expecting you yet.' And at this, Hannah gives a heave and hardens and I must pause for me breath, panting a little, overtaken by pain for a space.

'You are at your time. You should not be here.'

'Tell me,' I says between little gasps, 'what tha hast to say more of Isaac.'

'I hardly know how to tell you, a lady in your condition ...' He collects himself. 'Mrs Kendall, be mindful of your situation. Come. We shall go to the vegetable garden at speed. Should Mrs Marsden take it into her head to come out, we are doing only what she has agreed to, though somewhat earlier than she had in mind.'

I follows behind him. He stops by the carrot plantings.

'The seeds, Mrs Kendall, if planted in the coolest part of the day and sluiced with water, have most chance of germination here.'

I nods.

'By placing leaves like this, so, across the top, a little shelter is provided from the heat. Then another fine sprinkling of soil, here, in this way, and more protection from this murdering sun. If Mrs Marsden should appear, ask loudly of the problems of shortages of water.'

'Aye.'

Another swell of pain takes me. I breathes hard, then stops a moment to let the spasm be. Stockwell looks anxious at me.

'You should not be outside. You will be brought to bed today.'

'By nightfall, so I thinks. But tell me, sir, of Isaac.'

He hesitates over his hoe.

'I would you tell me and true. Better what I knows than what I dreams.'

'Perhaps.' He looks at me, grave and serious. 'You have seen the women here, at Parramatta?'

29

'The transports?'

'Yes.'

'Trollops and jades, all. Her that be the nurserymaid Milord Pelham would not have to drive his flesh-cart.'

'Some are better but most are as you say. And so it is with the men. Those that were not depraved before become so.'

'Depraved?'

'Men of ill repute. Wild men. Desperate men. And what have they to lose here in this hell hole?'

'Th'art not depraved?'

'Some of us are made a different way. I am a man of thought and speech; Isaac is a man of action. It is harder for the men of action. And Isaac . . .'

'He be your friend?'

'I knew him before, in Norwich and in Lincoln. When I would go to Lincoln, we would meet from time to time in The Butcher's Arms. Many a fat rabbit have I had from Isaac.'

'Then tha knows Sam, me brother?'

'Indeed, I do. A fine good specimen of a man.'

But at thought of Sam, me face do cloud. Stockwell mistakes it for the infant. Which have caught me already several hard blows, but that I must hear more of Isaac and be not showing the pain.

'It be nothing. Gone now. Tell me.'

'This is very hard for me to say to you. Isaac has become . . . different. More . . . fixed in his ideas. He has the notion – forgive me, Mrs Kendall: I know not how to put this better – that he must see you, that indeed . . . he is your true husband and Mr Kendall a usurper.'

'But how do he know I be in Botany?'

'In Botany, everyone knows all that takes place. Gossip and rumour spread fast in such a small inward-looking colony. Every ship and her company, all that come from Home, are remarked on and discoursed about by all. And Mr Marsden himself announced your arrival from the pulpit. The new missionaries of God.'

'But Isaac were in the Hulks waiting for the transportation

when I were married with Tom. And Tom a draper. How can he know it be I?'

'Someone has given him this intelligence, I know not how. And he is determined he shall reach you and speak with you. That you and he shall be reunited. Mrs Kendall, I am sorry. Perhaps it is wrong of me to tell you. But it seemed to me that if you could but write to him, convey him some message to calm him . . .'

'Visit him, tha means?'

'Under no circumstances. It must not be known to any other that he is related to you. It would be your ruin and your husband's. No, no. Merely send him word that you are well and happy, that you leave imminently for New Zealand . . . He seems possessed by the idea that you are ill, dying, and that he has been the cause of your sickness. The heat and the conditions here have turned his brain.'

'What other knows of this?'

'Only I. He is persuaded by me that his silence is necessary to recover you.'

I feels stabbed to me heart. Be seized by a cramp and rising vomit, and staggers behind a bush and loses me stomach.

He holds me urgent by the shoulders. 'Mrs Kendall, go in, go in. You are too near your time. I am sorry. Forgive me, I had no intent to harm you. And in your condition. I am a fool.' He takes me arm. 'Come. I will guide you to the house.' And then, of a sudden, he leaves hold of me, runs forward and entreats with Mrs Marsden, who he have seen coming towards us. In a shimmer of haze, I hears his voice far off.

'Mrs Kendall came early to examine the plantings and has been struck by her pangs, ma'am. Shall I escort her to the house?'

And Mrs Marsden, looming large by me, says. 'Help me, Stockwell, to lead her to the verandah.'

And rolling between them on a wave of pain and sickness, I somehow comes to the house and be taken by Tom and Sannah to the flat calm of the sheets and the bed, while Hannah rages and beats to be out and me whole body shivers

31

in that blinding heat, then heaves and tosses, a thing apart from me.

And I hears a voice, me own voice, screaming in me ears with agony, lowing like a Brocklesby cow, feels me hands clutching at the iron bed-rail, back arching, caught in a net, a man-trap of pain, tearing out not only me hair and me flesh but me entrails, me guts, me very self.

'Be calm,' says Mrs Marsden, a spirit on the edge of Hell. 'The lying-in woman will be here within the hour. Reverend Marsden has gone to fetch her himself.'

And all around, the heat. Hot, it be, like the inside of the baker's oven at the Hall. Not hot like sun that warms, nor hot like water nice to the touch, but a cruel heat. Wicked. A heat with madness in it, flies screaming at the ears. A harsh pursuing heat. The sun like hounds' breath after the fox, panting at me back, down me neck. Surrounding me. Whichiver way I turns, the heat rises up to snare me, trap me, hold me.

Me girls was winter infants, Thomas Surfleet, autumn; and the other two, spring, when all the soft white may were out on the hedgerows. But this one that ought have been winter, too, were a summer thing, born wrong at the other turning of the world, torn out of me by gasping heat into a place of fire and sweat. The transport lying-in woman, a dull drab beloved of Mrs Marsden, whose last confinement she have attended, thrusts him at me, red and bloody, all screaming pink throat, an owl-baby with a nose-beak and gaping, starving mouth.

And all I thinks be of that great weight gone from me at last and how I must needs get back to speak with Stockwell. Now. At once. To talk of Isaac.

'Lie down, Jane. Be calm,' says Tom, stroking me head. 'A fine boy. As strapping as God has ever given.'

I looks at the new little one. Another boy, thinks I, in disappointment. And says aloud, 'God had better provide, then, for how I shall, I knows not.'

'Hush,' says Tom, shocked. ''Tis not like thee, Jane.'

'I be not like meself now.'

'Doesn't yet know what she says,' puts in the drab, wiping

the blood and slime from this new one. 'Such a fine little one. I would he were mine.'

I looks at this hot, red, ugly thing torn unloved from me own body. 'So take him, then,' says I. 'Five I has already. Have this one. I gives him to thee.'

She looks at me, shocked-like. I sees how her mouth forms ready to run tattle-teller to Mrs Marsden.

'Jane,' says Tom, 'here's Sannah at the door to see her new brother. Take him to thee now.' He kisses the tiny thing as I latches him, reluctant, to me breast.

The drab bends over me. 'I would he were mine and all,' says she, low and only for me own ear. 'Thou'rt a bad woman. God will punish thee for what thou hast said.'

'God's messenger, art thou, then?' says I, nasty. Spiteful. All of me churned about by news of Isaac. 'God will niver be doing what thou sayest.'

But He did. Indeed He did.

Four days afore I be able to rise from bed and go to the garden. All me strength lost in sweat and heat.

'What wilt tha call him?' says Tom and I, listless, uncaring, says, 'Botany. Call him Botany after the place where he have sprung.'

'In England was he begotten,' says Tom. 'Not here. Come, Janey, try.'

This one be ugly. Large nose on him and cross black eyes either side. But Sannah loves him more than all the others together. Sings to him and rocks him when he cries. Which be often. Clasps him and smiles to him in the most tender mother's way.

'You do not like him, Mither?'

'Oh aye. I loves you all.'

Susannah stares grave at me from coal-black Quickfall eyes, says nowt but holds inside her head all she thinks. A deep one, Sannah, old beyond her years. Be as if all the love I canna feel for him she carries.

'Hold him, Mither. He is hungry.' 'Mither, I have changed

his swaddles. Sick, he was. And wet.' 'Here. I have brought little John. See how he nestles against me like a baby bird.'

'John, be it, then, miss?' says I, smiling at how she will try to turn me to the name. Seven years only, she, but like to a woman not a child. Lizzie, at six, be still a puppy, rolling and playing, hopscotching on the broad verandah, tangling with Thomas Surfleet, pushing, shrilling, flapping at Basil and Joseph. In everything Lizzie be loud, Sannah silent.

Sannah's eyes watches me now, dark, hoping.

'And what says thy father to John?'

''Tis a good manly name.'

'So it seems his name be John.'

She smiles. Her face lights up and shines from within. Plainer than Lizzie till she smiles, then she have the face of an angel.

'Get on with thee, miss. Basil be pinching Joseph. Take them away to the garden.' And as I says it, I remembers Stockwell and me own business in the garden. 'Take them by the purple tree and I will fetch thee all in meself later.'

'Th'art getting up today, Mither?'

'Near enough time, it be, for me to rise, surely?'

She smiles again, lays little John sleeping in the Marsdens' crib and skips away, happy, to the others.

It have been in me heart to tell Tom this latest intelligence of Isaac but I am feared what he will say. And that Isaac now believes hisself, not Tom, me husband do bother me. Isaac be a country lad but Tom be different. Educated. A tutor. Have turned his hand to drapery. And now to be a schoolmaster. When I married with Tom, it be not like with Isaac. Tom were shy and gentle, spoke to me. Told me what God be thinking of what us be doing. Hot for me always but brooding with it, where Isaac do catch me, tease me, and quickly do what be on his mind. And mine. And it do seem that Tom believes most truly I be ignorant of any knowledge of it afore him. So why tell him other?

'Here,' says me mither, on us wedding day. Gives me something well-wrapped in a cloth. 'Men is not like we. If

Thomas Kendall would have ye a full maiden, be so. No need for him to know owt of what be not his business.'

Mither do know about me and Isaac? She do know what I has kept so well hid I scarce believes it yet meself? I doesna ask.

'Chicken liver in cloth,' she says. 'Keep it by thee and after, make a use of it on thy nightclothes. And a little on front o' his nightshirt, too.'

'Belike he may catch me.'

She gives a great laugh. 'Mark me, girl, he be sleeping then. And heavy too.'

And right she were and all.

'Good morning to you, Mrs Kendall, and the Lord's blessing upon you that hath brought you safe through your travail.'

'Good morning, sir,' says I. 'I thanks thee.'

'And what is his name to be?'

'John, sir. Be Susannah have named him. She have a fancy to the name.'

'A good name, a strong name, a godly name. The name of both the Evangelist and the Revelationist. I shall baptise him myself next Sunday.'

Mr Marsden pours a little wine in a glass for Tom, and another for himself, then an inch within a small glass, cut fine and pretty, which he do give to me. 'Drink this, Mrs Kendall. It is good for the health. Builds up strong blood and nourishment.'

'I thanks thee, Reverend Marsden, but I hasna niver took strong drink.'

He presses the glass to my hand. 'Have no fear. It is not strong, merely sustaining.'

So I swallows it, choking a bit at the quick burn of it and feeling after a fire in me belly where it lies, but grateful to be thinking on some other thing else than what Stockwell have told me. Isaac. Him that I loved more than me own brother, that had me by the fields and by the dyke and swore to wed me but that the gamekeeper have took him first. And me lucky that Tom Kendall have so soon after set his cap at me and I were not left a mother and husbandless.

And what to say to Tom? Him that I has niver breathed one word to. Who loves Sannah dearest of all his bairns. A seven-month child, she were. Be lucky she were but a small infant. And have he not seed hisself me maiden's blood on his nightclothes?

Isaac had no knowing of it. It canna be for that he thinks I be his own true wife. Comes to me the feel of him against me, chest hard, heaving, mouth biting at me neck, which I so loves, but Tom may not niver do, being that he finds it coarse when I moans so and be worried how God may take it.

Yet if Isaac have the knowledge us be here, mebbee he have, too, intelligence of more of me life than I knows.

And if he should mebbee talk of it, speak of what were between us to any at the barracks, what then? If the Marsdens was to know, or the Governor, that Tom be related to a transport, that Sannah . . . I feels sick to the worry of it.

'Well, Jane, hast thou?' It be Tom.

I looks up. 'Hast what?'

'She is dreaming,' says Tom to the Reverend. And to me, 'Mr Marsden has asked you this twice now whether you have yet seen any of the North Cape natives.'

'Why, nay,' I stammers, 'not yet. I been in the garden with Stockwell, him that is the transport, to see to the growing of vittals.'

'So Mrs Marsden has told me and I am indeed impressed that one busy with her children, and so near her time, has been as industrious in her pursuits. You are a fortunate man, Mr Kendall.'

I sees Tom be pleased.

'These natives,' says the Reverend, 'are remarkable men. Great navigators, quick to learn. They are in no respect like the blackfellows here in Botany. Our aborigines are completely beyond redemption. They will never be brought to the Lord. But the Maori are altogether different. You will be safe in their hands, Mrs Kendall. And your little ones also. They have a most uncommon tenderness to their children. They are distraught to be parted from them, yet, even so, in the interests of bringing them to the benefits of our civilization, some of them have sent their sons, and daughters too, to me here at the Mission.'

'Most worthy,' agrees Tom.

I nods to shew I thinks same.

'They have grasped already,' says Reverend Marsden, 'under what sentence of potential exploitation, misuse and treachery their illiteracy places them all.'

'Illiteracy?' says I.

And Mr Marsden, not understanding, says, 'Yes, 'tis true, they are all, to a man, unable to read or write. An entire race without the written word. No Bible to comfort them, no classics, no poetry; of their heritage, not one word to commend them to posterity. Consider it, Mrs Kendall.'

I makes bold. 'Mebbee, sir, they has no need of what they knows not.'

'That, Mrs Kendall, is the definition of a Heathen. They are but as children, savage children. And like children, also, in their eagerness to learn and grasp the new.'

I does not look at Tom. I must now be Heathen too, a savage child. 'Belike you be right, Mr Marsden,' I says aloud. And, 'Dinner,' says Mrs Marsden, appearing by the door. 'Come, be seated. That was a fine uplifting address, Samuel, you gave us at this morning's service.'

'I am more and more sure,' responds her husband, 'that firmness and the rule of law are all these transports answer to. I have conveyed my sentiments to Governor Davy. The next one to break out, I say, must be made of to his fellows an example that His Majesty's Government does not tolerate mob rule. We want no Frenchie ideas here, eh, Mr Kendall?'

'No, indeed,' echoes Tom. 'But what example shall be made?'

'Flogging,' says Marsden. 'The cat. Good enough for disciplining His Majesty's Navy, good enough as well for His Majesty's transports. And for the greater breaches of the law, a public hanging or two will work marvels at maintaining order among them.' And as I looks at him, I sees his mouth working with the pleasure of his thought. 'We shall all attend the punishments to show our support for the Governor and let the transports see that the rule of Botany lies only with their masters.' He rubs his hands. 'Ah, mutton, my dear. A splendid touch of Home. Come sit, Mrs Kendall. You shall have first slice from the leg, and mint sauce from Stockwell's flourishing herb garden.'

I thinks I loves Tom most for his talk. Tells me what I niver knew. Full of thought and greedy for new ideas, he be.

'In Egypt, Janey, the pharaohs were the kings. Not Christians like us but sky worshippers. Buried in great pyramids after death with their belongings. All the innards plucked from their bodies and preserved in precious oils, then wrapped in bandages and sealed in wooden coffins painted with their images.'

'Oh, aye.'

''Tis true. Every word of it. See here, this picture in *Britannica*.'

Better than the Bible be that *Britannica* to Tom. The whole set have he carried here with us all across the world. I loves to see him at the reading of it. What happens now if Isaac do betray me? It crosses me mind for the hundredth time, if only . . .

If only the gamekeeper have not come out that night. If only Isaac have come home after the leveret, not stayed to poach them pheasants. If only us has had money to buy him free. If only . . .

And how can I, that knows not how to write, send to Uncle Silas word of Isaac? And what word to send? *Isaac be here in Botany. He be in a chain gang. He believe he be my husband, not Tom. His mind be crazed with this evil sun.* What do that for Uncle Silas? What use be them words?

And if it be found out I be cousin to a transport, what then for Tom? What will the Church and Reverend Marsden do? Send us back on that terrible journey, all us? Send mebbee only I? And Tom, who wants but to serve God and save the Heathen, ruined by his own wife?

I finds I be weeping with the vexing and confusion of it but I be walking again to the garden as I weeps. To the roses, and beyond, where the vegetables be planted and where I sees plain the broad grey-canvas back of a transport working there.

Stockwell seems a good and honest man. But I says to meself that, even if I didna believe so, still and all I would have to speak with him. It do come down to the plain truth which be that I hasna any other choice.

'Good day, Mr Stockwell,' says I. 'Thirsting I be to know all ye may wish to tell me.'

'Begin then,' he answers, but not looking up, 'by calling me only Stockwell, never Mister. At all times remember it.'

'Yes . . . Stockwell.'

His voice stays very soft. 'I heard you were safely delivered of a son.'

'Told you that to Isaac?'

'I have not yet seen him. Nor will I until Sunday next. But I think it not a good idea to convey that intelligence to him in his present low spirits.'

'So low?'

'So low. Better you find words of yourself only for Isaac, I believe.'

'But what do it be I must say to Isaac?'

'Write to him words of comfort; a note will be sufficient. Write of his mother.'

'She be dead these twenty year.'

'His father, then. Sisters, brothers.'

'None he have but us. And Uncle Silas.'

'He has it in his head he has betrayed his father. That his father will see him no more should he ever return. To hear from you will tell him this is not the case.' He raises his head and looks at me direct. I sees he have true honest eyes. 'You. . .'

'Aye?'

'No,' he says and turns his eyes away. Us be silent for a bit, then he asks, 'So you will write?'

I hangs down low me head. Shakes it nay. Says very quiet, 'I canna write. Read neither.'

'Ah,' says he. 'I am sorry. That was foolish of me. Because Isaac writes, I assumed . . .'

'Isaac canna write neither.'

'But yes, he does. And reads too.'

'Nay, he canna.'

'I do assure you, Mrs Kendall, Isaac reads. And tolerably well. Perhaps he has learned since he left you.'

'Reverend Marsden said,' says I, 'them that canna read be the Heathen.'

'Reverend Marsden,' says Stockwell, 'confuses far too often the truth with his opinions. If you cannot read, you may always learn.'

'I?'

'Of course. Isaac has done so. Now tell me what you would say to him and I shall write it for you. How will that serve?'

'Very well,' says I. 'And thanks to you.'

I looks at him again. A body long, sinewy and lean, with legs stretching far between boots and breeches. Shoulders he has narrow, so that his head do look the bigger upon them, though it be large enough and seem the greater for the sweep of hair atop it. This hair gives him the appearing of something I knows but canna remember. The burning of the sun have made his hair to be almost white and his face beaten to bronze so that his eyes looks the more blue within his face. He gazes at me steady from them eyes and inside me something rises up. I feels I mebbee knows him, though I doesna, and in me heart I trusts him complete, transport though he be. I drops away me own eyes. Me hands be trembling.

'Isaac,' I says, voice trembling too. 'How do he truly be?'

He doesna answer. I looks again at him and it do seem to me he be trying to speak with his eyes and, though I wishes to hear what he would say more than the world, I dares not.

'I want you to know,' he says, and his voice gentle and soft, tender-like, 'I am no common criminal. No harm have I done, nor would do, my fellow creature. I labour in this wretched place for holding and speaking my beliefs and for that alone. It is important to me that you know this.'

'I knows it already,' says I. And it be true. I does.

40

'Mrs Marsden has told you?'

'No person have told me save thee. But I knows it already. Afore that ye told it to me.'

He stares a long time at me and I canna take me own two eyes from his. It be like to me he looks into me soul, me heart, and sees me how I truly be. Naked. More naked than Tom have ever seen though I be fully clothed and bonneted.

'Thank you,' he says finally. He hesitates, then, 'As to Isaac, I must be truthful though I have no wish to cause you more pain. He is unwell. Not in his body but in his mind. It is the heat here and the conditions.' His face darkens. 'My dogs at home were better kept than men are here.'

I would I were your little dog, thinks I, then feels shame at the loss of thoughts of Isaac. No wonder brother Sam have cast me off.

Something rises up into Mr Stockwell's face. Of a sudden, he looks hungry, a face staring at me through glass, the gaze of that single hound which follows, favoured, at the huntsman's heel. And words comes falling from his mouth. 'You are very lovely, Mrs Kendall. As Isaac said.' Then his face grows red. 'I am sorry,' he says. 'I have no right to speak in this way.'

Somehow I be clumsy. 'No,' I says, pleased though. 'No more. Isaac have not seen me in a ten year. I be mither of six children. Old woman now.'

He laughs. A sound to listen for again. 'Oh no. Not you, Mrs Kendall. You will be lovely for ever. You have the bones for beauty that lasts.'

I touches me face. Then, 'It be a lion,' I cries, on sudden remembrance.

'A lion. What is a lion?'

'Why, thee,' says I, confused too. 'Tha hast a head like the lion in my Lizzie's little primer. "The noble lion hunteth where he will."'

'You said you could not read.'

'No more I can. Be Lizzie read to me.'

'But you have remembered. So you can learn as she does. Remembering is the most part of it.'

41

Of a sudden, I remembers something else. 'Little John,' I says. 'I has not fed him now since well beyond his time. I must go back.' And as I thinks on it, me breasts spurts forth warm milk which spreads and dampens all me bodice. Shame comes over me terrible hot. Red me face to me hair.

'It is nothing but a natural thing,' says he. 'Please do not be disgraced on my account, I beg you.'

This last so kind, tears comes in me eyes.

He pulls out his knife, sharp for the pruning. 'It may be Isaac will require proof that the message comes from you.' He looks full at me head. 'Will you?' I nods aye. He glances around for sure us be not seen, then reaches for a curl below me bonnet, shears it and slides it away safe in his breeches. I doesna look, just feels the little tug. Then silence. Still he holds his knife, and eyes at me like me mither's pet sheep. I nods again.

'But not for Isaac, this one.'

'I knows.'

Another tug.

'Come the day after tomorrow, if you can.'

'Assured be, belike I can, I will.' And Lizzie's little book comes up to me again. 'The lion is king of all the beasts.' And I laughs as I runs away in me soaking dress, back to Tom, little John, the other bairns, the Mission House. And marvels how I feels more like me, meself, than iver I has felt these three year gone and more. Iver since that Tom have come to God.

Early morning I wakes to find Tom holding me, stroking me. 'Come here, Janey,' he breathes in me ear. Sore still I be, and breasts on me like a milk cow, but he be gentle.

'Great talk I have had with Reverend Marsden. He tells me he is of the firm opinion I shall be ordained before a three year is out.'

'*He* will ordain thee?'

'No, indeed not. Only the bishop may do that. I shall return Home and be accepted as God's minister in the sight of my sponsor, Mr Wood.'

42

At this do a small stroke of fright touch me but I lets it fly unspoken.

'When goes us to New Zealand?'

'To Rangi-Houa? Not yet. We have much to learn first. In a ten week maybe. And with us will return some of the natives who, even now, are on their way to join us here at the Mission.'

I stretches. Thinks of Isaac. 'Better sooner mebbee. All us here is much for Mrs Marsden.'

'Ah! She is fitted well for it. And the Mission, 'tis her life also.'

'Thee said us has a little house there in New Zealand. At Rangi-Houa.'

'So has promised Mr Shunghie.'

'The chief?'

'Under whose protection we will lie. He comes to us here at Parramatta himself by the *Mary-Anne* on Friday. Mr Marsden had intelligence of it from the whaler which put in at Botany but yesterday.'

He strokes with his hand me cheek. 'Ah, Janey, Janey, thou art the best of women. Knows thee I love thee?'

'Get on with thee.' I pushes him with me foot. Playful-like.

And, sudden, there comes from the next room the sound of keening. A terrible low moaning. I be sitting up on the instant. Tom, too. Door flung open and Sannah standing there. In her arms, Baby John. I be across to her afore that I has taken breath. Cold, he be. And still. Lying in her arms like always but dead, marble dead. Little arm hangs stiff, bead eyes far off, mouth froze half-open and silent. And Sannah, fierce and brave, holding him like to force him back to life by willing of her love.

'Come, Susannah,' says Tom, very quiet. 'Give Baby to Mother. Let her take him.'

'No,' says she, clinging fast. 'She does not love him. I am his mither. 'Tis me he needs.'

'Little John is not well,' Tom says. 'Milk, perhaps, will help him. Put him to his mother's breast.' His eyes meets with mine. Us knows. 'Come, missie. Let me take him.' And holds his arms out, slow and careful. 'A good girl thou art.'

'He will cry in but a moment.'

'I think not.'

'I know it. Always he cries after waking and it is me he wishes. I will hold him so to quiet him. When he is cross, I sing to him.' And bends her head over the infant body, rocks the stiff bundle and hums to it the lullaby I meself has sung to her and me mither afore to me.

Belike I be in a dream and this have not happened. It be but a passing thing and us will wake and find it gone.

'See,' says Tom, 'thou hast hushed him, Sannah. Let us lay him in his cradle and leave him to his sleep.' He places his arm upon her shoulder and guides us all to the room wherein be her and Lizzie's bed and that of Thomas Surfleet and the other boys. All them sits silent in the boys' bed, watching us. By Sannah's side of the bed lies the little wooden cradle. On the pallet and the pillow still be showing dents where has laid his head and body, solid pressed by weight of death. Lizzie looks at me, bright eyes dark, holes in a blanket. Tongue still. Saying nowt.

'Sannah,' says I, 'thy brother be dead. He have gone to God.'

'Not God's,' says she. 'Nor thine, neither. Thou did'st not want him. Mine, he is.'

'God's now,' says Tom. 'An angel, he is, thy brother. The Lord has taken him for His own.'

'The Lord will give him back to me. Many He has but only one have I. I will hold him and pray that God restore him to me.'

'That God cannot do.'

'A miracle. Like Lazarus.'

'It cannot be.'

I finds me tongue. 'Why not niver so? She have Faith. Faith, says the Scriptures, be all that she requires. Why not like Lazarus? Tell me that, Tom Kendall.'

And Tom, head bent, says only, 'Hush, hush, Janey. Trouble enough have I with Sannah. Quiet thee now and take her next

44

door to thy bed. Lay him down now, girl, and cover him well, then lie with thy mother a little till I come.'

Sannah do place him most tender upon the old pressions, do cover him with his swaddling cloth and walk by me to the bedroom beside. Her face be an old crone's face. Such grief I has not seen since Uncle Silas.

Turns she to me at the door. 'I know well why my Baby John has been taken.'

I says nowt. Mebbee I knows what be coming.

''Tis a judgement on thee,' says she. 'The lying-in woman said. Not wanted, he was, save by me.'

'Wanted he was, like all of ye,' says I and shakes her roughly.

'Ah,' she says, 'then 'tis I did do it. Did not look to him diligent enough. It is judgement on me that was not his good mither.'

'Judgement on no one, miss,' shouts I. 'Hush thy mouth.'

'And thee, and thee, Jane,' cries Tom, come in behind us. 'Leave her be. She knows not what she says. Poor child is mad with grief.'

'Not mad, Father,' says Sannah, seven year old. 'Dead, I am, like my Baby John that God will not give back to me.'

And Tom weeps, like I has niver afore seen him in all us life together.

Now I knows what Hell be. I knows too that when I were in Heaven I knewed it not. Supposing I has begun me life in Botany and after has been transported to Brocklesby, I would be like one took from Hell to Heaven, rejoicing in its grace and pleasures, its coolness, quiet, lack of flies, abundance of water and vittals, its gentleness, the softness of its light. But, took from Heaven to Hell, I knows not how to be. Nor when it may end and Heaven be restored.

'It is a test of Faith, Jane,' says Tom.

But God knows that I has no Faith, no more. Why be He then testing me? This I thinks but says it not to Tom.

*

45

So it falls out that Baby John be born on Sunday, baptised on Sunday a two week following, and buried on Thursday after. Died only in the early morning and by night lay in his eternal bed hewed from hard dry ground, wrapt in his swaddling cloth in a coffin so tiny only Tom needs carry it.

'The Lord hath given and the Lord hath taken away,' says the Reverend Marsden. While his wife and Lizzie does loudly weep, Tom do only gaze ahead and I regards the littleness of that raw red hole in which he now must lie for iver, Sannah moves like one bewitched. Nowt says she, niver a cry escapes her, niver a tear. She, who have loved him best, have not left even the strength to grieve for him. Her heart be buried with him.

Judgement, I tells meself, it be. Judgement on me that wanted him not, that let come to me mind, unbidden, thoughts of Stockwell. Felt once more a wench, I did, a-coming from the garden. Thought meself to be again in Lincoln, like to the day of the Michaelmas Fair, sporting together below Castle Hill, arms linked with Sam and Isaac, ribbons in me hair and all the boys a-watching where I walked. The noise and jostle up and down Steep Hill. Jugglers, there was, and a dancing bear. Frenchies eating fire and swallowing swords, booths for lace and fairings, Punch and Judy fighting in their stall till Judy dropped the baby and Punch, a-picking it up, said that it were dead. Bad mither, Judy were, too. Yet us did laugh and laugh again. Isaac breathing and biting at me ear, making play to eat me neck, feeding me plums in sugar and quaffing back ale with Sam outside the Coach and Horses. Chased one another all amongst the carts and horses down Steep Hill, us did, with bells ringing above and behind from the Cathedral tower.

And it comes again in me ear, the voice of the drab: 'God will punish thee for what thou hast said.'

A great punishment for a small offence. And yet were worse to follow.

Witchcraft, me mither would call it. The evil eye, a cream-curdler at work. 'Change thy luck, our Jane,' I fancies I heared her say. And I puts a little salt by the windows and the door to the verandah, where it be hid from Tom but I knows it to be. Sprinkles water from the ewer over the surface of the crib, and when I sees the laughing bird alone on the purple tree I mutters very low, 'Excuse me, Your Majesty, excuse me, Your Majesty, excuse me, Your Majesty,' he being very like to a colourful jackdaw and mebbee a carrier of the ill luck.

Stays away from the garden, I does. Fear in me to speak again with Stockwell. Since the graveyard, I be in a dream. All us floating in a dream. Of heat. And red dust.

Then it rains. Of a sudden, the sky goes dark, wind sweeps through the Mission, hot and damp, an ugly breath. And after it, rain. Slanting upon the roses and the apple trees, the carrot plantings, Stockwell's tiny seeds.

And following, the sun. Then from the earth do spring out iverywhere flowers of blue bindweed, cushions of marigolds, feathers of green carrot, bursting up through the red soil. Fresh leaves upon the apple trees, the roses a-holding up their heads again, not bowed afore the sun.

And in the Mission meadow, where droops the two poor cows, twitching and flicking against the swarms of nipping flies, grass, true green English grass, do sprout and thicken hourly afore us eyes.

I sprinkles a little more salt, to be safe, but by nightfall I knows it be for nowt.

Comes from Botany at dusk, riding to Parramatta, two of the Colony officers, muskets clapped to their belts, from Governor Davy to Reverend Marsden.

Clattering and drumming of hoofs has all us to the gates, watching their approach.

'The dust,' sighs Mrs Marsden as a red cloud rises afore them. Even the rain canna hold the earth in place here.

Thomas Surfleet and young Charles Marsden has to be held back from rushing to the soldiers, so excited be they by the horses. 'Trouble, Captain Hales?' asks Mr Marsden, very grave.

'Aye, sir. Great trouble. The Governor has ordered us ride to you in haste. It is the transports.'

'What of them?'

'They have rioted, sir.'

'What? All?'

'No. Two gangs only and most of them recaptured. There yet remain just three men unaccounted. But desperate fellows these, and armed. It is thought they head this way.'

'To us? At Parramatta? Surely they will make for the inland or the North-East?'

The horsemen dismounts. Marsden orders the horses taken and all us goes within. A trusty takes the soldiers' capes and hats, brings wine and water on the orders of his mistress.

A slow fear be growing in me.

'Think you,' says Marsden, 'they are heading here to rally with our transports?'

'Preposterous,' says Mrs Marsden. 'There is not a one amongst our convict servants would fraternise with the hardened criminals.'

'It seems that one of them has here with you a sweetheart or a wife. Of those retaken, two have confessed under the lash it was not a planned uprising but opportune, upon the heat of a moment. One of the gang – a molly, so they said – took umbrage at the doings of another, a scuffle arose, and whilst the overseer pulled off one from the other the rest seized staves and clubbed him down.'

'The overseer is wounded?'

'Dead, Parson. Then one among them seized his musket and pistols and, with these weapons, they took the advantage of surprise and forced the overseers further down the quarry to yield their guns as well. Thus armed, they broke into the stores, took powder and provisions and made away. It was more than three hours before the authorities heard of it.'

Reverend Marsden have again upon his piggy face that look of secret pleasure. 'They shall pay for this, Captain Hales, I swear it.'

'As does Governor Davy, sir. But they are still at liberty. And you and all within your household may be in danger.

48

The Governor has ordered troops to guard you but the transports have the advantage of time. Grieve and I were sent before on swift mounts to warn you.'

'And grateful we are indeed. But surely the convicts are on foot?'

'Three horses were stolen from the stables by the quarry stores.'

'So they are horse thieves as well as murderers!'

'It may be prudent, Reverend, to call your servants here and question them. It is not impossible one be a wife or lover.'

I looks at Tom. Nowt do he suspect. But will when once he hears the names of them that rides towards us. A haze falls about me. I sways a little. The Mission parlour dims afore me eyes.

'Mr Kendall!' cries the captain. 'Your wife – she is faint.'

Tom and Mrs Marsden makes towards me and I sees me chance.

'It be the heat. I must lie down.'

'It is the shock,' says Marsden grimly. 'These convict devils. They will learn it does not pay to flout the laws of England.'

'You must take your wife to rest,' says Mrs Marsden. 'She is not yet recovered from her recent troubles.'

'You are most kind, ma'am,' says Tom.

And leaning heavily upon his arm, I makes escape. Oh God, I prays silent, let it not be Isaac. Let it not be Isaac.

In the night comes musket shot, a scuffle of men and horses. A scream. Another. Oaths and curses mingled; then, clear, a voice that I would know were it a twenty year, not ten, since last I heard it.

Me heart have squeezed and shrunk. I longs to run to Isaac, see again his face, clasp meself to him, weep tears to soak the shaggy chest beneath his shirt. But this be not Home. Us be in greatest peril.

Beside me, Tom be wakeful. I has not slept, nor he.

'Tom,' I mutters in his ear, 'I be feared that convict be our Isaac.'

'*Isaac*? Isaac Quickfall?'

'Aye.'

'But why should Isaac Qu—'

I stops with me hand his mouth.

He reaches to light the candle.

I battens down his hand. 'Nay, niver. Be no one here but thee and me knows I be Quickfall too.'

'Think you 'tis to seek for *you* he comes here?'

'Aye. It be possible.'

'You have seen him, here in Botany?'

'That I has not. But Botany be Botany. It be a world off, yet but a village in its ways. Certain, it be, he would know of me. And thee.'

'But why comes he here?'

'Mebbee ... he be crazed. By this heat. His life here. I knows not. But us must think, and that right quick, of what us says to Marsden. Or to the Governor's men.'

'But what can we do?'

He be sore troubled.

And I.

'If Marsden knows I be cousin to a transport, tha'art finished with God's work. Niver will any in Botany speak with thee, nor I, nor any of us bairns. Lie still. Say nowt.'

'Marsden may summon me.'

'Then it be Isaac's word or thine. List to me, Tom. Tha scarce knoweth Isaac. Would'st recognise him, thinks tha?'

'Nay. Your brother, Sam, indeed, but Isaac had been taken before I came to Brocklesby as tutor. It was only the once I saw him.'

Thinks I on that once. In Lincoln, at the prison. After the last Assizes. And the Fair a-rabbling all around. Tom and I sedate, only just a-courting, come with the others from Brocklesby in me uncle's cart. Goes us after sentence to the prison, where for a silver coin bribe us be allowed to bring to Isaac ale and pie and cockles, talk with him a half-hour, more or less, and give him news of Mither and little Hannah, Brocklesby and home.

From the yard below the prison comes the sound of

hammer blows where them that be to swing next day must look their last from the gallows being built. Up to the Cathedral, down to the town. Scenes there be around us of such misery and sorrow it be hard to find some words of cheer for Isaac.

'The transportation,' says he, over and over.

'It be but fourteen year,' says Sam. 'And thou art young and strong. Tha'll be back, Isaac, supping ale in the Coach and Horses, afore us knows ye've left.'

Uncle Silas saying nowt but clinging his arm about Isaac's shoulder like to fix it there for iver.

'Aye,' says me father, 'stout man thou art, Isaac.'

But Isaac, shocked-like into stillness, only mutters to himself again the sentence. What to say, I knows not. Afore them all, I canna lay a hand on him, nor he on me. Nowt says he to me till us be leaving, shepherded by the gaoler, and then he raises his head, gazes at me long. 'Tha'll wait for me, Jane? It be but a fourteen year. From Botany I swears I'll have a man to write for me to thee. Wilt wait?'

I nods, dumb, looks down at his manacle, canna say owt to him now of me own shackle, which yet be not shewing to any eye. He and me, both, be trapped. Like to foxes or stoats which waits in the pit only for the final blows to fall.

It be more than an hour afore there comes a tapping at the door and Parson Marsden calling Tom. Great show Tom makes of rising, a-lighting his candle, shuffling to the door. Whispered conversation, then he comes back, pulls on his garments and slips out, but murmurs loud enough for me to hear and comprehend, 'She sleeps now, sir. I am loath to disturb her rest.'

And Captain Hales' reply drifts in to me. 'No need for it, Mr Kendall. Better she is not troubled.'

But morning comes Mrs Marsden to me door. No sign there be of Tom's return and I be struck with terrible fear. Mebbee he have forgot hisself and told that I knows Isaac. Tom perhaps be now in irons, too. So when I hears her knock, I trembles so great she canna help but spy it.

'Ah, Mrs Kendall,' says she. 'A dreadful business indeed. One dead, one wounded and like to die from his injury, and the last apprehended. And he a madman. The magistrate has come and speaks at this moment with Captain Hales and Sergeant Grieve, and my husband and your own.'

At this, me heart turns over. 'Me husband, ma'am?'

'Yes, Mrs Kendall. And afterwards he wishes to speak with you.'

Goes I into the Marsdens' parlour, all me frame shivering though the heat be thicker than for days afore. Seems like I canna will meself be still.

'This gentleman,' says Mr Marsden, waving to him seated to one long side of the table, papers tied in bundles by, quill and bottle afore him, 'is Mr Cartwright, the magistrate.'

No sound comes from me mouth. At the window side of the room be seated Tom, and pale and ill he do look. Beside him, Captain Hales and Sergeant Grieve and in between them two, with heavy iron shackles to his feet and wrists, slumps Isaac. And I knows straight it be he, despite he be so thin, cheeks all sunken, hair wild, hands swollen and torn. Them hands it be that catches me gaze, chained together, fallen in his lap, palm to palm, fingertips puffed and near to worn away. Starving body, bloated hands.

Specks dancing in the window sun-shafts blinds me for a moment and I shakes me head. On the darkened side of the room be other folk, too, but I canna see who they be for the dazzle to me eyes.

'Pray sit, Mrs Kendall,' says Mr Cartwright. 'I must put to you one or two questions. It will not take long. Your name is Jane Kendall?'

I nods.

He writes something on the paper in front of him, powders it, blots it.

'You are wife to Mr Thomas Kendall?'

I nods again.

'You must answer, Mrs Kendall. Do not be anxious. These are merely formalities, required by His Majesty's law.'

I swallows, finds a croak of speech. 'Aye, I be his wife.'

'Have you had before a husband by another name?'

'Nay, sir.'

A terror has I now. What if he do ask me maiden's name? And comes to me I will say it were Edgewater, that being the maiden's name of me mither. But he do not ask it.

'You have seen before Captain Hales and Sergeant Grieve?'

'Aye, sir. Last evening afore I were took faint.'

Reverend Marsden do lean across to have his say. 'Mrs Kendall has been delivered but lately of an infant, now cruelly expired.'

'I am sorry to hear that, ma'am.'

A silence.

'Mrs Kendall, you see both Captain Hales and Sergeant Grieve within this room?'

'Aye, sir, there, by the window.'

'Between them is a man, the prisoner. Do you see him?'

'Aye, I does.'

I wills meself look straight at Isaac. What becomes of me children if I be took away? And what can I meself do for Isaac now? He lifts his head and looks on me with black Quickfall eyes, like to me own. And Sannah's.

'Do you know this man?'

Comes to me the face of Sam, me brother.

'Do you know this man, Mrs Kendall?'

It were the note have done it. The note writ by Stockwell. And me hair with it beside. Where be that now? Mebbee Isaac have had it upon him when he were taken. Were it but a trick to have me made a convict too? If I answers nay, belike the magistrate will lay upon the table, in sight of all here, that lock of me own black hair.

Sheep afore the butcher's knife, I rolls me eyes up, prays wordless to God who niver hears, who have took from me Thomas Kendall, draper, and give me back Thomas Kendall, missionary, since when I have niver had no good thing happen in me life again.

At the thought of God's treachery, I feels meself grow strong, calmer.

'I niver seed him in me life afore nor niver wishes I might do again.'

The prisoner raises up his head.

'Ah, Jane,' he says, 'tha'rt a cruel one indeed. To turn away from me so, thou that be me own true wife.'

'Hush your mouth, Quickfall,' says Captain Hales, 'or it will be the worse for you.'

Mr Cartwright sighs. 'I am sorry, Mrs Kendall. It is not uncommon with the transports they should have such fancies and notions. It is ever the same when men are brought low from their own base natures. You may leave us now. My thanks to you, ma'am.'

It be all I may do to hold meself upright. Thinks I to hear the cock crow as I stands.

No sound comes. Save Isaac. Who be weeping.

I leaves the parlour, Mrs Marsden by.

'It is clear,' says she, 'he has seen you at the Colony, perhaps at service, or the Governor's address, and he has had a mind to fix upon you. It is the greatest, greatest mercy Captain Hales and Sergeant Grieve were sent, for I know not what might have passed had we not been apprised of the transports' coming. I shudder at the very contemplation of it. Come, let us turn about the roses. I recall how much their scent revives you.'

And takes me arm. And I be forced to walk out there in the garden, in terror Stockwell may appear before us. Which he do but niver raises up his head nor betrays by any movement that he be aware of me nor of his mistress. And she, being minded to talk of nowt but the night's events, speaks not a word to her trusty rose-gardener that do make his way, pruning and plucking, watering and weeding, far from where us sits or stands, till he have disappeared from view into the vegetable garden.

*

54

'What do become of Isaac now?' says I to Tom. Night it be and a great shadow lying between us. And not from the lack of a moon, neither.

He sighs heavy. 'It seems it will be the long drop for them that survive.'

'And niver a pardon possible? Tha couldna ask for mercy?'

'Nay, nay, it would be utter foolishness. We must not shew by any mortal thing your kinship to your cousin.'

'But kin I be and all.'

'And because of that he came here and exposes us to the possibility of public vilification.' He turns his head from me. 'You are aware an example will be made of Isaac and the others?'

'Even if mad?'

'Here there are many mad and no Bedlam in which to confine them. This is a sorry business.'

Silence falls between us.

'It came to me to wonder,' he says, after a time, 'if perhaps, thee ... Quickfall and thee ... if, in Brocklesby, it might be ...'

Me heart jolting. 'Aye?'

'If it may have fallen out that thee and thy cousin ...'

I thinks of the ferret kept by me brother, Sam, for to stuff in his breeches and swallow up game stored in them if the gamekeeper showed. Stank, it did, and Sam reeking days after. Nasty twitching thing it were, too, and only tamed to Sam, a-coming at him when he whistled and darting up his leg. And I hears clear Isaac's voice.

'Terrible thing, Sam, if that ferret be chuzzled and mazed. Mistook by tender morsels in them breeches and gobbled up wrong bit of meat.'

And Sam, 'Know me reek, he do. Not touching nowt of I. But bite and devour any other thing that come his way, would that bugger. Niver seen a ferret in me life didna come out fighting and making for to attack.'

Like the ferret, I goes for to attack now.

'Tha means that tha believes him tha calls madman! Lunatic! Wife I be to thee but him that might mebbee be in Bedlam have the word of me in me husband's ear. Hast forgotten already me maiden's blood on thy nightshirt?'

I feels his shame beside me. 'Forgive me, Janey.' He reaches for me. 'I forgot myself.'

And I allows him make his peace with me though it be the last thing I desires.

Two it were that swung. Company at least had Isaac of another beside him.

'A necessary evil,' says Marsden. 'Tomorrow Mr Kendall and I shall ride to Botany, where I shall offer them the chance of repentance before they meet their Maker. And following, we shall watch these felons dispatched.

'I have ordered all our trusties attend the hangings. Such public examples as these work wonders for law and order in the Colony. Do not you agree, Mr Kendall? We tolerate no Frenchie notions here. Mark you my words, they will not riot again after this.'

Perhaps he sees the pallor upon me or belike he have mistook me guilt for fear.

'Set yourself at rest, Mrs Kendall. It is the heat and loss of Faith turns the minds of depraved and evil men so that even a pious Christian woman may become the object of their depredations. But this hour, a two day hence, the wretch shall be no more. And then he shall answer only to his Maker.'

'Aye, indeed,' whispers I.

Comes to me unbidden in me sleep a cart which do drive away from under a twisted tree, a groaning, visions of legs jerking and thrashing, of squawks and grunts like to them that John Tindall uttered as the rope tightened and twisted and squeezed from him his final breath. And I lies wakeful many and many a night. Better than close me eyes and let ride in them things that I canna bid to me will. Nor take back in me thought to what they was afore.

Seasons here us has none of. All around, the earth and trees remains the same; brown or greenish grey be the leaves and, as none does fall in autumn, so none does burst forth in spring. Yet it be coming back to hot and rainless, a drier parch in the air about us. Like to me that be out of me season also, with milk that still do leak and flow from me breasts though nowt has I now to suckle there.

And then do come Tom to me, in November, aglow.

'The greatest, finest news, my dear. It is settled. Marsden had it from the captain of the whaler *Queen Charlotte* but yesterday. Within a two day comes Shunghie, the North Cape chief, he that will take us back with him to New Zealand. In a month, Janey, we shall be upon the seas again and heading for our Mission to the Heathen. And we may begin, at last, God's great work for us.'

What can be me life to me now but ivery day to rise in the morn and hold fast to them small things by which I makes anchor to me spirit? Feeding of me children. Listening to the primer that Lizzie do read me over and over, though I knows not what say the black markings of them words within it. Sampler sewing give to Sannah. Sannah that looks now niver direct to me eye but rises her gaze only to me breast where dandled little John. Withered blue bindweed flowers have she strewed upon his grave, thinking me not to see when she slipped through the lych-gate of the little churchyard with them clutched fresh from the vine in her fingers. Silent, she be, but fierce. And around her shines like fire, invisible yet clear, a wall that she have raised between herself and all us here, mebbee even all souls in this world. And I might search and search all me days for chinks within that wall and find one niver.

If I looks within the glass, I sees me meself, Jane Kendall, that were Quickfall but niver now to say it so again, face and hair and eyes and mouth and colour all the same as allus were. Yet no glass shows within me what I be, how it do fall out all be not the way it were with me. And no soul here to know it nor to care, neither. If I pinches at me arm, I feels the snap and sting of it, the little marks shows up from clear to fade. But of the inside of me, where lies such cuts and stings and deaths and fear and ice-cold, ice-cold hate, nowt shows to no man. And mebbee better so.

I has seen the great chief, Shunghie, with whom we travels to New Zealand. With him have come the other native chief, Tuai, who have been here afore to the Mission. And great be the preparations and excitement of all them Marsdens when they has the intelligence of it that he were also on the vessel.

It were at supper us should have met together but I, in the afternoon, passing the straggling meadow well beyond the vegetable garden and, for shade, crossing it and walking beneath the eucalypts, were startled by a screeching. And did see what I has thought to be but grey-white leaves upon a dying stump uprise of a sudden all, revealing theirselves to be birds, parrots – sun-setting pink underwings displaying in the cloudless sky like to pale wild roses strewn upon a summer lake.

And I sees that, at the far end of the eucalypts, there strides a man, purple and so near to naked I believes him, for an instant, conjured by me fancy, no real man at all. And then behind him comes another, like to him but taller, thicker-set. I shrinks back by the bushes and they doesna see nor hear me.

Their feet be bare, their hair scrapt up into topknots, where be stuck in each a feather. Both they glanced about them, yet not to where I be a-shrinking by the shady edge, then they has disappeared into the bushland edging the fence. And so was gone when I passed by that same spot a three minute after. Gone like ghosts.

Shocked I were by their strange appearance, their bodies rude and bare. They didna look like poor and meek souls waiting for salvation.

Yet if they doesna want salvation, what be it they would have from us? Me whole heart be afeared by this Mission to New Zealand, yet I canna do owt to halt it. Where be there for me and me children now to go but off into that Unknown, since me husband have decreed it? I would I held me own fate, me destiny were not in others' hands.

Still and all, I tells meself, though me lost last-born I must leave behind here, I has us all the rest together. I be not like them whose men be gone to battle; who must sit at home and wait for their return or news that they will niver more be seen. So why does I be weeping now for trifles and why do me heart so often knock against me ribs for fear?

And when, on the selfsame night, I sees them two again in Parson Marsden's parlour, I canna feel no better at the sighting of them. Nowt of any Englishman about them. Purple-blue they look, these Maori Heathen. Cut deep and everywhere in curls and whorls and stripes about their bodies and their faces. And in the cuts some dye makes stains upon the walnut colour of their native skin, tinting them to a toad-flax blue. Hard to see it and not to stare. And bodies strong and muscled-hard like farming men or outdoor working men. Like Sam, me brother. Or Isaac when he were a Lincoln man: not starved and bloated like I seen him here, but skin brown from the hay-making sun, arms and legs hard and knotted, sinews tight, bum firm and strong. Working men has bodies lean and beckoning, not fleshy full and pudgy pale like Mr Marsden, Mr Wood, or the Governor here at Botany ... A cheeky thought besmirches me mind. Belike them Heathens' body carving do go so far it even be upon their danglers!

Both natives be in the parlour afore I enters. I doesna look at Mrs Marsden or her older girls, nor at the Maori chiefs. Keeps me face down as Tom leads me to Shunghie, our protector.

Below his waist, Mr Shunghie do wear a linen mat, fine wove, like to a skirt that comes above his knees and be wrapt tight about his lower body. Above it, he be partly dressed in Englishman's attire. On his breast – in the place where I has seen pinned Milord Pelham's battle medallions – a pointed fish tooth do pearl against the stuff of his dark frock-coat, and, hanging from a thong about his neck, where Milord do secure his stock with a stick-pin, there rests on his deep-scarred chest, a green and shining stone cut to the likeness of a hideous deformed infant.

'The mark of the Anti-Christ,' murmurs Tom, following me gaze.

Very strange the chief do look altogether, especially as he have neither shoes nor stockings upon his feet and the marks upon his walnut face serves only to show how shrewd and watchful be his dark-brown eyes.

English manners he have, too. Bends across me hand when I has offered it, at Tom's behest, and, 'Tena ko-e,' he says, low and quiet-like.

'He greets you good day,' says Mr Marsden.

'How do you, sir,' I answers, eyes fixed on them circles and lines to his face which to me own mind gives him the appearance of a groomed and parted thoroughbred horse whose mane be divided at the centre and plaited up equal to either side.

'Kood, perry kood,' he says.

'You see,' says Tom, 'already he speaks in our tongue.' And he himself do rattle something in Shunghie's native speech. Which pleases that Heathen chief greatly. His eyes sparkles and he laughs from his belly very free and easy. But most thing of all which I notices be how dear he holds his son, that Ha-Re-Shunghie which Mr Marsden have spoke of often that he be so diligent with the silversmithing and at the forge.

Such gentle looks flies between them and so tender, I be minded of a mother with her nursling, yet the son be all of fourteen year or more, so Tom have told me.

Careful I be to look away and not to gaze direct which Mrs Marsden have said they dinna find agreeable. And of his companion, Tuai, I doesna catch the eye at all.

And, looking down, I sees the great broad feet upon them, then the hands, hard and strong. Easy to throttle with hands like them, I thinks. And shudders in spite of meself.

All be ready now for us departure. I dreads the ocean voyage, though it be but a two to three week, according to the winds. Feels like someone dreaming, I does. Canna clear a fog from out me head though I knows I be packing boxes, watching the crating of chickens by which us will have eggs and poultry at

New Zealand, washing and storing of me children's clothes and mending of Sannah's woollen cape that she mebbee now have need of. In winter, so Mr Shunghie have said, there be cooler weather there. Wind. No snow, though. He have niver seen it: he do not comprehend what it can be, though Tom have over and over tried to bring it to his mind.

This morning Tom have come to me. 'I must talk to you, Janey.'

And I, suspecting nowt, says, 'Later, Tom. No time has I this minute.'

'It will not take long,' says he. 'It is but a small thing we must settle now.'

So I puts down me bundle of linen for the washing and sits, at his behest, upon the bed's end.

He pats me hand, gentle-like. 'A small thing it is, Janey, yet great as well.'

'And what be this thing?'

''Tis hard to tell thee, yet I must. Of only six or maybe nine months' duration is it, though at first it will seem like more. And it is God's Will.'

'Much be talked about God's Will round these parts. God sends Mr Marsden an angel, do He? Or tablets, mebbee, dug from the quarries by the transports? Brought direct to the Reverend for his examining. Why needs the Church archbishops when Marsden do make his say on things?'

'Hush, Jane. 'Tis hard enough already. It concerns our girls.'

'Sannah and Lizzie? What of them?'

'It is not like here in New Zealand. At Rangi-Houa.'

'Then God be praised for that.'

'It is rough, unmade.'

'Thou said'st us had a little house and made by Mr Shunghie.'

'And that we will have. But . . .'

'So?'

'Sannah will be eight and Lizzie near to seven.'

'Seven and six do yet their ages be. And younger still when all us embarked from England.'

'But at Rangi-Houa is nothing of our English civilization.'

61

'Not so here, neither.'

'Mr Marsden is of the opinion that … at Rangi-Houa … that it is better … that … they should for just a little time perhaps … stay here. In Botany.'

'Me two girls left behind? To stay here with the Marsdens? I be as like to leave a dog.'

'No, not here. In the main settlement, under the Governor's protection.'

'The Gover— Where, then, Tom Kendall? Tell me and tell me true.'

He swallows. Looks not at me. 'In the Female Orphanage, Janey. But for a few months only. And sent for as soon as we are settled. It would be a good thing. Better by far than—'

'Me girls,' cries I, near to shouting, near to hitting at him – me, that would not niver afore have hurt even a dumb animal – 'be not orphans. Mither and father has they both. Or, that be to say, a mither, at least. Since seems their father have lost all thought of them and cares no more for his own.'

And so it comes, the day before us leaves, Tom and me, in Parson Marsden's trap, rides into Botany and leaves me girls, who each do clutch her own small bundle, in care of Mr Hoskings and his lady, her with a face like the block to chop the kindling on.

'I know,' says Sannah, 'why th'art leaving me behind, Mither. But it was not Lizzie's doing. She has done no wrong. It is only I. Th'art not fair to punish Lizzie also. Only I killed little John.'

And Lizzie, me bright parrot that do dance and talk and sing, doth fluff her plumage and lay her quaint head to one side, engaging always with the world, sits dull and silent, moulting in the corner, and do not even raise her head goodbye nor watch to see us go, us that has caged them and abandoned them so far from their native land and home.

And now I knows for sure I does not love me husband, Thomas Kendall. Wife I be to him that loves his God but cares not for his own. His flesh and blood.

I has give up, for Thomas Kendall, all I has iver knowed and loved, held dearest. Me own folk, me own home, me own land. I has gone by his side across God's world to nowt. Away from Brocklesby, us little house in Thoresby, me mither and me father and me sister. No friend nor family has I here. And for sake of Thomas Kendall, and him alone, I has been cursed by Sam, me own dear brother.

For Kendall has I come to this wild furnace of a place with nowt and leaves with even less. Me infant son that, born in Lincoln winter, within his rightful place, might mebbee not lie burning, roasting, in his reddened grave deep in this convict Hell-hole earth.

And Isaac, that I loved but has so cruel denied, for sake of Thomas Kendall, be gone for iver now. I knows not even where his grave may lie but that it be in ground unconsecrated. Damned.

Sannah has I prayed beside while sleeping and put below her bed me little circlet of bay leaves, give me by me mither against the evil eye when us be leaving England. No taint nor ill luck has I suffered to come near her. No hungry ghost nor spirit that do walk abroad to claim her for his own.

How be it I may guard her now that she be took from me?

Bad enough I thought it when half me heart lay still in Lincolnshire and half be held by Tom and all me bairns. Now have me heart been split again, and part of it chained with me little girls in Botany, to the Female Orphanage. Even the name do have a deathly sound. Like 'workhouse', it be a knell, a doom. Suppose the typhus rages there and takes me girls? Her that be set to look after they have a face like granite, clothing harsh and rough, nothing soft of mither to her.

And what have Thomas Kendall done for me? And mine?

He have brung us here. Have watched me cousin swing. Have took away me daughters and placed them with the parentless. And now do carry me and me sons, with nowt for us protection but a Bible, to the savage purple Heathen's land. And what do he tell me daily? 'God will provide. Have Faith. We must trust in the Lord.'

It be only God he loves. Us, his own, be nowt but the

trappings of his life. And though he stands afore me, looking like to always, he do be gone from me now as sure as Sam and Isaac.

All I has left to me be me little sons. And this fierce pain that lies within me chest, me spirit, that niver will be ground away to dust, no matter how he seeks to bring it low.

Only twenty days be our journey across the Tasman Sea. Though I has prayed daily, hourly, that us might be becalmed foriver, a following wind have sped us to New Zealand faster than the albatross do fly.

Thomas Surfleet grizzles, whines for Sannah and Lizzie, Joseph and Basil scuffles and mewls and I, distracted, tries to keep them safe with me below and hold me mind from wandering.

What be afore us? How do go me girls what niver has spent a night from me? What be it I has done that all me life, so sure and safe and fine at last when I married with Tom Kendall, works now so out of kilter? Falling apart about me now, it be, and I powerless to stop it, to hold back the mighty wave of life that sweeps me off from all I loves.

I finds I be weeping.

Little Thomas wipes me face and strokes it. 'Sad, Mother?'

'Oh, aye.'

'Soon Sannah will be with us. And Lizzie, too.'

'Th'art right, Thomas Surfleet. That they will. As soon as I has set me foot upon New Zealand. And no more will thy father come to me till he have sent for them. I swears it upon the Bible.'

At the hatchway appears Tom's face, aglow like the sun.

'Come, Janey, boys, on deck. See our new land.' And stretches out a hand to me that pushes it aside and turns me face from him. 'Still sulky, then?'

'Not sulky, Mr Kendall. Ashamed of a father that so soon forgets his own.' I knows where to strike. Sees his look at 'Mr Kendall'. Pain, then anger.

64

'I have not forgotten my girls. They are constantly in my thoughts and prayers.'

'A great difference that will make to them, be sure.'

'They are in God's keeping.'

'Nay, they be in Mrs Hoskings' keeping. And thou and Reverend Marsden has placed them there.'

'Janey, you misjudge me. Be reconciled. Come up upon the deck. Take first sight of your new home.'

'No home it be to me without me daughters.'

'I am a-coming, Father,' says young Thomas, scrambling up the ladder and Joseph clawing after.

'Come, Mrs Kendall,' says Tom, 'I am your husband and I order you bring my sons on deck.'

Which I does. But joins not in the general rejoicing at the sight of a white cloud on the far distant horizon.

'Ao-Tea-Roa! Ao-Tea-Roa!' cries the natives over and over.

'"The Long White Cloud", they are saying,' explains Mr Marsden. 'It is their name for their land.'

No land does I see meself for some hours until the cloud lifts and a line of green-covered mountains stands high against the sky. The natives be by now all weeping copious tears and beating at their breasts. Mr Shunghie be the most affected and not by joy, or so it seems. He have pulled from his neck his shark-tooth ornament and be tearing and cutting at his body with it. Blood spurts out from the wounds and drips on to the sawdust on the deck, making it like to a slaughterhouse floor. And all the while he be giving out the most sad and affecting cries, till, without noticing it, I be so moved I be weeping too. Weeping for me girls, for Baby John, Isaac, me mither, Brocklesby and Home.

And all around us be natives tearing, cutting at theirselves and shrieking and crying most terrible. Then one of them gives a loud shout, 'Waka, waka!' and points below to where be advancing, paddled by kneeling natives, six great canoes, each mebbee fifty feet long.

And standing in the first canoe be a huge, ugly woman, breasts bare and sagging and nowt to cover her but a woven mat of brown and black slung low about her hips. Hair she have tied tightly to the top and feathered, and on her bottom lip, extending to the chin, a block of that tattoo marking which covers Mr Shunghie's whole entire body, even to the buttocks.

And at sight of her, that great chief raises hisself up, throws his arms to the skies and dives from the side of us ship into the sea-swell far below. And a mighty cry goes up from all the Heathen on board and in the canoes. 'Shunghie! Shunghie!' And Ha-Re-Shunghie, five seconds after, do follow his father into the waves, both swimming like to porpoises to the side of the canoe that be all cut with decorations and wooden adornments. Hauled up and into the craft, wet and all, they clasps theirselves to the woman and presses their noses against hers, the blood and sea water making her own breasts to turn bright crimson. And she lays back her head and cries, 'Tanga-Roa!', her face now being full visible, and I able to see she have eyes like milk and be blind and yet she do stand foursquare in the canoe and niver wavers in her balance.

'And that,' says Reverend Marsden, 'is Turi-Ka-Tuku, Shunghie's wife, reputed the most powerful influence in his dominions, greater even than his tohunga.'

'Tohunga?' says Tom.

'Witch doctor,' says Mr Marsden.

And I feels me skin crawl cold under the blinding sun.

Seems now a hundred years since I first set foot upon New Zealand. Seems it were some other wench, not I, were sat in that little black armed-chair and lowered down from the ship's side into the great canoe below. With Joseph wriggling and wailing in me arms, I be surrounded by natives, tattooed and reeking of rotten fish like to make me gag. Upon a sight of Joseph, several of the men leans forward to touch and stroke at him, smiling at him most tender and patting at his arms.

I looks around me. Us canoe be pulling to the shore of a great bay, the sea blue and flat calm, great high green mountains and hills to either side. Ahead be a wide sweep of sand and shingle beach, into which do run a little stream from the hills beyond. So green, it be, I canna believe it.

And to us left, high upon the hillside, be cut terraces and ledges with, above and below, three fences of great pointed sticks jutting up into the air. Everywhere be scattered low golden-brown buildings but not houses, being no higher than pigsties. And all along the beach ahead be beehives, with a great cluster of them to one end. Smoke do rise from the hillside in little puffs here and there and, at the high hill's very top, there spreads and straggles strange wild trees with long stalk trunks and fountain spurts of wide green grass from out their tops.

And as the canoe rocks nearer to the shore, I sees leaning to the water huge grey trunks of trees with clusters of grey-green leaves threaded through with bursts of blazing flowers, foreign and beautiful. A blood tree, I tells meself, the flowers rising through the leaves like swelling crimson from a wound. And Tom, seeing me look, leans to me and says quiet, 'Are they not glorious? Sacred trees they are and called, says Shunghie, "po-hutu-kawa". Further north, at Te Re-Inga, at the top of this island, is a single one of them hanging from a cliff into the water. The natives believe that, when they die, their souls travel to the tree and descend through its branches down into the water and thence to Purgatory. And after, to their Heaven. So all such trees are sacred to them and no man may cut a part of any one.'

But I looks at him cold, distant. He and Reverend Marsden has cut a part of me that be sacred. And no thought to me heart nor soul nor me girls' neither.

Upon the shore the beehives moves and swells. Rises. Shakes theirselves and stands. Natives, they be, wrapt about in matting, and sleeping seated on that shore.

But on a sight of Shunghie, they flings away their mats and runs, races, into the waves and swims like a great school of fish out towards us little boat and the canoes. And all them girls and women has not amongst them one garment to cover their breasts. Displaying theirselves above their waists as naked as the Lord have made them, they swims beside us and not a one shews a single blush of shame. I sees the Reverend

Marsden's look. It be hard to seem at the same time both greedy and disapproving but he do manage it.

Us has been here now this three month and Marsden have returned to Botany more than a six week since. Detest him though I does, I were feared more when he have left than at any other time afore, even than on that terrible journey out to Botany. Now it be but Tom and me and us boys that dwells here with the Heathen. And them so strange and wild in their customs, it be all I may do to hold meself out from being as a lunatic meself. Days I thinks, belike I be in Bedlam. This be but a dream and I be crazed, mad in me head. But then comes Tom to speak with me or me boys clamours at me knees for bread, and I sees how very little be that space between the crazy and the calm.

Now at Home, it be Eastertide. Tight purple crocus heads spearing through the earth, the meadow by the huntsman's house a green sky starred with yellow primroses. Yet here, though the weather be dulling and the winds springing up from a rough grey sky in the mornings, all be still green. Nothing here do die and restore itself yearly in soft pink and white blossom, burst into leaf, fade into russet fruit and bare itself for winter. Here it be always green, dark and light, green on green, yellow green, brown green, grey green, the bush dense and packed with springing trees and creepers. Brooding, sinister. Ivery tree a gallows, ivery vine a noose.

'Tapu,' says Shunghie, pointing to the dense hills behind his kumara gardens. 'Do not go into forbidden place.' And I needs no telling twice.

How to say how it were when we landed first upon the shore of Ao-Tea-Roa? Tom eager, fired, pulsing with throbbing Christian love, sure in his own thought that God were about to shew him the way to the hearts of them Heathen. Marsden, watchful, cunning, remarking in his mind what here he might mebbee turn to his own advantage. And right soon.

And stubborn. Rigid against Tom, who have seen at once

how us canna farm crops nor grow grass upon the land near the stream which be stagnant and muddy, the soil poor, the rank smell of thin and sour earth oozing from it. Though Marsden be a crofter's son, yet still he have ordered Tom that this be where us must set down and build the little Mission. And to no avail have Tom made argument to shew the folly of this choice. For Marsden be not swayed by any word. And since he be not the farmer here but it be us must daily engage in battle with such weak and feeble soil, why needs he take care to choose aright our patch of ground from Shunghie?

And though I feels that chief amazed at the Reverend's decision, he says niver a word. His countenance displays nowt of his thoughts, yet I sees clear how stupid he, too, do rate Marsden's choosing and how this do set Tom the smaller, also, in the eyes of our protector.

Beside us on the shore lies all us boxes, bundles, chicken crates, which has the savages clustered round for the wonder, and, double-boxed and perched above the others, safe and dry, the chest in which have come *Britannica* so far across the world. A table has us, three chairs, and of bedsteads, two. These does also occasion great interest from the savages, who hits and clangs upon the iron rails, the children clambering and swinging from the ends. Tallow candles has us, stored in two iron chests against the rats, and three more bound and hooped provision boxes with that quantity of flour and barley meal, oats and provender to use to bake us bread till us has set and harvested the seeds brung to plant out in us own crop fields here.

Seed potatoes there be from Parramatta and carrot plantings and turnips likewise. No roses, for which I thanks God. But no trusty for the watering neither.

I looks around me now, for a sight of that little house of which Mr Shunghie have so often spoke in Parramatta which, since it be no place near the poor stream of Marsden's choosing, may yet save us from dwelling in that stagnant place.

I has not lived within me own four walls since us be gone from North Thoresby and us little house with Tom's drapers' goods in the shop out front. A bell rang if folks wished serving and, when Tom were gone with his donkey cart upon deliveries, Seth Paterson, his helper-boy, would pass at speed from the back into the shop, a-tying of his apron and scuffing of his hands along his breeches to clean them off for the showing of the goods. And I meself might come to shew and sell, Sannah and Lizzie sidling up beside, dazzled by the fine muslins, the silky shine and dip of new French ribbons, the froth and cream of Brussels lace brought up by Tom from Norwich where the ships has carried it stored safe and clean in packing boxes sealed with wax. The smell of that waxen seal breaking rises to me now, a warm, tallow tang in me nostrils.

Shakes me head, I does. Clears it. No fine lace and ribbons here. Nowt but chests and boxes upon a foreign shore. I pulls at Tom's sleeve. 'Where be it?'

'Where be what?'

'Us little house. That Shunghie promised.'

He looks at me strange.

It comes to me again how he be not who I has all this ten year thought him. Smaller in spirit, far off from me. And fogged about, his eyes no longer looks at me straight and open as they meets me gaze.

'Janey, patience. We have but now arrived upon these shores.'

And then I knows what he have knowed all the while he were telling me other. Lying to me. No other name for it.

Us has no little house. Nor mebbee niver will. And tears rises and drizzles down me cheeks and nowt I can do to halt them. And it be not the house makes me to weep so but the lying and deceit. For now I knows that Tom be flawed and mean and selfish and all that he have said to me, of truth and love and us together, niver were so. It be he decides us fate, and lies to me to have me cede to his will easy, no quarrel. A dupe, a gull, I be to him. That, blind to any but his own desires, have wrenched me from me daughters, from me mither's hearth, me own kind, me own home, and tells me what he knows to be most false because it be that which he knows well I wishes most to hear.

Me eyes be wet but me heart be burnt dry, a scalding baking stone.

And, of a sudden, I turns to him, the chief.

'Tha promised, sir, a house,' says I. 'Thy word us had upon it.'

He looks at me and rapid talks to Tuai, his brother chief, who stands beside him.

And Tuai, speaking only now to Tom and Marsden, says, 'Tonight, you sleep in hut of his brother. Tomorrow, his people build hut, fine hut.' He waves his arm towards a little pigsty shack of reeds and mud, mebbee four feet high, with a small door where may pass an animal such as a goat or sheep or pig. 'Like here.'

'Like to that?' says I. Perhaps he do seek to insult us. Sleep us no better than his animals.

'That one, chief's hut. Very kood. You have house very kood like this. Soon, soon.'

So all them pigsties be people's dwellings. Drops of rain falls soft upon me head. Even a pigsty be better than no shelter.

'Remember,' says Marsden, who have the Mission House at Parramatta, 'our Lord was born within a stable.'

If I did have me brother's ferret, great pleasure would it give me to send it up the Reverend's trouser leg to attack and devour with its cruel sharp teeth his most delicate and tender parts. If he do have any. Which, saving Mrs Marsden and his children, it be very hard to credit.

And so us be brought to lie within a tiny smelly hut, with the remains of a charcoal fire in the centre, one small window, unglassed, and a doorless entrance through which us must stoop and crawl to enter. And all us be together, Tom and me, the children, Marsden, Tuai and Shunghie, lying clothed upon a woven floor that gives off such a damp and musty reek I feels I niver may sleep in all me life again. But I closes me eyes to rest, and when I has opened them daylight be streaming in at the entrance way and I has slept, with all me boys, a full twelve hour or more. Or so says Tom, bidding us all rise up and look about.

*

71

Trudging up to us plot of land I be, with the smell of good Maori meat floating to me from the pa above and to me side. It be long since us ate proper meat. Not since Botany.

And then it begins to rain like nowt I iver seed in all me life. I seed rain here afore. Gentle rain and sudden slanting squalls upon the sea. Rainstorms I knows from Home. Snow. And bitter weather. Ivery kind of weather. Or so I has thought.

But niver, niver, rain like to this. First it were hot, sodden hot like it have been all day and the day afore too, but no moisture, nowt but a splattering of drops. Then, sudden, a mighty sheet of water comes pouring out of Heaven so thick, so hard, I canna see the sea from where I stands. And hard the drops to hurt and sting the body where they falls. Cruel rain and merciless it be, like to 'ivery thing else here. And up off the ground do rise a smell of earth, mushrooms, sweet dung, green plants and dust all together mixed to a strange new scent. And not disagreeable neither.

The natives didna go for shelter in their huts but all goes rushing forth on to the hillside into the weather, a-holding out their arms and crying, 'Rangi, Rangi,' like to the name of our settlement here, Rangi-Houa.

Someone strides up behind me. I turns me head and makes out through the sluicing rain the figure of Shunghie. He have his arms held wide, a holy look upon his face. I bends meself forward into the wind and the drenching rain-sheets makes washing of me bonnet.

Shunghie raises one hand to Heaven, shouts to me. 'Sky-Father, Rangi, send good rain, eh-Modder. First boy child born after named Rangi. If girl, Mo-Ana, meaning, "great piece of water".'

He marches beside, nods at me bonnet. 'Maku. Wet, eh-Modder. Take off. Better no hat.'

Tom have already made suggestion I might loosen up me garments to the weather and conditions here. I be no Heathen, I be an Englishwoman. No savage parts me from me bonnet. I shakes me head nay, as rain flows over me face and head. Me frock and underskirt be sopping too but I sees the chief's flaxen mat garment be but glossy with the weather like to a goose's back.

He raises his hand to the sky again. 'Rangi.' Motions me to say the same.

'Rangi,' mouths I through the weather.

'Mo-Ana.'

'Mo-Ana.'

He cocks his head to ask me what they means. Us little plot of land in sight now.

'Great piece of water,' says I.

'Kood, kood.'

Mo-Ana, Mo-Ana. Me Sannah and me Lizzie be parted from me by a great piece of water. So no wonder how I weeps when I thinks on it.

This beating rain will mebbee wash away the sorrow from me heart. And, plodding through it, I finds I be praying, silent, only to meself.

Shrive me, Lord, shrive me. Wash away the stain of me denial of our Isaac. Cleanse me of me hatred of this world and all men in it. Wash clean me soul, I prays Thee. And send me daughters to me, I beseeches Thee. Dinna take me daughters for what I done against our Isaac. Thou hast already Baby John. Give me back me girls and I holds fast to love of Thee for all me days. I swears it.

Belike He do not hear. Mebbee like Sam, me brother, He have put me away from Him for ivermore.

'Not weep, eh-Modder. They come, your daughters. They safe. They come. My wa-hi-ne, Turi-Ka-Tuku, see them on the water. Tanga-Roa, the sea god, carry them here.'

Silent I were and spake not once, yet Shunghie have heard me ivery word.

I looks at him, afraid. His purple face be wild and savage, yet I fights away the thought lest he mebbee hears that too.

'Aiee, eh-Modder. You same as my people, my iwi. Not your tangata, this land, but one day you be like us. You, eh-Modder, not Keni, you, be like my people.'

73

RICHARD STOCKWELL.

PRINTER.

BORN NORFOLK,
1777.
DIED NORFOLK,
1859.

Man's inhumanity to man is the most wretched manifestation of our kind. Tom Paine – late fled to the Americas, and dead now, for all I know, buried as I am in this miserable place – saw it plain. Even the most ignoble savage would accord to his fellows those rights we Rational men deny one to another, driven as we are by greed, bigotry and self-interest.

It is, we know, an Age of Reason. And also of the Romantic. Mr Wordsworth's Odes lie pat upon the lips of every man of learning and of fashion. The elegance of our Prince of Wales is a source of common mirth. Yet all around us, poor and dispossessed wretches starve, the new machines encroach upon men's livelihoods and soon will come a day when labourers and the lower orders of working men will have no employment for their little talents. Their idle hands will stretch for bread they can no longer earn by honest toil. The workhouses will be filled, the pages of the Poor Register increase, as more and more are flung upon the streets and one machine commands the work of ten or fifteen men.

And yet it is as Tom Paine says. Each of us has the right to his own soul. No man is born to be the slave of another, to have his food plucked from his mouth by those who have much.

Our laws are made by old men, fixed in their opinions and their thinking. Nothing they see around them has the power to sway their souls. They desire only that which they know, not that which they may bring to pass. The common good, the embracing of the new, the fire which springs alive in young men's bellies, all are damped and crabbed about by pettiness and self-interest, the overwhelming need of old men to preserve their properties and estates against the altruism and commonality of young men's ideals.

My father and I parted company on all things. Were I to support in any discourse the views of Mr Fox, on the instant my father would extol the virtues of Mr Pitt. Of the Revolution in France, he would brook no comment beneath his roof. The despair of beggars aroused within him the most uncharacteristic vitriol. In all things, so it seemed to me then, he must be my opposite.

I was born in the smell of ink and leaden-type at No. 2, Farthings' Gate in Norwich, the first son and third child of my parents. My father, bound to Hugh's in London, on his release went journeyman compositor to Appleby's, and having by diligence and his marriage to my mother accrued to himself moneys enough he removed to Norwich, where he set up on his own account. And, for his fine eye in the setting of type and the laying-out of pages, all of which work at the start he did himself with but one coz and a travelling journeyman, by degrees he prospered until, several years after my own birth, Stockwell's house had become a local byword for a manuscript of quality and economy.

Norwich was prosperous, work plentiful. By the time I was

five years of age, my father had beneath him three journeymen and five indoor apprentices.

One of my father's friends was Master Abbott. An honest man but of the Highest Tory persuasion, Master Abbott was certain that should ideas of liberty and equality be let abroad in England the heads of all such as he would be seen upon staves at Tower Bridge, the old king's waxen countenance atop the rest. To Master Abbott, on all things French must fall the very blackest of suspicions, the darkest whiff of treason.

Bound for seven years as apprentices to Hugh's in London and released at Stationers' Hall together upon a single day, my father, John Abbott and Luke Hansard remained close friends throughout their lives.

While Hansard stayed in London, both my father and Abbott found employment in Norwich, setting up in friendly opposition. Between them they hatched a plan, each to have his eldest son articled and bound to the other. And at the end of seven years, freed, we should return to our family firms, there to succeed our fathers.

In my father's house, we had, from Master Hansard, the intelligence of most that passed in London. He, having been born a Norwich man, came often to our city to visit with his mother and sister, living still in Hungate.

And a Hansard's coz, John Meredith, told me first of Thomas Paine.

Sent from London to Norwich with a pannier full of pamphlets for Abbott's to finish at our cheaper provincial rate, Meredith sat chatting with us after supper. From eight at night till morning, our time was all our own, though we might not leave the house without permission of our master.

Everywhere now, outdoor apprentices were employed as cheaper labour and in London, said Meredith, journeymen were setting up and signing petitions and demands for better wages. 'It's a bad business,' he observed gloomily, spitting in the fire, which hissed and sizzled in agreement. 'A quartern loaf is up again and flour is taxed. And oats and ale as well.'

'Same here in Norfolk,' said Johnson. 'First, war in America, now, war in France and always the common folk that pay.'

'The masters claim,' said Meredith, 'the wages for their labour bills are risen more than double in a ten year.'

'And a quartern loaf has risen fourfold within the same time,' said I. 'Many here are struggling for their basic necessities.'

'While the Prince of Wales plays at dice and closets with his tailor in pursuit of yet more fashionable waistcoats,' said Meredith.

He pulled a snuffbox casually from his pocket, flipped back the lid and stuffed a pinch up either nostril.

Despite the brown snot trickling on Meredith's lip, Johnson and I, impressed, watched this fine display of London sophistication.

He tossed the box across to me. 'You take it?'

I would not, for the world, have admitted my ignorance. With all the elegance at my command, I lightly took a smattering of powder between my fingertips and pressed it up each nostril in imitation of his manner.

It was as if a charge of gunpowder had exploded in my head. For fully a minute, the room and all within it dissolved before my vision, my ears and eyes disposed of all their functions, my frame fell quite apart and reassembled.

'A fine pinch, is it not?' said Meredith. 'From Amsterdam. And harsh and strong like all that's Dutch.' He nodded at me to pass the box to Johnson.

Through watering eyes, I pitched it at his wavering form and had the satisfaction of watching him snort and choke in a manner most unpolished.

'They say,' said I, determined to show that we in Norwich lacked nothing of knowledge of affairs of the capital, 'that Prinny has asked the Parliament again for money to pay his gambling debts.'

A froth of brown appeared at Johnson's lip. He struggled for his breath.

Meredith shrugged. 'It may be. He is the most extravagant, loose-living fellow ever was. But the Parliament will not grant him more until he agrees to marry.'

'I would,' said I, 'that the Parliament would settle on *me* an income of fifty thousand pounds a year when I am come of age.'

'And another sixty thousand for your debts,' said Meredith.

'But Prinny is married already,' put in Johnson, clearing his throat.

'No,' said Meredith. 'Vehemently denied by all the Whigs.'

'The Prince of Wales,' said I, 'has the Whigs within his pocket. I heard your Master Hansard say so to Master Abbott.'

'Better a Whig in the pocket than a High Tory master,' said Johnson feelingly.

'Agreed,' said Meredith. 'My master rails against the Frenchies every day.'

Johnson returned the snuffbox.

'They are all frightened for their heads if radicals breed revolution here. And for their pockets too. But Prinny is already married.'

'They have been living together,' said I, 'for nearly a ten year.'

Meredith shrugged. 'Then why should he deny his marriage?'

'Because she is a Roman Catholic. And it is not so long since the Parliament granted him for his debts the sum of two hundred and twenty-one thousand pounds.'

'After he had denied contracting any marriage with his mistress,' said Johnson.

'I think,' said I, 'that I might lie to the Parliament if such a sum were at stake.'

'Perhaps he does not lie,' said Johnson. 'It may be Mrs Fitzherbert *is* but his mistress.'

Meredith took another pinch of snuff, inhaling this time from the back of his hand. He sneezed violently. Yawned. 'It may be he considers, as Prince of Wales, he is above the need for truth. For kings to keep a mistress is not the same as for the common man.'

'We heard that Farmer George insists now that he marry his Hanoverian cousin. But that he refuses,' I observed.

Johnson's heart was touched. 'Then at least he is a man who

believes in marriage for love, not for convenience. And that must be uncommon in a prince.'

'No,' said Meredith. 'It is certain he will marry with his cousin. His creditors pursue him hotly and though he cannot abide her, they say, neither is he in a position to resist the pressures of his father.'

'Whom he also detests,' said I.

'Indeed,' said Meredith. He lowered his voice and glanced briefly at the door as if to ascertain the servant did not linger with his ear pressed to the panelling.

'The king was mad again for a little space but last month. We had a most highly guarded document delivered to my master by a courtier with instructions it be printed in four copies only and not to leave his possession till the original and all four copies be taken up next morning by Mr Pitt's own manservant.'

'So how came *you* to know its contents?'

'By stealth. And native wit. I was a-setting of type when the messenger came and I went on very quiet about my business so none was much aware of me. The messenger handed it direct to Master Hansard and . . .'

'And . . .'

'Master Hansard, later going to obey a call of Nature, his regular habit every day at that hour, slipped it within the topmost drying rack beneath another manuscript. I raced across – with beating heart, I tell you – and deciphered with difficulty the script of the King's doctor. In which he said His Majesty again was taken with the ravings of a lunatic, his piss was purple and he complained incessantly that the sun had seared his skin. And this in February!'

'If Hansard had caught you at it, that would have been an end to your apprenticeship.'

'Men have been hanged for less.'

'Treason!' said Johnson. 'Transportation for you if you had been apprehended.'

'Which I was not,' said Meredith, good-humoured, 'it being I am such a flash and foxy lad. But tell me, what think you of your Norwich man, Thomas Paine?'

'Our master,' said I, 'calls him the poxiest rapscallion scoundrel unhung.'

'Which, coming from such a right-wing Royalist,' said Johnson, 'some men might deem a compliment.'

'Abbott lives in daily fear of revolution here,' said I. 'He is more touchy upon the subject of the Colonies than Mad George himself.'

'Aye,' said Johnson, 'so all we know of Thomas Paine is that he is a drunkard and a great fomenter of public disorder. And that he has fled back to his Frenchie friends.'

'Those are slanders upon him. What he has to say is greatly interesting. His arguments are reasoned well. His sentiments are afeared not his arguments.'

'He wishes us,' said Johnson, 'to behead our monarch, I believe.'

'Not to behead, merely to remove. And, as in the Americas, we would elect a President.'

At this, we all laughed merrily.

'He says,' continued Meredith, 'all men are created equal by God.'

'Not in this printing house,' observed Johnson and I together.

'Nor in St Luke Hansard's neither! But surely you have read Paine's manuscript, *The Rights of Man*?'

'It is banned,' said I.

'Of course,' said Meredith. 'But all us London prentices have read it.'

'And what think you of it?'

'Compelling and convincing. He wishes to deliver the poor and enslaved from bondage and their lot.'

'Not likely any here among our rulers would embrace such ideas.'

'Never. In France, Monsieur Robespierre was out to have his head upon a pike, so they say he has fled back to the Americas. In England, he was the scourge of the government and the king, going about the countryside and expounding to any who would hear him.'

'He wished to foment them with his philosophy?'

'No. He is the very persuasion of an orator by his under-statement. What he speaks, not how, apprehends the ear. I heard him only once, before he sailed for France, and every word he uttered struck into my heart like the angel's flaming sword.'

'He has an imposing presence?'

'Not at all. He is a little man, quite ugly. Underdressed.'

'Our master says he was but a staymaker and has whalebone ribs where his intellect should be.'

'Your master is indeed no advocate of Paine.'

'But did not Master Hansard forbid you attend Paine's address?'

'I omitted to tell him I was going.'

'And if he had found you out?'

'How so? Whenever I need my freedom, I place a bolster in my bed and slip off through the servants' gate. No fear of St Luke Hansard's presence anywhere *I* might wish to go in London at night. And, as soon as ever I may, I shall place into your hands a copy of *The Rights of Man* so you may read it for yourself and judge its worth.'

'But it has been suppressed. There are heavy penalties for its possession.'

'Oh, tish. You country lads are all alike. Trust me, there is no risk in it.'

'He is a Quaker, they say.'

'His father was a Quaker. He has abandoned all religion.'

'A dangerous course.'

'But one that he himself commends.'

'No wonder Master Abbott wishes to see him hanged.'

Johnson threw coals upon the fire and poked it with his foot. 'I would I could see London.'

'And I,' said I fervently.

'It is the greatest of all places,' said Meredith. 'And daily I go out within it on deliveries of manuscripts or ordering of the plaster for the type-moulds or running of the usual little errands for the house. And so I acquaint myself with all that passes in our mighty city.'

'And by what comes within the house in privy form.'

'Of course. And it is a mercy for that, or all the finest gossip of London-town would pass me by. And what would you country noodles do then for your news?'

Abbott's Works, though smaller than my father's printing house, was renowned for the quality of its setting and its fine compositing. Abbott, High Churchman, High Tory, low paymaster of compositors and pressmen, was a fair, though rigid, master. Of the old persuasion, he held all his apprentices in his house with him and fed and kept us well enough.

Three daughters, he had, each one plainer than the last, a son before and two after. The eldest, Charles, whom my father had had six years as an indoor apprentice, would within a twelve month be released from his articles. Then he would return beneath the paternal roof and in time take over from his father as master of the family works.

Mrs Abbott was distinguished chiefly by her teeth, which, being of dentiform polished wood and ivory, we might not take a meal but that her chewing and general mastication be punctuated by clacks and clicks, slippings and slidings. And a stream of spittle, unchecked by any victual, must accompany it. And greatly did the prentices take mirth in her situation. It was the sport of those long-placed to set the newest lad at his first supper well within the range of Mrs Abbott's teeth and greatly to enjoy his vain attempts at suppressing his discomfiture whilst ducking from the sluice gate.

The ceremonies of induction of apprentices being secret, I had not, though I lived within a printing house, been privy to any part of them before my own initiation at Abbott's.

I was led, blindfold and wary, into the printing room where my eyes were uncovered and I beheld all the chappellonians marching ceremoniously about the room, right arms through the lappets of their coats. A wooden sword was thrust into my hand and I, bearing it, was pushed to the head of their line, where I trod timorously before them.

'Kneel, Coz,' cried the Chapel father, Mr Thomson, chief of the compositors, and thereupon did squeeze over my unsuspecting head a swollen sponge of liquid, the taste of which, as it dribbled down my hair and ears and passed across my lips, I found to be of ale. At once, I stuck out a questing tongue and licked my chin and cheeks wherever it might reach. And much did all the chappellonians laugh at my antics.

'And now, good Coz,' said Mr Thomson, pulling me up, 'your name be Duke of Farthing Gutter, Pisspot Lane, and provided you keep that tongue close in your head concerning our actions here, not revealing what has passed to any man outside these walls, no harm will befall you in the world again.

'You shall not fall into the river and be drowned, no cart shall run you down, no horse shall never kick you, your wind will never break in church, and every drab, upon the espying of you, shall jostle and plead for your favours.'

At this the others roared and laughed and toasted me the Duke of Farthing Gutter. And then came Mr Thomson and pushed me to my knees again, and, with their arms held through their coats as before, all solemnly marched about me in a circle, singing some kind of babble rhyme of ba-ba, ba-be, ba-be-bi and so on throughout the letters of the alphabet. And so much ale they plied me with, I scarce could stand next morning for pain within my head.

Here in this terrible heat, as moisture runs from my scalp and brow down across my cheeks and lips, I think often on that trickle of ale to my head but my tongue touches only the briny tang of sweat where I long for the quenching sweetness of hops and malt.

Memory invades my senses. The recollection of that night we three sat round the master's fire discoursing as do young men, with boast and swagger, each aggrandising himself in accordance with what he has not yet known, each with his printer's mark of graphite hands, gunmetal grey and slippery to the touch.

And rising all, next morning, to the early clash of clogs across the cobbles beneath the casement, the signal of the fishers to the sea.

Yet, within a twelve month, being sent by Master Abbott upon the stage to London, there to lodge at Hansard's for a three day, all my life was changed. The pleasure of Meredith at my arrival was warming to my spirits and, 'Later,' he whispered, aiming a sly wink at me as he made excuse of an errand to pass the table at which I sat flap-dragoning half a loaf and butter prepared for me by Miss Hansard.

What a wondrous place is London! How much I wished my father had sent me to Hansard's for my apprenticeship that I might daily taste the life of such a city. The sights, the smells, the cries and crowds, churches, theatres, coffee-houses, ale-houses, all manner of conveyances and folk abroad. Sheep driven down this lane, baker's hot waft down that, saucy knowing girls on every street, fine folk with their laces, satins, silver-buckled shoes, the great concourse of the Guild-hall, St Paul's, the Monument, Newgate Prison, where black-clad lawyers hovered, their purses on their backs, the jostle and the jumble of the sellers with their wares, the houses crowded hard together and the great, great river winding all about.

And, promised Meredith, he would take me out upon the town after the house lay down for the night to sleep.

Which he did. And took me to a bawdy-house, where such lewd goings-on were enacted I thought to blush for shame. And after, on the payment of a sixpence, I was led into the basement, to a little curtained antechamber – of which there seemed very many – where a jade with auburn curls and dugs like giant apples bursting from her bodice let me make free with her, which, in truth, I never had done before, though I had boasted of it often. And, when she let me snatch her purse at last, I felt such pride and pleasure in my manhood that she observed that for a threepence – it being all I had left, and I being so fine and vigorous a young man – she would let me repeat my performance. As she did. Not once but twice, so that it was all I could do to muster strength to stumble back to Great Turnstile, where I fell into a hearty sleep from which I was awoken far too soon by Meredith. And spent all day following examining myself privily for signs of the pox.

The morning of my departure came Meredith to our chamber and slid into my hands a package.

'Tom Paine's writings,' he whispered and shook my hand farewell.

I fell asleep within the stage and did not wake till we were near to Colchester.

How dull was Norwich. Proud and prosperous, staid and secure it seemed, with none of that teeming, pulsating tide, the grime and filth, the lustre and the low life of the capital.

I took my forbidden manuscripts, secreted them beneath my pallet and, by degrees, made my way through them. How great was my admiration at the clarity of writing which shone within them, the noble sentiments they conjured forth: 'The contrast of affluence and wretchedness continually meeting and offending the eye, is like dead and living bodies chained together.'

It is no wonder, thought I, our times are called the Age of Enlightenment when men write pamphlets such as these.

Justice demands we should all hold rights in equal and common parts. But where about me do I see this justice? Though I and all my family be comfortable within our situation and never have I had to beg my bread nor had my shoes with flapping soles and buckleless, I need but walk along the poorer Norwich streets to see the wretched swarming all around, snatching and plucking at what morsels they may find, whining infants pale upon the shoulders of their mothers who wheedle ingratiatingly for a little coin, or offer themselves to any who pass that they may have the wherewithal for sustenance. And men without paid labour spill from the taverns where they may drown themselves in gin for less than a quarter of what they must pay nowadays for a loaf of bread.

And, as I set my type, I thought, too, of the fly-boy, Joseph, Master Abbott's devil, a perpetual blackamoor from the ink, who passed my box to carry the sheets to dry as they came off the timpan, from whence he would after place them in an orderly heap. For a nugatory sum he performed this work, deemed even below the offices of a coz such as I, and poverty only was his spur to labour. His father, a printing workman never bound, smouted where he might at one house or another with, it could be, one or two days' work only in any week. At home, there lay a mother and another ten, all with mouths that must be fed. On market days, had I not seen with my own eyes Joseph scavenging for fallen fruit and scraps about the stalls? And felt a flicker of distaste, disgust even, for his activities. Which, Tom Paine saw plain, were animated only by the forces of necessity.

A wave of shame now rippled over me. I nodded companionably at him as he passed. In answer, he grunted like a pig. Looking up, I saw that the press-man, Tinkins, had come into the room; in his grasp, the metal mould ladle.

The ink-maker, spying Tinkins, also gave a loud grunt, hastily transmuted to a cough on sight of Master Abbott hard behind him. I busied myself with binding about the finished copy in my frame.

'Put these papers into a coffin for me, coz,' called Mr Thomson.

Master Abbott strode into the room. Something in his demeanour caused us all to scurry the harder while giving the outward seeming of normality. He balanced between his fingers a manuscript, holding the edges only, as if the thing were poxed.

Waves of icy fury flowed out from him. He took up a stance within the centre of the room and stood there, his very silence bespeaking danger.

Every man among us strove the harder to cleave to his work. Not a one but did not have both heart and hands trembling. From the sides of my downcast eyes, I watched him observing us all. He seemed to be regaining mastery of his temper only with greatest difficulty. He spoke.

'Stockwell,' he said, in a voice of steel.

I laid aside my mallet in my tray with all my letters, headpieces, tailpieces, slips and blocks, and moved to take up the manuscript he held out to me. But, even as I reached for it, I was halted in horror by the ribbon tied about it. A narrow ribbon, satin and green as grass. Given to me as a token by the friendly jade of the bawdy-house.

A roar from Master Abbott sounded through the printing house.

'Stockwell, thou wretch, stand forth!'

At this the room fell utter silent. All ceased their labours to observe and overhear. I took another wavering step towards my master. His face flushed violent angry red. The fingered manuscript twitched with venom.

'Is this your property?'

'Yes, Master.'

'Where did you come by it?'

'I . . . I . . . do not know, Master.'

'Simpleton. You know indeed. Who gave you this piece of excrement?'

'I . . . have purchased it, sir. In London.'

'And how paid for it?'

'I . . . bartered for it, Master.'

'You bartered what?'

'My silken handkerchief, Master.'

'*Your* silken wipe? Does it not stipulate in your indentures, plain and clear, that while apprentice-bound you and all you have shall be the property of your master?'

'It does, sir.'

'For which, in return, with your labour, he shall take you as his own into his house and there feed and educate you in the ways of your trade?'

'Yes, Master.'

'And you have bartered *my* silken handkerchief for this? This piece of mad delusion, these ravings of a lunatic who seeks only to bring down his government and his king!'

I believe now that if I had but thrown myself upon his mercy, repented with lamentations of my folly and abased myself, my master would have ordered the workmen take me by force on the spot, lay me athwart the Correcting-stone and solace me there with a paper-board. And, if it had been so, and I had humbly submitted to my correction, still might I rejoice within my native land.

But young men are hot and precipitous. Their wills inflame their tongues.

'I read here, Stockwell, thou ingrate, of notions from France and the Americas being seeded in feeble minds and held up as equal to the proper truths of England and her government and monarch. A century before we would have burnt such as Paine, and a fine thing too. His pestilential propoundings rot the very ears of those who hear them.'

Alas, the foolishness of youth!

'My own ears are not rotted, sir,' said I, quavering, false-bold, 'and Thomas Paine remarks that monarchy would not have continued so many ages in the world had it not been for the abuses it protects.'

The apoplexy seized my master.

'Insolent donkey. You are speaking of your king. This is treasonable talk. I will not hear it in my own house.'

'It is but the truth. And nowhere in my articles does it say I may not speak the truth. Indeed, it is expressly stated I must do so.'

Master Abbott swung his head from side to side like a waiting carthorse.

'It is also expressly stated, coz, you shall not bring your master nor his house into disrepute and yet I find, with your own brazen hand, you have brought beneath my roof the works of that heinous madman Thomas Paine. Works banned within this realm. And, worse, you have seen fit to print here upon your own master's press, copies of part of this seditious desecration.'

It was Meredith had copied several pages and placed them with the manuscripts, and careful study would have shown that Hansard's was their origin. But how could I incriminate a friend? I stayed my speech.

'Answer me, sir.'

Still I stayed mute.

My master's colour deepened to brick red. His voice shook with his fury.

'To act against your master is a felony, to act against your monarch and your country, treason. Too many young men nowadays hold with these Frenchie ideas. Destruction stalks in secret in our country waiting but to shatter and destroy all

that is best of our English heritage. These Continental mad-
nesses, these foreign notions, ideas of the Americas. What
need have we of these? Is not our country mightiest on the
globe? Do not our laws espouse, and the Parliament uphold,
the very notion of our sovereign supremacy? Let all here who
disagree with me stand forth.'

Not a one of them but did not root himself to the spot.

'Then each who holds as I do, call forth his aye.'

At this, from Mr Thomson to inky Joseph, burst out the
cry of 'England!'

'So,' said Master Abbott, gratified in his support, 'let him
who would have Frenchie ideas go to France. And see how
long he keeps his head upon his shoulders there! I will not
have my authority flouted, my country and my government
brought low.

'You have not shown a fragment of remorse, Stockwell.
And so, no more shall I. You are no longer apprentice here.
Your name shall be erased from the Hall Book and your
indentures destroyed before a meeting of the Council of
Stationers.'

At this, there was a gasp throughout the room.

'Mr Thomson,' ordered my master, 'fetch me a bailiff. This
seditious wretch shall be arrested and tried.'

And so, for my beliefs, at the age of one-and-twenty I came
to be consigned with those my equals – yet none of us equal
under law – to His Majesty's Hulks. From whence I would be
taken and transported to His Majesty's Colony at Botany
Bay, in New South Wales, for a period not exceeding the sum
of twenty-five years, and there to be engaged in hard labour.

From my daily life in the smoky smells of the printing
house, the dusty catch of the plaster stirred for the moulds,
the acrid tingle of hot lead in the nostrils, the rattle and thump
of the presses, the joggle of characters in the boxes, the swish
of the rope noosed round the block for binding, I passed,
within a twelve month, to the vile excremental stench of the
Hulks with their reek of filth and despair, the grieving clang
of chains on balls, the wailing of the crazed and damned.

A seditionist was I now, so designated by the laws of England. I had known myself a printer with words to set and bind, to print in settings beautiful by reason of their symmetry, but now I found myself abased, despoiled, rejected. The very he I thought myself – erased.

And yet, though my outer form today be leaner and more haggard to the view, by all it has been forced to encompass, the inner has gained in breadth and stature.

My father and my sisters came to the prison in Norwich but once. My father referred to my situation as 'such a heart-rending disgrace'. My sisters wept over me, Anne presenting me with a Testament and a Prayer Book, Livvy with a nosegay which was stolen and shredded before the night was over.

And, within a month, came Master Abbott to see me also, a most unwelcome visitor. I braced myself for remonstrances and sermons and was stunned to find him clutch my hand and beg me for his pardon.

'Ah, Stockwell,' said he, 'your father is my dearest friend and now I have betrayed him by my foolish heat of temper. I shall have you pardoned. I am determined on it. I shall not rest until I have bought you out. It was never for a moment in my thinking that you should be subjected to such a terrible, such an unjust, punishment. The shame of this has brought your father low. And I, too, can only pray and ask forgiveness of my Maker.

'Be strong, lad. My lawyer, Mr Markby, is speaking with the magistrates and we shall have you sprung from here before another month is past.

'Your folly was but the ignorance of youth.'

I confess I clung to all he said though I was in greatest shock at the unexpected severity of my sentence.

'It is because of Tom Paine and his discourses,' said Meredith, visiting me more than a six month later in Norwich prison where I still awaited transporting to the Hulks. 'But be assured, you surely will be pardoned. Your father and your master are seeking every day to buy you out. I cannot tell how bad I feel it was I copied the pages. I meant them only for Johnson's scrutiny.'

I felt like one in a dream who knows he soon must wake and then all will be well, that his terrible apparitions must dissolve in the light of day. And when, after an interminable space, I was removed to London, to the prison at Newgate, I clutched at the belief that this was a sign. That daily, hourly, my freedom yet marched towards me.

So it was in a daze of unbelief that I entered, some long time after, the rowing boat which carried me to my new quarters, the Hulks, those desolate, half-dying ships, once bearing names to rouse the cheering of a nation, now lying rotting on the marshes out of Deptford, a ghostly fleet of spirit ships such as might appear in dreams as warning of catastrophe.

Aboard my phantom vessel, I suffered the indignity of all my clothing ripped from me at once and pawed about by my gaolers, one claiming my shirt, another my breeches or my buckles, until all that had covered me was gone and I stood before them mother-naked. At which, to great ribaldry, was brought in a barber, himself in convict garb, who set about me with a razor, shaving my head and afterwards my privy parts, my underarms and chest, even the bum-fluff of my buttocks, and nicking and blood-letting as he scraped.

This degradation finished, two of them led me out upon the decks, where they threw over me pails of icy water, then handed me a coarse and ugly convict uniform which tore at my newly shaven parts as they roughly dragged it over my shivering frame. And a transport smith was brought to set about my ankle a manacle, on which he secured a ball and chain, the weight of which I could not have believed so heavy were it not anchored to my own leg.

Time now lost all meaning for me. Each day I told myself the next would see me freed, a rowing boat must come to take me off this dying ship, return me home.

But slowly, with nothing of familiar routine to mark out the passages of time, day ran into day, month into month, year into year, like jumbled letters marking little incidents, meaningless strings of words standing ciphers to my confusion, a continuous manuscript with only sunsets and sunrises delineating the edges of its pages. And if I try now to recall that time upon the Hulks, thousands of pages rise up to me blank, unmarked by any recollection of when it was that first I understood all hope of mitigation of my sentence had been lost to me.

It is one matter to hold to ideals of equality within the comforts and security of home. Another quite to be confronted on every side by the vileness and depravity of debased ruffians.

The common man, with but little education, is much taken up by all his basic needs and, placed within the confines of imprisonment, such petty concerns obsess him as the dimensions of his rationing of bread, the space about his iron cot, the jealous and ferocious guardianship of the trifles left to his possession.

And so, cast out from my own society and into the company of felons, became I, too. The savagery of our daily life upon the Hulks from whence we were ferried each morning to dredge by hand the reaches of the River Thames, the sting of the whip about the shoulders of the sluggard labourer, do not bring forth in Man that kindness to his fellows which ought to be his hallmark.

In such a company, the loutish bully will be king, the others, weaker, subject to his rule. Norton, an aged Devon man, both built and brained like an ox, held reign of terror upon our broken ship. By night he might command whatever he chose from those under his yoke: a little from each man's rations, secreted in the day to buy off Norton's wrath, the blanket from another's freezing bed that Norton might be warm.

And he that refused would find himself abused, accused of infamies never committed but sworn for by many.

Man is a pack animal, like to a hound, who cannot stand beside his equals but must lie within a hierarchy, top dog to underdog and the pack in between. And thus is it, too, with our Government. He that heads our state has much by which to live and more to pay his debts, while the cur at the bottom must forage for his scraps.

Upon our ship it was different only in that it was Norton, not George, who would be king.

So that when, at last, they took us from that damp, unhealthy ruin and placed us on our transport ship, it seemed as though the conditions of our life must be improved, if only for the fact that our vessel was the healthier and sturdier.

And that this was a fallacy I did not learn until a two day after, by which time our ship had set her sails, slid down from Tilbury to the open sea and started out upon that nightmare journey to the Antipodes and all that lay beyond.

And by my left side, where we lay, shoulder to shoulder, was manacled Isaac Quickfall.

Memory is all I have left to me now: memory, strangest of all our senses. As life itself fades from the body, that which lingers last must be the drift of recollection: single characters impressed upon the soul, making no important sentence or paragraph. Scattered idle letters – the J of a scent, the T of a fleeting vision, the Alpha or Omega of a sound, some more deeply printed than others.

What makes an instance of the past be so remarked it can, unbidden, spring into the mind, bringing instant joy or grief, transporting us in a moment to another time, another conti-nent, another life? It is not merely the magnitude of a thing that causes a man to remember and be moved.

I strive to recall my last sight of my mother, laid within her silk-lined coffin, a smile fixed on her cold lips, white roses clasped in her still hands. But from its parts, I struggle to bring the sum of that melancholy sight to its whole. Yet, in an instant, uncalled and free, leaps to my mind's eye my little self dancing upon her lap, the feel of the stuff of her dress recollected in the soles of my feet, her tender smile alive to me. All as vivid now as then, by virtue only of memory, which no more may be commanded and bound than may be the wind by the becalmed mariner.

Upon the typeface of *my* soul will lie at the last a J. For Jane. Merry, dancing, her black curls falling under her bonnet. Just as I saw her at Lincoln Michaelmas Fair, Isaac and Sam on either side, arms linked as they made their way down Steep Hill among the jostling crowds.

I had observed her before though she had not a notion of my existence. Of all the lasses thronging at the Fair, she was the most striking for her beauty. Black curling hair, black eyes like her brother Sam's, sharp and glossy as coals. And her skin as soft as peach flesh. I knew they came from Brocklesby, Lord Pelham's great estate. Old Quickfall was head kennel-man there and Sam a bailiff's prentice. But Isaac laboured in the fields. He was built for it. A back as broad as oxen shoulders, bull head and hands like hams. Stubborn as a donkey, too. It was common enough local intelligence that if you wanted a Lincolnshire pheasant, plump and juicy, a brace of hare or even, rumour had it, a fine milk doe, no questions asked, none answered, Isaac Quickfall was your man.

But to see Isaac there, where he stood four square, part of the Lincoln landscape, no man might imagine the merciless breadth of his fate.

It is the lot of some men to be born in troubled times, times which shape their destiny. So it has fallen out with me. And with Isaac, also.

For the duration of that voyage I watched the very markings of myself falling from me, little by little, as the lead-grey colouring of my hands was worn and chafed away, until, upon our anchoring at Port Jackson, my fingers had once again assumed their forgotten colour, the tiny hairs that thatched between the knuckle and the wrist reborn from ancient gray to virile black.

It is a bitter irony, and one I much contemplate, that Master Abbott, by whose intercession my situation here at Parramatta is so much ameliorated, is yet the very man by whom I have been brought so low. The terror of sedition that drove his anger against me was the selfsame terror that held his contemporaries from any mitigation of my sentence.

But, having failed in his plea to save me from transportation, Master Abbott wrote to Governor Davy, to plead my case for clemency. And Mrs Marsden being in want of a trusty for her garden, and her husband, the Reverend Samuel Marsden, that gorbellied hypocrite, in want of respite from her demands, it was agreed I should be taken from the Botany chain gang and be sent to Parramatta, to which decision I probably owe my life.

And it was a full four years after, in the Marsdens' Parramatta garden, I recognised, with shock, that my fingers nevermore would be of printers' grey. Under the blazing, blinding sun, scrabbling and pulling within that foreign soil, they had darkened for ever to ochre, like the terracotta digits of an ancient pot dragged unwilling from sleep within its native earth.

THOMAS KENDALL.

*TUTOR &
DRAPER.*

BORN NORTH THORESBY,

LINCOLNSHIRE,

1778.

DIED NEW SOUTH WALES,

1837.

I am a man of God. There you have it, the very kernel of my life contained within a nutshell.

Coming over Headling Ridge in the high summer of 1811, trimming along in my small draper's cart, I, Thomas Kendall, was vouchsafed a vision. I saw what is given few men ever to gaze upon – the Face of Almighty God.

It was a day of mixed weathers, at the one moment showering rain, then hard upon it blustery wind, and following, pockets and patches of bright but heatless sunshine. Scudding grey clouds billowed and shook above Headling Ridge, sailing before the wind to the horizon. I whipped up my beast who clipped her heels and tossed her head as the cart swayed and clattered behind. Raising my glance to the Ridge and, above it, the sky, the better to observe the coming weather, at that very instant I observed the clouds to part and a shaft of blinding sunlight ray to Earth. The huge doorway of clouds piled to either side of this great beam served only to increase its brightness. Dazzled, I dropped my gaze, lifted it once more and saw for the space of a moment, in all Its awful radiance, the Visage of my Maker.

Blinded, I tore off my hat, sank on the instant to my knees and bowed my head. Beside me, my little donkey lowered her own head and sank to her knees also, humbled in the presence of Him whose earthly means of transportation she and her kind had been.

'Only show me Thy Will, Lord,' I prayed, 'and I shall obey.'

In echo, my donkey's sweet hay-laden breath blew forth an animal hymn of praise to her Maker.

The light of God flooded around us as we knelt on the soggy turf. I felt it spread to touch my feet, my back, until it dropped, a benediction, upon my naked head.

How long we thus remained, I know not. But on my return to my dearest Jane I informed her of this miracle and instructed her to pack at once for me a small bundle, that I might make my way that very night to London, there to discover what of God's great work it was required for me to do.

Ah, London is such a city of sin that a man called to serve his Maker might find his very mission there among its streets that teem with vice and wickedness.

With little idea of where I should go but placing myself entirely in the hands of the Lord, I made my way to a lodging house recommended me in Dew Lane, off Great Turnstile, taking care to watch about me for pickpockets and press-gang men who, it is well known, frequent the streets of the capital seeking out gulls and country bumkins such as I.

And, so great is the goodness of the Lord to them that believe in His everlasting kindness and have but faith in Him, upon that very evening Providence turned my steps to

Marylebone, where, passing a chapel of ease, the Bentinck, I was suffered to hear singing new to me and delightful. I stepped within, sat and opened my ears. My attention was arrested as out of a long slumber during the solemnity of the service when I was told so plainly and impressively the one true remedy for sin and misery. My Saviour Himself had led me thither.

I returned next day to Lincolnshire, disposed of all I had, and within the four month had dispatched myself and my little family to the capital, there to live as near as I might to those means of grace that could lead me to hope of glory.

And it was the same Reverend Wood, whose stern and silver-tongued oratory in London had first aroused my soul, who turned my understanding towards the deplorable state of the Heathen world, that citadel of Satan, where poor ignorant savages must struggle against the forces of Darkness bereft of the knowledge of the loving kindness of their Lord.

I had already taken upon myself the duties of the Sunday School at Bentinck and much enjoyed my frequent discoursing with Mr Wood upon the nature of Christ's love. It came to me now that I might be called by God to preach Salvation and the doctrine of the Cross unto my ignorant brethren. Do not the Scriptures themselves prophesy that the Lord should set His hand the second time to recover the lost remnant of his people? For this I had been formed. Had not my mother's dear proscriptions, her exhortations and admonitions, her true and ever-held belief, been that I, her younger son, the child of my father's dotage and her own declining years, had been marked out at my birth by the Hand of God for His service?

Even the vile sin of my youth, the fall for which I nightly still beseech my God forgiveness, the stumbling of my steps in Grimsby, that wanton city, rank with the reek of fishwives and their wares, the coarse cries of carousing whalers in search of rum and trollops, had been but a preparation for my destiny. For how can he who is spotless understand the temptations of the sinner?

*

Reverend Wood, seeing clear in me also the vocation of the missionary, wrote on my behalf to the Church Missionary Society, where he is a personage of some influence, and thus was I introduced to that august man the Reverend Josiah Pratt. He, in turn, corresponded with the Reverend Samuel Marsden, then seeking to raise the first Mission to New Zealand.

And Reverend Marsden having at his Mission House in Parramatta in New South Wales, a number of these Heathen, of chiefly rank and desirous of availing themselves of the knowledge and love of God, and Reverend Wood having spoken of my ability in learning new languages, it came about that, I not yet ordained but with the certain promise of it ringing in my ears, we took leave of our dear ones and our fellows and sailed with our five children and Jane already four months gone with a sixth. She had exhorted me to remain in London until her confinement but God's work cannot be held subject to man's needs. 'Was not,' I reminded her, 'Elijah in the wilderness fed by ravens? Only have Faith and believe and all shall be given unto you.'

Faith, it is, moves mountains; by Faith are we raised up. It is Faith and Faith alone leads man towards the knowledge of his Lord.

My own sweet mother, having passed before into that glorious kingdom where she may claim the true and just reward of a virtuous Christian soul, did not see this happy day of our departure. And yet her presence about us was so palpable I whispered as our vessel drew away from land and our first faltering steps were set towards our goal, 'Thy Will be done. Bless me, my dearest Mother.' And fancied I heard her answer float to me upon the wind, 'Well done, thou good and faithful son.'

When I first saw the New Zealanders, however, dressed as they were in native raiment, their appearance was by no means any recommendation to me. Their wild forlorn looks were distressing to my feelings. How I longed to bring the blessings of civilization and the message of Christ's love to those poor lost souls.

I must confess, as well, my disappointment at my first meeting with the Reverend Samuel Marsden. Upon that long and frightful voyage, starved of those discourses on the nature of Christ and His love, the state of the Fall of the Heathen, and similar burning questions which I had daily enjoyed in London at Bentinck Chapel, I sustained myself by envisaging the earnest and eager conversations to come with my new brother in Christ. For Jane, whilst a worthy soul, is but a woman, with neither the skill of reading nor the gift of rationality. God has not seen fit to grace her sex with the understanding of scientific enquiry.

Conceive, then, of my distress when my tentative advances were rebuffed by Reverend Marsden in most plain terms, he informing me very curtly of his disaffection for chapels of ease such as the Bentinck and of his opinion that all within them were Evangelicals of the Low Church persuasion with whom he would not consider himself cousin, much less brother.

Deprived thus of the nurture my soul sought, I was set forthwith by the parson to study the calling of a sawyer, he being of the opinion that this occupation would be much required in New Zealand and that conversion of the Heathen Maori must first be preceded by the bringing to them of those skills and artefacts which would most persuasively seduce them and engage their interest.

So, when later I was sent out with a servant and the traveller Mr Nicholas to New Zealand upon the *Active*, which ship Marsden had purchased with his missionary funds to ply between New South Wales and New Zealand, it was with iron nails and tomahawks, axes and blankets, I travelled, not with the Word of God. A tradesman he sent me thither.

And upon my return from that first exploratory voyage, he did not come to greet me at the shore, sending in his stead Stockwell, his garden servant; then, at my entering the house, he summoned me to his study where he berated me most cruelly.

I had, shortly before leaving, been granted an audience with Governor Davy in which he saw fit to invest in me the powers of a magistrate at New Zealand. A proud moment, I do confess, but, surely, justifiably so.

During the voyage and upon our arrival, the deplorable and unjust treatment of some of the natives by certain Europeans had been brought to my attention. The chief, Rua-Tara, implored me to understand that the massacre and subsequent terrible fate of all aboard the *Boyd* was the direct consequence of the beating and chaining of his cousin, Te Pahi's nephew. Who, when that vessel first left the Bay of Islands to sail south, had been press-ganged aboard it, then flogged when apprehended trying to escape over the side.

This nephew being of the highest rank within his tribe, the equivalent would be the Duke of Clarence held against his will by natives and lashed with the cat when trying to bid for his freedom.

And inasmuch as His Majesty and the Prince of Wales would vow vengeance against the perpetrators of such an act of treason, so did the relatives of Te Pahi seek to avenge this insult to their own native prince when, upon his return, he conveyed to them the history of his ill-treatment.

Bearing gifts for the captain and crew, Te Pahi's relations allayed the Europeans' doubts, treating with them in the most affable manner, said Rua-Tara, but, returning under cover of night, they swarmed the ropes and fell upon all aboard, women and children included, and slew them.

Te Pahi sued for the right to the sole survivor, a woman, whom he placed with his own hands upon a whaling ship bound for Port Jackson. Whereupon Governor Davy, apprised by her of all that had befallen, sent a gunboat to New Zealand. And it was thus, through his merciful action, Te Pahi sealed the fate of his own cousin, principal chief of the tribe.

I had, upon receipt of this information, written, in my new magisterial capacity, to Governor Davy. I have the text of my letter by heart.

His Honour Governor Davy,
&c. &c.

I would suggest to your Honour that many fatal occurrences have taken place in the South Sea Islands in consequence of the ill-treatment which the natives have experienced from unprincipled Europeans, and many valuable British seamen have fallen innocent victims to that usual mode of retaliation which they adopt after receiving an injury, and with respect to the New Zealanders it is well known that after they have been some time from their home they are exceedingly desirous to return, and every unkind disappointment of their wishes tends greatly to excite their resentment. It cannot be supposed that they are acquainted with the binding nature of an article at the time they sign it, and they must in certain cases on this very account deem the restraint a great hardship upon them.

> I am,
> Sir,
>
> Your very obliged, and obedient Servant,
> T. KENDALL

Mr Marsden, at Parramatta, foursquare in his study, back to the wall, threw down to me an immediate gauntlet.

'Mr Kendall, you have seen fit to trouble Governor Davy with your unsolicited opinions of the native mind and heart.'

'I do not deny it.'

'And in what capacity do you set yourself up as mouthpiece for the savages of New Zealand?'

'As one who has at heart the well-being of his pastoral flock, sir.'

'Mr Kendall, may I remind you you are not an ordained minister of the Church of England. Nor of any other church, in so far as I am aware.'

'No, sir.'

'Therefore you have no "pastoral flock". You are bound, under my authority, *my* authority, Mr Kendall, to the setting up of a school and the education of the children of the natives of the Bay of Islands of New Zealand.'

He passed to me a paper. 'Here is a letter to the chief, Rua-Tara, which you will be charged with carrying upon your return. Pray pay particular attention to the second sentence.'

I read as follows:

Rua-Tara King,

I have sent the brig *Active* to the Bay of Islands to see what you are doing, and Mr Kendall from England. Mr Kendall will teach the boys and girls to read and write. I told you when you are at Parramatta I would send you a gentleman to teach your Tamoncekees and Coeteedos to read. You will be very good to Mr Kendall and his family. They will come and live in New Zealand if you will not hurt them, and teach you how to grow corn wheat and how to make houses, and every thing ...

I am,
Your friend,

SAMUEL MARSDEN

'None the less, Reverend Marsden, Governor Davy has appointed me magistrate at the Bay of Islands and in this capacity I shall write to him as I judge fit and right.'

'Governor Davy returns to England within a three month and will be succeeded by Governor MacQuarrie.'

'Then amen to that.'

'Mr Kendall, I advise you, trim your sails lest the wind overturn you.'

And within a nine month following I returned with Reverend Marsden, my wife and sons, two Maori chiefs and assorted native princelings to that very shore of New Zealand where earlier I had set foot. I did not fear for our safety as I could not learn that in any acts of violence the Maori had been the first aggressors.

We arrived upon a Sabbath, Christmas Day, and Marsden at once set up to hold Divine Service on the beach of Rangi-Houa. Words have not the power to describe the great wave of emotion which threatened to engulf my heart as I knelt upon the shingly sand to receive the Host.

Around us swelled our congregation of Heathen drawn

already by the Divine Light from that Outer Darkness into which they had so long been cast.

'Take, eat,' said Marsden, consecrating the Bread, 'this is my Body which is given for you.' He took up the Cup. 'Drink ye all of this ... This is my blood ...'

He placed in my suppliant hands the Host. 'The Body of our Lord Jesus Christ ... Take and eat this ... and feed on him in thy heart ... The Blood of our Lord Jesus Christ ... Drink this in remembrance ...'

As I raised my head to the Cup, I saw the tears which coursed down the tattooed face of our protector, the chief, Shunghie. Our Saviour Himself had touched his pagan heart. The Lord moves in mysterious ways.

I vowed anew to set myself yet harder to the task of mastering the Maori tongue, which study I had commenced at Parramatta. And greatly taken were the Rangi-Houa natives with my attempts to convey to them in their own language the meaning of the ceremony of the Holy Communion.

Here we now rest in a hut built for us by Shungie's people, Marsden having returned alone to Parramatta.

Shunghie is my friend and constant interpreter of their lore and customs. My tiny school is built beside our hut but it is no easy task to give instruction there. The children sleep often in the schoolhouse with but little or no clothing to cover their nakedness, and their unwashed and unkempt state is difficult to bear. I have requested Marsden frequently for suitable clothing to be sent but none has yet been vouchsafed me.

When a teacher amongst the Heathen is surrounded by a number of children, and while perhaps one is repeating his lesson, another will be playing with his feet in fascination with their whiteness, another taking away his hat, and another his book, and all this in so friendly a manner he cannot be angry at them, yet it requires some study how to introduce a salutary discipline. The children do not come to study every day and I have not the means of feeding them to retain them here.

It is a constant source of affliction to me that, in order to secure our food supplies, I am already tempted daily into trade. The Maori longs for nothing so much as muskets. And the whaling and sealing vessels that from time to time put in at Rangi-Houa, here in the Bay of Islands – which traffic is now increasing since time has eclipsed the memories of the *Boyd* – scruple not to give the natives what they demand in weaponry in exchange for pigs and sweet potatoes. So that we here at the Mission cannot tempt them to sell food to us for any less, yet am I loath to engage in any trade at all. And I have writ most often upon the subject to Marsden, pleading that he send us those supplies we need. But to no avail. He is deaf to my entreaties.

It is remarkable how the Maori have adapted themselves and their life's necessities to the conditions here. The weaving of their linen flax is entirely superior to anything I ever saw. And, sure, I was a draper before I was called by God.

Their nets, too, surpass any I have seen in Grimsby. They fish by many different means but in the use of the seine net they are particularly skilled, all the tribe joining together to haul in the largest nets with their wriggling harvests trapped within. The old men are often to be seen upon the shore mending these nets, which are of the very finest stranded filaments so that keen sight is required even to find the rents.

And in this, again, I have noticed the superiority of the Heathen. Their eyesight is so much more developed than ours that the old men have no difficulty in carrying out this task. And men and women alike have an acuity of vision which makes it possible for them, upon examining the Heavens at night, not merely to see all seven of the main stars of the Pleiades quite clearly but also to locate many of the surrounding smaller stars with the naked eye.

Shunghie, upon being shown Mr Nicholas's telescope and apprised of its function, pronounced himself severely disappointed, since it showed him nothing he had not already seen before with his own unaided eyes. One sharp, still night in autumn, as we stood on the hillside, he pointed out the rings of Saturn but, try as I might, I could not see anything, the planet itself being but distant and blurred to my own eyes.

He has taken upon himself the charge of instructing me in the native tongue and I now am able to converse with him on many subjects with little hesitancy or stumbling in my speech.

Yesterday, he proposed we should go fishing together in his canoe. This is smaller far than the great war-canoes, though still of some twenty feet in length and, carved only of a single tree trunk, lies flat and low upon the water. To assist in the paddling, came three of Shunghie's slaves, though he himself wielded one of the paddles as hard as they whilst I sat idle in the bow of the vessel.

My English garments being heavy and absorbent of water, Shunghie suggested I might adopt a flax kilt like his own for the expedition. I concealed my natural distaste at this barbaric notion, merely stating that God forbade his ministers from exposing their bodies to the elements in such a fashion.

Shunghie appeared nonplussed by this and wished to know if my God Himself wore clothing. I endeavoured to convey to him a vision of the Lord in His raiment of majesty, seated amongst heavenly clouds upon the throne of glory, but Shunghie's only comment was that, since cloud is absorbent of water, should God decide to go fishing on the morrow He would be better served by His garments than I might be.

Our expedition proved most productive, both of fish and in our discussion together.

I have been greatly exercised in mind by the manner in which I might go about my conversion of the Maori. Though Shunghie insists that every one of the natives attend Sunday School, and himself listens to my Bible-readings self-rendered in the native tongue, yet he appears, as do they all, indifferent to the Word of God. He has a most disconcerting habit of asking questions to which it is not within my compass to give answer. To wit, does God enjoy music and dancing? Has He a wife? If Mary is not God's wife, who is Jesus? I confess I find these most awkward of reply and there appears nothing in the Catechism to assist me.

Yet following upon our fishing expedition, I am more comfortable within this place than I have been before.

We set off from the shore at Rangi-Houa and, having left the Bay of Islands, headed north-north-east along the coast. The wind was light, the air fresh but warm. The surface of the ocean lay unruffled all about us.

As we rounded the cape into the open sea, I looked up at the great sheer cliffs that flung themselves into the churning waves and inwardly remarked how impossible it would be to descend on foot from the land at their heads. The depth and compass of them was awful to behold. They towered above us, a reminder of how insignificant a creature is Man, yet still the greatest of God's creations by virtue of his immortal soul.

Shunghie, following my gaze, seemed also to comprehend my thought.

'Above, the domain of Ta-Ne, below, of Tanga-Roa.'

'They are brother gods?'

'Two of many brothers, all the sons of Rangi and his wife Papa.'

'In England, papa is another name for father.'

'Not here in the Maori world. Papa is the mother and Rangi is our father god.'

'So Rangi is the lord of all creation?'

'No. Over him is yet another.'

I was greatly curious to know more of this supreme god but further on that topic Shunghie refused to be drawn.

I asked him of Tanga-Roa, the sea god.

'He is the fourth of the sons of Rangi and Papa. Before him comes first his eldest brother, Ta-Ne. It was Ta-Ne who brought the stars from the First Heaven here to the Twelfth, the Heaven of Rangi, the Sky-Father. And laid them down upon his father's body. And over Rangi now move all the stars and planets, the Whanau Marama, the children of the moon.'

'Why did he put the stars upon his father's body?'

'To give light to man. The sun is on Rangi's head, and the

moon is in his left eye-socket, and the stars are spread all over him like a sacred cloak. And Rangi makes them shine on us.'

'And Ta-Ne is his son?'

'Ai-ee.'

'And also the god of the forest?'

'The god of many things. Ta-Ne, the father of trees and birds, Ta-Ne, the father of man, Ta-Ne, the raiser and holder of the sky.'

Much interested by this, I told him of the myth of Atlas, propping the world upon his weary shoulders. He listened intently.

'Not like Ta-Ne. He uses four props to keep the sky up high. Atlas does not think. Ta-Ne is clever. He does not carry the sky about with him so he is never tired.'

'And after Ta-Ne?'

'Tu, the god of war and battles. Ha-Re-Shunghie, at his birth, was dedicated to Tu, Tu-Kai-Taua, eater of the war parties. It is Tu who brings success in battle. I myself was also consecrated to Tu. This is why I am such a mighty warrior.

'But Reporo, my second son, is given to Rongo, brother of Tu and Ta-Ne, the god of farming and of peace and plenty. He it is who guards our kumara crops and causes them to yield.'

'And Tanga-Roa . . . ?'

'Ai-ee. He holds the tides within his hands, the fish, the sea and all within it. He casts the fate of sailors and of fishermen. Like us. You must never put out to sea in your canoe taking cooked food with you, lest you anger Tanga-Roa.'

I looked about at once for the bread I had carried with me. Jane bakes it in a Maori oven upon a flat hot stone and, though it has an earthy taste, it is palatable and sustaining.

Seeing me, Shunghie laughed. 'It is upon the shore, your food, placed high in the crevice of a rock, awaiting your return.'

In all the time of embarkation I had been near him, yet had not noticed this little sleight of hand. In answer to my unspoken question, he opened in the stern a kit of flax in which were berries of the fuchsia plant and little shoots of fern, young and delicate, which I had eaten before and which, though tasteless to my own palate, are esteemed by Shunghie's people a delicacy.

Our proximity to the surface of the sea in this low-lying vessel caused me some unease. We appeared to be at a level with the water and I feared that if a large fish were hooked it might, in its run, tip our craft, and ourselves with it, into the depths of the ocean. And I have never learned the art of swimming, there being little call for it in North Thoresby.

We were, however, well placed to observe the slap and swell of the currents and I was surprised to see rise of a sudden from the water a fish, about a foot in length, closely followed by others. Their tiny fins appeared to act as wings, propelling them upwards for a space, then sweeping them below the surface as they plunged down. Diving and sporting thus in the waves, but for their disproportionately large and ugly heads they might have been cherubim springing in the sky.

'Kaha-wai,' said Shunghie.

In expectation, I lifted my hand to my baited line, which was trolling from a float attached to the bow of the canoe.

Shunghie shook his head. 'No. Wait. Bigger fish will come soon.'

I examined again my unbaited fish-hooks. The line itself is made of dressed fibre flax rolled into a double thickness of ply, then twisted, and each hook is attached by a snood-lashing wound in a figure of eight round the shank and point. The shank is of stone or bone, fronted with an iridescent piece of shell.

'To catch the fish's eye,' said Shunghie, watching me.

I had earlier, before we set out, made him a present of several different sizes of our metal fish-hooks, which are greatly prized by the natives, and four iron nails. One of these nails he had bent by hammering at it with a hard stone to force it into a crude curve with the point exposed. He drew my attention to it now, attached to a large shank of wood on a short line at the end of a wooden rod. What he intended to catch with it I could not imagine. Pehaps he had seen at some time a European rod and had made for himself this quaint simple version of it.

We paddled on a little further up the coast, then Shunghie dropped anchor. From the length of its rope, I realised that we sat in several fathoms of water.

I saw my drifting line jerk. Shunghie nodded to me and I clutched at it, excited at the prospect of my imminent catch. The fish pulled, and I hauled my line hard towards the canoe.

'No, no.' The chief moved position beside me. 'Let him go.' He saw my disappointment. 'He will not swim far. He has eaten your hook.'

I released more line. It relaxed in the water. The fish had, after all, slipped off the hook. But several minutes following, again the flax cord tautened and threshing was seen at a little distance. I looked for assistance to Shunghie, who indicated I should pull in gently, slowly.

'Deceive him. Let him think you do not want him; then, when he is lulled into false safety, take him. And he is yours.' He raised his tattooed brow quizzically. 'Not for nothing is the war god, Tu, brother of Ta-Ne, keeper of the ocean.'

And so it came about I caught the first fish of my life, a good specimen, some five or six pounds in weight, or so I estimated.

'Te ika,' said Shunghie. 'The fish. And this large island on which we live is named Te Ika-Nui, the Great Fish. The great fish of Maui. Such a fishing expedition did Maui and his brothers make. For many days and nights after he had hooked it he fought that great fish, all across the Ocean of Kiwa, the Pacific, and, when at last he caught and raised it, where his hook came out was formed in that huge hole a lake which has no bottom. No end. And if you travel far enough south, to the lands of the Tu-Wha-Re-Toa, there you will find that lake today. Taupo is its name.'

'Maui,' said I, 'must surely have had a mighty fish-hook.'

'A sacred fish-hook. Magic. Tapu. The jawbone of his revered grandmother. And, with it, he hooked that fish, our land.'

*

My expectations of returning to Rangi-Houa with my fish were dashed, however. No sooner had I detached it, with Shunghie's help, from the hook, than he took it from me, held it gently facing the ocean, murmured over it some words I could not catch and tossed it back into the sea.

Anger seized me momentarily at this summary disposal of my prize.

'This is the first-caught fish,' said Shunghie. 'It belongs not to man but to the god. We have given it back in thanks to Tanga-Roa. And now he will send others for us. A good thing it was not so big, being the first.'

It would not have been politic to complain though I confess it seemed to me a sizeable and most respectable specimen.

Within an hour or two, I had indeed caught several others, as had Shunghie. The slaves did not participate in our fishing but I do not know if this is ever the case or was merely so for that day.

Shunghie ordered the anchor raised and we had just set a course for home, when one of the slaves gave a loud cry. 'Look! There. Te pu-hanga to-hora. The spume of the whale!'

Some two sea miles away, the spout of a huge whale played above the waves. The spray shot high, diminished, blew again as the paddlers laid down their implements and we watched the wondrous display.

Shunghie shook his head. 'And soon they will come, your white brothers in their ships, with large iron hooks to stake it and pull it from the ocean and cut its flesh and hack at it until it dies in agony, moaning in the waters. We hear them, these whales, crying to Tanga-Roa for vengeance for their suffering.'

I was at pains to dissociate our Mission from such as these crude, rough men. 'These whalers are not brothers, nor never could be. They are of the lowest breed of men. They do not know God as I and Matenga, Reverend Marsden, do. They are men of little learning, rude and unlettered. They are not men of God.'

'But you are of the same tribe. Horhi, your chief, is their chief also. They told us so when they put in at Rangi-Houa to trade for water and kumara and pig.'

By this, I understood him to mean King George and hastened to explain the king's dominion over all his subjects. I do not think he took my meaning very plain. And, the whale having finished its spectacle, we paddled off again.

We had not yet rounded the cape which takes us into that enormous Bay of Islands wherein lies Rangi-Houa at the north-eastern side, when Shunghie's attention was caught again by something which I myself could not discern.

This time no cry arose from any of our company, but all froze, silent, where they sat and watched as the chief stealthily took up his primitive rod and cast it far out into the sea, twisting it so skilfully that the hook with its bent nail threshed upon the ocean's surface.

And up to snatch and swallow it rose a giant barracuta, of hideous visage, perhaps some twenty pounds in weight. It gobbled down the simple baitless lure, whereat Shunghie flung up and back his rod and within five minutes had landed it on the canoe's prow, stunned and dispatched it.

And never have I tasted finer fish than that barracuta cooked within leaves in a native oven – which, we along with Shunghie's people, did eat that night, at a feast upon the shore, where was recounted the story of my catch, the first, and the good fortune it had brought us with our sighting of the whale, our noble complement of kaha-wai and Shunghie's landing of such a prize, which, he was gracious enough to concede, he owed in no little part to the magic properties of my gift, the nail.

It came to me, sitting there among the savages, that I have never had before such friends as these. And many might conclude that Heathen lives were not as dark and godless as we in our far-off domains believe, who have enjoyed, in truth, but little of their society.

Thomas Surfleet has a spinning top, fashioned for him by Shunghie's cousin. It is made of a gourd inlaid with the iridescent native paua shell. The pith and seeds have been removed through little holes, and a stick, passed through from top to bottom, projects at the base to form a spinning point and at the top to make a shaft for the cord, which is of woven flax. When it is spun, the holes give out a loud and vibrant sound and great is Thomas Surfleet's joy in it. He will not be parted from this top: night and day it accompanies him wherever he be.

Yesterday came Shunghie to the school-hut to tell me he and his warriors would depart in two days with a war party to exact utu, vengeance for a murder perpetrated upon his cousin some three years previous. The warriors, led from time to time by Shunghie himself, have since performed in the pa and upon the shore the most bloodcurdling war-dances, which they will continue almost until the hour of their departure.

In this time the male warriors may not touch their women, nor the women warriors their men, the more to preserve their strength in battle, says Shunghie, who brought us to the water to observe their ceremony.

The warriors stand in lines, one behind another, as do our English soldiers. There steps forth one of them, who twirls and brandishes his jade club with many subtle manoeuvres, then leaps forward suddenly, gives a hideous scream and begins to chant in guttural tones some kind of incantation. I cannot convey how terrifying this sounds, the sonority of his own voice and those of the other warriors who then join with him, producing a compelling and fearful noise.

The eyes of all stare fixedly, glaring towards the watchers and, as the chanting swells into a universal shriek, the warriors, as one, roll back their eyes into their sockets, protrude their tongues as far as they are able and raise their hands as if to attack.

The truly awful aspect of them has struck utter fear in me for the first time in all my acquaintance with Shunghie. They remain frozen in their terrible contortions for some minutes, then the leader withdraws to the ranks, his place is taken by another and a variation of the same begins.

'They are calling upon Tu, the war god,' said Thomas Surfleet, intent upon the spectacle. 'He will make them victorious.'

And Basil, poking forth his own small tongue, stamped his feet in time with all the Heathen.

But Jane drew little Joseph closer upon her knee. 'I do not like it,' she said and, clutching him against her breast, rose, seized Basil by the hand and led them to our hut. Thomas Surfleet and I remained some time beside the rocks, observing the growing frenzy of the dancers and the slaves stocking up the great war-canoes.

And from my talk with Shunghie I have discovered that they are also bent upon other purposes, not merely war. 'Harvesting,' said he. 'We shall go harvesting.'

As they departed, I was much amazed to see that with Shunghie, who had earlier pressed noses with me in a truly brotherly fashion, went his blind wife, Turi-Ka-Tuku, clasping a paddle of the great war-canoe, all of seventy feet in length, which led their flotilla out into the Bay of Islands. And as they drew away she and the other women rowed with the strength of male warriors and gave no signs of weakness or fatigue.

I confess myself wary of this venture of revenge and theft. And, should Shunghie be defeated, what then and how precarious might our own position be here at Rangi-Houa?

'But, eh-Keni,' said he, 'we shall not be defeated. Te Kemara, my tohunga, has read the omens. Success will attend me.'

I watched the carved prows of the canoes disappear around the promontory and prayed they might be successful in their battle. Does God allow me, a Christian missionary, to pray for a Heathen savage to triumph in the field of war?

JANE KENDALL.

MISSIONARY'S WIFE.

BORN BROCKLESBY,

LINCOLNSHIRE,

1784.

DIED NEW SOUTH WALES,

1866.

'The Lord is good,' says Tom. 'Free will is given to man that he may make his own choices in God's world that He has created.'

'Oh?' says I. 'And if Thomas Surfleet do be beating Joseph with a club, does I stand there saying nowt? Free will, boys, it be.'

'Not the same at all,' says Tom, in great bad humour. 'These are but children that need guidance. And later, from that guidance, will make their own right and just decisions.'

'Thou hast told me the natives are but children, and so says the Reverend Marsden, but I does not see him, nor thee neither, telling Shunghie to stay his hand from any mortal thing he may choose to do.'

'Be not so simple, Jane.'

'Thy pardon, I do beg thee. Simple indeed I be that do see so plain thy duty to thy fellow man.'

''Tis different with the natives.'

'How so?'

'In all their customs, manners, society, they are not as we. Civilization is what we come to teach them. And the word of God.'

'Thy God that flogs a poor man if he steals a hare? Transports a man for pheasants and a leveret? Thy God that hangs His children for a loaf of bread? Thy God that makes the Reverend Marsden fat and I and me boys to forage for the fern roots here like to rats in a cornfield? That snatches from me that loves them me own two little daughters and leaves them in a baking convict Hell-hole? Thy God?'

'Be silent. Hush thy mouth.' He takes up his hat and leaves.

And I do cry such bitter tears even the salt be rancid on me tongue.

It be mebbee now a ten day since I passed beside their kumara fields and saw a stripling, age of me own little Lizzie, a-fretting in the heat. Climb hard from us plot of land up the hill which lies below the pa and past the stream, under the lee of the hill, and there the land do level on to flat afore it rises, steep and winding, to the first level of the pa palisades. And there, behind the hill, hid from the sea, they has their fields of kumara, the sweet potato.

Nowt I had to give the child to still him but a little piece of it, steamed, which Shunghie's girls had brung to me piled in a woven native kit of palm leaves. The child have devoured the piece as one so famished that, full of pity, I have give him another, like to me last.

At which he do put his little arms outstretched to me and, 'Kai, eh-Modder,' he begs me.

Whereat comes up one of the native women digging there, for hours they spend a-working in their kumara fields, and clips and cuffs him hard about his head, pointing at him and saying the while, 'Cookee, cookee,' which Tom, when later I tells him of it, says do mean us slave. And young and tired and starving though he be, in all that heat I seen him digging, pulling, hoeing with a tiny stick, when I went down after from the stream.

And on another sight of me, the child cries out once more, 'Eh-Modder, kai,' and stretches his little hands for food.

At which a Heathen takes from his mat his greenstone club, which they do hang at all times round their waists, and with a single blow to the side of the little one's head, fells him.

The day following, being of a mind to treat with Huia, daughter of Mrs Shunghie, her that is blind, I mounted up the hill beyond the stream and there, careless strewn across the flattened track, I seen a little human hand. Me stomach rose, me heart turned over, when I spied it, and further on, a forearm, small as me Lizzie's, and hacked, it did seem, in pieces. And across from it a foot. I didna travel on but stumbled back from whence I begun and, calling Tom make haste, bid him come and view.

The which he did and seen it likewise and went swift to Shunghie's cousin, who assured him nowt had befallen but that a grave have been worried at by native dogs.

They cooks their food here in a manner passing strange. The men and women, both, digs out a deep, straight-sided pit. And in the base they lays out several stones – large and flat – and on them builds a fire and stokes it till it burns up fierce and bright, then dwindles into embers. And then they lays across them embers a layer of thick green leaves of their nikau palm trees and places within the hole their meat or fish or kumara, well-wrapt in more green leaves, covers the food with yet more leaves and another layer of stones and fills the pit with earth again.

Then off they goes and leaves it till the morrow, when they returns, digs out the earth and leaves, and lifts out the green-wrapt food, which do taste, as I meself may tell, better than any I have eat anywhere afore. And Tom be of the same persuasion. Hangi, they calls it, this way of cooking, and the oven itself be named umu. And if Milord Pelham have had his venison done so, in an umu, he niver wouldna had the bakers' ovens cleared for after hunting but had, instead, the game-keepers dig such a pit behind the Hall. And none of us would go with two-day bread while all the ovens be took up by the deer.

Stands I on the hillside, feet planted in barren soil amongst them withering vegetables I be trying to coax to live, sun beating down on me bonnet, boots like to last mebbee two to three months more at most, already showing wear and cracks to uppers.

Three children has I here and nowt will grow to feed them. The cow have took terrible sick and though Shunghie's witch-doctor tohunga have pointed sticks of bone at her and took her off to feed her bitter herbs, I knows in me heart she willna live. Hens hasna laid one egg since us come and though us be eating the hens theirselves now, what has us after?

'Have faith in the Lord, Mrs Kendall,' says Marsden a-taking hisself off to Parramatta.

'God will provide,' says Tom as he sets off daily on Marsden's business.

Nothing to put in me children's bellies but what Shunghie takes it to his mind to give. And he gone now six days with his great war party, his blind wife and tohunga and all them warriors from the settlement.

'Mother! Mother! Come quick!'

Thomas Surfleet have run to us plot from the water edge. He sounds somewhere between joy and terror, which brings me to him at high speed.

'What be the matter?'

He pants for breath to answer. Points down the hillside to the great bay below. 'There. See.'

He have become already like them: in a three month, he have developed the keen sight of the savages. Nowt shows to me own eye.

'What?'

'Their waka, Mother. Look. War canoes. Shunghie is coming back home. He has won.'

'Hast told thy father?'

'He is gone to see to the felling of trees on the far eminence there.' He points to the little promontory near the po-hutu-kawas. 'He has taken his sawyer's axe. The sharp one with the killing blade.'

'The killing blade?'

'Aye, Mother. If you but struck a man one blow to the neck or throat with it, he would be dispatched on the instant.'

I shakes him roughly. 'Tha'rt niver, niver, to lay thine hand upon that axe. Dost hear?'

'It is too heavy, anyway, for me to raise above my knees.'

'Too heavy, not too heavy, tha doesna touch it. Niver. Be that clear?'

He nods his head. Looks down, sullen.

I gazes again at the bay. Still nowt show to me own eye. 'Tha'rt certain of what tha hast seen?'

'Aye, there. Look. Before the little island is a shape. And following it, another. And another. Six in all, there are, with others tied behind them, and the same six that are leading are those that departed from our shore.'

A dreadful thought do come to me. 'Mebbee it be not Shunghie but his enemy who have won and come now to claim us for his own?'

'But, Mother, I see him, standing in the first canoe. And look at the pa,' and here he points above him to the hillside where the palisades of pointed sticks aims upward to the sky. 'The Maori are streaming out down the hill. Father must see them where he stands. They are but across from his view. Look how they are descending.'

'And so will us then, too,' says I and takes in mine his hand. Which he draws to hisself like to stung.

'Nay, Mother. The native boys laugh at me. They say I will never be a warrior if a woman directs me.'

'They tells thee true. Thou wilt niver be a warrior but a scholar. Dost hear?'

'Aye, Mother. Do not shout. I hear you well. But here there are no scholars. Only warriors.'

Down the steep hillside us goes, I trudging, he skipping and jumping beside.

'When I am grown,' he confides, smiling to me, 'I shall have the moko.'

'And what be the moko?'

'The purple tattoo. Shunghie says I shall have it all over my face and body. Just as he does.'

'Thou'rt prattling, Thomas Surfleet.'

'Nay, Mother. Shunghie has promised. He says his own carver himself will tattoo me. Look. Now everyone is come to the beach. And there is Shunghie standing in the first canoe, just as I told you.'

Six great canoes dips over the surface of the ocean, each with another tied behind. Their paddles rises and enters the water together, perfect as the hounds of Brocklesby trotting in their pack. Front leg, back leg, front leg, back leg, like to one large hound of many parts. So the oars rises up, dips in, hauls back: forty oars which seems like two oars only. Helmsmen crying 'Ho-yah! To-yah!', splash of the paddles, swish of the great boats flying forward, floats clear to us across the water. And Shunghie, like to a single hound, the half that do lead the pack, standing afore them all in his great canoe.

'And he has prisoners. Prisoners-of-war, like Boney!' cries Thomas Surfleet.

Fear takes hold of me heart. But not of Thomas Surfleet's. He breaks from me side, races down the hill, across the shingle, and wades out into the water, shouting and screaming like one of their own. Which follows him into the waves, thrashing and yelling.

'Capital!' roars Thomas Surfleet. 'He has won. He has proof.'

And I seen that Shunghie do swing a censer back and forward in his hand, shouting his joy of victory.

And the fear in me becomes a terror that I must push down and hide afore I sets foot upon that shingly shore.

*

By evening, as I were descending from us gardens to us hut, there, ranged about the beach and rocks, sits captives, bound together by ropes of flaxen twine, in rows, their heads downcast, as some great parley were carried on by Shunghie and his brothers. Pointing at this one, that one, Shunghie be choosing which should go for slaves. And great were the weeping and agony of them whose wives or children was took away, divided as spoils of battle. And Shunghie and his brothers did take for themselves the youngest and most comely of the women to add to all their wives.

Them that be not taken be slapped and pinched and hit about with staves and led, still bound together, uphill to the pa.

And as I stands watching, a woman from the prisoners takes regard of me and remarking, so I supposes, me difference from her captors, weeps and cries, a-holding out her arms to me like one desperate, and though I knows but little of their tongue I understands right well she begs me for her life.

And Shunghie, seeing me, and that she have called to me, cuts with a shell her bonds, seizes her and flings her bodily across the shingle at me feet.

'Take, take. Your cookee.'

I shakes me head nay. 'I has no need of a slave.'

But the poor creature clings to me and weeps and willna be took away from me so I be obliged to bring her back to us hut. And she have slept outside it iver since and have set herself to help me in us plot and guard both Joseph and Basil with such care she might be took, but for her colour, to be their natural mother. Yet no other woman from the pa but does not spit at her as they passes by and nowt of them do speak with her nor offer her no word of kindness.

The morning after Shunghie's return from battle, of the prisoners, men, women or children, there be no sign. And, Shunghie coming to us hut to seek for Tom in the forenoon, I has asked him most polite and careful what be going with the captives.

'Kone,' says he, waving his hand for dismissal. 'All kone.'

The day following I hears the sounds of the digging of many pits, and us be kept awake all night by great singing and carousal. And Tom and I be minded to cling together, not him nor I do dare to utter what mebbee in our hearts. And all next day, Ngaio, me slave, weeps inconsolable and canna be comforted by nowt, not Joseph's caresses, nor even by Tom's a-reading of the Scriptures, he, like Thomas Surfleet, having by now great fluency in the native speech.

If I been a bold, brave woman, I has gone to the pa on the day following and seen if what I feared be true indeed. But terror of what were mebbee there froze me feet below the bottom row of them palisades. And Tom didna venture up there, neither. And none of the natives did come within the kumara fields nor to the beach nor the ocean. It were as if none of them had niver been. And though us could hear the sounds of revelry above, niver a one of them did us sight.

I thinks, and often, on that tiny hand, brown, the soil around it, where it lay, a darker ochre from the blood which have oozed from it when it were severed. I seems to see the ghostly stripling clinging to the earth behind it, all of him a spectre but his little hand, gone from the pathway now I knows not where.

'Mother,' says Thomas Surfleet, 'Reporo and Ha-Re-Shunghie are not come to sport with me. I shall go looking where they be.'

'Tha doesna stir from here. And if tha disobeys, tha shalt be shipped back to Botany to Reverend Marsden,' shouts I, harsh, too loud. 'Much there be here to do. Assist thy father.'

'But, Mother, it was you that said I might not touch the axe.' He looks at me, a-frighted.

'Tha hast no call for an axe to gather kindling. And great need will us have of such when autumn draws full on and us be cold of nights.'

And that were truer than I knew I spake.

THOMAS KENDALL.

MISSIONARY
&
MAORI SCHOLAR.

BORN NORTH THORESBY,

LINCOLNSHIRE,

1778.

DIED NEW SOUTH WALES,

1837.

It was with a rising heart, while working felling trees upon the promontory, that I saw return, some ten days later, Shungie's huge war canoe and the five that had accompanied it, with several others towed behind.

In the leading canoe, balanced upright by no visible means but the grasping of his bare feet, stood the chief – an arrogant, imposing conqueror – swinging in his right hand a censer on a black rope, backward and forward, forward and back.

Across the calm ocean surface his voice carried clear. 'Tayo!' as the oarsmen raised in unison their paddles. 'Ayo!' as the craft sped towards the shingly beach and the censer swung against its steady motion.

Bareheaded in that foreign forest, I was of a sudden

transported to the great cathedral of my dear, dear Lincoln. Up before my eyes rose the rubies, sapphires and emeralds of its windows, in my ears sounded the pealings of its majestic bells. Came to my mind its watchful sandstone gargoyles, its abstracted alabaster saints, the heavenly gaze of the cherubs of the choir stalls, the angels of the transepts rising on carved stone wings eternally to Heaven.

I lifted my head as if to catch the sudden smoky whiff of frankincense pouring from the censer, Papist protection from the Devil and all his works.

On the instant, my vision of the Cathedral dissolved in the tang of salt, the reek of fish-oiled bodies and the heavy smell of the mud and red ochre with which our Heathen dress their hair. All these drifted, blending, across the water, but of frankincense there came no trace. Yet there clung in my nostrils a strange, metallic odour, underlying all these others, like iron or sea-weed, undefinable yet faintly known.

Down the hillside towards the shore from the garden plot, I saw come Jane with Thomas Surfleet. Breaking from his mother, he raced into the waves, straining towards the returning warriors, churning in the sea with the wives and children.

Yet for all their wild activity, the older natives were strangely silent. It is their custom upon the return of loved ones to cry and wail and hack themselves about their bodies. This they did not do but ploughed through the water, mute, until, within a hundred yards of shore, Shunghie abruptly ceased to swing his censer and gave a single piercing cry, which was answered by all in the water, these being the old and women with children, the men and women warriors having gone with the war-party. He swung back his right arm and, with a single mighty movement, propelled his censer all that great distance on to the shingle shore.

From the people came a shout of 'Te matenga!' Since this is the name by which they call Mr Marsden, I scanned the war vessel for sight of him, but to no purpose. It may be his name has other meaning, thought I, for certain it is that Marsden is at this moment still in Parramatta.

From my vantage point I saw Jane, of a sudden, draw back,

turn and go quickly from the shore. Thomas Surfleet by now was dancing in the waves as one demented, echoing the shouts and actions of the native boys. I laid down my axe and resolved to join them.

As I approached from the east, the huge canoes drove north so that we met beside the shore at the perfect junction point. Hatless as I was, for me at that time a rare thing, Shunghie, perceiving me, took it as a sign of my own jubilation. 'Eh-Keni! eh-Keni!' he bellowed across the water.

As we drew together, the paddlers raised up their oars to the sides of the canoes, lifting and floating now of their own volition shorewards on the incoming tide. Our North Cape savages, still in full war regalia of flax kilts, and ochred hair tied in topknots speared through with huia-bird feathers, displayed every evidence of ferocious and victorious barbarism towards their captives.

These huddled together in the bottoms of the canoes, hands tied behind their backs with flax cords. There were upwards of sixty men, women and chidren, all of whom suffered from their captors random kicks, tweakings and shoving, even the smallest children. In the midst of this human misery, one young woman stood out from all the rest. Beautiful, had she not sported filthy, matted hair and wild eyes, she suckled an infant no more than ten days old. Her arms and thighs were hacked about with wounds, the wounds of war, or so I thought, but saw on closer approach they had been but recently self-inflicted with a shark's tooth.

I gazed at her with compassion. There hung about her an air of pure grief, palpable and most affecting even to those such as I, who knew her not.

One of Shunghie's younger sons now proceeded to kick at his father's censer with his bare feet, then snatched it up and, with a truly prodigious throw, flung it back across the water into his father's great canoe. The strength and mighty physical power of the Maori would have gladdened the eye of Monsieur Rousseau.

'Te matenga!' shouted everyone again, my young Thomas included. Shunghie, suing for my attention, leapt into the waist-deep water and made towards me. 'Eh-Keni! My hoa! I am the victor. See!' And raising aloft in his hand the censer, he brandished it again.

It was only then, with horrified revulsion, that I saw it to be no Papist holy object but a human head, heavily tattooed, the cords, by which he had swung it, its oiled black tresses.

He brandished ferociously his great greenstone club, rolled back his eyes at me, protruded his tongue. For a second a flicker of fear possessed me. Only a second. Long enough.

The warrior king swished in his flax kilt through the water and embraced me, the head still lolling in his grasp. For reasons I cannot know, my donkey and my little draper's cart appeared before my eyes, dissolving almost at once.

Shunghie flung wide his left arm, encompassing the entire party in his sweep. He spat into the water. 'Pah! The Wai-Te-Mata! What is the power of their ranga-tira against my warriors?'

He swung the tattooed head so high it momentarily achieved a level with my own. The eyes, I saw, were closed in peaceful sleep, though the mouth hung open. No sign of decomposition could I evidence.

'This is their paramount chief, father of them all.'

Within the canoes the natives bowed their heads. In shame, I supposed. All save the woman with the suckling who fixed upon Shunghie a direct and proud challenge of her eye.

'She,' continued he, 'is his daughter. That, his moko-puna, grandson.'

From where she sat, the sole prisoner with hands untied, that she might hold her infant, she gathered up her lips and spat a contemptuous gob on to the water by my protector.

I waited, trembling, for Shunghie to avenge this deadly insult. He swung the head back and forward, forward and back, then, without warning, released it so that it fell heavily into the canoe beside her. At which, with the most affecting cries and lamentations, the equal of any I have heard before or since, she laid the infant across her knees, seized the head in both her hands and pressed its nose to her own, moaning and muttering to it the while as to a living being. And in the canoes, all from her tribe wept silently along to her lament.

Shunghie, his face alight with the joy of victory, stood beside me pointing to the cargo of three of the captured canoes. 'Here, look! We have harvested.'

And I saw that in each of the vessels lay dozens of severed heads, warriors, women, children, each cut through at the throat and tossed upon its fellows, a bloody yield so barbaric I must turn my face from it to recover my composure.

It may be long before these Maori are brought unto the Lord.

Marsden has arrived at Rangi-Houa on the brig *Active* from Parramatta, whence he has ordered me return with him in a month.

This is his first pastoral visit to us, yet his only words of greeting to me were: 'I have done as you have charged me, Mr Kendall, though much against my will and better judgement.'

The more I meet with him, the more do I recoil from him. His eyes are shrewd and calculating above that high, pinched nose. He seems not troubled by doubts or misgivings but is most sure and certain of his rightness in all things. A hard man, with whom, were I a draper still, I should expect to have to drive a hard bargain for little profit.

He intends to make an expedition to Kiddi-Kiddi, south of here, but insists that first I must accompany him on his walk to the Hoki-Anga, which journey Shunghie tells me is of three to four days' duration as the Maori walks. I translate this to a distance of some eighty-five English miles, an arduous but interesting proposition with, so Shunghie says, a plunging cascade and several small lakes upon our route. Marsden means to take his sextant and plot our position from hour to hour and to sketch our way with the aim of sending his findings to London, to the Admiralty Office.

'The Admiralty,' said Janey, when told of this, 'be surely but concerned with the ocean.'

'Ah, nay,' said I and instructed her in the wider workings of that august institution.

Marsden will send out a convict trusty from Botany to assist her whilst I am gone back to Parramatta in the autumn. It will be preferable to have here with her another Englishman, albeit a transport, to succour and assist. Shunghie has afforded us several natives for the purpose, but since I have seen the heads within the canoes my heart rests easier to know she will have a Christian to whom she may apply.

'I am grateful for your generosity,' said I to Shunghie, 'but it will calm Mrs Kendall to have with her also one of her own kind.'

At this he replied most enigmatically; a compliment to my wife I must construe it. 'Eh-Keni, soon, soon, Modder will be one of our kind.'

This eased my mind greatly. Jane has shewn a deep hostility to her surroundings here. Perhaps it was foolish of me to have left behind our girls at Botany, yet thought I only to spare them that privation so vexing to the female sex, which, being weaker, cannot cope as easily with the unknown. And, too, she has but not long since lost an infant, safe now in the arms of Jesus but gone for ever from his mother's bosom.

Thus engaged in thoughts of familial concerns, I swung with eager step to the small wha-re wherein resides Marsden upon this visit. He motioned for me to enter. I crawled upon my knees through the entrance and sat, uncomfortably, upon the flax matting with which the floor is covered. Its intricate and varied patterns give great occupation to the eye and I was engaged in its perusal when Marsden spoke in a manner unanticipated and startling.

'I have summoned you here, Mr Kendall, that I may speak with you more freely than is possible outside this dwelling.'

I am mindful of how little privacy is afforded us at Rangi-Houa at any time. Janey has often remarked with irritation upon the native habit of comment and intrusion in our lives. Quiet within our small hut, we will of a sudden be disturbed by a head at our window, exclaiming loudly, 'Eh-Keni! Eh-Modder! Tena kou-rua!'

'I am at your service, Mr Marsden.'

'I shall be blunt and to the point, Mr Kendall. I am dismayed to see further developing in you what I have already observed at Parramatta. The sin of pride.'

I admit our departure from Parramatta came very timely, I and Reverend Marsden having daily become more like unto the iron pot and the earthen pot carried on by the same current – we must not come near each other in haste lest one of us be dashed to pieces.

But I was unhanded by this accusation of which I had no expectation. Unprepared as I was, I endeavoured to defend myself. 'I am dismayed, sir, that you should find it so.'

'And I, too, Mr Kendall. It had been my fervent hope that here, at the Bay of Islands, you would find your destiny and your place in God's Holy Service. And yet I see you consorting with the Heathen as a brother.'

'But,' expostulated I, 'surely it is only as a brother I may bring them to the love and knowledge of God?'

'That is for God to judge, not you.'

'But does not God instruct me I must be my brother's keeper?'

'You would assume the will of God as your own, Mr Kendall?'

'No indeed, as I live. But it is only by winning the confidence and trust of the Maori we may show him our God. His own gods are so powerful and pervasive an influence that the Lord Himself is hard put to compete with them in the native mind.'

His gaze upon me caused me to feel quelled and belittled.

'I cannot believe I am so grievously abused, Mr Kendall. I shall be frank with you. At Parramatta, I saw disturbing and disquieting evidence of your stubbornness of mind, your will to power, your disobedience in the face of the opinions of your superiors. Obedience, sir, must be your lesson. The humbling of your pride to that of your betters. Do you hear me?'

'I do, sir.'

'You are dealing here daily with savages. Rude natives

fashioned, half-finished, in the image of God. But untutored, Mr Kendall, unlettered, primitive of belief, wanting only the knowledge of God and his Son, Jesus Christ, to turn them from their evil ways and bring them from Outer Darkness to the knowledge and redemption of the Lord. Salvation must be your aim. To bring light to their darkness. To burn for them. And burn again.'

'But the natives have already a most complex and advanced form of belief and it is idle—'

'I despair of you, Mr Kendall. Where is your Faith? Never forget that the Maori is but a pagan. Made in God's image indeed, but flawed. A rudimentary Christian. A pre-believer. We are here in the name of the One True Church but hard upon our heels come the Papists, the Jesuits, who would deceive our native friends with false visions of the Almighty. Shunghie is a remarkable specimen, a Noble Savage. But a savage, none the less.'

'But, Mr Marsden, sir, I have spoken with him much. He considers *us* to be savages. Primitives. And it is true that, without their aid, we cannot survive on their land, upon their oceans, as they do.'

'This survival of which you speak is not the yardstick of the enlightened Christian. *That* is the knowledge and love of God, belief in Redemption, distinction between good and evil, the imposition of English law and order and obedience to the Sovereign and the Realm as representative of God on Earth, which brings forth a well-ordered and well-balanced society.'

'But it is well known in all England, sir, that King George is now quite mad and the Prince of Wales—'

'Silence, Mr Kendall. His Majesty is Supreme Head of the Church of England. Will you deny this?'

'No, indeed, but—'

'I hear you aright, Mr Kendall? You claim that the Supreme Head of the Church of England is a lunatic?'

'No ... no, indeed. But the natives here already adhere to all that you have just described. Within their own society.'

'The natives do not know God.'

'I do not speak of our god but of their gods.'

He looked at me aghast. '*Their gods!* Their gods are pagan idols.'

'No, they are not all idols. The concept of their atua, their supreme god, is not dissimilar to our own. His laws—'

'Mr Kendall, this is sedition. Attend to your own heart, sir. Go now and pray. I cannot tomorrow administer to you Holy Communion until you have purged the sins of your proud and wicked heart. You are in greater spiritual danger than your native charges.'

Within that cramped and fetid space, he turned himself away from me. The pinched tip of his nose had whitened to fury and even his broadcloth admonished me silently. I rose and slunk, like a native dog, from the wha-re.

My despondency of spirits only increased as I drew near our little hut. Outside, at a distance, Basil and Joseph played in a patch of ochre dust. Of Thomas Surfleet there was no sign; no doubt he sported somewhere with Shunghie's younger sons and the other native boys. I stooped low and crawled beneath the wooden lintel. The interior being no more than four and a half feet in height, it is not possible to stand upright once inside. The raupo flax matting which covers all the earthen floor gave off the musty smell of reeds, the small fire in the centre of the hut spiralled its smoke towards the hole in the roof and its excess acrid clouds brought smarting to my eyes and pulled at my throat. Everything of our clothing and coverings, and even Janey's and the children's hair, smells at all times faintly of this smoke. Because of the wisping grey-blue haze within, it was a time before I understood Jane to be lying in the far corner on a blanket. More time elapsed before I ascertained that she was weeping.

My first thought was that she had, in some way, had intelligence of Reverend Marsden's dialogue with me and had become, by this, distressed. I approached her on my knees and, squatting uncomfortably beside her, took her hand, patting it and enjoining her be strong and believe in me. I could not help but observe how calloused and ingrained with dirt her little fingers had become. There was, too, a new hardness to her skin.

She pulled back her hand from mine and turned her head from me.

'You are weeping, Janey.'

No answer.

'What troubles you?'

Again no answer.

'I charge you, Jane, to answer me as a wife should her husband and her master.'

'Not me husband nor me master neither, thou.'

'What ails you?'

'Nowt,' says she with bitter irony. 'A mere trifling thing. Two trifles. But nowt that should touch a father's heart.'

'Thou hast punished me an hundredfold, Jane. God Himself is not such a stern and cruel judge.'

'God Himself sheweth mercy. Or so say the Scriptures. Though I seen it not. Nor Isaac neither. Nor those, me little daughters, orphans with both a mither and father living, yet abandoned to the mercies of a jade.'

I heard myself stiff and formal though I wished for all the world to speak to her free and friendly as before.

'Mr Marsden has but now spoken with me.'

She made no reply.

'He has charged me with the sins of pride and arrogance. He instructs me to pray and repent.'

Closed and cold her face remains.

'He has informed me, also, that, acting upon my express written instructions delivered from the hand of the master of the whaler *Jenny*, and greatly against his better judgement, he has arranged a passage for Sannah and Lizzie on the *Mary-Ann* with a trusty to accompany them. Given a favourable wind, they should have left Botany these five days previous.'

Even through the eddying smoke her mouth shews softer, a little life returns to her eyes. But her voice, when she speaks, holds still the same hard edge to it.

'And when do come this ship to the Bay of Islands?'

'It will put in here at Rangi-Houa that our girls may be set down with us.'

'So when be that?'

'Much depends upon the weather. But Shunghie claims the wind is set fair for half a month at least. Let us say within a four week they will be here.'

'If the sea do not rise up and claim them nor the natives rise up and slaughter them.'

But a weight has slipped from her.

'Come, Janey,' I say, and make to hold her to me. 'Truce, eh? Thy daughters are even now on their way to thee.'

For a moment her body yields but only a moment.

'I has told thee, Thomas Kendall, and I has told thee true, as God be me witness, I wouldna come to thee, nor thee to me, until the day me daughters stood again afore me. And that day have not yet dawned.'

But she suffered me, for the first time since we left Botany, to rest an arm across her shoulders and to place a chaste kiss upon her cheek.

After which, I went outside again to find a quiet place in which to pray.

JANE KENDALL.

MISSIONARY'S WIFE.

BORN BROCKLESBY,

LINCOLNSHIRE,

1784.

DIED NEW SOUTH WALES,

1866.

Marsden have come back from another expedition to Kiddi-Kiddi and Tom have spoke with him most earnest on what mebbee have befell the prisoners from the war. Marsden were of the firm opinion that there be other explanation. Could be them prisoners was marched to the interior or carried away by night by sea. And Tom and Marsden both was took up some time with quizzing Ngaio, who, averring she didna understand them, wouldna, for her life I thinks meself, utter a single word on owt of it.

Us has gone into the pa on the topmost hill for the first time since us come here. Marsden have asked especial for this visit and he and Tom both has donned their broadcloth and I me better bonnet and me Sunday skirt. It be Marsden's wish to question Shungie about his anthropophagy, a new word I has learned, which means to be eating human flesh – that be to say, a cannibal.

Thomas Surfleet have come with us but Ngaio be overseeing Basil and little Joseph. Afore I leaves the hut comes Joseph crawling to me and in his hand a feather. 'Mama,' he says, a-clawing at me skirt for me to raise him up. Which I does, and I not yet being bonneted he places the feather in me hair at the topmost point of me head, like to how the chiefs here do dress theirselves, and, 'Pretty,' he says, pointing. I fears he must grow even more like them Heathen than Thomas Surfleet, who have, at least, a recollection of his true English home.

Us has gone down from the smaller hill whereon do lie us hut and the school-hut by and climbed up again to the first of the three great hills – mountains them would be in England, but not so here, where even the higher peaks juts up like the backbones of giant scraggy cows wheriver us looks to the inland horizon.

Them three great hills be where the pa be set and only when us has climbed a halfway up the lowest, does I see how overlooked us be by Shunghie's people. If I glances down and back, there be me young boys waving, ant-sized, and Ngaio, a brown doll, beside them.

Ahead be just a steep incline, but to me left, below, lies a view so magnificent it looks to be a painting, not a true and real place where folk abides. There falls away beneath us feet the sheer and mighty mountainside, dropping to the sea, so blue and calm it mebbe be the sky, and here and there upon it lies lazy canoes, drifting in the warmth and calm. And far as me eyes do see be nestling bays and arms of land which stretches out to the ocean. And all that land be green but for some little clearings and the stakes of palisades on the hilltops where there be other pas and settlements.

Away to the south, the hills falls down to flat land and the wide Wai-Tangi River.

'What means its name?' I has asked Tom afore. And he have answered, 'Weeping waters.'

He says he thinks it be like the tears that washes down the mountain's face and into the ocean.

But I has seen how red the sea have been by Rangi-Houa when Shunghie have come back from his war and I thinks meself there mebbee have been other cause for the naming of that river.

Be farther than it looks, the pa. Hill steep and nowt of the Maori out to greet us. Be only when us reaches the first wall of pointed sticks and sees dug out behind it a deep pit filled with stones and rocks, and raises up us eyes again, I realizes them three hills be not so at all but one hill only, mountain-size, cut in three places and fenced about at each, the better to give protection to all them that might seek shelter within the pa.

And if a one of them had took a mind to toss at us them rocks as us be climbing up the hill, then over that sheer rockface us be sure to topple, smashed to nowt.

On us climbs to the second row of sticks and now can see to the inward land side, down to Shunghie's kumara gardens and the stream which flows, I sees now, from a little lake farther inland, shewing to us from here, but niver seen afore, it being us has niver ventured beyond them farthest kumara plantations.

I sees that great protection has them gardens, ringed about by hills, and none might come to set a foot upon them without that someone of the pa would have the seeing of it.

Then us has come, still without no sign nor sound of any of the natives, through a gate – open like them other two afore – set in the final ring of palisades and into a flat open plain, like to a field or great meadow, upon which be the pa itself.

Strange it be. Nowt like a Lincoln village. Ivery hut be tiny, smaller than a standing man at its tallest part and coming to a point at its centre where be an upright balancing the roof board, above which, on the one hut only, there be a small carved figure, having a large head like to a man's, smaller body, with two hands, yet but three fingers upon each, and all the face tattooed in a likeness to Shunghie's own countenance.

The roof of each, made all of thatch, comes forward afore the door for mebbee two feet, making a little porch space against the sun or bitter weather. And in these huts, I knows now, they lies for some time in the day, heads beside the door-space or window – in which they has no glass, there being nowt such known here – and there they watches all that may befall about their village.

Them that be not chiefs, which be the most of them, has all alike the same huts, mebbee smaller, but with no carved figure at the roof point.

And round about be long forked twigs stuck hard into the ground, on which they hangs their bundles and their roots of fern, which they eats as a delicacy. And hangs there also any other thing they desires escape the depradations of the rats or of their little dogs.

Platforms they has as well, of woven mats of flax, raised up from the ground. And kumara and fern lying upon them also.

By the far end of the palisade wall, away from all the rest, be a smaller, lower hut that stands upon but two legs in the centre and seems, at first sight, like to a little church with a pointed steeple but made of straw and flax. And where the cross might be upon the church be a long and carved-out piece of wood, painted the red they smear upon their skins and fashioned to wicked faces, grinning like the Devil, eyes wild, made of shell, and tongues hanging like panting dogs' from their mouths. And all them facing boards be carved and stuck with shells, with curves and curls and spiral decoration. And to one side be a carving of a man and wife and made so very lewd that I must turn away me gaze lest Mr Marsden sees me glance upon it.

And as I looks away I sees, to the other side, a large, long hut, high as any English house, with, afore it, a clearing. And silent there, a-clustered to one side, stands a clutch of women in their mats, flaxed and feathered giant molehills in their shape, and children, stark, uncumbered by any clothing. All them quiet, waiting for I knows not what. And still us takes no sight of Shunghie.

It be several moments afore I sees there be none of their men in any place and with a sinking heart I plucks at Tom's sleeve to say what it be I fears. Then, sudden, with a scream to chill the blood, leaps Shunghie hisself forward from out that great long hut into us view, mother-naked but for a little skirt of flax, through which his greatly tattooed thighs be shewing. And in his hands a long and sharpened spear of wood.

He gives a great cry and I be near to swooning with terror at sight of him thus. Tom and Marsden likewise oozes the smell of fear as he do move towards us, rolling back his eyes into his head, a-sticking out his tongue and screaming and grunting most terrible. It be only Thomas Surfleet remains unmoved, indeed do enjoy this spectacle as much as Captain Hales' horses in far-off Parramatta, which daily now do seem like Paradise when that I looks at me life here.

Advancing with his spear and shouting iver louder, Shunghie comes within six feet of where us stands, rooted all, and making a most prodigious leap towards the skies, he flings the spear with all his might, so that it flies like a giant arrow through the air and comes to rest, point into the ground, but six inches from us. And all the lance above the point be trembling and shaking, yet the spear holds fast in the earth.

Both Tom and Marsden starts in alarm and I, pulling Thomas Surfleet, be quick to cower behind them two. Yet Shunghie remains afore us, tongue poked out, eyes rolling in their sockets, and both his hands swings together to one side of him, knees bent, so that the little skirt he wears do barely cover his nakedness.

In a voice to remind me of Lincoln's bishop calling the creed at Eucharist, Shunghie recites a question. Be some moments afore Tom regains composure enough to answer and then, since it be in the Maori tongue, I be not privy to its meaning.

'He says,' whispers Thomas Surfleet, a-seeing me confusion,

'"What is your name? Who was your father? From whence do you come?"'

'He *knows* us names,' hisses I.

'Hush, Mother. We are not permitted speech at all. And you are a woman and should wail for all our dead as you go into the meeting-house.'

If us has been in us hut, for that insolence might I have cuffed his knavish little ear.

And after, comes from out behind the great long hut, their meeting-house, all the men and some of the older women of Shunghie's tribe, whooping and screaming, half-naked in their little skirts, and stamps and dances and throws about their spears, all which has sharpened and deadly points enough to kill a man. And all them when they turns has naked backsides on them, prick-marked purple with tattoos.

Then comes the girls, wa-hi-ne, singing and making little balls of flax to dance about on strings. Their music be sweet and pleasant to the ear but, of the men and how they dances, all I can think on be how like villains and footpads they do seem and how I am afeared of ivery one. And as to the women's dancing, they do sway and bob about with dugs all bare, but seeming not to feel the shame of it.

Then us be led inside the meeting-house. Dark it be in there. A long black cavern which wraps its dark about us like us be infants in the womb. And when me eyes be settled to the dark, wheriver I looks there be more of them lewd carvings I has seen on the two-legged house. Wild monsters, terrible things, come out from dreams, and on all them carved men, great long ram-rods, huge as iver I seen in me life, hanging between the legs on them or poking out like they has no shame. And no clothes to cover them neither. And what they be doing to them women, I canna bring meself to say.

Thomas Surfleet stares like one bewitched, then puts a hand across his mouth to smother back his laughter. Me girls be niver, niver, to see such things. Nowt to wonder at that all them Maori be Heathen with carvings like such about them.

And a great lot of talking do go on, nowt of which I understands. One do speak and after him another. And

Thomas Surfleet fidgets by me side at the length of time us sits there.

I looks again at the carvings by the walls and I sees that they be not all the same as looks at first glance, but different, each one with a face on him unlike his brothers, special to hisself. Some be looking full at me and some to the side and one have his little dog beside his feet. The bodies on them, long and twisted out of shape, puts me in mind of them angels I seen in Lincoln Cathedral, though the faces on them be more like to the wicked Lincoln Imp. Spirals and curves makes up all their parts and faces: even the dog have spirals to his back.

And after a time, I finds they grows on me, them carvings. I be looking to find the ones I likes the best.

And then Shunghie do rise to his feet again; and Tom and Marsden, beckoning us to follow, makes hongi with their noses with him and, after, all the men from Shunghie's tribe. And I and Thomas Surfleet likewise. And then, when us has come out in the light again, and greatly has me eyes strained because of it, us sees they has made for us a feast of pig and kumara and I did watch the slaves, both men and women, pounding at the fern root. Soft and tasty, it be, like to us kale when sweet and young. And everyone did eat and drink but for their witch-doctor tohunga, that, in consequence of the war, were still tapu, which means to say he be sacred, apart, forbidden to come within the confines of the pa, and must stay in a little hut or wha-re, as they calls their dwellings. And his wife, with her kit of flax, have come and, after Shunghie have invited Tom and Marsden, then made hisself his choice of best meat, she, for her husband, makes next choosing.

'And,' says Thomas Surfleet, 'she will feed it to him from a long stick. She may not lay one finger upon the food. All that goes into the tohunga's mouth must not be touched by human hands.'

And he says it like one of the Maori, telling it to an Englishman, not like an English child amazed and curious, but like one who believes this be the proper way of life. And I be sick at heart for it.

*

Te Maaka, from the pa, have caught his secondary wife in adultery with his cousin and she be stoned to death and all her body hacked and scattered for the kuri, the little native dogs. Her mother wanders on the shore, a-tearing at her flesh with shells and wailing for the shame of it.

At Brocklesby once, a hound have went lame from falling down a dyke in bitter weather, and as the leg couldna be set the huntsman shot the beast and buried it in consecrated ground at the behest of Milord Pelham, whose churchyard it be, so he may have lie in it who or what he will.

And in the heat of summer, us upon Milord's estate has a picnic all, upon the grass before the Hall, and wears us Sunday best, and ale there be for everyone and food and drink enough and more, and, after, us makes merry and dances upon the soft grass. And the night breeze do blow the smell of roses and gilliflowers from Milady's garden all about us.

And now have come Tom, to tell that he and Marsden, with Shunghie to accompany, will set out the day following this one to Wai-Aniwa-Niwa, the greatest of them waterfalls of the Bay of Islands, and then to the River Wai-Tangi, mebbee thirty mile by land from here, which route Marsden be determined upon taking, though by canoe upon the sea it be a mere four-hour journey.

So I must be left alone with Ngaio and me little boys while Marsden and me husband goes off upon the duties of the Lord, though what the Lord have need of at the waterfall I knows not.

And Tom will leave me thus, yet he and Marsden both has seen the awful remnants of Te Maaka's wife and all us seen but yesterday, upon them three tall stakes within the pa, set like to scarecrows with mats draped round about the poles, the heads of some of them that Shunghie lately conquered.

RICHARD STOCKWELL.

CONVICT.

BORN NORFOLK,

1777.

DIED NORFOLK,

1859.

I awoke to the most beautiful sounds a man might hear this side of Paradise. A chorus of birdsong swelled upon the wooded hills and a chiming bird gave out a song which rose from this choir like a soloist calling to his Maker. Such beauty in music I never heard before, yet here, in New Zealand, it sounds forth every morning.

Our ship, having crossed the turbulent Tasman Sea and reached New Zealand, followed then to the south a coastline of gigantic cliffs, rounded a headland and headed due west. It was as if, suddenly, we had entered a secret yet enormous hidden inland sea, dotted about with tiny islands and bounded in the far distance upon each side by forest-covered moun-

tains. Small habitations perched in clearings upon their pinna-
cles and clung to the crowns of the islands all about us. We
sailed across this wide expanse, the open sea far behind, and at
length I saw ahead the slow descent of the mountains to hills,
then to a narrow coastal plain, until we dropped anchor in a
tranquil little bay where Reverend Marsden was ferried out to
us in the bum-boat of an anchored whaler.

This, the captain told us, was Kiddi-Kiddi, and, having
collected our human cargo, whose first words to me were not
of greeting but of the necessity of mindfulness of God in my
altered situation, we tacked north-east across the bay until, at
last, we sighted Rangi-Houa.

All upon our voyage from Parramatta, whilst little Lizzie
daily rose in spirits and skipped about the deck, the older girl,
Susannah, sat silent in the stern gazing upon the ocean and did
not suffer us even a smile when we informed her the settlement
of Rangi-Houa had come in sight at last. And, while Lizzie
crowed and waved at the figures now discernible upon the
distant shore, Susannah placed herself against the vessel's side
and stood there mute. It was only when I glanced at her the
better, I saw the tears that, coursing down her cheeks, had
soaked the bodice of her little frock.

''Tis Mither,' was all she said, and yet it brought a lump so
great of pity to my throat, scarce could I suppress my own
unbidden tears.

The closer to the shore we drew, the more my heart knotted
in my breast. The gentle coolness of the breeze about us and
the general softness of the weather uplifted me. And the
prospect of my greater liberty gave a natural quickening to
my spirits. But over and above all other considerations rose
the knowledge that, so soon, I should see Jane Quickfall, Mrs
Kendall, once again.

Out upon the ocean to greet us came three miraculous
native vessels, great canoes, all upwards of sixty feet long,
hewed each from a single giant tree. And in them, clamouring
natives, hacking and cutting at themselves and screaming as

they rowed. Standing erect and proud in the foremost was Shunghie, the Bay of Islands chief, who shouted as he drew alongside our bows, 'Matenga. Matenga, haere mai.'

'I it is he calls,' said Marsden, in whom the sin of false humility will ne'er take root. 'I am Matenga, the head, the leader, and haere mai means welcome.'

One of the chiefs, Tu-Taki, who had crossed with us from Port Jackson, greeted his closest relatives – or so I assumed them to be – upon the deck of our ship. Their manner of salutation was most curious. Leaning forward, they pressed their noses together and remained in this position some several minutes without speaking and with no other bodily contact. On several occasions, tears fell copiously down their faces, yet they uttered never a sound. It was as if they were figures in a tableau.

Shunghie scrambled up the ladder to the deck, greeted Marsden and indicated that he, with the Kendall daughters, was to travel to the shore in the chief's own canoe.

Marsden, who has been in the Bay of Islands some four weeks already, conducts himself as one who might be thought the lord of this domain, his proprietorial air of condescension extending even to those things one might deem the sole province of the Maori. He did not scruple to precede Shunghie in the disembarking from our ship, which I saw that chief remark, though he held his peace.

And as Susannah and her sister were lowered and handed into the canoe, their brother swam through the waves like a Heathen child and scrambled in there with them, a feat much applauded by the Maori. But for disapproval it would have been hard to better the expression on Parson Marsden's face.

It was most affecting to witness the reunion of Mrs Kendall and her daughters. She stood, plain to see, at the ocean's edge, her gaze fixed only on the canoe which bore them to her. Though I could not from that distance discern the workings of her face, it was plain from every aspect of her body that she could barely hold herself back from plunging, like her son, into the water, the sooner to clasp them to her.

And when, at last, they were set upon the shore, it seemed

as if she had neither arms nor tears enough to express the fullness of her heart towards them.

'Mother!' shrieked little Lizzie. 'Mother, Mother, Mother.' And, plying her parent's cheeks and arms with kisses, she hung and clung upon her. But Sannah stood stiff and awkward within the circle of her mother's arm and must be coaxed to lay her head upon her parent's shoulder, the which, when she had done, unleashed from the child a torrent of tears. And all the Maori standing about them wept along with her, and I, too, must swallow hard and hold myself in check to keep at bay the grief of my own loss.

Having been ferried ashore in another canoe, and a more stable and comfortable journey I never had before, I stood alien upon the shingly sand, my box beside me, my bedding roll upon it, and gazed about me at the verdance of the landscape with its rolling hills which fell to embrace another series of little bays all held within the arms of a sheltered harbour.

And after I had been greeted again by Shunghie, the chief, and several dusky maidens had eyed me very favourably and wished me 'Haere mai', one pointing to herself, then to me, and after to my bedroll, Mrs Kendall, who, having been so occupied with her daughters, had not so much as noticed me, turned and started at the sight of me. She blushed; confusion overspread her face. And it came to me suddenly, she was afraid I might betray her.

'Ma'am,' said I, conscious of the sweeping eye of Marsden, 'I have had the honour to escort your daughters hither and am detailed by Reverend Marsden to assist you here when your husband returns with him to Botany.'

At this she grew pale. 'Me husband return to Botany? Without ... But when? He have niver said nowt ...' She stopped, aware that Marsden was within hearing.

'Thanks to you ... Stockwell,' she said, with an effort.

I confess myself shocked at the sight of her, her black eyes, even in the joy of reunion, troubled and dulled to grey. I have seen such dullness before. As if a light has been extinguished; the spirit deadened, blinding itself to sights it can no longer bear to witness. Common, it was, on the transport ships. Not so much seen in the Hulks, where men clung still to the belief they might be bought away or pardoned or that, despite the shackles, the starvation and the rats, their stubborn hope itself might bring them a reprieve.

It was only aboard the convict vessels that spark of hope was seen to have withered to extinction.

And so it seemed with her.

I turned from Jane Kendall and looked about for her husband. He strode forward and clasped my hand.

'I do not consider it seemly, Mr Kendall,' said Marsden, 'that an intending clergyman, such as yourself, should extend the hand of friendship to a felon. We must, at all times, remember the example we are setting the impressionable Heathen.'

'But Christ Himself went out amongst the sinners, sir.'

'And when you have become Christ-like, Mr Kendall, so may you.'

As the evening was drawing in we made our meal upon the beach, where the native women brought us, in cornucopias of woven flax, steamed pork and sweet potato so delicious that my spirits rose at the thought of residing here, away from the violent heat of Parramatta and its filthy dust.

Night came down upon us, the sky transformed into a velvet canopy hung about with crystalline stars so close upon us lying I felt that if I but raised my arm above my head my hand would brush against them. And from the hills beyond came the throaty husk of a native owl: 'More-pork,' it cried, 'more-pork.' At which I observed Jane Kendall start, then settle back beside her daughters who nestled both against her, little Lizzie babbling still and prattling, Susannah with her silent head laid in her mother's lap.

The weather being clement and the air both fresh and balmy, at Marsden's bidding I unrolled my bedding and set it, my box alongside, further up the beach. And having bid goodnight to all, and twice dissuaded ladies from joining me in my slumbers – Marsden's views on this being very plain to see and I not anxious to disturb my chances of advancement in my freedom – I fell asleep amongst the Heathen, whose habit it is to wrap themselves about in their flaxen cloaks and, sitting upright out-of-doors, to chatter merrily and incessantly amongst themselves before they fall asleep, remaining all the night in this position.

As I lay down, greatly did they pull at and examine my bedroll and possessions and laugh and make great good-humoured sport of me and all I owned. It seemed they did not yet know I was a convict. This intelligence, no doubt, would be soon imparted by Parson Marsden, whose company I was spared by virtue of his departing up the hill with Kendall, intent upon sleeping in one of the native huts at his disposal.

This country holds an air of spacious freedom. It is uncultivated for the most part by the hand of man, though here and there the natives dig and set their kumara fields and fell the native kauri for their great canoes and dress and work the raupo flax for all requirements of their clothing and dwellings. And, too, they grub and pluck the fern, the unyielding roots of which their lower orders pound and beat into a pulpy paste.

A man may walk along the shore around the promontories and encounter not one other member of his species and see about him only the density and profusion of the native flora, none of which is in any way familiar to me.

It is as if the Heathen here live in such harmony with their land they account themselves another part of it. They are Pantheists like the Noble Savage so applauded by Monsieur Rousseau, who, if he had visited this country, would nowhere have found more worthy prototypes and proponents of his ideals.

The people themselves are strong, above middle height, with lustrous hair, black and curling, worn long by men and women both, sometimes upon their shoulders but frequently swept up by the men into a topknot, stuck about with shells and feather decorations.

These Maori strike me as a most industrious people and I

am determined to set about learning those fragments of their tongue I may readily assimilate.

Shunghie has already seized for himself a cockerel which travelled with us here, crated with its fellows. He has tied it to his wrist and intends to tame it to him, as he has a native wood pigeon which he uses to ensnare its wild kindred. The cock, however, he proposes carrying with him in his canoe, the better to entertain his kinsmen by its crowing, which sound the natives find a source of convulsive mirth. The two cocks which remain with the hens, all now in the charge of Mrs Kendall, attract a daily quota of marvelling visitors and at their early-morning calls to greet the dawn Shunghie's laughter is heard clear across the bay, so prodigious is it.

The very morning following our arrival Marsden proposed a journey to Hoki-Anga, which lies on the western coast, opposite our eastern situation here. He has already recently visited this place but sees in it many possibilities of trade, since its harbour and river offer deep-water access to ships and it is plentifully stocked with the kauri, a straight-trunked tree of sixty to a hundred feet in length.

But the captain, mindful of his need to embark for Port Jackson within the fortnight, insisted the time required for this venture was insufficient and dissuaded him from it.

I confess my disappointment. It is so long since I walked freely about a land, I should have liked it mightily. Kendall, observing my crestfallen demeanour, assured me that upon his return we might make the journey, he and I together, charting the land about us as we went. Whereupon Marsden bade him again heed the nature of my position and his own.

Mr Kendall spoke only from enthusiasm and his need for the friendship of his kind, yet it was plain that Marsden believed him calculating and self-willed. It is ever our worst faults we attribute to another.

Kendall appears much possessed by this place: his friendship with Shunghie, his duties as a sawyer and his attempts to establish the Mission School – which august institution has its location in a little hut by the Kendalls' own – his fervent study of the Maori tongue and frequent excursions with the chief to unmapped places in the Bay of Islands, all render his interest the keener.

It is left, so it seems, to Jane Kendall, her servant, Ngaio, and the children to forage and gather food for them all, the plot of land that Marsden has selected for them being of such poverty in its soil and so windswept in its location that it is hard to conjecture one less calculated to be fertile. Since Marsden is a crofter's son, his motives in selection suggest, to one unencumbered by the burden of naivety, that he hopes his deputy will not be successful in his absence.

I am freer than I have been these last eighteen years, five months and three days.

Kendall is a man of vivid passions of the intellect who, having once seized upon an idea, will cling to it and its expansion despite the most earnest entreaties of moderation. He believes the Maori may be descended from Egyptian seafarers, and this hypothesis, with the aid of his *Encyclopaedia Britannica*, he strives to prove at all times. That he is a man of great potential but seriously wanting in his education is very evident. He has rudimentary Latin but no knowledge of Greek or hieroglyphics. And Marsden, who might direct his enthusiasms, seeks only to grind his theories into the dust.

Kendall reveres Shungie all too openly, listening attentively to discourses in the native tongue, and plucking from them everything that his roving interest deems valid to his own suppositions. As a recorder of facts, Mr Kendall leaves much to be desired, but he has already, with his mercurial mind, attained a certain fluency in the native language. Which fact, far from being applauded by his vicar, has marked him out for cavilling and censure.

In his isolation, Kendall falls daily further under the spell of Shunghie, a clever, wily man, and powerful here at this place, who must surely see within their friendship some chance – I know not what – for his own advancement.

*

Upon my third day here, Marsden took me to the Kendalls' hut, there to set about instructing me in my protector's duties.

I confess Mrs Kendall looked unkempt. Salt-water stains blurred the hem of her skirt and her bodice bore the grey bloom of grime about it. She kept her eyes cast down, betraying to us nothing of her thoughts.

Kendall again assured me of his gratitude that in his absence I should be standing in his stead. To his wife he barely spoke, nor she to him. There was a hostility between them, concealed yet strongly felt. It was in my heart to wish I might indeed be quite supplanting him, a thought I banished almost before I had formed it.

Marsden, having warned me against the depravity of the Maori wenches and of my immediate recall to Port Jackson should I but once succumb to their freely offered charms, continued that I must be sure I did not 'wink' at them. Can it be but by the squeezing of his eyelids he has begotten six children upon that harridan, his wife?

It is well known amongst the transports at Botany Bay that he most assiduously attends the floggings, frequently enjoining those laying it on to exert themselves further. I shall be the merrier when he has departed.

For my skills within the Marsdens' Parramatta garden, I am charged with making this barren plot of land yield food. But here, to fetch the water, I am given by Shunghie three cookees, who run back and forth on their bare feet over the shingle of the little river and fill their gourds and spill them on the plants with unfailing good humour. One of them is so heavily tattooed it is clear he has been at some time a person of consequence in his own tribe. Kendall explained he is the brother of a chief defeated but lately by Shunghie in battle. Taken prisoner, he is obliged to perform tasks so much below his rank that death would have been for him more honourable. Yet he seems cheerful enough. His brother's head, severed and preserved, lies within the precincts of the pa. And such proximity to his brother's remains upholds his spirits.

Ngaio, by means of signs and rudimentary English, gave me

this intelligence as we worked alone in the garden, and I have not passed the information to any other; nor will I, since she begged me not to do so.

Upon the far end of the shore this morning, I observed Mrs Kendall and her daughters, all three running and skipping lightly across the sands below the great trees which march away across the hills to the interior. Laughing, they were, and frolicking like lambs. Susannah spun a stone across the water and Lizzie, attempting to repeat her sister's feat, threw in a small boulder, which sank with a splash, spraying her mother and sister, who screamed in jest and chased her round the promontory. It is the first time since I came here that I have remarked either the mother or her older daughter laughing, and my heart soared to see it.

Mrs Kendall, in high good humour, later sought me out in the garden plot. She appeared lighter, more like the carefree creature who had danced so long ago upon Steep Hill in Lincoln.

'Stockwell, I be come to thank thee for thy goodness to me girls. Sannah says tha did tell to them the tale of Gamma that took her pig to market, and Tom-Tit-Tat and such.'

'It was nothing but a pleasure to me to entertain them so. They are most charming little creatures.'

She smiled upon me for the compliment. 'Hast tha bairns?'

'Nay, m'am. And no wife either. Neither married nor fathered before I was taken to Botany.'

Something in what I said dulled her face a moment.

'It mebbee better so.'

'Perhaps.'

She turned upon another subject. 'I sees thee be watering but nowt do flourish. Water do soak away and the ground stays thin and weak.'

'There is no body or sustenance in this soil, that is why. A poorer plot I could not imagine.'

She shrugged. 'Be Marsden have chose it, not me husband. Nowt will niver grow here. But by there, at Shunghie's field, iverything do burst with nourriture. Whativer he plants do grow.'

'This position is too windswept and the sea air drops salt upon the soil. His gardens are protected by the lea of the hill.'

'Aye, that be true. But I . . .'

'Yes?'

'I wonders . . . times . . . if there be witchcraft in this soil. All here be their land and they puts spells always upon their own gardens.'

At this I laughed. 'I think not. It is science and reason which determine whether crops will flourish, not the incantations of a savage priest.'

'Aye, but look to how Shunghie's crops do be and us with a few poor stragglers only for all us labours.'

'I believe the fault lies somewhat in the soil but also with the types of crops you are endeavouring to raise. Wheat will never flourish here, nor barley. And how will you thresh and mill it should it, by some miracle, succeed?'

'I knows so. But it be Marsden again that says us must put in them English crops here. He wants us self-sufficient in us own vittals and provender before a year be out.'

'A year to accomplish such a task! The man is a lunatic.'

'Oh aye, indeed. But a lunatic with vittals upon his own plate in his own house.'

'I will speak with Mr Kendall. If Shunghie will but yield to us some plantings of their sweet potato . . . What is its name?'

'Kumara.'

'And if even kumara will not grow in this plot, your husband must insist that Marsden allow him to move your gardens.'

'Shunghie will mebbee give thee plantings. He have many. They be a-setting them since the last new moon.'

But when I had spoken with Kendall and he, in turn, with Marsden, and the great chief's plantings had been sought, none could he be prevailed upon to supply.

With much smiling and good humour, Shungie assured us that we should have as many kumara plantings as we might desire, but: 'Tomorrow, eh-Matenga.' 'Tomorrow, eh-Keni.'

'Tomorrow, eh-Tokere.' 'Tomorrow, I bring,' he promised. And tomorrow was always tomorrow, even when I stood by his gardens, pointing at a pile of plantings and asking to carry them with me on the instant.

'No, eh-Tokere, they no kood. Tomorrow I bring.'

And it became clear, even before Kendall and Marsden had departed for Botany, that kumara plantings we should never have.

The kumara is a most original vegetable. Pink and cream-skinned when first dug from the ground, cooked, it turns a soft dull yellow. Its flavour is sweet, somewhere between a potato and a beetroot, and it is highly esteemed by the natives here, being their staple item of diet.

It is astonishing to me that Shunghie, who prizes most highly his position and distinction, personally tends his kumara fields and oversees all farming activities therein. In this he puts me greatly in mind of Farmer George. Like our own king, his pride in the cropping from these fields is so great that the size of his harvest is his constant boast.

'You have the second sight, sir,' I told him. 'You know beforehand which plots of ground will yield you most.'

'Second sight?'

'An inward eye which sees within its own world and divines the future.'

'How do you know this, eh-Tokere?'

'It is but an instinct.'

'My wa-hi-ne . . .'

'Your wife?'

'Ai-ee, she, Turi-Ka-Tuku, my chief wife. Has no eyes.'

'Blind.'

'Blind. Always. Eyes turned, so, back in her head. Sees things inside. Things to come. Like a tohunga. And this is why I am great warrior. She sees before battle. She knows his thought, my enemy. She tells me how he fights.'

'His tactics?'

'Ai-ee. Turi-Ka-Tuku, my tapu chief wife. What she has, mine, what I have, hers. So I, too, have second sight.'

And, seeing my interest in his words, he proudly went on to tell me more of his powers.

Whenever he was the victor in battle, he said, he would cut the head from the vanquished chief – and here he made a slicing movement with his arm across his throat – and then would pluck from his enemy the left eye and eat it. By which means he ingested the power of his rival and prevented the eye from being translated to a star in the heavens. The other eye he dispatched, and, in so doing, deprived the dead leader of sight in Paradise. With their chief unable to look down on them and protect them, his entire tribe was utterly brought low.

As he spoke, I tried to conceal my revulsion and terror. I could see he meant most earnestly every word he uttered. I have known that kind of fear before, waiting in the dock for my sentence to be passed down. Perhaps he felt my unease. He laughed. 'No worry, eh-Pakeha,' he said. 'Not eat you. Too salty.'

Here, in Ao-Tea-Roa, I have felt free again. Yet the country has a wild and disturbing juxtaposition of landscape that mirrors the nature of its native people. The melodious singing in which they constantly engage together soothes like the swell of the quiet sea; their laughter and openness flow like their pleasant streams. But the savagery of the jagged, soaring mountains, the blood-red soil, the sudden beating storms of wind and rain, all reflect their casual cruelties and brutish practices, the eruption of their sudden violence one to another. It is a very alien place.

Formerly I have pushed such observations from my thoughts, refusing to dwell upon them for my sanity's sake, but now they crowd upon me, unbidden. And, too, those remembrances which I believed buried in my heart for ever come flooding through my dreams and will not be suppressed.

Each night as I watch Orion, called by the Maori the Great Canoe, striding, sailing, through the heavens, there rise before me the spectres, clear and substantial as living men, of those who with me crossed, like the stars this sky, the wild and turbulent Indian Ocean.

Isaac Quickfall, his huge collar-bones jutting like hangers from which his skin, an ill-fitting garment, crumpled upon him. Irish Billy, touched with madness, first to die. His leg was greened and stinking with gangrene, and so much by then had pity fled our hearts that we joked as he was flung into the waves, a hasty prayer muttered over his shroud by our captain. And we wagered how the owners of the circling fins that bore in upon the ripples might puke upon his verdigrised flesh.

Euphoria seized us. We had cast off an evil omen. Relieved of his suppurating stench, rotting though we were ourselves, we breathed the air below the decks as if it were sweeter, purer.

And yet, at a week's end, when the cavernous ocean had swallowed utterly another seven, all of whom nightly arise in sad procession before me, there shewed visible in the rest, despite each man's effort to disguise it, that dullness I saw clear, on my arrival, in the eyes of Jane Kendall.

Like a pestilence, silent, feared, Despair moved among us, claiming as its own any who would succumb to its cold touch. Man after man bowed forever over his manacles, fell sideways, lifeless, upon his neighbour.

Panic pierced our ship's master. He commanded the doctor attend all injuries, gave orders for the exercise and four-hourly relief of every convict. With more than half his cargo gone, he would not collect his bounty on arrival at Botany Bay. Within the Roaring Forties and a three-week sail to New South Wales, in an effort to save of his charges what he could, he ordered our leg-irons struck off and each man's rations doubled. Too late for those truly wretched who haunt me now by night.

SHUNGHIE IKA.

PARAMOUNT CHIEF
OF THE NGA-PUHI
OF AO-TEA-ROA.

BORN *1772*.

DIED *1828*.

The first pale men I ever saw came clambering from their
sailing ship, a vessel unknown to me, Shunghie Ika, given to
Tu, the war god, navigator of mighty war-canoes in which I
have sailed to attack and defeat the Tai-Nui, the Arawa, the
Ngati-Awa.

There stood I on the sands of Koro-Ra-Reka, my summer
pa, gazing at the ocean and the strange many-masted vessel
tossing upon it. Like a large chest bobbing high on the waves
– no carved prow leaping clear of the water, no men wielding
paddles – wide and cumbersome it lay, a burden on the sea.
Crowding the decks were men, bodies covered in tight-fitting
cloth of strange colours. Pale, bleached men like curing flax. I
peered to see them better and one of them raised an arm in

greeting; then, as I watched, from the ship's side swung out on ropes a shrunken blunt canoe, pale as the men seated inside it.

This was a thing already known, spoken of by my mother and other old ones, but thought to be fantasies or visions of dancing minds. I shouted from the sand for all to come to view, we launched canoes and paddled to meet them. In such a way did we set out to embrace our fate and that of our whanau for ever.

Turi-Ka-Tuku does not trust them. She wishes me to stay far from them and all they offer us. But I tell her this is an impossibility.

They *interest* me, these white men, fleas, Pakeha, so strange and ugly. Not their whalers and sealers who come to rot our women and destroy our sons. But the ones we see now at Rangi-Houa with their notions of one Heaven and one God, their legends of virgins seeded by opportunistic angels, dead men revived, their submissions to a god who does not display himself in land or sea or air, who holds them in such cruel bondage they cannot move their limbs freely to dance or sing or couple. Such a heavy Lord.

We are disturbed by their strange behaviour one to another. Passing by the wha-re we have given to Matenga, I heard him and Keni in hot anger within. I spoke of it to Turi-Ka-Tuku.

'They are arguing amongst their tribe. But what they say I know not.'

'I hear them.' Her eyes roll back. 'And I feel them yet more.'

'Strange, this brother against brother.'

'It may be they are not, as you suppose, brothers.'

'I am certain of it. They are chiefs of the same blood.'

'Keni and Matenga? They are not chiefs. They are serving men.'

'They are chiefs. Have I not seen with my own eyes at Parramatta?'

'And what is their tribe? Who is their iwi?'

'They are tangata of King Horhi of England, a wise and

famous chief: greater than I, greater even than your own father.'

'Then why does King Horhi not send letters asking for protection for his people? Matenga alone comes to us; we have not seen this Horhi. No word have you had from him.'

'Do I send myself to sue for peace after battle? Is it I who carries forth the head of my enemy on a pole offering truce?'

'We have had no battle. Nor yet the head of their king. Be cautious, Husband, heart of my heart. I do not trust what I smell. Now when I walk in our kumara fields, the land clings to my feet and will not be brushed away. It is breathing against my every step, calling on me to guard it, protect it. Never to desert it.'

'You wrong Matenga. And Keni. They do not want our kumara fields.'

'You wrong my vision. They want our kumara fields *and* our souls. And if you let them, they will take away our gods as well.'

'They want us to have knowledge of *their* god. It is not our gods that interest them.'

'It comes to the same thing. Tell them nothing lest you weaken and destroy the power of our gods.'

'I would never betray our gods.'

'But, Husband, you do not always see as clearly as you believe you do. Pride is your enemy. Do not display our gods. Speak not a word of Io or our atua or any sacred things. Our gods will grow angry and abandon us. Keni is dangerous to you.'

'He is a good man, an honest man.'

'And that is why he is so dangerous.'

'Matenga has brought us a tree.'

She turns her blind eyes to me. 'I am curious. What does he look like, this Matenga?'

'Even for a Pakeha, he is ugly. His nose is not wide and generous but high and pinched together. Like this.'

I gather in the sides of her nostrils and pleat them up. She laughs, pushes away my hand.

'And his lip, the top one, is almost gone. From below his nose to this lip is a long, long journey. Five days as the huhu grub crawls.'

I trace with my finger the crease below her nostrils, slide my finger over her lips and caress her moko. Four sacred spirals, waves of the ocean, growing life, the emerging fern head, the everlasting renewal. Of these she has a clear vision. As the carver traced the patterns, then struck with his sharpened stick and shell, there emerged before her inward eye the sacred markings of her moko. Even the colour, which she has never seen in all her life, she has described to me as that of the feathers of the huia.

'How do you know this?' I once asked her, long ago.

'I held a huia-bird in my hands as a child. Through my fingers, I could feel its purple darkness.'

Mutunga, her father, a mighty chief of highest mana, gave orders that she, his favourite child, be brought all manner of objects to understand by touch, that she might have knowledge of a secret order, to compensate her for her sightless eyes. After his greatest battles he ordered brought to her by his tohunga, within curving shells, the blood of his enemies that she might distinguish them, one from another, by their smell. Of all our children, not one can she fail to identify instantly when she has inhaled his approach.

Her spirit breathes on my fingertips.

'What is this tree Matenga gives?'

'An apple.'

'Apple? This is their holy tree. The tree of their Adam and Eve.'

'So Keni tells us.'

She laughs. 'Bring me this apple. I shall eat it, and if Keni speaks the truth the whole world will be revealed to me.'

'You know already the nature of the world. Better far than those who see with eyes.'

'And I have told you, they will starve our land with their "apples", these Pakeha crops. And then they will steal the land from us. Already they take our whales, our seals, our sons.'

'You wrong Matenga. He does not steal our sons. He is

teaching them how to read and speak the pale men's language. Did not Ha-Re-Shunghie live within Matenga's own house at Parramatta?'

'Matenga smells harsh and sour. You have told me how pale and wan he looks. The colour of mashed flax, you claimed.'

'And so he is.'

'Yet you would trust him? Of course Matenga will take our sons to his own hut. That man has a greedy breath. His sweat is treacherous. I have sat beside him and I know. First he will teach them the Pakeha speech, then he will teach them of his Te Ariki, Jesus. Next he will ask for prayers for Te Ariki, fish and kumara for Te Ariki, land for Te Ariki. So it will begin. And it will not cease till Te Ariki has the whole of Ao-Tea-Roa in his grasp. And then he will fight our gods. And Te Ariki has muskets.'

'Matenga has a likeness of Te Ariki at Parramatta. Te Ariki does not believe in killing and muskets.'

'Matenga tells you this?'

'Indeed.'

'But he himself has muskets. And Keni, too. If their gods say they are tapu, why do the missionaries have muskets?'

'I had not thought of this.'

'Then think of it now. Before it is too late.'

'Too late for what?'

'Too late for us. Send them away. Do not let your curiosity and your pride place us all in peril.'

Sighing, I place my nose against her own, breathe and rest a moment.

'It is already too late. I cannot send them away. If I do not befriend them, one day they will take us and all we have by force of their muskets. I have seen the fate of the blackfellows at Botany Bay. Matenga's tribe has guns and we have none. We have no choice. Better we are their friends than their enemies.'

Turi-Ka-Tuku shakes her head. 'When I was a child, my honoured father kept at his side at all times his first tohunga, who had lived so long his sight had faded, his ears had closed and his juices leaked all from his body. Only once, perhaps twice, in a season would he speak, to prophesy. And these predictions were so twisted and difficult they resembled most the scented po-ananga vines that weave their way through the trees of our bush so no man knows from which root flows which vine.

'But three times he made the same holy utterance. And each of these times I, myself, heard his voice, so feeble all must strain to catch the frail flight of it.

'"Maui", he said, "is our hero, he who hauled up our island, Te Ika-a-Maui, the great fish of Maui, using for his fish-hook the sacred jawbone of his most revered ancestor, his paternal grandmother. For us men took he fire nine times from the fingertips of the fire goddess, Mahu-Ika, who pursued him so that he flew for protection in the shape of a hawk to Rangi, the Sky-Father, who sent a great flood to save him.

'"And when the fire goddess threw her dying sparks into the topmost branches of the drowning trees, Maui it was who broke with his beak these branches and brought them to Earth for men to rub together to know the secret of creating fire.

'"Maui it was who tied the Sun with great ropes to force him to move more slowly, to let the day be longer.

'"And now are coming from the north, even as I speak, great canoes, pushed by the wind, in which sail flax men, sand men, men who will change about our times and seasons, who carry twigs of fire by which they will conquer us, my people. Oh, my whanau, beware these men and their fire-twigs."

'I am afraid for us, Husband. Very much afraid. Not for you, not for me, but for Ha-Re-Shunghie, Reporo, Huia, for all our children. And for their children. And their children's children.'

'Fear Matenga if you must. But Keni is my friend, my hoa.'

'Matenga is far from here but Keni lives amongst us.'

'He is a different breed of man from Matenga. Matenga has more power but Keni has more understanding. He tells me that their Devil is a powerful tani-wha who lives below the ground in caves of smothering heat and fire that smell of sulphur like the lands of the Arawa at Roto-Rua.'

'Te Kuru, the Arawa chief, does not think himself a tani-wha.'

'I believe he may be. He lives amongst fire and smoke and the stink of ancient rotten moa's eggs.'

'Then he is a very visible tani-wha. Does Matenga's Devil also show himself abroad like Te Kuru?'

'By magic he assumes a foreign shape to tempt the erring. And then he leads them down into his sulphur cave and boils them alive in greatest agonies.'

'Like Te Kuru by the bubbling mud of Whaka-Rewa-Rewa. For an instant, so my father said, he shows himself to the enemy, then lightly leaps away across the secret paths that only he knows. Following, his enemy falls from the way, into that giant boiling pot.'

'So he is a tani-wha!'

'And this apple tree of Adam and Eve, so Keni told you, Husband, had also a tani-wha twined around its trunk. One man, one woman, one apple tree, one tani-wha clinging to it, whispering, whispering to that woman: "Hear me, eh-Woman, I am rising, climbing up. Place your hand, eh-Wa-hi-ne, here, on my tani-wha's head."'

And while she speaks, she is sliding her hand in amongst the heavy strands of my flax mat.

'Aiee! Here is that tani-wha, there his head. See, his eye turns to my hand. He is holding his apples for me to suck upon.'

'Do that longer and I myself shall bring you the tani-wha and his apples.'

She laughs at me. Her foamy eyes roll back into her head as her fingers play upon me as on a flute.

'Aiee, he sings!'

And she withdraws her fingers, rolls to her knees and crawls at speed to the wha-re entrance. Quicker, I seize her, roll her back and pull her to sit on top of me.

Eh-Turi-Ka-Tuku, no other woman is like you. No other wife comes near your beauty, your smell, your laughter, your sharpness of mind and softness of body, your great warm belly, your dark, seaweed, fish-scented hair lying in oiled locks

162

across my shoulders as you rock and swell with me here upon the floor of the wha-re. Your cries of pleasure are the sea, the gyrations of your hips against me are the rushing, swirling waters of the cascade, Wai-Aniwa-Niwa.

'Turn me on my back, then lie on me and come into me as Keni does it to Modder.' Her stomach heaves with amusement.

'They never do it. I think their god forbids it.'

'Before, no. But since her daughters came, they do it often – when Matenga is not there.'

'How do you know?'

'Rerehu and Huia told me. They were curious, so they peeped through the raupo chinks of Keni's wha-re. It is true. This is how the Pakeha does it, every time.'

She falls on her back and I collapse on top of her. So hard is she clinging to my ure, I can no longer resist. Like the cascade I spray down inside her as she rises under me, a wayward canoe.

Ah, these poor Pakeha: their God does not allow them to rejoice in their sensuality. A sad, sad religion. It is little wonder Keni wishes to know of our gods.

THOMAS KENDALL.

MISSIONARY.

BORN NORTH THORESBY,

LINCOLNSHIRE,

1778.

DIED NEW SOUTH WALES,

1837.

Being determined upon completing at least one further expedition before we depart for Parramatta, and the ship's captain having most firmly stated that he would not wait for our return should we be delayed at Hoki-Anga, Marsden has settled upon a march to a not too distant lake, called by the natives O-Ma-Pere. This lies to the north-west of Kiddi-Kiddi – as far as we may ascertain from Shunghie, who will accompany us.

Jane's coldness to me, which had thawed greatly since the arrival of our girls, has once again manifested itself. She refuses to understand that my return to Parramatta is at the behest of my spiritual overlord, Marsden, and I am powerless to say him nay. All my attempts to reason with her, and to reassure her that Mrs Marsden is at this moment in the same husband-less state she herself laments, fall upon deaf and graceless ears.

It is a thought I endeavour at all times to tamp down, but yet it springs wantonly in my head that Jane perhaps has not the natural temperament and humour of the true missionary's wife.

I remarked a little tartly, to my shame, that she herself might set about the lifting of some of my more burdensome duties and take it upon herself to instruct my Heathen pupils in their English catechism in my absence. I shall not repeat her response to this most reasonable of suggestions. Suffice it to say it was not the reply of an obedient Christian wife and I have chided her strongly and urged her pray on this subject in my absence.

Stockwell, our convict, an educated man, here interposed to offer his own services, but, mindful of Marsden's horror should he find a seditionist engaged in such a task, I reminded him he was already greatly encumbered by the charge of guarding, in my stead, my wife and children. To which he most graciously replied it was but a privilege and a pleasure to him to be so occupied.

He has the manners of a true gentleman. Unlike that upstart Marsden, who accords to himself airs and graces, yet is as rude in his bearing and comportment as the blacksmith he surely would be still, had he not left his native land to better himself.

A curious event took place at Lake O-Ma-Pere. At the very time of death of any of the Maori a singular performance of weeping takes place which I have heard several times since our arrival in New Zealand. It is a most musical but melancholy lamentation in which all join and it is very affecting to hear. This mourning for their dead continues several days and nights whilst the cloaked body of the deceased remains seated on a sacred platform on the marae before their meeting house. At the final obsequies, a woman of the tribe comes forth and makes a single long and haunting cry to call the spirit of the dead to listen to its final ceremony upon this Earth, after which are many speeches and much weeping until the same woman again gives her long strange cry and bids the soul depart for the next world. Tangi, they call this ceremony and the greater the mana or prestige of the dead man, the longer does it last.

Upon our near arrival to the lake, Shunghie insisted we divert our way a little to a pa some miles from our route, where his kinsmen reside. Marsden, mindful of the shortage of time at his disposal, was much annoyed at this, reminding me he must collect both specimens and data at our proposed destination.

It was agreed that, in order to prevent offending Shunghie – which we can, in truth, in no wise sensibly afford to do – I should accompany him whilst Marsden and the other two chiefs who made up our little party pressed on to O-Ma-Pere, there to await our arrival in a two day.

It had occurred to me already that Shunghie seemed to have some hidden motive for this visit and I surmised it might be that he wished to display me to his relatives. He speaks of me in his own tongue as 'my Pakeha' and I am grateful of the compliment bestowed. Being of a different hue and, unlike most white men – whom the natives encounter but rarely, if at all – being able to converse with them in their own tongue, I am something of a curiosity.

I therefore set my course with him with interest and vigour, eager to meet this new tribe. But as we drew nearer to their stronghold, Shunghie's face grew grave and he shook his head. 'Eh-Keni, we are too late, too late.'

And echoing his words, the lamentations of the bereaved cut through the air towards us.

We quickened our pace and found on our arrival at our destination that, seated at some distance on the marae, raised on a platform, with a feathered mat draped about his person, was the deceased, Shunghie's cousin, who had expired some time earlier.

Shunghie's tears were copious and I took myself off that he might have the privacy of his grief. Seeing that all were much engaged in mourning and in greetings, and likely to be so occupied for some time, I thought to walk beside the small creek flowing nearby which led into a sheltered glade of native forest.

I wandered there until the dusk set in, then retraced my steps beside the water. I estimated myself to be within half a mile of the pa when I was surprised to see walking purposefully towards me a tall man, strongly built, well-wrapt in the feathered mat of a chief. As he drew nearer, I saw his face was heavily tattooed, with strange and singular arrow markings above each eyebrow, his oiled and ochred hair dressed with huia feathers.

He seemed to be striding urgently, as if in haste, and, unusually for a Maori, upon my timidly offered 'Haere mai' of greeting, merely nodded gravely, inclining his noble head towards me but neither speaking nor pausing in his pace.

I turned my head discreetly to watch his passage and was surprised to see him veer from the bank and set his course directly into the denser part of the forest.

I watched as his figure faded amongst the trees, then slowly I returned to where the mourners sat and wailed. Shunghie, at my approach, rose with tears coursing still and drew me aside to tell me this was the body of his honoured cousin, a chief of great mana, that he had had upon him since early that day, as we headed for O-Ma-Pere, the premonition of impending doom and that, as we approached, he had felt the presence of his cousin's spirit and recognised he came too late.

'But,' said he, 'I have spoken with him now as he sits dead and we shall meet again in the spirit world.'

'You are not the only relative who was in haste,' said I, in an effort to console him. 'Just now I passed another of your cousins hurrying home.'

He regarded me strangely. 'My cousin? Where so?'

I indicated my former path.

'This one you saw. How did he seem?'

'I should say he walked with determination. He was firmly set upon his course.'

'You spoke with him?'

'I greeted him but he was travelling quickly and did not

stop to answer. He merely nodded to me civilly, then headed for the forest.'

'The forest?' I felt his agitation. 'Did he pause or stop when he had seen you?'

'He did not hesitate a single step. It was as if I was but a shadow on his path.'

Shunghie took me through the group of mourners to the side of the dais, where sat the dead man.

'Do as I,' he said. And spoke, to my surprise, in English.

In English I answered him, 'Yes.'

I followed where he led, closer to the corpse. I had not looked upon the peaceful dead since first my father, then my mother, passed away. The others I had seen, the victims of Shunghie's massacres, hanged men like Isaac Quickfall, a drab in London stabbed in a brawl slumped against a wall with her mouth agape, Baby John frozen in mid-cry, rose up now within my head. It seemed a hidden thousand ugly images floated there.

I recalled how at Bentinck Chapel in London Reverend Wood had told me of a Frenchie, fled to London to save his own skin, who had seen, or so he claimed, the severed head of the French Queen held up to the crowd and had watched as her lips tried desperately to form words, struggled to speak. And this, said Reverend Wood, some three or even four minutes following the ghastly thud of the guillotine blade.

In the little time it took for Shunghie to lead me nearer to the body and instruct me to glance quickly at the dead man, not letting my gaze to dwell on him too long, and to wish his spirit a safe journey to the Underworld, all these sights crowded in my head.

'Each of us, when we die,' said Shunghie, 'must make the journey north to the po-hutu-kawa at Te Re-Inga, the entry point to that world wherein the soul is purified before it journeys on to the spirit world. Where live all the ancestors who have gone before us.'

'But this is a Christian belief. You speak of Purgatory.'

'Hush,' he said. 'Pay your last respects to this great chief.'

I looked across to the body. Saw to my horror, as I almost swooned, the exact likeness of the chief whose path had crossed my own. The arrows above his eyebrows marked him out and all but his grave brown eyes, now closed, pronounced him the selfsame man.

'Te Re-Inga,' said Shunghie, supporting me, 'lies north-north-west of here, beside the stream, then through the forest. Towards the path of the setting sun. But you did not halt or deflect him. No hungry ghost can take him from his journey if he did not stop nor stumble.'

'He did not waver from his path,' said I.

I have tried to make other explanation of it since we returned but none can I bring to mind. It seems I have seen a ghost. And not merely a ghost but a Heathen shade. And yet it seemed quite human in its mien. I cannot cast it from my mind. And Shunghie has not spoken of it since. Nor dare I mention it to Marsden.

At the lake, a most beautiful, tranquil spot with a small pa at its farther end, Shunghie greatly angered Marsden by refusing to speak in English at all and using only his own tongue. Whilst Marsden has a smattering of Maori, he is by no means fluent and thus has been forced to rely on me for his translations, a source of great resentment to him.

And as we sat beside the shore, the three of us together, Shunghie was moved to ask me of Christianity.

'What does your God say is the start, the beginning of all things?'

'In the beginning was God and His Holy Word.'

'His breath?'

'Yes.'

'So God has his wai-rua and he breathes it for man.'

'In a manner of speaking, yes.'

'What says he, Mr Kendall?'

'He asks me about the Gospels, sir. "In the beginning..."'

'Then tell him of Genesis, Mr Kendall. "In the beginning God created the Heaven and the Earth."'

I translated this.

Shunghie nodded. 'Twelve Heavens, there are. And the nearest is the Heaven of Rangi, wherein lie all the stars.'

'He says . . .?'

'That the stars are in Heaven, Reverend Marsden.'

'The simplicity of our Heathen is a little hard to bear.'

Shunghie returned to the New Testament. 'So this girl, this wa-hi-ne, Mary, had a baby but no husband for its father.'

'God was its father.'

'So the grandparents took the baby, and Mary after found a husband and all was well?'

'No, no. Mary was a virgin.'

'She could not be a virgin and have a child.'

'It was God's child . . .'

'And now, Mr Kendall?' A testy tapping of his foot.

'He speaks now of the Annunciation, sir.'

Shunghie smiled. 'A clever girl, Mary. Her lover will have trouble if the tribe knows she is pregnant. Her lover may be married and, for his adultery, killed by the father of Mary. So in this manner she saved him and herself, too. Yes.'

'No. This child was divine. Like Maui.'

'But Maui had not a human mother.'

'Maui,' said the Reverend, interrupting at his catching of a known native word, 'is a Heathen demigod. He has nothing to do with the Word of God.'

'Aiee, I like this Mary. She was resourceful.'

'Now he praises the sanctity of Mary, sir. I do not think you have taken my meaning plainly, Shunghie.'

'I think I understand you very well. Tell me, eh-Keni,' he beamed at me and Marsden, 'is it true that intelligent men in England *believe* this story?'

Yesterday, while Marsden was instructing Stockwell on the locking and securing of our muskets, Shunghie took me upon an expedition to a most singular place.

I have observed, in various remote areas, single posts carved and painted in the same red ochre as the storehouses in the pa and have requested Shunghie to tell me what function these bear within his society. At all previous times, he has evaded my questions, but now he has revealed to me what purpose they hold.

They are memorial posts to the native dead. This, in itself, caused me no anxiety. Do not we ourselves raise monuments to our own departed loved ones?

His further discourse it was which so exercised my spirit. Bidding me follow him, he led me to that area to the north-east of our settlement here at Rangi-Houa, to the stand of native bush which he has most frequently and earnestly enjoined us all to eschew, it being tapu by reason of its being a burial place.

Following him with trepidation, I pushed my way between giant ponga ferns the size of small English trees, the tripping, clutching supplejack vines and the vicious barbs of the native lawyer-plant, until we came upon a huge cavern hidden within that green and gloomy bush. On the back wall of this cave ran ledges like the shelves on the walls of my little draper's shop and, stacked upon them, row on row – where I would have shown my muslins and my cambrics, my ribbons, buttons, laces – was piled a display of human skeletons. On the floor were laid several small canoes wherein rested more decaying and revolting remains. All save one, in which lay a pile of bones with a skull placed upon the top. Some of the bodies were rotting within their burial mats: others appeared to have been removed and laid in the canoes. And further into the cavern, on a wooden stage, sat the headless body of a man, also partly wrapped within a flaxen mat.

At this unexpected and repulsive sight, I having had no inkling of the object of our journey, my gorge rose, and it took all my efforts to suppress it. Mindful of the honour accorded me by Shunghie in allowing me to view this sacred place, I had no wish to deter him from reposing further confidences in me.

Shunghie now led me deeper into the twilight of this macabre vault, to yet another cavern, where lay upon an elevated platform a chief's head in a state of perfect preser-vation, hair tied in the topknot, and dressed with red ochre and sacred feathers. Below, on a small ledge, there rested many bones, which I ascertained to be those of three or four people, though I have but a rudimentary knowledge of anatomy. This, said Shunghie, was the tapu of tapu area, the burial place of chiefs.

'What,' said I, cautious in my questioning lest I offend him, 'becomes of these bones?'

But he declined to answer.

Upon our return to Rangi-Houa Shungie took me to his whare in the pa and, drawing down from a little shelf a handsomely carved box – which I had observed before: there being but meagre furniture within their houses, any thing of it shows immediate to the view – he opened it before me, displaying therein a bone flute and long thin red feathers, which, he told me, had belonged to his father's most chiefly enemy, and were his most sacred, honoured and valuable possession.

It was several days before he once again approached the subject. And then he remarked only that it is the custom of other tribes in the area to bury the bones of their dead in a temporary shallow grave, and, when decomposition has set in, the friends and family of the deceased collect the bones, scrape them clean, place them in a woven flax kit with the skull at the top and take them to secret caves. This he called the hahu, the taking-up of the bones, a rite that must be performed to appease the spirit of the dead man. And after it has been completed, his tribe holds a great feast of commemoration. But if it is not done, the dead man will become a ghost and haunt them all.

I was bemused by his shewing of these Heathen practices yet I must account it, too, a singular honour.

In but three more days we depart for Parramatta. I shall miss our expeditions and our discourses together when I am gone. I have promised to Shunghie a gift upon my return.

This morning, early, Shunghie and I went fishing from the rocks around the headland to the west beyond the pa. I am gaining skill in the use of the native rod, which, belying its fragile looks, can support the strain and weight of a heavy fish. Shunghie was in discursive mood. He cast into the frothing surf as sea gulls wheeled and shrieked about the falling bait.

'From there, the north, came our ancestors in their great canoes. From Hawai-Iki, cradle of our race. But first came Ku-Pe, fleeing with his wives and children to escape the wrath of his rivals, sailing south in search of the fish of his tupuna, Maui. And, after many weeks without a landfall, his senior wife saw one day a cloud, long and white, in the far distance. "Ao-Tea-Roa, Ao-Tea-Roa," she cried. And from this comes the name of our land.

'But Ku-Pe, when an old man, grew homesick for Hawai-Iki and went home, where he told of these islands at the edge of the southern seas. And so set out his ure, his descendants, Nuku-Ta-Whiti, with his nephew, Rua-Nui, in their canoes.'

'And did they get here?'

'Yes, indeed. And after them came many more canoes...'

'Yes?'

'And in those canoes they brought with them the plantings of the kumara. Plantings such as you and Tokere have need of. Perhaps, in Parramatta, you will find some plantings for your garden.'

'They do not have the kumara in Parramatta. Those root crops which they do have will not flourish in this soil. They are English vegetables: the potato, the turnip, the carrot.'

'I should like to go to England to see these interesting vegetables.'

'If it will please you, I shall try to carry plantings back to you from Parramatta. But I think they will not grow here.'

'Later, I will give to you some kumara plantings. They are very precious, these plantings. I need a musket to protect them. Do not bring me the English plantings. Bring me a musket for your gift.'

'It is forbidden,' said I, smiling at his deviousness, 'to supply muskets to you or to the blackfellows of Botany. And I am a man of God. I go to Parramatta to deal with matters of God, not matters of warfare. God wishes us to live in peace together and love one another.'

'But Matenga does not live in peace with you.'

I felt a sudden tug upon my line, so great that it slid me down upon my rock. Shunghie seized me about my waist and together we pulled against it. The line arched, bowed, fell slack as the huge fish feinted, then tautened as it hauled and headed out to sea.

'He is too big for us. Never will we pull this one in,' said Shunghie. He took his whalebone blade and severed my line. I felt a stab of sorrow, till I glanced down and saw we were already almost in the foaming water which sucked and pounded on the jagged razor shafts of the nearby rocks.

We sat silently together as he deftly spliced another line upon my dangling thread. Then, 'Why should your God love you?' he asked.

Surprised by this unexpected question, I endeavoured to find a worthy answer. 'Man is set within his place below the mighty Heavens. It is not God's duty to love and honour Man. Man must hold sacred the immutable laws of God. God loves us and has died for us sinful men.'

'This sin, eh-Keni, I cannot understand it. You tell me to lie with more than one wife is a sin. Why?'

'It is against the laws of God.'

'If God did not wish man to have sexual needs, why has He made this thing so pleasant?' Briefly he squeezed at his crotch. 'Why has God made man and woman to be so shaped between the thighs? And to be desirable each to the other?'

'Your married women do not commit adultery. Adultery is a sin.'

'It is not a sin. It is a crime.'

'Against God?'

'Which god? It is a crime against the authority of the chiefly partner. Man is tapu, sacred: woman is noa, profane. She has her own tapu. Each man is one, a singular, but women are all together, in common.'

I struggled to take his meaning.

'I am the chief, the ariki of my tribe. This you know.'

'I do.'

'I am the head, the singular, of all my people. They are together, in common. You understand me?'

'I am attempting to do so.'

'The land, the whenua, we hold in ownership together, but I alone am the leader, though my tohunga and the council of the elders advise me. So, in the end, my people are the chiefs of me – their chief.'

'And your senior wife, too, advises you.'

'Turi-Ka-Tuku? This is true. She is the daughter of a great, great chief and so she holds his mana, his power and his prestige, in her own person. She is a woman and is noa, but as the daughter of her father she is sacred. And because she is a tohunga who sees the future, she is very tapu.'

'I cannot understand it.'

'As I cannot understand this missionary sin. Why must I not be naked and walk about?'

'It is a sin against God.'

He threw back his head, laughed at me, but kindly. 'He is very small, your God.'

'Not so. God is omniscient. He is everywhere.'

'Then he is in your body and in your nakedness.' He flashed me a lewd glance. 'Even in your ure, eh-Keni.'

I cast my line again into the water. The Church Missionary Society in London, when speaking of the Heathen, does not begin to comprehend the complexity of their arguments.

SHUNGHIE IKA.

PARAMOUNT CHIEF
OF THE NGA-PUHI
OF AO-TEA-ROA.

BORN *1772.*

DIED *1828.*

Turi-Ka-Tuku is angry. She has spoken no harsh word to me
but her actions make it plain. She turns from me when she
senses me near her; she does not speak of familiar things. So
polite she is to me but with frost upon her breath, like the
South Wind.

It is the Pakeha have brought about this rift between us.
She knows that I go about with Keni, walk with him, eat with
him, fish with him, talk with him, and this she does not
like.

'What is the matter, Wife of my heart?'

'Nothing is the matter.'

'But you are cold to me.'

'I?'

'You, Wife. You.'

'You wrong me, Husband.'

'Come to me, then, and sit upon my lap.'

'I am busy. I cannot spend time in useless chatter. I must cultivate our kumara gardens. Someone must see to them, since you are always fishing.'

'Put away your anger.'

'I am not angry. I am occupied with all that I must do.'

'Then, if you do not like my company, I shall spend the night with Tangi-Moana. She is not always gardening.'

'And you will make any excuse to give your favours to my sister.'

'It seems you do not have the sense to want them.'

'It seems *you* do not have the sense to know when you are putting all of us in danger.'

'You wrong me. All I desire is utu. Revenge.'

'Oh, no, I know you better. It is I who am wronged. All you desire is supremacy and power. Utu is not your sole desire. You wish for more than your just portion. And for this, the gods will punish you. If you cannot be careful for yourself, be careful for your children, for your whanau.'

'You talk the greatest nonsense. I am going now to Tangi-Moana. She will sing to me and entertain me. I shall not be caught in the trap of these stupidities you utter.'

'Go to Tangi-Moana. She feels as I do. But without a principal wife's right to speak, what can she do but try to lull you back into your senses?'

I bent and crawled beneath the lintel.

'You,' said Turi-Ka-Tuku. 'You do not deceive me. I can smell you and your every thought. Already you plan your voyage to the north. But it will be your undoing. And ours, as well.

'Suck at the sweet fuchsia-berry words that Tangi-Moana feeds you. And then, like any foolish glutted pigeon, waddle out and fall into the snare. Pah! I am glad you are gone.'

I did not go to Tangi-Moana but walked a time alone upon the shore beyond the promontory.

*

Keni must go to Parramatta although he does not wish it. Matenga has offered me passage also but I cannot now be gone. The omens are too unpropitious. Te Kemara, my tohunga, has seen a star biting the cusp of the new crescent moon. An enemy force is moving towards us, waiting only for my absence. I am mounting precautions now against a surprise attack.

Perhaps the Ngati Wha-Tua will seek to make a raid, to sack the pa, steal our women and all our crops and stores of kumara.

They will claim it is for their utu but it is I who seek utu against the Ngati Wha-Tua.

I shall, I swear, have back my brothers' heads from them. On my life as a warrior, I pledge it.

It may be Turi-Ka-Tuku is right. Matenga must be senior to Keni in rank within their tribe since Keni obeys him utterly. And Matenga speaks of King Horhi as his te ariki so this Horhi is the one I most desire to meet.

Tokere's position I do not comprehend. I think perhaps he is a conquered enemy chief now condemned to slavery. His manner and his bearing bespeak a higher rank than he enjoys and I have seen how Keni and Matenga, both, defer to many of his opinions.

I have not had the opportunity to speak with him on matters of philosophy but when Matenga and Keni are gone to Parramatta I shall seek him out.

Keni seems a man who has no tribe, no brothers. A lonely man. He is not a hero, merely mortal, yet he talks of this god of his as if he were his own father, not the great protector and ancestor of his iwi.

And he is strange and clumsy in his actions. He cannot bait a hook well, nor swim, nor man a small canoe. And yet, he is sincere. He wishes to be good, to be acceptable; he thinks about the nature of the gods, the questions of the universe. I did not think that I, a warrior, would stoop to value friendship with such a one as he. But he interests me with all he says, his theories, his thirst for understanding, his desire to know our world.

It may be that the gods have sent him to me as the instrument of my revenge. Unbidden, he arrived upon this shore, my shore. Can it be by simple chance he has come to me now? At this very time?

And whatever Turi-Ka-Tuku may say, we must accept these pale men. They are coming, coming to our land. Every year, more of their ships seek sanctuary in our harbours. Their whaling vessels put in here for food and shelter. Water. And, for all that we can supply, they will trade with us.

We are more highly civilized than the Pakeha. Our knowledge is much greater; in our skills upon the land and on the ocean we far surpass them. It seems they have but little culture: in music, dancing, poetry, oratory, they are most sadly lacking. As Turi-Ka-Tuku daily reminds me.

But she does not see, she will not acknowledge, that they have iron and blacksmith skills, the wheel, the forge. They have large dogs, hounds, such as I saw in Parramatta and this wondrous animal, the horse, on which they ride about, which pulls their carts and carriages.

'We do not have the need of carts,' she says. 'What use would they be here? We have canoes. Canoes that exceed these pale men's ships.'

And this is true. Yet if we had the cart *and* the canoe, then might we use the cart as well. And their iron nails are far superior to anything we know.

And, more than this, above these marvels, something else has the Pakeha. More powerful, most desirable of all his treasures. Without which, I am nothing. With which, I shall be the greatest chief in Ao-Tea-Roa.

Turi-Ka-Tuku is wrong in her fear of the Pakeha. He has many things to offer. And I shall take them all. All. Whatever it may cost me. My heart is set upon it.

RICHARD STOCKWELL.

CONVICT.

BORN NORFOLK, *1777.*
DIED NORFOLK, *1859.*

Kendall has departed, sailed with Marsden and two of the chiefs on the schooner, *Erasmus*. And I am left alone with Jane Quickfall – and five small children and some two hundred savages.

As the vessel disappeared around the distant cape, I saw that Jane was weeping. 'If I would be give again me time, I niver wouldna come to here.'

'But how could you know it before you made the journey?'

'All what I has done be gone sour, spoilt, like old dairy milk and canna niver be made right, niver go back into the churn and made sweet again.'

'You cannot blame yourself for your life here.' And a

sudden rage against Kendall rose in me. 'Nor for Isaac, either.'

She raised her eyes to me, dark in her delicate face.

'Nay,' said she. 'I be no more that she I were in Lincoln.'

'Not your doing, Mrs Kendall. It was not your decision to cross the world to convert the Noble Savage.'

'It be not that. It be how I lives here. Me children ragged, like to natives, me garden that willna grow nowt, the cocks and hens that do die and niver lay, the Heathen and their wickedness.'

'But you are living here in difficult conditions. It is only natural that you should feel despondent from time to time.'

'Thinks tha truly so?'

'Indeed, I do. You must not blame yourself for the circumstances of your life here.'

'It be that I feels when summat have gone awry, be I must set it back to rights again.'

'So all the world must rest upon your shoulders?'

'Nay, but be I must see to the growing and to me children. I hasna time to worry nor fret about God's Will. Talk be not a belly-filler of bairns.'

'Your husband is resolved upon staying here?'

She sighed. 'Aye. And when he be come back from Parramatta, he be set to go about with Shunghie on matters for the Admiralty.'

'The *Admiralty*? What does he with the Admiralty?'

'He will plot their courses for them. But upon the land.'

'I see. He is set to mapping routes for them.'

'Aye.'

'Better he set himself to matters here. His domestic concerns.'

'I wishes for nowt else. But he be iver about God's business. Or Marsden's.'

'But can you not reason with him? Speak to him? It seems you take upon yourself all Kendall's foolish decisions. This is not a place for women and children.'

She lowered her head, rebuked. And I felt the injustice of my speech. How should I presume to judge her actions? Did

I not deny my friend, her cousin? Did I not myself lie shielding a dead man a day and night that I might savour double rations? Back to back with his corpse and inhaling his dead stink, but even that preferable to the pangs of hunger and desolation on that damnable journey. Who am I to judge my fellow creature?

'Forgive me,' I said. 'I spoke in haste. It is not for me to judge the wisdom of your actions.'

She smiled at me. The rare delightful smile of her elder daughter.

'Nay, I be not out of humour with thee. All what tha says be true. But I be a-thinking now only on how I may shift for meself and me own. And Tom away to Botany.'

'You fear for the children now?'

'That be not all I fears for. Tom, it be, also. More and more, he have changed from hisself. He be like a stranger since they was at the lake. Shunghie have worked some spell upon him. Tom were telling me afore he were gone to Parramatta that he believes in their tohunga magic. He even were of a mind to believe in their gods. Tanga-Roa, it were, he said, brung us girls safe across from Botany. And usselves, too. Shunghie's tohunga seen to it Tanga-Roa were made happy and so he gives good crossing to us and us own. Great talks Tom have with Shunghie. Gods this, gods that. Spirits, tapu . . .'

'What is this tapu?'

'Their word it be for sacred. Forbidden. Something set apart from others. Shunghie be tapu. Not a one of them that may lay a hand on owt of his. And if they does or touches his person, even by a mistake, they be killed.

'Their heads be tapu, too. Look how they dinna touch them against their dwellings when they goes in or out, no mind that the space of them doorways be very small. And when they cuts their hair, they makes the ceremony upon the beach and the hair, being of the head, be tapu also. And the shell by which they do cut it. He that cuts it be tapu, too, for a time. And must be fed by a long stick and canna go about within the pa. And all the little shavings of the hair be took up in mussel shells and burnt so none may make witchcraft with it.

All their power that comes from their forebears, they says, do lie in their heads.'

'It is true the head is the repository of Reason and Logic and ideas.'

'All the men and women warriors be tapu when they goes to war, but the women who stays, niver. Noa, they be. Like to say, ordinary, not sacred. Except when they be newly delivered of an infant.'

'These are very singular ideas.'

'And in the wars, so Shunghie did tell to Tom, his old blind wife and his tohunga and hisself, when they have slew an enemy chief, the tohunga takes a blade and cuts him open round the chest and takes out bits of him from inside there which he do look upon very careful and by them he knows who it be that be set to win the war. And Shunghie and the others eats the heart and pieces of the chest from out the chief and so gains all his power.'

'He told me some of this himself.'

She shivered. 'Aye. And it be true.'

I looked full at her. Caught her gaze. The feeling that was between us in the Parramatta garden had not diminished.

'Listen well,' I said. 'We are not in England now. Home is far away. Nothing at Home prepared us for what is here. Judging yourself by the standards of England is an impossibility.'

She turned her face up to me. 'What be thy name? Thy given name?'

'Dick. But no one has used my given name for such a time, I have almost forgotten it myself.'

'Call me Jane and I will call thee thy name also. Th'art kind. Tha'rt good to me, Dick. Better than I deserves.'

Fish we had for our evening meal, steamed in the native green leaves. Bartered for iron nails upon the shore. And afterwards, the natives everywhere around, well-wrapt for their evening slumbers and calling as we approached, 'Tena-ko-e, eh-Tokere, tena-ko-e, eh-Modder,' we walked along the sand with all her children, even little Joseph, who stumbled against the twisted po-hutu-kawa roots as he sought to keep up with his brothers and sisters, crying after them, till Susannah turned and swept him up and bore him off with them.

'You see the stars above us?'

'Aye, I does.'

'Do you see the Seven Sisters?'

'Aye. Same as in Lincolnshire. And here, says Shunghie, they calls these the Seven Chiefs. Each have had his eye plucked out after battle and flung by his people far into the heavens, and there the eyes lies for ever to watch over their tribes until the world might mebbee end.'

'This is only superstition, Jane.'

'Oh, aye. But still and all, Lord Nelson's eye were taken by them Frenchies. And then his arm were gone. And after, they has killed him at Trafalgar. Without his eye, he couldna set to save his life. Nor mebbee mind his own.'

'Be summat I would ask thee, Dick, mebbee tonight when all me bairns be sleeping. Mebbee thou wilt talk privily?'

'Indeed I will.'

'I be a-coming by thy hut then.'

'I shall expect you.'

'What said Isaac when tha gave me note to him? And me lock of hair?'

I cannot bring myself to tell the truth. Upon the Sunday, at the barracks after service, I had searched in vain for Isaac. And, asking after him, was told he languished two days in the lock-up for insubordination to an officer.

And so it was I never saw him before he sprang upon us at Parramatta, where, to my everlasting shame, I renounced him for the saving of my own skin. All I can now hope is that the turning of his mind rendered him insensate to his fate. It seems only just I should have been forced to witness it. And never shall I forget it, either, that jerking and thrashing on the rope, the slow strangulation of the twisting collar, the robbing of a man of his only true possession, his life.

'He could not believe his good fortune in finding you again,' said I.

An anxious look. 'But dost tha think ... mebbee ... it be because of that he went to find me there, at Reverend Marsden's? Mebbee if I hadna niver sent me hair ...'

I sought for words to comfort and convince her. 'He was, even then, determined on coming. And nothing you or I could do ever would have dissuaded him from it. Be assured, Jane, there was nothing might have saved him. I have written to his father to say he died of the fever.'

'That were kind.' She paused. 'Very strong, were Isaac. Neck on him like to a bull.'

I knew of what she was thinking. I braced myself to lie to her again.

'Tell me ... were it ... quick? He didna suffer long?'

'He strangled very fast. It was merciful.'

'I hasna had no friend nor none other than thee to talk with.'

'We have much time to talk together now the others are gone to Parramatta.'

'Aye. Shall it be I comes to thy hut again?'

'Take heed of any natives who may be by.'

'By night they sleeps upon the shore.'

'Be careful still.'

She laughed. 'Parson and Mrs Marsden be a good sail off.'

Nearby, the children slept inside her dwelling and Ngaio, sitting upright outside it, snored a little as we, in my hut, silently reached for each other through the dark. I have but little experience of women, yet she felt to me as warm and yielding as ever I had dreamed her. Every day following, I longed, I lived, for our dark, soft, wet nights.

And, upon the third time that we lay together, breathing hard and spent, a great desire to confess to her my own weakness filled my soul. I longed of a sudden to tell her what had lain so long upon my heart.

'I have none other to speak to either. No one in whom I may freely confide.'

'I be not thy equal and at Home I knows I wouldna be judged fit company for the likes of thee. But if tha wishes to confide in me . . .'

'Then will you listen to what I tell you? What I have told no other living being? And after, you may judge me as you will. Decide whether I am fit company for you, not you for me.'

She gazed at me, uncomprehending.

'Whatever I tell you, whatever I disclose of my baser nature, will you still account yourself my friend?'

She nodded.

'You are sure of this?'

'Ah, Dick, it be hard for me to think the less of thee.'

'Then I shall throw myself upon your charity.'

I swallowed, took her little hand, found strength to speak.

'After we left the Hulks, bound for Botany . . . we lay upon our convict ship shackled in pairs, two by two. Like Noah's animals but less well fed and cared for. And certain it was we were not selected by God for preservation. I had thought the Hulks to be the lowest in human degradation until the day we set sail upon that evil ocean.

'You know already . . . the horrors of that voyage. I need not distress you with recounting it, reminding you. But manacled as I was, the rubbing of the shackle at my ankle slowly bit away my flesh and the sea spray, which drenched us constantly, burnt the wound deeper.'

'Aye,' she said.

'The pain . . .' At the recollection of that pain, my stomach contracted.

'Aye,' she said.

Shame came over me. I longed to tell her but I could not bear to have her flinch from me.

'If we had not lost so many already from the dysentery, my ankle would have been left to fester and to rot. But more than forty had been consigned to the Indian Ocean and, on the captain's orders, all those with wounds now were treated.

'The ship's doctor ordered my ankle cleaned. The scraping, with a knife-blade, was like the pain of Hell. Then came the overseer with a poultice. A bread poultice. To draw away the matter.'

'Oh aye. Me mither often used such upon us chests in winter.'

'Mouldy bread, it was, with salt piled upon it. The overseer slapped it on my ankle; and pus, with blood and matter, oozed forth from the wound. Soaked out into the bread. And in the night...'

'Aye, in the night?'

I hesitated. But the urge to be rid of the secret was too great. I longed to have her understand me, shrive me.

'In the night, like every other night, I lay tormented by the pangs of hunger. And of thirst. Grown men called for water and food like little children starving on a dunghill. And in the night...'

It rose before me now the vision of myself, alien as the figure of another; the moaning of my fellows pierced again my ears; their reek hung foul in my nostrils. And hunger tore once more at my stomach. Misery and despair overwhelmed me. Abandoned by humanity, I sank to the level of my own starvation.

'Aye?' she said quietly, balm upon a wound.

I shook my head to clear it, closed my eyes against her contempt.

'In the night, when no other could observe me ... I ate the poultice. Filthy, diseased with my own oozings. I ate it. And the next poultice. And the one after.'

I felt her face wet as she buried it in my chest and held me.

'So?' she said through tears. 'Bread be bread, when all be said and done.'

She sighed, ran a gentle finger along the twisted rim of the scar about my ankle. Then she bent and kissed it.

'A bracelet, this be, Dick. Thy wedding bracelet. Holding thee to me. I would tha were me husband. Th'art kind and good. Me one true friend in all the world.'

*

187

And, about a five week following, on a day so unseasonably hot and humid for the end of October that I remember thinking, as I hoed, of snow and ice and the cold of Norfolk winter air, I felt the presence of someone at my back, and turned, half expecting to see a frozen English countenance. But there stood Shunghie, the carved lines of his face drawn into a ferocious scowl.

I clung the tighter to my hoe.

'No kood, no kood, eh-Tokere,' he growled. 'She tapu to her husband. I have second sight. I tell you this thing now bad. Very bad.'

And he vanished along the path.

But how did he know? Even Jane herself was scarcely sure.

JANE KENDALL.

MISSIONARY'S WIFE.

BORN BROCKLESBY,

LINCOLNSHIRE,

1784.

DIED NEW SOUTH WALES,

1866.

Us be alone. Rare thing for Rangi-Houa. Us has climbed up the hill behind the promontory, from where us looks now far out to the open sea. If it be I had eyes like the Maori, I might mebbee look clear across to South America, or so says Dick, who be striding ahead. Seaward side of the hill have but little of dense growth to it. Only nikau palms and pu-riri trees and, down below, by the water's edge, gnarled po-hutu-kawas, bending to the surface of the ocean.

Us sits down on the spiky crab grass near to the hill top. The sea be far below now and great cliffs to the left and right jags theirselves, rocky, into the creamy water. The sun be warm and a little breeze blows me hair across me neck. Dick lifts up the fallen brown frond of a nikau palm and waves it like to a fan. South, by the great cape, I sees a twig, a canoe, the spider webs of its nets flung out from the sides. Comes to me, I feels happy. Content-like.

I looks at Dick from the sides of me eyes so he doesna see what I be doing.

Tall, he be, and of an upright bearing, with a rugged, manly countenance. His face have lines carved deep in the skin beside his mouth, upon his cheeks and across his forehead. A moko from the Parramatta sun.

Nothing of the delicate to him but for his eyes, which iver do look with gentleness and compassion on me.

'You are peeping at me, Jane.'

I laughs. 'Oh, aye.'

'A farthing, for your thoughts.'

'A sovereign's worth, them be.'

'Had I a sovereign, I would pay it for them.'

'A farthing, then.'

'Ah, even that I cannot pay.'

Us is silent a bit. Much between us, though. Then, quiet and deep, he says, 'It is a fine, calm day.'

'Aye.'

Sun be glinting on the little heads of the sea waves, making them to shine, sparkle, like they be frost upon English earth.

'It be a Lincoln field, that sea.'

'The sun upon the frost.'

Me heart swells with the recollection of it. Lowing of cows across the meadows, barks and yelps from kennels behind the huntsman's house, ewes and lambs calling low and high to each other, thick bleating, poor lost baaing, little hoofs a-clattering across the stones of the brook. And the early Lincolnshire morning sun spreading thin fingers west over the frost-covered fields. Sparkling like to Milady's rings in little gleams of sharp light that has melted to moist by mid-morning and dried to nowt by noon.

'You miss your own kind.'

'Aye. I does.'

'And I, too. Only it is not the country that I sigh for but the city.'

'London?'

'A little, sometimes. But Norwich it was for which I had a mind.'

'I has been but once to Norwich. To the Fair.'

'And often to the fairs in Lincoln.'

'Oh aye.' I smiles at him.

'I know it. It was in Lincoln at a Michaelmas Fair that first I saw you.'

'Tha said afore tha seen me there.'

'Indeed. And remarked, along with all the other swains, how pretty a creature you were.'

Pleased and sad I be at the same time. 'But were that truly I?'

'Without a doubt. And still I would know you as the same.'

I hears how his voice have fallen softer, touching me, making me chest to tighten and me breath to quicken. Like I has a weight within me breast that have a sweet ache to it.

I canna speak. Knows not what I might mebbee say if I does.

He have a hold of me shoulders. He looks full at me face, at me eyes, and I sees their blackness reflected in his blue. And sees again plain what I has fled from afore. Be like a heat between us. A silence that do hum and breathe and move, swelling like to a wave, lodged someplace in us chests. Unseen and yet I sees it clear. Feels it too, and the beating of it to be free, be give a shape and form.

His hands upon me be shaking like he be cold, freezing, yet they feels as hot as the sun. He clasps me the tighter, pulls me to him.

A smell be coming off him – sweat, heat, a man-smell of grass. Summat ripe and waiting. He clutches me hard against him and me nose, against his chest, sniffs up warmth, arousing, need. Such a need I has not felt clear in him afore. And sudden, me own need rises up too, knocks at me heart and do struggle to be known.

Hard he be against me belly. Hard that I wants and knows I wants, and he, too. I feels it like it were spoke aloud between us. Not need just for what us be about to do. Us has done that nights afore. But need for another one who feels the same, who knows how it be for me, knows me like I knows him. Who have the understanding of me.

And nothing has I iver knowed afore nor longed for like to this. It comes to me that for all us be so different, yet I be very like to him and he to me.

And the memory of them carvings in the meeting-house springs up into me head. Them that was of their Heathen Creation – of their Rangi and their Papa.

And Marsden saying loud, 'Arrest your eyes, Mrs Kendall, for your soul's sake.'

Which I has done. But not afore I has clearly seen the man with his dangler carved long and stiff, squatting above, and her below him, carved like to Shunghie's hei-tiki but with her privy parts open to public display and his rod pushed deep into her, carved there for iver, that all or any Heathen might look upon it as free and often as they would.

And then Dick have held me tighter and us has fell together to the ground below the pu-riri tree. Side by side and gazing still at each the other's eyes.

How long us has laid there I knows not, the wide bright pain of me chest making it like to a voyage out of time.

And he lies upon the reddened ground and slides his hands, which be trembling still, from me ankles to under me skirt. And I be shaking in great spasms. And he pulls me against him, on top of him and whispers to me ear, 'Ah, Jane, Jane, how much I do love you.'

And I him.

And us two like to the carving and he rises and falls in me like me own breath and I cries out and cries again. Loud, like to lowing. And over me own voice comes his: 'Hold me, Jane. Hold me.'

THOMAS KENDALL.

MISSIONARY.

BORN NORTH THORESBY,

LINCOLNSHIRE,

1778.

DIED NEW SOUTH WALES,

1837.

I have returned from Parramatta a nobler and a better man, in no wise Marsden's doing. I am pleased to be free of his society at last. Our convict trusty, Stockwell, returned upon the brig which bore me hither.

I am gratified to find that Jane is once again with child. Within that brief space before my departure, when our estrangement ceased upon the arrival of our girls, she has conceived what may, God willing, become the first English infant born upon these New Zealand shores.

Shunghie himself came paddling out to greet my return. He has such a gentle, mild countenance it is difficult to conceive of him as the barbarous conqueror I know him, at times, to be. He clasped me to him as a brother and welcomed me in the warmest terms of friendship. And though I have returned but two days only, we have already made a fishing expedition together.

He having shewn in New South Wales a most uncommon bent for silversmithing which would be remarkable even in an Englishman, I carried back with me from Parramatta a little cartridge-box, a present to him. His joyful cries upon receiving it were most affecting and he will not now suffer it to leave his possession even for an instant. Despite the prohibitions and admonitions of Marsden, our friendship has but increased and flourished in our absence from each other.

He has shewn, too, the most intelligent and lively interest in the theories which I have formulated in that time available to me for reflection upon the vessels carrying me to and from Parramatta.

We have spoken together much of Maori superstitions, our discourse being initially occasioned by a most strange incident that took place almost at the moment of my departure from the Bay of Islands.

A fellow chief of Shunghie, who had long desired to visit New South Wales, at the moment of our embarkation espied a little lizard on the decking of our ship. At sight of it, this mighty tattooed warrior was in the greatest fear and trembling and would not set his foot upon the brig. And no amount of cajoling from either myself or Marsden could alleviate his anguish or prevail. At length, the patience of the captain being tried beyond endurance and the wind threatening change, we were obliged to leave without him.

And Shunghie, speaking with me privily now, has told me the reason for the terror of his brother chief. The lizard is the symbol of their atua, their holiest of gods, the First State of Divine Being in which all life is present but quiescent, in a state of being about to be brought forth but not yet so. The essence of Life to come and World without end. And so tapu is this knowledge that the lizard himself is strictly tapu also and his presence seen as heralding some great disaster.

I knew already of the Maori belief in the atua but never had I understood it to be represented visibly in any form. Unlike their lesser gods whose carvings decorate the meeting-house, the storage huts and the marker posts for the dead, the atua is not shown. And Shunghie has been reluctant ever to speak for long with me about it.

The nga-rara is the name of the little lizard. But also of the serpent, which creature is known to them, and yet there are no snakes within this land. And, too, Shunghie has spoken of a giant saurian, the tani-wha, which lies within lakes and rivers, ready to seize and carry off those who venture within its territory. I thought, at first, this was merely a wild tale, but he has described the creature in such terms and detail I realize it now to be a crocodile. It is a ferocious amphibian, so he claims, and was here before the Maori peopled the land. Many warriors have been lost to the jaws and razor teeth of these beasts whilst seeking to rid their territory of them. Of such a monstrous being I have seen no evidence, but this story and others of which he has told me have led me to my musings on the origins of this Heathen race, the Maori.

How might they know of the snake, the crocodile? How is it that their sun is called Ra and daily rows across the heavens in his canoe? And, Shunghie says, they have two classes of knowledge of their gods and legends. One for the common people of the tribe, another for the chiefs and priestly adepts.

Iri-hia, he tells me, is the name of their ancient homeland, older far than the ancestral land, Hawai-Iki.

'Could this Iri-hia,' I mused aloud, 'be, in a corruption of their speech, Egypt?'

'Be India, more like,' said Jane.

I sighed. 'Pray do not interrupt me in my thoughts. These are most difficult scientific matters.'

I have had the hope that she might share with me these most important theories I am formulating from my obser-vations and my books. I confess it has been a disappointment to me to find her in such a lowered state upon my return. She seems to lack the heart to rouse herself to anything. Even my discourses have failed to lift her spirits. And, it must be said, her enthusiasm for our intimacy together seems again entirely lacking.

This is ever a fault with women. The emotional axis of their natures renders them so often prey to fluctuation of intellect and temperament, it is not to be wondered at they need the stable hand of a man to guide and direct them.

When Jane is safely delivered of this infant, she will, I have no doubt, recover her spirits. And, too, its presence will be compensation to her for the loss of Baby John.

My conversations of this morning bore but little fruit.

'I wish I had been better educated in the Classics. So much of my learning is self-determined.'

'But what matters it if the Maori be Egyptian?'

'Not themselves Egyptian. Descendants of that ancient race.'

'Aye. So?'

'Of greatest and most scientific interest.'

'But why so?'

'No man before has thought this.'

'No man afore have surely lived here with the Heathen as us be forced to do.'

She is, I must acknowledge, entirely without intellectual curiosity.

I persisted. 'The Maori have not the wheel, but it may be that knowledge was lost during the migrations of the great canoes.'

'No carts, no mills, no pulleys like them us used at Brocklesby.'

Brocklesby, Brocklesby, each and every day. And such a sullen countenance upon her. A more impatient man might well have lost his humour with his wife for less by now.

'The natives here have no pyramids, as such, either. And yet their pas perch always on conical hillsides with rows of fortified stakes pointing up to Heaven. The impression of the pyramid is much heightened by this. And they worship the river as sacred.'

'Tha hast read to me that be what the Heathen of India thinks also. When tha told me of them bones upon the towers.'

'Parsees, they are. Of Persia and of India.'

'Aye. So tha said. Be they of Egypt also?'

Jane, who has no book learning, yet has the disturbing habit of remembering such facts as bear but little witness to a greater truth.

I have composed a letter to Reverend Pratt in London to acquaint him with my early musings on the possibility that the Maori are descended from the Egyptians. It is a topic of the very foremost scientific interest: I must return before too long to England, there to present my evidence. If I do not go, it is certain that some other scholar, in my absence, will seize and develop my researches. But when I was in Parramatta, I spoke nothing on these matters to Marsden. He is no scholar; he is an artisan.

A weight has fallen from me. I have broached most delicately with Shunghie the possibility of his journeying with me to England. I suggested to him, cautiously, that together we might make a voyage Home. He assured me he wishes most earnestly to assist me in my work of compiling a native lexicon. Professor Lee at Cambridge will rejoice at the chance to interrogate such a one as he.

Shunghie pronounced himself most desirous of obtaining 'all the good things which the Pakeha have', most especially, it seems, a large hound. It is this upon which he has set his heart.

And so to England I shall return with my Noble Savage. Shunghie is fired with enthusiasm to make this visit. Indeed, he himself precipitated my question to him by remarking how much he longed to see the country of Te Ariki, Jesus. It is a mark, too, of how much he desires the knowledge of the Scriptures that he wishes to travel to work upon them in his own language with Reverend Professor Lee. What need have I of Marsden who neglects us and ignores our plight here at the Bay of Islands? He is but a minor cleric, powerful indeed in the transport society of Botany Bay but in England, an underling a mere vicar.

And whilst I am in England, I shall be ordained. And nothing can Samuel Marsden do to gainsay it. As a man of God, I came here. *Truly* a man of God, I shall return.

The Church Missionary Society will hail me and my converts. I shall show them the truth of our New Zealand Mission, not that arrogant distortion penned for their scrutiny by our absent Christian overseer who deigns not even to supply us with food and sustenance, who leaves us to fend alone with hostile forces, who forbids us choose even that land best suited for our own farming. Who grows ever fatter, a black spider extending his web of land and property, whilst those of us whom he has sent to the front line of battle for Heathen souls do struggle against the forces of Darkness, bereft of the light of Godly illumination from him who should be our bulwark and our guide.

Jane I shall leave here with all our children, under Shunghie's family's protection. I thought she would rejoice with me at such an opportunity. It was she who wished me a man of God, who has, in former times, conducted herself in a manner supportive and understanding of my aims. And yet, some jealousy, a worm, has entered in her heart. She turns away her sulky face at my every attempt to reason with her.

I do not understand her fears. I am not proposing this voyage before another six or seven month at least. She will have been well delivered of her infant, our garden will be flourishing and she, herself, will have more fluency in the native speech. At the suggestion that Thomas Surfleet might accompany me, she became so very violent in her protests I gave in upon the matter, not wishing to tax the strength of a pregnant woman. She is fast becoming a stranger to me.

Did I not request a trusty to assist her in my last absence? Yet when I asked her if the matter lay with Stockwell, had he assisted her in every way, been diligent in his service, she made but churlish reply: 'More diligent than iver thou.' Intending, in her present mulish state, to seek to wound me.

I turned the other cheek, took out *Britannica* from its box and set about my study of the hieroglyph.

I shall use the duration of our voyage Home to speak most

earnestly and piously with Shunghie and instruct him ever deeper in the Christian faith that he may turn from his atua and his gods and embrace the One God, Father, Son and Holy Spirit, Who alone may herald his eternal Salvation.

I shall bid him teach me the deeper labyrinthine meanings and turnings of his own tongue that, upon my arrival in Cambridge, I may turn my hand to the compilation of that Maori lexicon by which the Scriptures may be translated and brought to the Heathen in his native tongue.

And I shall broach with Reverend Professor Lee, tentatively and with greatest delicacy, the matter of the Egyptian fore-bears of Shunghie and his brethren, the similarity of his pagan gods to those of the pantheon of Ancient Egypt. His interest may be provoked in no little measure by my humbly offered theories.

It is clear to me now why I have been led by God to this far-flung place. Why I have been guided and steered to New Zealand, where the eyes of pious Christians have not until now penetrated. Herein lies my destiny.

All has not passed as I have dreamt and prayed. Like one who sets out to scale the heights and has almost reached the summit, I see now with dismay and loss of Faith that I stand not below the mountain top but merely at the peak of another foothill.

Marsden, who holds himself in such high esteem and crosses with his staff the hills from here to the Hoki-Anga, who sees himself Moses in the Promised Land, is but the son of a humble crofter and blacksmith. As I myself saw plain in Parramatta, he works a bellows still with no mean hand, yet he chooses to act the fine gentleman and raise himself above his humble origins. I shall not have *him* thwart me in my intentions.

I am resolved upon my journey Home. God's Will be done. And may He be praised Who, in His Infinite Wisdom, has shewn me my path so plain.

JANE KENDALL.

MOTHER.

BORN BROCKLESBY,

LINCOLNSHIRE,

1784.

DIED NEW SOUTH WALES,

1866.

Once, at Home, in the early morning, I seen a grey skein of wild geese honking through the raw pink sky. And Noah, Uncle Silas's old white yard gander, did look up too and twang and hiss, flapping and spreading them great wings on him like to arms.

But no matter how he might strain and yearn, he niver did rise up to join them wild ones flying so free above him, it being that his wings be cut too short.

Nowt sadder than a bird of flight that hasna wings.

Same to me now that do watch the ship that carries me husband and the chiefs back Home. And I, left behind like Noah, can but wave me arms, useless, as they do fade from sight.

SHUNGHIE IKA.

PARAMOUNT CHIEF OF THE NGA-PUHI OF AO-TEA-ROA.

BORN *1772.*

DIED *1828.*

How strange, Turi-Ka-Tuku, was my first glimpse of England. This morning, on the north-west, we sighted its southern coast. I was the first to discern it from the deck.

This country is very flat, a green lagoon of grazing land atop a few low hillocks sheering into the sea. Like the inhabitants, the centre of the land is colourless. Where it is cut away and fallen into the ocean, there is no red ochre, no volcanic fertility. White and dry, crumbling, it buckles before the assault of the waves.

The sailors became very agitated at the sight of this flat, pale land and displayed much emotion, a thing rare with these people. Wai-Kato and I had already been obliged to wrap ourselves in our mats against the cold, these over our English clothes which, at the suggestion of Keni, we have affected since Rio.

Keni himself was unable to contain his emotion at the sight of the home of his ancestors. Hoa Keni, friend of my heart. He understands our tongue with a considerable degree of skill. Alone he stands, apart from such as Matenga.

From the deck of our ship, Wai-Kato and I watched the small boats coming towards us. As we moved gently up the Estuary we slowly understood that, of all those present on the little boats accompanying us in, not one contained any brother, father or relative of those on board our vessel.

'They will be waiting for us at the docks,' said Keni when I questioned him. 'They could not all come out in boats.'

A strange country with strange customs. The docks were entirely full of ships. Remember, Turi-Ka-Tuku, our great war expeditions setting out. Twenty war-canoes and more, each full of men intent on their purpose. You have heard yourself the din of voices, paddles, chanting, the clatter of the gourds being loaded, the slap and rattle of the kits being lifted aboard. Imagine this ten thousandfold. But not for war. Merely for trade, and every day, is this bustle, clamour, excitement. Truly, until I saw it, I could not have imagined a harbour with such shoals of vessels, such numbers of men.

They were not all white-skinned. One of the first I sighted had narrowed eyes and skin the pale yellow of a steamed kumara, was small and very thin with trailing wisps of beard upon his chin. Several more were black so that at first Wai-Kato thought them to have smeared their faces with charcoal ash. These have fine large teeth, mouths very full and wide, and filmed brown eyes the colour of your own. We saw a number of the same in Rio. They are very strongly built with the muscles of fine warriors.

I am troubled by your sorrow. Though you did not speak of it as I left you, I know you are angered by my leaving: I know you have seen danger in this voyage, danger for me, danger for Ha-Re-Shunghie. I have yielded to you in the bringing of Wai-Kato and not Ha-Re-Shunghie, though he begged me for the honour of accompanying his father, as is a principal son's right. In that way, as I told you, you could not lose us both. Indeed, I consulted with Te Kemara seven times before departure. He cast the omens, asked of the bones and seven times came the reply that Shunghie will live to avenge his brothers and all great success will attend upon his battles. That Ha-Re-Shunghie will, as my general, avenge also the murder of his great-uncles. How could I dismiss his words?

Ask yourself, Turi-Ka-Tuku, how I might defy the prophesies of a tohunga of such mana. Witchcraft has caused you to doubt. Some spell from a sorcerer of the Ngati Wha-Tua is bending your wisdom away from me. They know, these Ngati Wha-Tua, I will be avenged, I will have back my brothers' heads. They know how I love you, honour you, heed your words, and by sorcery and stealth their tohunga seeks to bewitch you.

Think how I gathered our forces to avenge your father's bones, how I slew all, all – the chief, the tohunga, the brothers of the chief, all who had turned your father's sacred relics into fish-hooks – until they cried cessation of the utu, acknowledging their defeat. How I carried back your father's noble head, how you wept at the sight of his moko, tracing your fingers over the patterns of his cheek and jaw.

Wife of my heart, before you conceived Ha-Re-Shunghie I dreamt the skull of my grandfather lay on the ground at my feet, adorned with white crane feathers which fluttered and swayed as I gazed, by which I knew both of the coming conception and also that your infant would be a warrior child.

I see you in our kumara gardens, hoeing, digging, pulling up the weeds in your hands, feeling with your feet for where they have fallen and throwing the red earth over them where they lie.

In Rio there were parrots shrieking every morning and evening but here on the waters of the Estuary no birdsong floats to my ear. Perhaps there are no birds in England.

Tomorrow, we shall disembark and see this mighty city, London. Parramatta is but a little pa by comparison. And later we shall travel by land to Cambridge. Keni is much possessed with this Cambridge. Living there is his tohunga, Professor Mr Samuel Lee, sacred in his pronouncements.

This great city, London, you could not begin to dream of. For a beginning, there is much of everything. Many people, many boats, many buildings. We have not yet left the vessel but already we can see that the river is long, longer far than the Wai-Tangi, and all along its banks lie buildings, dwellings, trading houses. Everywhere are trading houses. This is a great city of barter. I desire very much to walk about it and to see Mr King Horhi. Here I will find muskets, Turi-Ka-Tuku. I have seen it in my dream. And muskets we must have. Without muskets we are nothing, a dying race.

With muskets, my mana will be supreme. I shall be invincible. I shall swallow the eyes of those who devoured my brothers.

And here, hidden in my heart, I shall store all that passes, to relate it to you upon my return, so that you, too, will have made this great journey as I have done.

I will come back to you, Turi-Ka-Tuku. This I know for certain. I have already dreamt it.

THE MEETING
OF
MR KING SHUNGHIE
WITH
MR KING GEORGE IV
1820.

Took Communion in Our apartments and transacted early business with the Minister of the Interior and His Grace, the Duke de Richelieu.

The damnable *London Packet* tells Us, 'People are leaving the Church because the Queen is not prayed for. They desire Her Majesty's name restored to the Liturgy.' Eleven columns of loyal addresses follow. Then a final charming touch. 'God save the King! God save the Queen!'

We have it on early intelligence from Their Lordships that the

Queen will on Thursday next be pronounced guilty of licentious and adulterous conduct. Hah!

Luncheon at the Guildhall. Concourse packed with carriages. Since the late ugly display against Our Gracious Presence, We have taken to distancing Our Royal Self from the attentions of the mob. The attractions of Brighton, save those sadly faded, weigh greatly over this inelegant capital.

Received this day to Our presence two most singular persons accompanied by a third of the gloomily utilitarian United Church. The visitors were native New Zealanders, held in high esteem in their own Dominion. They were fashionably dressed in black clothes but their faces much disfigured by tattooing. In consequence of the scars having been rubbed by some vegetable acid, there was a polished green hue upon the natural copper ground of the skin which gave them a most novel and extraordinary appearance.

They were rather above middle height, with well-formed features, hair black and bushy and their appearance and conduct equal to those of any of Our noblemen.

The younger of the two, Why Rato, aged twenty-six, spoke but little English and was of a more generally reserved disposition. But the elder, Shunghie, who, so the Reverend Mr Kendall, the mean retainer, informed us, is a principal Chief in the Northern parts of New Zealand, had most earnestly and frequently pronounced himself desirous of an interview with Our Gracious Person and had much to say for himself.

We have heard accounts of these Chiefs at both first and second hand in the preceding months, many ladies of the Court having engaged in speculation as to whether the art of tattooing extended to the buttocks or, indeed, to any other farther parts, but none being as yet able to confirm or deny rumour.

The Chiefs' tattooing placed Us in mind of the curved and spiral laying-out of design by Mr Nash and We have arranged for this gentleman to meet with the New Zealanders before their return to the Dominions. 'An architecture of the face', We have described it to Mr Nash.

Mr Shunghie was in but indifferent health, our climate being not to his liking and the air lying hard upon his chest and causing him some labour of the breath. Nevertheless he remained at all times alert and sensible of his surroundings.

Upon being presented, he held forth his hand and intoned in a deep and sonorous voice, 'How do you do, Mr King Horhi?'

Mr Kendall here interposed to explain that the limitations of his own language caused Mr Shunghie to be unable to render with his tongue the sounds G or J of our speech but that his intentions were all exquisite politeness, a fact his entire demeanour served only to confirm.

'How do you do, Mr King Shunghie?' We replied.

At this, the Chief seemed seized by some deep emotion and, leaning forward, pressed his nose almost against Our own, muttering a babble of unintelligible sound, with all the while copious tears flowing from his eyes.

The younger Chief, seemingly similarly afflicted by tears, gazed on at the scene whilst the Reverend Gentleman, himself in no little confusion, hastened to explain this to be the most noble form of honoured greeting offered in those parts from whence the Chiefs had but so lately come.

'We could only wish such devotion and sensibility of feeling from all Our loyal subjects,' We remarked to Mr Kendall.

Mr Shunghie, stepping back, then embarked upon another most remarkable performance. Fixing Us with a severe and concentrated gaze, he proclaimed loudly, 'Have we not con-quer'd? By the vengeful Sword?'

Surprized indeed to hear the opening of Mr Wordsworth's Thanksgiving Ode from the lips of such a savage, We waited with anticipation for the lines following. These, however, were not forthcoming and the Chief, having relieved himself of this single utterance, stood patient for Our approbation.

'"Worthily sustained",' answered We with a slight bow, at which the Chief bowed also.

Unmindful of the custom of the Sovereign's initiation of

conversational topics, Mr Shunghie then proceeded to inquire of Us whether We 'had many slaves'. At Our negative reply he seemed much gratified and stated that he had 'many, many'.

Did We have many muskets?

'A considerable number. At Woolwich,' We replied.

At this he expressed a deep wish that he might be permitted before he left Our shores to see them, a wish We were minded to grant that very hour, much to Our noble Chief's delight. Though he speaks but rudimentary English and has the simple mind of the Noble Savage, yet he contrives to make himself well understood and appears to comprehend very much of our speech.

Upon our arrival at Woolwich, both Chiefs shewed great excitement at the sight of the Armoury, Mr Shunghie exclaiming loudly in his native tongue over the cannon and double-barrelled muskets.

Mr Kendall informed Us that Mr Shunghie, while in New South Wales, had exhibited no little skill in metalworking and silversmithing and shewn a most uncommon aptitude for the mechanical arts.

This seemed to Us a most unlikely possibility and We resolved to put his statement to the test.

Mr Shunghie was examining with deepest interest the iron chasing of a cannon. 'Perhaps, Mr King Shunghie,' We remarked lightly, as if in jest, 'you would care to show Us your skill with a piece from Our Armoury?'

We flatter Ourself We are much admired within Our lands for Our delicacy and the ease at which We place Our subjects, a skill self-taught entirely and in no wise ingested at Our Parent's knee, He being in possession of none of those elegant and sympathetic graces which should mark out the natural-born gentleman.

The savage inclined his head towards Us as if signifying agreement. We ordered musket, powder and cloth brought, and all repaired to the courtyard, the Chiefs jabbering excitedly together.

'Now, Sir,' We requested, motioning for the musket to be

placed in the hands of Mr Shunghie, 'let Us admire your skills. What say you, Mr K?'

That man of God seemed somewhat unhappy. 'Perhaps Your Majesty would deem it discreet to stand at a little distance.'

We had already resolved on this most sensible course but We are not in the habit of being dictated to by clerics. 'No, no,' We assured him. 'You have said yourself, Mr Kendall, that this noble gentleman has uncommon skill in the twin arts of war and metalwork.'

The clergyman's gloom further deepened. 'Your Majesty,' he muttered, 'does great honour to both Mr Shunghie and Mr Why Rato and even, by extension, to my humble self, but should any unforeseen incident occur ... the musket ball be deflected from its true course ... the hand of Providence intervene ...'

'Providence, Sir,' We rebuked him, 'must surely be seen by men of religion such as yourself to be on the side of kings and not of unwitting assassins. Besides, Sir, We have your recommendation.'

The increase of his discomfiture greatly heartened Us. Whining fools, all clerics. From Charles Cantuar down, there is not a one of any of them to be trusted, whose word is not hung about with deceit, lies and self-advancement.

Mr Shunghie, who with Mr Why Rato had been engaged in the most serious study of his weapon, now broke silence to exclaim loudly in his native tongue.

His chaplain seized upon this diversion. 'Your Majesty,' he entreated, 'it is not merely that we are within such an enclosure' – here he waved his black-beetle arms to encompass Our entire Woolwich courtyard – 'but that, whilst both Shunghie and Why Rato lack nothing in ferocity on the field of battle, and with their own weapons their skill is unmatched, yet ... [a glance at the Chiefs to ensure our privacy of speech] ... yet ...'

'Have done, Sir. Bring it forth,' We encouraged.

'The Maori, Your Majesty, in the matter of aim when using the musket, have been known from time to time to be somewhat arbitrary. I fear only for my Sovereign's Gracious Person.'

And, at this, the fellow sank upon his knees in supplication before Us.

The Chiefs, startled by this event, immediately fell upon their knees also but, perceiving our courtiers to remain standing, Mr Shunghie raised himself to his feet, flashed at them his considerable teeth and commanded them with the single word 'Down!', this accompanied by such an imperious gesture of the right arm We confess even Ourself momentarily minded to obey.

The consternation of Our courtiers was a sight most wonderful to behold. After several anxious glances at Our Royal Person to seek assistance on the protocol of necessity of obedience or otherwise (which assistance We steadfastly withheld, being minded to see them forced to their own decision), each one, swept by the ferocious eye of the Chief, dropped down to the stones of Our courtyard, Lord Arbuthnot's struggles to achieve his desired position being the height of the entertainment.

Mr Shunghie now knelt also and, in a voice bold and strong, began to intone what to Our astonishment We recognised, with some difficulty, as the words of the Lord's Prayer, the courtiers, transfixed by his gaze upon them, following feebly his sonorous lead.

We bowed our head attentively until this unlikely company reached the conclusion of its performance, whereat Mr Shunghie, still upon his knees, cried loudly, 'Koti save te Kingi!', leapt unexpectedly to his feet and, without warning, discharged both balls of the musket he was holding.

The resonance of the shots within the walls gave more of the impression of a cannon's having been fired than a musket. The entire company rose in terror, Lord Arbuthnot ascending, so We observed, considerably faster than he had gone down. All retired toward the walls, Ourself included.

Mr Shunghie, unconscious of his effect, said some word to his brother chief, then strode towards Us proclaiming the virtues of the weapon, which he pronounced much superior to any he had handled in Ao-Tea-Roa, by which name he calls his own land.

Boredom, Our principal and ever-present enemy, having been routed by this capital occurrence, We laid our hand graciously upon Our subject's arm, noticing as We did so that he flinched. Undoubtedly his extraordinary body markings cause him pain when touched. It is such scientific and logical researches which further distinguish Us from Our late unlamented Parent.

'Splendid, Mr King Shunghie, Sir!' We cried. 'A worthy spectacle indeed. Accept Our gracious thanks and the gift of two dozen muskets from Our Armoury.'

The savage leaned towards Us and again all but pressed his flattened nose upon Our own. The proximity and heat of his breath caused Us some momentary unease. For a single moment, We entertained the extravagant thought that the noble Chief was on the point of devouring Us with his teeth. It is a consideration most sobering and philosophical that such a splendid specimen, made in the image of God, does from time to time ingest with evident enjoyment (or so We are informed) such parts of his fellow man as he considers delicacies or trophies.

Unaware of the course of Our thought, the Chief drew back and spoke in his Maori tongue.

'He thanks Your Majesty in the name of his ancestors,' explained Mr Kendall, translating. 'In battle, when using these muskets, he will call upon Your Majesty's strength and power to mingle with his own. With King George of England as his brother, how can he fail to defeat his sworn enemies?'

Pleased at this pretty speech, We resolved to add to Our generosity. 'As a mark of Our most particular favour and in recognition of the devoted loyalty of Our most worthy subject,' We announced, 'We grant also the further gift of one of Our own silver-chased muskets and a suit of chest armour.'

That this keenly annoyed Arbuthnot was evident. We dispatched a keeper to procure the firearm forthwith.

The Chief's emotion at the sight of it was deeply affecting. Holding the weapon to his breast, he wailed aloud to Heaven.

'This my hoa,' he cried in a voice of great emotion. ('Friend', translated the ever-helpful Mr Kendall, whose pallor had greatly intensified since his arrival.) 'My kingi musket. My heart.'

We bowed, made some apposite remark to turn him from the topic and began to lead the way back to Our Armoury.

As the company passed below Lawrence's portrait of Ourself on horseback, Mr Shunghie stopped, gazed at the picture and spoke rapidly to Mr Kendall and Mr Why Rato in the native tongue.

'What says he, Mr Kendall?'

'He remarks upon the portrait, Your Majesty.'

'And what, Mr Kendall, is his opinion of it?'

Mr Shunghie looked full at Lawrence's vapid offering, turned to Us with an intense scowl and shook his bushy head. 'No kood,' he stated.

'And why not, Sir?'

For some moments he struggled for the word in English, but was obliged to have recourse to Mr K. That that gentleman was reluctant to convey his message was abundantly clear. The savage prodded him. 'Tell, tell,' he urged, staring at Us solemnly.

'He wishes Your Majesty to know that the painting is not a good likeness. It does not do Your Majesty justice.'

'No kood,' repeated the Chief. 'Too much ... too much ...' He indicated that the clergyman find his missing word.

'He says,' stumbled that unhappy man, 'that Your Majesty is too pretty.'

'Like woman,' said Mr Shunghie. 'Not king of war.'

The courtiers, as a single body, drew in breath. Mr Kendall braced himself. It gives Us great pleasure to observe these little evidences of the awe in which We are universally held. We allowed several moments to elapse before We spoke.

'We congratulate you on your excellent judgement, Sir,' We remarked. The courtiers audibly exhaled. 'Sir Thomas was the favoured dauber of Our Parent who Himself commissioned that facile piece of canvas when We were but Prince of Wales. We, Ourself, do not like this portrait, which is why We have had it hung here in Woolwich and not in Our Royal Apartments.'

The Chief looked puzzled. 'All here muskets, kuns. Here is Kingi Horhi's power. Here must be king of war picture.' And, at this, he amazed Us yet further by adopting, below the Lawrence, the exact pose and gesture taken by Ourself for the fine portrait executed by Mr Stubbs. Before Our eyes, this remarkable savage appeared to ride an invisible horse, his right arm to brandish an unseen sword.

We spontaneously applauded this tableau of representation. Mr Shunghie held his position. There was tittering amongst the courtiers and, indeed, posing thus in his dark frock coat and English apparel, yet tattooed and bare of foot, the Chief made an incongruous sight. At this slight sound of mockery, however, whilst still maintaining his tableau in all other respects he turned his savage visage towards his detractors and in the most terrifying and bloodthirsty fashion imaginable extended his tongue, rolled up his eyes into their sockets and uttered a chilling guttural scream.

'Better he is a friend than an enemy,' We observed drily. 'And now, Gentlemen, let us dine. We have ordered a cold collation.'

Which sustenance the Chiefs appeared most greatly to enjoy, and, following, took their leave.

We must admit these gentlemen interested Us considerably. Mr Shunghie was well pleased to carry off his silver-chased piece, for which We have promised an engraved silver plate commemorating his visit. We have resolved to place this matter in the charge of Arbuthnot. A fitting example of poetic justice!

We shall summon Our tailor on the morrow, with the aim of incorporating into Our coronation dress some such feathers as the Reverend Mr Solemn Kendall tells us the Chiefs use to adorn their topknots in their own country. Peacock, perhaps. We favour the colours of the peacock.

* * *

I have secured for us muskets. Muskets, Wife. The golden yield of all the harvests. Sweeter than kumara, swifter than eel, deadlier than shark. Ai-ee, muskets. The greatest of the white man's treasures.

I have beside me where I sit, my chest armour and the mighty silver weapon presented this night to me, Shungie, King of Ao-Tea-Roa, by George, King of England By the Grace of God. Very satisfactory. Yes, indeed.

Just as I saw in my dream, I met with this great king. We went to a meeting-house all together to observe the counsel of their elders. Lords, they call them. We sat 'below the bar', in the seat of strangers, and watched them challenge each other and practise their oratory on this sacred ground. We were not called upon to speak or give our lineage, though afterwards many of these elders wished to see us and even to touch us.

Imagine, if you can, my tapu person touched as though common to all. But here, it is the custom.

The tohunga professors in Cambridge and even Mr King George himself place their food in their own mouths with their own hands at all times. Yet they are still regarded by their people as sacred. And all they have used they will wash and let be touched by others. In the house of their great warrior, Wellington, I dashed my little cup to the floor after I had drunk from it, and this, I quickly understood, they did not like. Such things seem strange to us but I and Wai-Kato must do here as the natives do.

Until I came to England I did not understand the nature of the white men they have sent us.

In Ao-Tea-Roa, we have their lower classes, their workmen. And only those workmen they have chosen for us. Sawyers, whalers, they cut our trees, take our fish. But not for us. For them. 'Send me an armourer,' I told the king.

We know already some of the Pakeha, the rough ones who come in ships for whales and seals, the ones upon the French ships, the ones who live with us at Rangi-Houa – Matenga, Keni, Tokere, so beloved of Modder. But these are the only white men of whom we have had knowledge. I had thought

Matenga and Keni to be of the same rank as those clever ones, the French, but this is not so. And Mr King George does not know Matenga. Even the missionaries are workmen. We do not have their ranga-tira, their educated men of high rank. Matenga and Keni we see as great men, powerful men, as, indeed, they see themselves, but here I know the truth.

I am no fool. I see this King of England, clever with his book-learning but fat, unhealthy, suspicious and vain. So vain.

He picks his way across the carpet like a pukeko, a swamp hen. Plucks a compliment here, pecks at an enemy there, clucks nonsense from his beak. But powerful, so powerful. This pukeko has muskets, cannon, soldiers, ships, armourers, tribute, mana. Yet if I were to strip him to his skin, cover him with porpoise grease and tie his hair into the topknot with adorning feathers, place in his hands my stoutest greenstone me-re and my sword spear, my tai-aha, then set him at the head of his army, he would fall over. He could not lead his warriors into battle, strike a blow himself. For this he has generals, admirals. Other men go to war for him though he has his likeness made many times over, holding his sword while seated on his horse.

Their horses are driven into battle with men riding on their backs.

'Surely,' said I to the King of England, 'this is an error in warfare? For those firing the cannon and muskets will shoot only at the horses to unseat their riders and thereafter kill them.'

'Unsporting, Sir,' said the king. 'My officers, I hope, are gentlemen of honour.'

War is sport? A game? I do not think so. War is life.

Savages, they call us. Rough. Primitive. Uncultured, unman-nered. Anthropophagi, said Mr Basil Wood of the Church Missionary Society. Cannibals. Eaters of *human flesh*. And this is what so occupies their minds. They do not say, 'Tell us of your culture. Tell us of your gods.' They have not exclaimed in awe over the majesty of our bodies, regarded the beauty of the patterning, the carver's skill. No indeed. As they whisper behind their hands, shudder excitedly as they view us, cautiously return our greetings, there, shivering behind their eyes, trembling beneath their wigs, hangs the question all long to ask. I have seen the greed for that knowledge in their eyes.

You know they do not breathe with each other nor greet as we do: I have told you of their ceremony of pressing hands. Each time one of them takes my hand, I feel, in his thin, white touch, the faintest tremor of unease, the merest convulsion. 'This is the hand that has held and eaten human flesh.'

Even His Majesty, King George By the Grace of God, allowed himself the luxury of curiosity.

Falling behind Wai-Kato and Keni at his Armoury at Woolwich, he lingered by a cannon and murmured to me as we gazed at the chasing of the ironwork, 'They tell Us, Mr King Shungie, that you are a connoisseur of human flesh.' I answered nothing but inclined my head slightly as I had seen him do earlier. He leaned towards me closer and asked me from the very side of his mouth, 'How does it taste, Sir, We wonder?'

'Much like pork, Mr King George, Sir,' I answered, 'which is no doubt why some call it "the long pig".'

'Have you,' said the king, 'tasted the flesh of ... white men?'

'Not I myself. But those who have tell me it is not so good. Too salty.'

He laughed. I noticed how his belly wobbled.

'Too salty, eh? We should have pickled Our Parent and sent him there. Something for you to chew on. An old boar, if ever there was one. So blue-blooded it even came out in His piss.'

I did not let him see the shock it caused me to hear him speak so of his ancestor.

'Keni told me, Mr King George, that your father was a great farmer,' said I.

'Correct,' said the king. 'And a great lunatic. Doubtless Mr Kendall has told you that, too.'

'I see, Sir,' said I, 'that the gods have not favoured Your Majesty in family matters. I have heard from the newspapers and from our visit to the House of Lords that there is much trouble with the Queen. Myself I have four, five, wives and no trouble from any of them.'

'Then tell Us your recipe, Mr King Shungie, Sir,' cried the king. 'Tell Us your recipe. In and out of the pot. If We could but send the Queen back to New South Wales with you, Our troubles would be greatly eased. A capital idea, Sir. Capital.'

The thought of this made him very happy. He repeated it to all present, who laughed and cheered greatly. Excepting myself, Wai-Kato and Keni.

'Come, Sir King, answer,' called the king.

Their ironwork is very superior and much exceeds anything we know. I drew my eyes with difficulty from the cases of muskets and the cannon.

'Send me an armourer, Mr King George, and I will tell you.'

'Fine fellow,' said the king. 'Not just an armourer but a suit of chest armour and a silver-chased musket in honour of Our favour. Now, Sir, the recipe.'

'If she is your secondary wife or a prisoner-of-war wife,' said I, 'you must beat her. Then she will be obedient to you. But if she is your chief wife or the wife who is the sister of your chief wife, you must consult with her for her opinion on your affairs and honour her on behalf of her noble ancestors. If she becomes too much trouble, you must send her back to her father.'

'Send her back,' said His Majesty. 'We only wish, Sir, that We could.' He pointed to a musket at the side of a case. 'There, Sir. It was with that weapon Captain Cook silenced the savages at Otaheite.' He seemed to need no answer. I judged he was thinking. 'She is so damnably ugly,' he said. 'But the people love her and rally to her everywhere.'

I have seen Queen Caroline. She seemed to me a fine, handsome woman.

'Drooping breasts, huge stomach, face like a horse.'

'I should like a horse,' said I.

'Take the Queen,' said His Majesty. 'Ride the Queen. Could be the making of her.'

In this there was some joke I did not understand, but the

manner of laughter of the courtiers caused me to believe I was insulted.

I looked again at the Armoury around us.

Muskets, I told myself. I, too, will exercise supreme power. The gods have ordained it. I will have my own armoury, my own powder, my own muskets. I will have utu for the dead of Mo-Re-Mo-Nui. The bones of my brothers will lie at peace. The Ngati Wha-Tua shall feel the power of the Nga-Puhi. I shall make them return my brothers' heads. I shall make them plead for peace.

I laughed with the courtiers.

The great King of England spoke again of his wife. 'We have excluded the cursed harlot from Our coronation.' His face was red with the pleasure of hatred. He breathed quickly. 'She will come, she will try to come. But We will have forestalled her. We will have her turned away. She will not win over Us.' He leaned towards me. 'The Queen will understand, Mr King Shunghie, who is her master.'

Utu.

His Majesty, King George By the Grace of God, King of Great Britain and Ireland, not King of America, took my flesh-eating hand and held it below his own.

'Here we have a saying, Mr King Shunghie, "Revenge is sweet".'

I know, Mr King George of England. I know.

RICHARD STOCKWELL.

CONVICT TRUSTY.

BORN NORFOLK,

1777.

DIED NORFOLK,

1859.

As a Rational man, I cannot take kindly to the notion of the Will of God. Can it be the Will of God that His children starve, that wars are waged such as the last miserable battle we have seen against the French? That there exists in every society such a gulf between the oppressor and the oppressed? That some have too much and others have nothing?

If God is the loving Father His spokesmen would have us believe, where is His sense of justice, His compassion? Men are slain, their children starve and suffer, and clergymen claim it is the Divine Will of God. Were their own infants sickening for want of sustenance, then might their Faith in an unseen deity so lacking in that compassion He demands from His adherents be tested to its limits. Then might they rail against Him Whose random hand had struck their own.

But yet, when Parson Marsden called me to his study and I, braced against an onslaught on the ravages of the rose caterpillar, heard with incredulity his proposals that I might sail again to Rangi-Houa, there to assist, for an eight month or more, the wife and children of Thomas Kendall whilst he journeyed, in violation of Mr Marsden's wishes, to England, I was minded to believe most deeply in this volatile Lord. I became but a man of my times in whom Reason was overtaken by the Romantic.

I knew from Mrs Marsden, who had had it from the master of the *Active*, Captain Hansen, that Mrs Kendall had been delivered fifteen months before, of as fine a boy as was ever seen, the chief, Tuai, later telling us of the child's head of Viking hair, his blue-green eyes, the utter partiality of his sisters towards this paragon, and his mother's joy in his every particularity. And great had been my own desire to see him, and his mother.

My unspoken petitions to an unknown God had, so it seemed, been granted in an excess of wondrous favour.

How earnestly did I assure the parson that I would bear again without complaint the privations of Rangi-Houa. How leaden and how weighted seemed the days till my departure.

And yet, when I arrived in the Bay again, Jane's demeanour to me seemed wary, hostile – even, it could be said, guilty. And I was much distressed by this, having thought her joy in receiving me would be equal to my own on seeing her again. She clutched a new-born infant at her breast, a shield against the outside world.

The older infant, whom she has named Samuel in honour of her brother, is of a most equable temperament and moves my heart whenever I espy him.

This latest enterprise of Kendall may render her a widow. And, before long, I shall be again a free man, with property in Norwich to my name. Providence would seem to favour me at last.

My ire at Kendall upon my arrival was very great. Ten days and nights we lay outside the entrance to the Bay while all about us raged the blustering Forties. And when, at last, we put in to that lovely spot and tacked towards Rangi-Houa, and I was landed with my stores and provender upon the sands, and Jane had almost swooned at the unexpected sight of me, I saw he had left them with almost nothing of sustenance in his absence. All of them, from Susannah to little Samuel, seemed hollow of eye, weak of frame. Of flour and barley, Jane had none. Kendall, she said, had told her Marsden had a ship upon the water, heading to her with supplies even as he left. Yet on my arrival, eleven weeks following, no vessel had put in to lift her famine.

The natives, she said, had fed her in the absence of her husband and her vicar. She fell upon the stores sent with me from Parramatta as one distraught. Kendall is a most selfish man. For this carelessness, this want of feeling towards his own, I cannot censure him enough.

Within a week of my arrival, all had settled with us into a familiar pattern. My joy in her and, subsequently, hers in me, my admiration of the little Samuel, grew as we made a pattern of our days. Replenished in supplies, secure now that she might feed her own, my Jane became as one restored. We passed our time as I had been charged by Marsden, and the carrying out of those small domesticities served but to bind us closer.

A ten day into my tenure, she told me how the infant, Laurence, had been conceived in the short time that she and Kendall had tried to be together after my earlier departure. 'What manner of man is it,' said I to myself, 'who leaves a woman, a suckling and six other of his little children thus to shift for themselves as they may upon an alien shore whilst he disports himself about God's business in another hemisphere?' But naught I said to her.

How much, in Parramatta in the weeks before departure, I had wished for myself the liberty of a free man's estate. I longed to carry to her a bonnet in the fashion, a gown to replace the grey-bloomed and tattered garment she had worn when last I saw her. Items for her children, the trappings of little luxuries. Yet all these were denied me by reason of my situation.

I set about, with cunning and with thought, to apply myself to how I might procure them. And, engaged with Mrs Marsden in the business of the roses, I remarked, with much apology, how far from the influence of civilization, from Mrs Marsden's own Christian daily influence, was poor Mrs Kendall. Recalled to the parson's wife how much Mrs Kendall had admired her lovely blooms. Perhaps, insinuated I, that worthy lady might find it within her province, should she wish, to send to Mrs Kendall with me – and greatly should I deem it an honour to discharge the slightest command of Reverend Marsden's wife – a parcel of clothing, that modesty and decency, English standards amongst the Heathen, might be upheld by Mrs Kendall and her family by virtue only of Mrs Marsden's Christian charity.

And greatly did the lady embrace such ideas, pronouncing them by the end of the day her own, so that, in the evening, when Marsden returned to supper, he must endure a homily from his wife upon the nature of denial and brotherly love, culminating in his being obliged to part reluctantly from several well-loved items of his clothing. And Miss Marsden and Miss Charlotte likewise were put to sort their wardrobes and those of the younger girls and little Charles, so that, on my departure, I carried with me a quantity of garments that evoked the rapturous cries of Jane and all her children upon my arrival.

All but Marsden's second stovepipe hat, which he had relinquished with the greatest reluctance and which, it being several sizes too large for Kendall, I was pleased to see later upon the head of a native chief, he having bartered us a kit of shellfish and two others of kumara for its possession.

In her weakened and single state Jane has become more like the Maori with whom she daily must consort. Their native superstitions have worked much upon her mind, a thing scarcely to be wondered at, considering her recent vulnerability.

Hearing the faint whistle of the wind about the hut, she assured me most solemnly that it was the voice of an atua, or great spirit, and would not be dissuaded from her belief whatever rational explanation I might bring to bear upon it.

'It is Whi-Tiki calling about our walls,' was all she would say. And I, thinking it best to humour her, made no argument.

Thomas Surfleet and Reporo, the second son of Shunghie, play together almost every day at draughts, which game the Maori have known since long before the Pakeha's arrival. And great is the native skill in it. Thomas Surfleet, too, is no mean opponent, as I myself discovered when trounced by him two nights ago.

Ngaio, the servant, a comfort and a friend to Jane, and who formerly relieved her of many of her burdens, before my arrival stole away by night and swam to a whaling ship, which has carried her back to her own people. Or so says Jane. And I can only wish it be so indeed and that no worse fate has befallen her.

From Ngaio, her mistress has learnt some rudimentary Maori, though in matters requiring skill the children, in their father's absence, translate for her.

The older children are fluent in the native speech and have undertaken my instruction in it. They play in the way of their companions here and Susannah is a favourite with the Maori. She has at all times with her a charming jumping jack – ka-re-tao is its native name – carved for her, at the insistence of Reporo, by his brother, Ha-Re-Shunghie. This little figure is a most ingenious toy, its arms worked by strings passed through the shoulders and manipulated from behind. Susannah makes it dance and leap like a live thing. And much do the natives delight in her enjoyment of it. She is a grave and solemn child, but, playing with her puppet, she becomes as one transformed, creating laughter everywhere about her.

And all of them, even little Samuel, daily go flying kites with the children from the pa. These kites are fashioned in the shapes of birds and soar, like them, to the skies. Even the men here take their kites upon the hillside, some of them ten or twelve feet wide within the wing-span, fluttering in the heavens. Jane tells me she has seen, on occasions, kites with human heads adorning them atop the wings but this macabre sight has mercifully been spared me.

Jane, reflecting upon the fate of her lost servant, related for me the story Ngaio had told her of her sister-in-law's jealousy. In all of their huts, termed by them ka-inga, burns a hearth in the centre for warmth alone, since it is tapu for them to cook and eat within their dwellings. And her sister-in-law, having obtained by stealth and deviousness some clippings of Ngaio's hair, which the natives deem tapu also, made a spell and buried the hair by the edge of Ngaio's fire. Whereupon this witchcraft began to take effect and Ngaio's husband to find fault with her. And no matter how she stoked her fire, the hut was never warm. So that she herself, suspicious, sought the assistance of an old rua-hi-ne, who told her to lift the soil from round her fire and cast it away into a tapu space far from her ka-inga.

This she did, and, following, went again to the rua-hi-ne, who bade her secure some special item of her sister-in-law's clothing and return to her. Whereat the old woman mumbled out a spell and instructed Ngaio bury the stolen garment at the very mouth of a distant cave.

And, following, said Ngaio, her sister-in-law was seized with such a violent toothache that nothing could relieve it until the tooth, a front one, was pulled. Which ruined her beauty utterly.

Today, upon a rock, Jane drew a likeness of an English sheep in answer to a plea by Basil. And made a baaing noise to match the drawing. At which all those nearby in the kumara fields laid down their hoes and crowded round, letting out gales of laughter at the sight and sound, and would not allow Jane to leave the place until she had used up her charcoal and her patience with further sheep, a cow, a goat and kid. The natives much enjoyed this unexpected entertainment. And if they should be passing they baa at us, then scarce can move for laughing.

A horrid trade has grown up here within the Bay of Islands since my last visit. The tattoos of the people, being unique to this land, have been the occasion of much interest from mariners and others on the ships which put in from time to time for supplies. I saw that some of the girls who came across from Kiddi-Kiddi had English sailors' names tattooed upon their arms. The carvers here would never stoop to do such decoration: upon inquiry, I found they were rendered by tattooists on the ships and marked the names of those who have had the favours of these ladies. Here, unmarried girls may spend their nights with whomsoever they choose. There are no prohibitions on them. One of the girls had seven such tattoos upon her upper arm. And most bizarre it was to see writ upon her gold-brown skin the names of William Jones, Thomas Dawkes, James Evans and all their companions carved there for posterity. These sailors ply the girls with rum; a sad and stupid folly.

But worse by far, and sadder, is the hideous trade in severed human heads. Some upon the visiting ships sought, on a sighting of these frightful objects, to purchase them as curiosities and quickly did the natives see their value.

The chiefs' heads, which bear the finest, most distinguished patterns and therefore command the highest prices, are greatly in demand. But, since they are sacred objects of inestimable value to the chief's tribe, the supply of such well-tattooed heads is, of necessity, very limited. And so the natives have hit upon a novel and gruesome solution to this problem.

Being aboard a whaler with Thomas Surfleet, who was skilfully translating for the captain, I was surprised to see clamber up to us two brother chiefs of Shunghie, each most strikingly carved about his face and person, and with them a fine, handsome young man, his face unmarked as he was but a lowly slave of menial rank. He was, however, in beauty and physique, a matchless specimen and stood beside his masters, patient and uncomprehending, while, to my horror, they bartered with the ship's master a price for his head when it should be tattooed.

Their attempts to have Thomas Surfleet broker this deal for them led me to remove the boy immediately from the vessel. But meeting with the master some three days later, I was told by him his purchase would be ready within a week and was being decorated even as we spoke.

My stomach turned and my every sensibility was shaken by this repulsive deed. And Jane tells me several of the young and handsome slaves who used to work with Ngaio in the kumara fields are missing.

At night, as we walked, the two of us, along the moonlit beach, I carrying little Samuel, the native children sported and swung on vines suspended from a pyramid of long strong stakes they had constructed upon the sand. 'For all the world,' said Jane, 'like to an English maypole.'

The Maori do not check or punish their children, since they believe it will break their spirits and they will never learn the courage to be warriors. And, certainly, they are a people fearless and bold.

Lizzie skipped with a clutch of little girls in a long rope held by two of them, and, casting about for Sannah, her mother spied her lying alone on her back upon a rock.

'Hush,' said she as we approached. 'Do not interrupt me. I am watching the woman in the moon.'

'Tha mean'st the man in the moon.'

'Nay, Mither, it is a woman. Rona is her name. She made the moon so angry that he snatched her up and swallowed her.'

Seeing the cloud upon Jane's face, I took her arm and drew her, on a pretext, away.

She strives to cleave the children back to English thought with little of success to crown her efforts. Clearly, she is troubled they may grow too like the Heathen. Which I myself should have thought inevitable, given their situation here. But have not said to her.

*

It was more than four days later that Lizzie, resplendent in a muslin frock that had been formerly in service to one of Marsden's daughters, came rushing, breathless, to the garden plot. 'Mother, Mother,' she cried. 'Come quick.'

And Sannah, panting up behind, was scarce less agitated than she. 'It is Te Imu-Rangi has appeared!'

Both Jane and I went forth at this intelligence to scan the sea for the canoes of a warrior foe. But naught was to be seen. The ocean's surface bore no hostile enemy.

'No, not upon the waters,' said Lizzie, capturing her breath. 'In the heavens.' Pointing above the far peninsula.

'The red demon travels there,' said Sannah. 'An evil fate is certain to befall us.'

High above, a red luminary, perhaps a comet or a meteorite, burnt a passage through the sky. The gathering dusk threw up its scarlet colouring as it sped along its course towards the north.

'That is but a heavenly body in the sky,' said I. 'It bodes nobody ill and by tomorrow it will have passed away.'

'No, no,' said Lizzie, certain of her ground, 'it was Huia told us. Everyone is going to the pa. And there the tohunga will make for them a special charm to ward off any evil.'

'Then we shall all be safe indeed,' said I.

'And nowt to fret on, miss.'

'But, Mither, we are not at the pa, so we shall not be saved,' said Sannah.

And such was their agitation at the thought, for pity's sake we took them to where the new tohunga, Manu, Te Kemara having died whilst I was back at Botany, was making a most elaborate ceremony to swerve Te Imu-Rangi and its power away from us. And since, by the early morning, it was gone, I cannot know whether Nature or Manu was the instrument of it.

This reading of natural omens is of uttermost importance in the native life. All sickness, they believe, is caused by evil spirits, an observation not so much removed from ideas of witchcraft held by certain classes of our own society.

Their year does not commence in January but in June and coincides, in this part of the country and maybe everywhere, for all I know, with the cosmic rising of Rigel which is known to them as Puanga. At which time they hold a festival and celebrate with singing and with dances, haka, done by the women and the girls, bare-breasted, twirling, with most surprizing dexterity, balls of flax on cords both long and short. And they offer to the star young kumara plantings, such as I never had from Shunghie.

Their knowledge of the stars is very great. Even the children are educated in this. Thomas Surfleet, asked by Reporo our name for Canopus and the Belt of Orion, was quite nonplussed and could not make any answer.

Still nothing thrives in this garden plot. Some of the plants are brought to growth but it is almost impossible to cultivate even the turnip. I do not know what may be the matter with this piece of ground but it is in no way fertile. And I fear never will be, despite all our efforts.

Two days ago in the morning, shortly after the men of the pa had set off on a three-day journey under Ha-Re-Shunghie's leadership, the rains came, lashing us and saving the cookee slaves the chore of watering. By early afternoon, the downpour had ceased and all across the bay at Rangi-Houa lay a wondrous double rainbow, almost complete. A cry of 'U-E-Nuku!' went up from all the Maori, which I thought at first to be a sigh of admiration such as I myself had felt upon first espying it. But soon I understood the sight of these shimmering arches was the occasion of general fear and consternation. And this, they told me, was because the bows were incomplete, which rendered them doubly malignant and would ensure the onset of some dreadful event.

Great spells were made and further omens cast until it was deemed the danger had been lessened. And everyone set off again about his doings.

And then, the day following, with the men still away at Kiddi-Kiddi, when the bow had vanished and I had quite forgotten even of its former existence, a watcher on the shore gave out a shout.

Paddling across the bay to us came a company of canoes.

'There are all the men returning,' I observed to Jane.

But she, paling, replied that these were not the canoes of Ha-Re-Shunghie.

'How can you tell?'

'Be by the carving on their prows.'

Her agitation grew and, laying down her hoe, she set off to gather up her children, instructing me to follow.

Within the shortest space of time came everybody from the shore and fields and mounted up the hill at speed to the pa, Jane and the children mingling with the others, as on the water swiftly advanced the alien canoes.

The general air of fear was most infecting. I concealed our tools beneath a bush and hastened to form the last part of the tail that snaked uphill.

The slope to the pa is very steep and, it being divided into three quite separate palisaded parts, it is not possible to see the topmost area till entering through its gates.

And in that highest part, beside the entrance to the meeting-house, calm amid the panicked throng stood Turi-Ka-Tiku with both her daughters flanking her. A shepherd to unruly sheep, she herded all inside save for the slaves, who did not, so I noticed, attempt to gain entrance also but scattered themselves about the other buildings there and hid.

Seeking a place of concealment and certain I should not be allowed inside the meeting-house with Jane, I took myself to the storehouse on its single wooden leg and crept below the grinning post carved above the door. With no one to observe me, I buried myself as much as I was able within the piles of kumara.

From my hiding place I commanded a view of the front of the meeting-house and the pa gateway both, so that I plainly saw Turi-Ka-Tuku, having hastened all within, instruct her daughters enter also, which directive they seemed very loath to obey but yielded to at last.

There came not a whisper from the meeting-house. Not a

one of those crowded inside could be heard or seen. Turi-Ka-Tuku, standing alone, her head tilted slightly back, listened intently to some far faint sound my own ears could not catch.

Cramped within the tapu space of the storehouse, where I should not ever have been, my knees doubled to my chin, I scarce dared breathe for fear her keen ears might detect my presence.

But it was not for me she listened. From far below, a slight noise floated up that fortified hill. I realised with a sudden shock that the pa gates were unmanned. Open. Should I now reveal my hiding place, rush down the hillside shutting gate after gate behind me? Could I, one man alone, without their warriors' strength, move back into position those huge wooden structures?

Fear held me in my place as the sounds below came more distinct. The war party, secure in the knowledge of Shunghie's absence, was ascending to claim his women, plunder his food supplies, decimate his people, burn his looted pa. Such treachery from a sworn foe would have been at least expected, but these were his neighbours, his cousins, those he had charged with guarding his own. Or so had said his daughter when raising the alarm.

A terrible thought came to me. Would Jane be spared by virtue of her colour and her race? Or would that make of her a greater prize, to be seized and borne away I knew not where, to what dreadful fate? I had not even a musket with which to offer a token of resistance, a little show of defence of her.

A stirring by the meeting-house drew me. Moving rapidly for one of her immense size, Turi-Ka-Tuku was feeling with wide-spread fingers for the base of the diagonal ridge-board at the front of the meeting-house.

Locating it, she unclasped from her shoulders her upper mat. It dropped at her feet and she kicked it to one side. Her huge and pendulous breasts swung bare as she pulled from her lower body her other flax garment and flung it off her so that now she stood, mother-naked but for her father's hei-tiki, at the side of the meeting-house entrance. Still no sound, not even a baby's cry, came from within. Had I not with my own eyes seen them all entering some little time earlier, I should not have believed anyone to be there.

I could not draw my gaze from Shunghie's wife. She was, in truth, a mighty and impressive sight, tall and immense in girth with layer upon layer of flesh encircling her, her great belly and trunk supported on legs like giant pillars. As I watched, she seized the flat board beside her in both hands and, with unlikely lightness, hauled up her vast bulk on to the narrow top of it.

Higher she climbed and higher. I observed her progress, naked as God had fashioned her, ascending, merely by the clutching of her hands and feet, the side of the meeting-house, until she arrived at the joining point of the ridge planks, where, with the skill of a delicate acrobat, she swung herself upright.

Fascinated now beyond the bounds of decency, I watched, unabashed. Holding on only by her feet, she raised her huge body until it straddled the apex. A more imposing and dramatic sight I have never seen before or since as she remained standing balanced there, her arms outstretched, like some Heathen version of the risen Christ.

It seemed to me some sign now must be vouchsafed from Heaven, yet nothing passed. The calm and quiet all about hung dense and heavy in the air.

Till into it broke, clear in that silent place, the shouts and cries from those below, now upon the fortified part of the hillside and ascending.

The princess, Turi-Ka-Tuku, stood silent still upon the roof.

War screams of the raiders, the clatter and the violence, the clashing of their spears, increased. There seemed within their shouts and cries a jubilation, the lusty power of conquerors about to pluck their spoils, the scent of blood and victory upon them.

I shifted my position a little to the other side, careful to remain withdrawn into the interior of the storehouse. From thence I might watch the invasion at the topmost gateway and meet my fate full face, not cowering like a weakling.

231

Resembling nothing so much as a native wooden carving, upon the roof the majestic goddess held her own position.

Loud chants of intimidation and the raiders were upon us. They poured through the entrance gate, then halted on the flat marae before the meeting-house. Their leader raised his head. Lowered his weapon. About him the hubbub ceased. That company of fighting men of a sudden stood still and silent.

Turi-Ka-Tuku fixed her sightless eyes upon them. Though I could understand only some of the words she spoke, the proud contempt of her tone and her face told all.

'Haere mai.' Her voice was calm and level. 'Welcome. For what do you come here?'

Their leader made no reply.

She pointed at him without the slightest disturbance of her equilibrium. 'You are my husband's kinsman, charged by him with our protection in his absence.'

She waited but again there came no answer.

'Within this sacred place lie those, unarmed and defenceless, to whom you pledged protection, but now you come to slaughter or to carry off by force. Take them, all of them.'

Disconcerted, the warriors looked for guidance to their leader. He shifted his gaze so that his heavily tattooed countenance looked earthwards. Shame, it seemed, had overtaken him. Behind him, in their ranks, another spoke, stepped forward. An altercation grew. It was clear that, while some were undecided, others, excited by imminent conquest, advocated action.

'You stand upon sacred, tapu ground,' said Turi-Ka-Tuku. 'Should you argue and quarrel here, you will offend the gods. Stand back.'

The leader stepped from the holy ground, his warriors following behind him.

'Go in,' said she again, 'and take my people. Your own people. But know that in order to do so you must pass between my legs spread out above you. I am my father's daughter and my husband's wife. All their mana I carry. As my father's daughter, as my husband's wife, I am tapu. Pass, if you dare, below my sex.'

And at this, she opened wider still her heavy thighs, exposing to their view, and mine, her privy parts.

I expected at this challenge, which might indeed be deemed as well a deadly insult, the warriors to rush and topple her from her perch, to storm the meeting-house and seize and slaughter all within. But no man moved to pass beneath her.

'Go in,' she said a third time. 'I am unarmed but for the tapu that I carry. If it is your wish, take us, break that tapu. The choice is yours.'

Nobody moved or spoke. It was as if a silent combat were engaged between the princess and the raiders. Until, at length, the leader backed towards the gate where he turned abruptly and, followed by his men, retreated down the hill.

She stood some further time in her position, listened a little, then descended.

From within the meeting-house, with eyes downcast, averted from her person, came Huia and Rerehu, her daughters, who went to her and re-arrayed her in her garments, then, one on either side, stood beside her in the doorway as all came slowly out from the interior. And every one, Jane and the children included, made hongi with her, inhaled her noble spirit, as they passed and filed in silence down the hillside back to the shore. From whence could be seen the departing canoes of the vanquished. And, over and above them, the faintest outline of a double rainbow.

A nobler thing I never saw. Had but Louis had her for his queen and not the vapid Marie-Antoinette, his head and hers might yet have been upon their shoulders.

I did not leave my own hiding place until I ascertained that all had left. And did not mention one word of what I had seen to Jane, it being that I had most seriously offended against their laws by my choice of hiding place and my viewing of the nakedness of Shunghie's wife. Better Jane does not ever know of it.

I told her instead that I had hidden myself below the raupo matting in a hut, since the earthy, musty smell of kumara clung strong about my person and I must have some credible explanation for its presence.

And on the shore at night, alone, I begged forgiveness from their Maori gods for any transgression I had made. It seemed to me both courteous and expedient.

HONGI HIKA

PARAMOUNT CHIEF
OF THE NGA-PUHI
OF AO-TEA-ROA.

BORN *1772.*

DIED *1828.*

So, Turi-Ka-Tuku, I have been to this Cambridge. I now can write with my own hand my name, Hongi Hika, Hail Fish, not only by the tracing of my moko but in English words.

'A proud moment,' said Keni. At which I laughed greatly. I do not need to write my name to know who I am.

The settlement itself is something of a marvel, carved all in stones. Their carvers rival ours in skill and execution, as, in some ways, do their musicians. On my return I will trace for you all the patterns and designs I have observed here and sing for you some wai-ata of Mr George Handel. These wai-ata are very pleasing to the ear but never change in note or form, being written down and therefore every time the same, like all the words the Pakeha read in their books.

Having observed how stiff and frozen they are as they dance, which, in truth, they rarely do, I was not surprized to find their music so formal and unchanging.

We attended a speech delivered in a church on Sunday by Mr Basil Wood. It seemed a long time in the telling and I found myself eager for its conclusion. His body, as he spoke, did not seem to be the servant of his head, his legs and feet the body's slaves. More, it seemed, the rigidity of his body held his jaw and lips and tongue in bondage. There is a great inhibition in the movements of every one of the Pakeha I have so far met.

They do not start as we do with the basic notes in their music or the words already known within their speech and, placing themselves within their words, their songs, take them for their own to suit the time or ceremony where they may be, but they have what they call a 'text' such as Keni reads us from their Bible. And this remains the same at every reading. Here, they do not embrace change as we do. A fortunate thing for us that we are so flexible and they so fixed.

It is, for these reasons, very dull to listen to them speak. Their voices are full of apology to the poor trapped words and their faces, too, are most uninteresting. When I or a brother chief rises to give utterance, our voices tell one colourful and mighty story, our faces tell another. How often have I scrutinized the countenance of an orator and sought to match his story with his genealogy traced within his moko. How satisfying is the tension created by a master orator who matches the profundity, the wit and narrative of the two, satisfying at once the ear and eye and heart of his listeners. When I return, I shall have much to say!

Within these buildings sit the tohungas of all the people, the wise ones, says Keni, of the whole of this land. But how ugly, how little, how uninspiring, Wife, are these so-called great men.

Most wonderful of all that I have seen here is the carving and the music in the Chapel of the College of the King, where Keni went with us to eat the body and blood of his god and where the people gazed only at Wai-Kato and me as we sat and listened to their chanting. I saw, across from where we sat, carvings of dark wooden angels, like those Keni has so often described to us. They appear very strong and warlike, these angels, with wings like the ko-tuku, though black. They wear long garments like Englishwomen, skirts like Modder's, and I observed to Mr Basil Wood that this must make it very difficult for them when flying about the Heavens. Mr Basil Wood turned red at this and started to explain something to me, but the music began about us and he fell silent. It was, indeed, the most wonderful sound and I wish only that we could carry back with us some of their musical instruments and their musicians. Their music is what I wish most that you might hear.

These Pakeha are a strange people. Alien. They study a great deal but they do not comprehend their own natures. I see that Professor Mr Lee hates and wishes to destroy Mr Basil Wood but his tongue tells us otherwise; and it is the tongue Keni so foolishly believes, not the heart. The outside of a man may be seen but the inside may not, and in the matter of thus listening, Keni does not know.

These are men whose understanding comes all from the pages of their books. In silence, they ingest their learning.

But we who do not read must take our knowledge from those who speak their hearts and minds aloud, who hold within their tongues and not their hands the mighty weapon of communication.

Think how this frees the hand! And finely shapes the tongue that darts like a fish through the silver waters of speech. The magic jawbone sinking into the sea of oration hooks a great fish from the shoal of thought and heaves it up, up, through the bowels, through the stomach, through the heart, into the heavenly vault of the mouth, from whence it breaks free on the tongue and darts away into another shoal, another mind, another heart.

And until you have hooked him and raised him to the tongue, you cannot know what manner of fish you have snared. You may guess. Hunt in the hapuka grounds and you will likely hook hapuka. But sometimes, stealthy in the hapuka grounds, comes the great shark. Hook him on your jawbone and you may become a ranga-tira, an ariki; sometimes, perhaps, a tohunga prophet.

Why do I befriend and protect them, these white men who cannot speak from the heart? I have pledged myself to gain utu. And to succeed, I must have even more of the Pakeha's muskets.

There *are* birds in this land, Turi-Ka-Tuku, but they do not often sing.

It was Keni's wish that we should return early to London so that we could meet again with Mr Basil Wood, his hoa and his chief.

Wife, I must tell you, they are not all we believe, these white men. Here in their own land, I see them clearly and I see how we are deceived. It is not you, but I, who have been blind.

Mr Basil Wood is no great tohunga. His understanding is trapped as in a child's casting net. Inside that net rests everything he has caught and the net, Turi-Ka-Tuku, is small, small, small. Only little fish in a little net.

This man despises what he does not know, hates what is not of his tribe; and, I tell you, he is dangerous to Keni. Though Keni himself does not comprehend this and respects him as a wise father.

While Keni was calling again upon Mr Basil Wood, I and Wai-Kato went together with a Frenchman, Baron de Thierry, to look at the inhabitants of this vast settlement, London. The people do not work and farm as we do. Trading, begging and whoring are their principal occupations. On every corner, by every door, are children, women, old ones, clawing, whining and wailing. I have seen elders who live without a tribe, in the open, by stinking pits of filth and human excrement, which, I am obliged to tell you, they throw into the path where all must walk and some must make their dwellings. And these old ones live alone, mocked by those who pass. Who will bury them, and raise and honour their bones when they are gone?

Too many of the people are drunken and unhealthy. Even their children they feed with gin or wine or porter. Strange – the missionaries here preach, like Matenga, against strong drink but their tohunga, Jesus, makes wine from water. I do not understand it. Neither does Wai-Kato.

You remember the animal which Matenga brought from Parramatta for Keni and Modder? For the milk for their children? And how it lived upon the dried grass which he had sent with it, then fell sick and died? And not even the wisdom of Te Kemara could save that beast? Here it is much different. Held by iron chains, the poor creature must inhabit a small interior space within a dwelling-house and never go into the light and sun. Its keepers feed it straw and water and in return this excellent beast produces milk for its keepers' tribe, who daily come with bowls to carry off the frothing liquid. Thinking it to be a delicacy, by reason of its foam and salty smell, I drank a little. All day following, the weight and grease of it lay heavy in my stomach, on my tongue.

Not far from here, they tell us, there are ships, old so they can no longer put out to sea. And in these waka live prisoners with iron weights upon their legs. And amongst the ships, the vessel of their famous tohunga navigator Cook lies rotting there with all the others, no sacred burial place, no funeral rites performed, only a decaying carcass holding the dying husks of slaves. What can be sacred to them? Where are their gods? Have they no tapu?

Wife, I have seen true wickedness. Cruelty in its most dreadful form. Yesterday, we were taken to a part of London where their prisoners are punished. These are not prisoners-of-war but those they call felons, whose crimes seemed often harmless to Wai-Kato and to me. I ventured this to Mr Wood, who accompanied us. At which he made plain his shock and said it was the will of their all mighty god that such sin be punished. But how can it be sin to take bread if one is hungry?

239

I reminded Mr Wood of the gospel which Keni has often read to us and the story of the bread and fishes given by the tohunga, Jesus, to his starving tribe. At which Mr Wood became warlike and wished to explain that Jesus was of the spirit, therefore not as we.

'But,' said Wai-Kato to me, 'surely bread is bread. Does he mean these hungry to eat spirit?'

I did not think it politic to translate this to Mr Wood, and nor, I saw, did Keni.

At first, when we reached the ritual punishment place, I was much impressed. I imagined it to be a hangi or a feast, from the general demeanour and the ceremonial dress of the people. Huge crowds thronged at the spot, momentarily causing me great pain in my heart as I remembered the holy moment of departure of our war canoes to defeat the Tai-Nui, the Arawa. I am a warrior; my destiny is war. Why am I standing far from the home of my ancestors, dressed in English clothing, my feet trapped in boots?

Then my attention was caught by an unknown noise. Like thunder and the rattle of stones together, it rose above the screaming of the gin-sellers, the shouting and the roaring of the people. Before any others, I and Wai-Kato heard it, and we knew it to be the sound of avenging death. As its note became audible to the crowd, the people's frenzy and excitement increased, yet that great mass of them nevertheless pulled apart to create a channel, through which slowly, slowly, appeared a pair of fine black horses pulling behind them a wooden cart, like a canoe with iron wheels.

And in this cart, clad in white English linen flax, their hats and heads decorated with flowers, and more flowers clutched in their hands, stood four people – three men and a woman – each with his neck garlanded with a flaxen noose. And beside them, a black-clad man, intoning sacred words from a book he clutched tightly against the bumps and janglings of the cart.

Behind the cart came others, all with inhabitants covered with flowers. From the crowd rose cries and moans and some broke rank to run beside the vessels, snatching at the hands of the occupants, members of their iwi.

At length, at the foot of the wooden structures I had observed when we arrived, the leading cart stopped, the flaxen ropes were strung across it, the driver whipped the horses and the cart pulled away, leaving the poor wretches jerking and leaping on the ropes like fish struggling to return to water.

And worse even than the sight of their faces, first red, then the dull purple of my moko, then black, the lips frothing like cow's milk, was the noise of their inhuman gasping for air and life.

This they did to all these prisoners and it was much enjoyed by the crowd, amongst which were even tiny children. I cannot conceive of a more repulsive act, yet around me the people cheered and clamoured for more. And had you but seen the blood-lust upon their faces, you would not have wished to stand for long amongst such primitives. 'The mob', these ones are called.

And Keni tells me that before such a fearful death the unfortunate prisoners are kept locked and chained for many moons unknowing of their fate; whether they shall be sent to Botany Bay or the rotting ships or whether they must suffer this indecent humiliation of public ritual strangulation. I tell you, Turi-Ka-Tuku, this I could not inflict even upon the killers of my brothers.

Wife of my heart, here it is night. You are waking now, alone, in the morning, on the far end of the shore where you swore to sleep till my return. The sun has stroked your face and warmed you and the small breeze from the ocean has blown the cold sand against your sleeping cheek, calling you. You have unfolded your body from your cloak, shaken dust and sand from the feathers, and reached for those familiar things – your flax kit, your hoe. And even now as I think of you and long to touch your skin, your hair, you are feeling with your hands and feet the path to our kumara fields, smelling around you the mingled earth and salt and bitter curing fish, the lighter echo of that harsh and wondrous smell you carry deep within you. Do you think of me also, Turi-Ka-Tuku? Put away your anger, I beg you. Let your heart rise again towards me as I stand here in the dark of this far, great city.

Soon I will return to you. You will lie close against my huia-feather cloak, lay your face amongst the feathers, clasp me between your thighs and cause me to groan in agonies of sacred love and pleasure. I yearn for you, Turi-Ka-Tuku.

Remember, Time will bring us what we most desire. Wait, only wait, and plan, and we shall have, at last, our utu.

RICHARD STOCKWELL.

CONVICT TRUSTY.

BORN NORFOLK.

1778.

DIED NORFOLK,

1859.

How sweet is the domestic life. When a man is thrust, as I am now, into the everyday concerns of family, the administration of a tiny kingdom, then strange indeed would be he who was not engaged and won by its weavings and interlacings, the rivalries and squabbles among its little subjects, its touching intimacies, its solidarity and its affection.

We sat, Jane and I, the picture of felicity, little Samuel fast upon my knee, the infant Laurence nestled against her breast.

'Aye,' she said, smiling at me. 'Love Sammy dearly do his sisters, Sannah most particular. Though at first she wouldna come nigh to him. Afeared, she were, that he might die, like Baby John. Be Huia, Shunghie's daughter, did cure her of her fears. She have made for Sannah a little stick with feathers on. And Huia's mother, Turi-Ka-Tuku, have took it away to Manu, then sent by Thomas Surfleet that I must go to Manu with Sannah and Samuel only of me bairns, and Huia with us. And us has climbed up to the pa where be also Turi-Ka-Tuku.

'And Manu do say the words of a charm across the head of Samuel and do take up a gourd and sprinkle water upon his little brow, and after, Sannah says, holding him to her for the first time, "He be safe from harm now and no spirit may take him from us."'

I held the child tighter upon my knee. He squirmed against me. A swell of feeling took me. I kissed his sweet soft cheek, pressed him to me, breathed in his warm smell of contentment.

Though I had heard, finally, in Botany, of Samuel's safe delivery, I had spent many anxious hours in contemplating Jane's situation. A sole Englishwoman being brought to bed within such a lonely place. Mrs Marsden, too, expressed her concern to her husband.

'But, my dear,' said Marsden, 'Mrs Kendall is a strong, healthy woman. She has been delivered of six children already. Why should we fear for her now?'

And off he strode to have his horse fetched that he might ride into Port Jackson for luncheon with the master of the barracks.

'Tom were gone again from Rangi-Houa,' said Jane, in response to my questioning her of her confinement. 'And I were took early, as with John. Sannah have called to Ngaio in the kumara gardens. And Ngaio did come running and took me outside our hut and wouldna hear it that I wants to be within.

'"Tapu," she said. "Tapu." And shook her head.

'And as I wasna in no condition to have me way, it be outside I must go.

'But when she have took me out, she didna set me down there but have led me a little distance to another hut, small, which I has seen some of the slaves building a two week afore.

244

And I goes in with her. And hard it were indeed to squeeze me belly enough to get below that lintel. And, at me pangs growing more severe, Ngaio did send away Sannah, who have come back with an old rua-hi-ne. So ancient were this crone she hasna a tooth left in her mouth and her hair be thin and wispy. And when I seen her entering in the hut, I like to thought her a witch. And shrieked aloud.

'But she, coming close, have brushed a large leaf across me brow and did sprinkle a strange brown liquid across me belly.

'Long they were, me pains of labour, and I were weakening and tired and Tom still not returned, when, sudden, I hears bees humming outside the little hut. Sweet, it were, that sound, like they was happy, content. And the humming grewed louder, sweeter, until I were took off in it, like I were swarming with them bees, floating, drifting in a blue English sky. And me pains has slipped away from me, all. And I falls into a deep sleep. And when I awakes, "Push, push," I hears a voice a-calling, which I does, and feels the infant sliding from me body. And the rua-hi-ne lifts him and hands him to me and he do look up at me with eyes the colour of that sky.

'Beautiful, he were. And are. And all us loves him dear.'

'And the bees?'

'There niver were a swarm. Be Ngaio, outside, did make a native spell and hum it to ease me pangs. Them Heathen be kinder to me than iver were me own.'

HONGI HIKA.

PARAMOUNT CHIEF
OF THE NGA-PUHI
OF AO-TEA-ROA.

BORN *1772.*

DIED *1828.*

I was not succoured by the English climate. All across the South Atlantic with cold and damp and raging rain and winds about us, I have fought to shake away from me the fog blanketing my chest, smothering my breath. My voice is a frog's croak.

If our ship would but speed as fast towards you as do my thoughts, Turi-Ka-Tuku, I should be even now entangled within the net of your arms and legs. Above me, set in the sky, I see the Stakes of the Heavenly Net, the Pakeha 'Milky Way', which they say spilt from the breasts of a feeding goddess. Our Stakes they call Magellan Clouds, in honour of their great navigator. I did not know before that they had any other seafaring ancestor but Cook.

I am learning many Pakeha things. Keni has been speaking to me of the god Hermes Trismegistus. He is not Christian but Neo-Platonist, which is to say he wishes men to turn aside from enjoyment, that by suffering torment in their bodies and denying themselves all things which are of pleasure to them they may free their souls for their God.

Keni has warned me I must not speak of it to Matenga as it is forbidden to the followers of Jesus, being against the beliefs of Christianity. But Wai-Kato and I remarked to each other how much the same it seemed.

Of the Ancient Greeks, too, I am learning. They are very like our people – warriors, navigators, orators, philosophers. I like them more and more. Their gods are similar to ours, though their sea-god, Poseidon, has at all times with him fifty wives!

Twice now I have crossed the world's great oceans. On the outward journey, over Kiwa, we followed the ara-mo-ana, the great sea-road of Ku-Pe and the ancestors.

Kiwa is called by them the Pacific but the fury of the waves which tossed our ship gave the lie to it. And, though I strained to see the night sky above us, dense clouds obscured every star. I was greatly disappointed but I recited aloud the navigating instructions of Ku-Pe as, for nine hundred years, we have all learnt them from our infancy.

'Keep the sun, the moon or Venus just to the right of the bow of the vessel, and steer nearly to the south-west.'

And Captain Strachan told us that, were our journey to be reversed, this would indeed plot a true course to Ao-Tea-Roa from the north. At this, our hearts were full.

Sailing home south across the Indian Ocean, I have with me here in my cabin my muskets and my suit of armour from King George. Every member of our ship's company has been to view and admire this armour. If any tani-wha rises to threaten my people I shall don it, go forth and slay the monster, like the Englishman Saint George.

Is he an ancestor of the king, Saint George? Recollecting the king, I think not.

Turi-Ka-Tuku, this is a tapu night. The night of my life that stands far apart from any other. This night I have seen a wondrous vision!

Keni and I were playing chess, a game I greatly favour for its being like our draughts but with more powerful war strategies, and Wai-Kato lay asleep upon the deck. To the hatchway came the captain and called us to take a grog with him. Keni went at once but I, who cannot bear its taste nor the dulling effects of it, said I would stay on deck with my cousin.

As I lay upon my back and looked up at the Broad Path of Ta-Ne, the souls' track that you and I must walk, in time, to join the spirits of our ancestors, I saw the Northern star, Hoku-Paa. And, at the selfsame moment, on the far horizon, shone Ne-We, the pointer of the Southern Cross, our new guide calling us.

And there came to me, in that moment, the exact knowledge of where I was.

Above me was the most sacred place of our ancestors, the Pito-a-Rangi, the great Navel of Space. The birthplace of the mighty god himself.

My emotion overcame me. Weeping, I woke Wai-Kato and we scanned the sky for those marker stars of which we have learnt through generations. And all, all, showed clear to me. I have been chosen by the ancestors. I, Shunghie Ika, paramount chief of the Nga-Puhi of Ao-Tea-Roa, have been thus honoured by the gods.

I knew at once, Turi-Ka-Tuku, I must speak with you, must share with you this tapu moment.

I set about the summoning of my powers. And in this ancestral place, where seemed the stars so close that they might lie upon our heads, I felt the sacred link which held me to them. And to you.

He who has great mana may, if he can command it, cause a halo to appear about the moon, a signal to those who wait far away. Once only I saw my father perform this feat. When I was a small, small child.

I called silently upon Ta-Ne, upon Rangi, upon Hi-Ne, the lunar goddess.

And slowly, faint at first, then shining visible, a mighty ring appeared, a noose around the moon, by which you may know I am here but that I am also with you, with our ancestors, with our race.

Keni, reappearing, was afraid.

'And as,' he said, 'Turi-Ka-Tuku cannot see it, what use is it?'

Ah, the Pakeha. So very little.

'She has no need to see it,' said I. 'She knows it is there.'

These things are signs to me.

I have travelled the routes of the Great Migrations of our ancestors. Of Ku-Pe, Nuku-Ta-Whiti, Rua-Nui. I, too, have made these epic voyages. I have seen our most sacred place. I have summoned a ring about the moon.

I am a man of destiny.

THOMAS KENDALL.

MISSIONARY.

BORN NORTH THORESBY,

LINCOLNSHIRE,

1778.

ORDAINED LONDON,

1820.

DIED NEW SOUTH WALES,

1837.

Such a voyage we have made. I have achieved all I desired. Even more than that of which I had dreamed. I am ordained a minister of God, I have met with His Most Gracious Majesty, discoursed with him, had the honour of the touch of his hand. My sovereign himself has commended my diligence and vision. Marsden cannot begin to boast of such.

I did not return to Lincolnshire while at Home. I could not face the arduous journey, the slow grinding of the coach as the horses struggled their way up Gonerby Hill. And little there was to draw me back to the simple life of Brocklesby or North Thoresby. For every door of high society in Cambridge and in London now was open to me and to my Noble Savages.

But that which I had before admired and never questioned seemed suddenly stiff and cold. How simpering were the ladies. The stupidities of fashion and of manners jarred upon me. Society, even that which had formerly been most agreeable, seemed stilted, meaningless, to me now.

And, I do confess, I longed most greatly for that liberty I enjoy in Ao-Tea-Roa. In this country of the Heathen, I am free from those constraints which hedge me round in England.

What man among these posturing English would philosophize with me as does Shunghie? In Cambridge, though I saw my Grammar greatly approved by Professor Lee, was I once sought out for my opinions? Might I there continue my researches?

And what of my friendship with the chief, my acceptance in this place as the man I truly am? I am not the he I thought myself at Home. I am another he, stronger in the Lord. A missionary. And none within the Church Missionary Society is there who daily treats, consorts as one with the Heathen, more than I. Marsden, safe in the counterfeit English fastness of his Mission, encounters no blackfellows, no sons of Satan. His dealings are all with Englishmen!

It is I am in the vanguard of the true defeat of the Devil and his legions. I who must daily, hourly, engage in bitter combat with the forces of Outer Darkness.

Consider but the words of Shunghie on our voyage back to Ao-Tea-Roa.

'According to our belief,' said he, in answer to some trivial word of mine, 'there is no limit to the world. Man must die, even the great kauri trees must fall and decay, but the stars live for ever. And in all things there is a pattern. The lesser gives way to the greater. By night, the moon rules the heavens. But in the day, the moon belittles itself in the presence of its superior, the sun. Its brightness is absorbed in the sun's light. In this way, neither becomes too great. Each is the complement of the other.

'And to show this, the sun and the moon have many names. As do the gods. That men may remember they are always in a state of change, in a state of becoming something other.'

'But surely the sun has not more than one name?' said I.

'Yes, he is Ra and Ra-Tu-Oi and Ra-Kura. He is Tama-Ua-Whiti. And Tama-Nui-A-Rangi, his ultimate title.

'And so, too, with the moon.'

We sat by night upon the deck, the stars like candle flames above us. And much did his talk of Ra, he that was also the Egyptian sun-god, excite my interest.

'So each of your gods,' said I, 'consists of many faces.'

'True. But for our greatest god, the Hidden One. He that is even above the atua.'

My interest quickened. No word before of this overlord had ever been vouchsafed me.

'This Greatest One, how is he titled?'

And his answer opened wide the floodgates of my thought.

'Io is his name.'

I am bound to tell of my disappointment in the response of Reverend Wood to my attempts, in London, to sway him to my own beliefs in the matter of the Maori and his origins.

'Better,' said he, 'we dwell but on their Christian conversion, upon the rescuing of their souls. Cast aside their Heathen roots and consider only their coming swiftly to the Lord.'

And further, he told me it was not the Will of God that I should pursue this line of study. 'The Catechism stands a bulwark against their unbelief, Reverend Kendall.'

Ah, Reverend Kendall. How sweet it sounds to my ear. Alas, that my dearest Mother never lived to see the happy day.

Professor Lee and Reverend Wood, though differing in their other opinions, were of a like mind, certain the beliefs the Maori hold are those of simple primitives.

And I, whilst with them, must agree. And yet, when I speak with Shunghie, or Wai-Kato, or any of their brethren, it seems no longer so. The halo Shunghie caused about the moon I saw with my own eyes. And no man of the crew had seen its like before. Nor could any one among them find other explanation for it.

*

Shunghie, lying gazing at the sky, asked me our name for Pewa.

'Pewa?' said I.

'The bird snare. Those three bright stars are its shaft and Puanga there is the sweet blossom in it for the lure.'

It was Orion's Belt and Rigel that he designated thus. And the more I gazed upon them in those deep and mystic skies, so clear the captain claimed he too could see the Moons of Jupiter with his naked eye, the more I saw it true that these resembled little a belt but very much a snare.

As we were blown south across that ocean vastness, how my spirits lifted at thoughts of my impending reunion with my wife. How great were my hopes of domestic peace and reconciliation as I made out the first sight of her with my family and the convict, Stockwell, upon the shore at Rangi-Houa.

And I saw, as we drew closer, that she was unbonneted, her lovely hair caught only with a loose green ribbon so that the ends hung black and curling upon her breast.

'Ah, Jane, my dearest wife,' said I, stepping from the canoe upon the shore and clasping her to me, 'here returned from his voyaging is your husband, the Reverend Thomas Kendall.'

But she, barely raising her eyes, merely replied apathetically, 'Oh, aye.'

I sat, the morning following our return, disconsolate upon the shingly sand of the beach. Shunghie padded towards me on his great bare feet, his visage newly ochred.

'You are troubled, my hoa.'

I sought to answer, to reassure him of his error, but on the instant that his eyes met mine I could not dissemble. The cruel recollection of how Jane had turned so coldly from me in the night, had closed herself so resolutely against me, struck at me anew.

''Tis Jane, Modder. But a passing incommodity. A nothing.'

He regarded me with gravity but spoke no word. Of a sudden, I wished with all my heart for his counsel. But how could I betray my poor Jane? Indeed, cried my heart, where is my own poor Jane? And where are our children for whom I have so longed and dreamed? All of them strange and staring-eyed, filthy, ragged, almost like unto savages.

What have I done that, on the very heels of my ordination as a man of God, my children are become as the Heathen?

It is Jane has wrought this wicked change in them. Their own mother has not kept them in the paths of the Lord. Consider my dearest Mother who nightly prayed beside me and spoke to me daily of my Saviour's goodness, urging me turn my face from sin. A purer woman never lived and breathed. And this must be the recompense of all her Christian labours. Unchecked, unheeded in my absence, Satan has come amongst my own and single-handed must I seek to drive him out.

Thomas Surfleet and Joseph do prattle not only with the Maori but even *between themselves* in the native tongue. It is as if there exists in them no knowledge of the Englishman's estate to which they must one day be heir.

My little Joseph, told of my meeting with his sovereign, asked me solemnly, 'And does he lead his army in his great war canoes, Papa, our King George?'

Mrs Marsden's children be not so. Mine, whilst I have been gone on the Lord's business, have developed even the sidelong glance of the native children, and my Lizzie gazed too long at me with eyes that, though of English hazel, mimicked the limpidity of the brown-eyed misses with whom she daily learns her letters here.

And what am I to say, above all, of that which has so changed between Jane and me? As God is my judge, I stayed a pure man through all the temptations of Home – and great they were indeed, most especially from the ladies of fashion in both Cambridge and the capital. How oft was I led to believe by the fluttering of the eyelashes, the soft gesture, the sliding glance of invitation above the fan, that I should be most greatly rewarded, nay, welcomed, in my lady's chamber?

Did not Lady Arbuthnot herself press me in the most endearing of terms to come to her dressing room to examine with my own eyes a text believed to be early Coptic? Which I eschewed with excuses of a prior engagement with Professor Lee.

'Ah, sir,' says Milady, 'it will not be every day the Copts will wait upon you.'

And I, flushed at her purported meaning, stumbled for an answer and did think most earnestly upon my faithful Jane.

Traversing the towering waves across the cruel Atlantic, in the buffeting winds of the Indian Ocean, how did my heart beat faster and faster as we steadily drew near our goal. How leadenly did pass the days from New South Wales to the Bay of Islands. How sweetly sang my heart hymning its way back to my Janey.

And what found I there upon the beach at Rangi-Houa? No rosy-faced wench in clean and sober muslin but a sullen, hostile creature in skirts of salt-stained black.

'Modder,' said Shunghie, breaking in upon my thoughts, 'is a woman and noa. You, eh-Keni, are a man, tapu. You are my hoa, my friend. You protect my mana and have your own. Have we not met with King George? Passed below the Navel of the World? Why are you now brought down by her, your wife? Do as we do – take a secondary wife! And let Modder have her slave husband also.'

I saw how he sought to uplift my low spirits. 'No, no,' I said. 'Modder will become herself again in time.'

'Never will she be, eh-Keni. I understand her, Modder. She is like my own people. More now than before.'

Recalling my first sight of Jane on the shore, sullen, unkempt, I could not but in my heart agree with him.

'You are unhappy, eh-Keni. You must take to you another wife. Put away this Modder whose heart has turned to frost. I will find you a secondary wife who will sing to you, smile at you, give you those agreeable pleasures we men must have within our lives.'

He looked at me so lewdly I felt myself discomfited.

'I am an ordained minister. I cannot take another wife. It is against the laws of God and man.'

'But we are not in England. Here you may do as *our* gods decree. I have five wives. Am I brought low by the gods for this? I am your brother. I shall find for you a wife of fitting rank. And you shall be my kinsman.'

'I cannot ...' I began. But he had turned from me and padded away, unhearing.

HONGI HIKA.

PARAMOUNT CHIEF
OF THE NGA-PUHI
OF AO-TEA-ROA.

BORN *1772.*

DIED *1828.*

The winning of a war depends on many things. On strategy and timing, propitious omens, the courage of the warriors, their skills, their weapons and the mana of their chief.

Since my return, I have armed my warriors with muskets, I have donned my suit of armour, our war parties have sailed to engage in legendary battles. And every one was ours. On every one we have harvested. So many heads, we must pile them one upon another. No chief has ever lived who carried such fear before him as I do now. At my name, on sight of me, fighting men flee before us. Since I have commanded the moon's halo, I am invincible. My power lies in my armour, in my kingi musket, in the mana which has come to me from the ancestors.

*

Turi-Ka-Tuku, who greeted me at first with ecstasy, with passion, has angered me by refusing to accompany me again to war. She says that she cannot sleep for dreams of blood. She called upon the spirit of her father, who turned from her and would not be summoned. And it is I she blames for this.

She does not like our wars, she says. We are too powerful, too greatly armed.

'Wife,' said I, at this, 'would you have me tell my warriors to lay aside their arms, fight with their spears, their greenstone clubs?'

'With your greenstone club you made yourself a hero. Why must you now conquer all? Stretching a net will widen it but make it thinner, too. And, sooner or later, it will snap and break at its weakest points.'

'And if you keep a fish from the sea for a day, then throw him back, the salt water will never revive him. He will not return to what he was. And so it is with me and with my weapons.'

'You put us all in peril. You with your desire to be a god.'

'Be silent, Wife,' I told her. And went to Tangi-Moana.

Turi-Ka-Tuku is angry, too, at my talking to Keni of Modder.

'Why should you be troubled by this?' said I. 'Did not Modder go to the bed of Tokere, their slave? If Modder were my wife, I would have had her stoned.'

'If Modder were your wife, she would not have the need of one to talk to, to guard her, to take her about with him. And though Tokere appears to be their slave, he is a nobler man than Keni. Listen to how he speaks. The words he uses.'

'You do not know their tongue.'

'I know enough. And of you, too. It was Keni who found for you so many muskets.'

'No. It was I, myself.'

'I do not believe you.'

'You wrong me and my strategies. For these I went to England. It is the will of the gods that I should have all these muskets.'

'Since you have been to England, you are different. You are

arrogant, vain. You forget yourself. Be careful the gods do not forget you, too.'

She is jealous, that is all. Because it is not she, but I, who have passed below the Navel of great Rangi.

THOMAS KENDALL.

MISSIONARY.

BORN NORTH THORESBY,

LINCOLNSHIRE,

1778.

ORDAINED LONDON,

1820.

DIED NEW SOUTH WALES,

1837.

I have turned my mind away from my troubles with Jane, though, in truth, it is very difficult. Barely does she speak to me, despite my every attempt to placate her. Instead, I have most determinedly set myself to further my discoveries of the origins of the Maori.

Most days I am gone about examining the spiral markings on the rocks at the far end of the shore. They bear more than a passing resemblance to Egyptian hieroglyphics. I am assembling them into a collection for my scientific researches.

Immediately upon my return to Ao-Tea-Roa, I wrote to Professor Lee in Cambridge to acquaint him further with my conclusion that the Ancient Egyptians were the forebears of the Maori. I displayed to him the many parallels existing in their beliefs: the sun-god, Ra, in his canoe, paddling the arc of the heavens; the Pythagorean idea the natives hold that the stars contain the souls of the departed; the crocodile transformed into a tani-wha; their corresponding legends of the Moon and such. And, over all, Great Io.

My letter, necessarily long, took me more than a week to compose and I personally charged Captain Florance with its safe delivery when the *St Patrick* put in at the Bay.

I eagerly now await Professor Lee's reply. As a man of erudition, he will be most drawn to the studies I have made.

Would Jane but relinquish her hardness of heart to me, how content I should be here at Rangi-Houa. I had forgot the magnificence of its mountains, the shining blue-green of its waters, the cloak of green upon green thrown across its contours, the freedom and the gaiety of its people, their joy in seeing me again. 'Eh-Keni, eh-Keni,' I have heard on every side.

And Shunghie and I have once more set out upon our fishing expeditions, though he has lately been gone away often upon his expeditions of war. And I have been obliged to absent myself from the shore on his return that I do not see for certain what may lie within the canoes of his warriors.

If I could but enjoy here the benefits of English society such as I was introduced to with Shunghie and Wai-Kato, roast mutton upon my table, a carriage or a stagecoach to transport me, the crispness of linen sheets about my body, the familiar pointing of a church spire, the comfort of books, the discourse with my equals, the fellowship shared with my ordained brothers in Christ, how happy might I be to live out all my days in this place.

Problems have come crowding in upon me, clouds dull my Paradise. Marsden has sent me word from Parramatta by the master of the whaler *Heart of Oak* that the Governor himself has spoken to him of rumours that Shunghie has engaged in trading land for muskets. He instructs me to investigate this matter in my capacity as magistrate here.

There is, he says, arrived a three week since in Botany, the French nobleman with whom we dined at Cambridge, a student there of the law, Baron Charles Hippolyte de Thierry, and a company of Frenchmen with him. And, says Marsden, angrily does he claim that Shunghie and Wai-Kato, whilst in England, sold to him half the land of Ao-Tea-Roa in exchange for money enough for two hundred muskets.

The baron swears upon his oath this transaction took place and wishes now to embark for Ao-Tea-Roa with his men to found a kingdom here of which he will be ruler. In Cambridge, he expounded very greatly upon the merits of Utopia and, having narrowly escaped from France with his head in place upon his neck, told us he wished but for a land wherein he might set up a true and honourable system of government. An admirer of Monsieur Rousseau, he was greatly interested in my Noble Savages and took them much about in Cambridge and in London, assisting and entertaining them when I must be with Reverend Wood or with Professor Lee at work upon our Maori lexicon.

Shunghie has assured me, upon his solemn word, the baron's story is but a fabrication and a pot of lies.

How comes it Shunghie has so many muskets? As I myself may testify, His Majesty presented him with a number of these weapons and his suit of armour with them, and he sold in Botany for handsome sums all those gifts such as the silver coffeepot, the garments of fashion and three of his four tall hats, his ivory toothpick and brush set and similar. And with that money, I confess that I myself assisted him to buy yet more muskets. But we must survive in this wild place and he, under whose protection we lie, must have the wherewithal to ensure and defend our safety.

And, again, the whaling and the sealing ships will surely supply our natives here with weapons, which renders it almost impossible for us, their catechists and only bulwark against Satan, to barter from them our food supplies. So that it was only to uphold our Christian settlement and mission here I acted as I did. I am an ordained clergyman. Who might doubt the purity of my motives?

Shunghie is my friend. He has the right of my loyalty. Even were I to believe this nonsense of a story, I cannot act against him.

I have written to Marsden and the Governor both to say I am satisfied this Frenchman lies, that all his attentions to us in England I see now were but to ensure his own most devious ends and his talk of having bought the land here naught but cant. That we met with him is true indeed and also that, assuring me of his sympathies with the Heathen and his most Christian desire to lighten their Darkness, he made to them, through my offices, a present of twelve axes and a bolt of red cloth, which goods I have carried here and distributed among them as Whare-Po-Aka and Shunghie will freely testify. But of money or payment, neither I nor the chiefs have had aught.

Shunghie coming again to visit me and I being engaged in the transcribing of certain rock spirals into my journal and matching them to the hieroglyphs listed in *Britannica*, I told him I am writing a paper on the origins of his people.
　'But this you know very well, eh-Keni. Many and many a time you have heard me recite my lineage. Why must you now make a paper of it?'
　And I could not convey to him, though I tried, the importance of my theory. In this, he is very like Jane.

Professor Lee has not responded to my letter though more than a ten month has passed since he must have received it. This is a bitter disappointment to me. At each arrival of a ship, and they are few and far between, I eagerly await that reply from him which might uplift my battered spirits. But nothing comes to my hand. It is isolated here and hard to order those thoughts which would most benefit from the free exchange of intercourse and society, the exercise of Reason and the ideas of the mind that Englishmen enjoy daily but for which here I must grub and forage where I may.

Shunghie today has told me that my unhappiness causes him great sorrow. As he accounts me his brother, he cannot, he says, be but saddened at my continuing melancholy countenance. He urges me again to take to myself another wife.

It is Jane's own coldness, her lack of duty to me, that has brought about my downcast state. She does not read her Bible and it is but a nonsense to claim she cannot, since she must know by rote those verses which would succour and support her.

I confess it had been my high hope that, in my long absence, I might return to find Jane had taken upon herself some of my pastoral cares and duties. That she might have taught to the native infants those verses from the Scriptures which she herself lisped as a child at her parents' knee. And yet, such is her stubborn turning from my life's calling, she has not even instructed our own little ones. To Samuel, whom she dotes upon, as do his sisters, she sings indeed, but only her Lincolnshire ballads and lullabies, no Christian teachings, so that, though his hair be white as English snow, his little soul is black as any Heathen's.

I can no longer believe she is truly Jane, my own wife. She seems like one bewitched. She will not pray with me, indeed, she barely speaks to me. Today, whilst I was copying the markings of a rock, she snatched the flask of grog from the pocket of my coat and poured its contents upon the ground.

And on my remonstrating with her that it could be long before I might acquire another, she dashed the flask against the rock, scratching and spoiling all the spiral engravings upon it. God had bent my steps towards that very rock. He had ordained that I should find and transcribe those holy markings.

Jane has thwarted His Divine Plan. The Lord Himself wishes me to carry out my researches. To set them before the world. But Jane, no scholar she, must set herself to block my every step.

*

264

'Tis Jane has led me to this pass in life, to this despair.

'Come, eh-Keni,' said Shunghie, his voice in my ears sounding musical as the sea, 'I have brought my niece to you, a present. A wife for you of fitting rank. She is my own brother's daughter. Beautiful. Seventeen. Take to you Tunga-Roa, of the god Tanga-Roa. She shall live with you and do all for you that your heart desires.'

And as she stepped shyly towards me with lowered but inviting gaze and I caught the dolphin tang of her, I felt arise within me the holy knowledge that here was my only salvation.

'I cannot,' I said huskily.

HONGI HIKA.

PARAMOUNT CHIEF
OF THE NGA-PUHI
OF AO-TEA-ROA.

BORN *1772.*

DIED *1828.*

Ha-Re-Shunghie, dedicated at his birth to Tu-Kai-Taua, eater of war parties, is the true son of me, his father, Shunghie, the true moko-puna of his grandfather, Te Ho-Tete, his grandfather's father, Auha.

Immediately upon my return from my Great Voyage, Ha-Re-Shunghie led me in triumph to the pa, where, displayed on poles, hung not only the heads of the principal chief of the Manga-Whai and his three brothers but those of our traitorous kinsmen who, in my absence and his, had attempted a raid on our territory.

At the very moment of his own victorious return from the Manga-Whai, apprised of this treachery Ha-Re-Shunghie had rallied his weary warriors and led them on a mission of utu against these wretches, not ceasing until he had razed their territory and not a one of their tribe remained alive.

He wears like a cloak the mana of his noble ancestors and the courage of Tu, the war-god. My pride in him is great.

As my general, he accompanies me at all times in my mighty war-canoe; his tactics and his strategies of war are unsurpassed. Together, we are setting plans now for the defeat of every other tribe. I shall not rest until we have taken all the lands to the south, until we have conquered right to Ku-Pe's Ure at the farthest end of this great island.

Then, with my very name striking terror in their breasts, the warriors of Mo-Re-Mo-Nui shall watch me fall upon them, devour them in vengeance. Then shall I have my utu.

And it came to me that following, when I have begun to build my monument, Ranana, my great city, my London, upon the banks of the Wai-Tangi River, when the whole of Te Ika-a-Maui is under my rule, when I have, in my armour, with my kingi musket, established my total supremacy over all the tribes of Ao-Tea-Roa, then might I, with Ha-Re-Shunghie, make again that voyage to England. And dedicate my eldest and favourite son once again to the gods in our most tapu place, below the Navel, the Pito-a-Rangi.

Mr King George is not virile. That great stomach folding above his breeches' buttons does not bespeak a warrior or a man who fathers many children. He has begotten no sons, only a daughter who sickened and died. But his father was very vigorous, as are certain of his brothers.

Mr Prince Clarence, with whom we also dined, though having a most deformed face – particularly about the nose – commands his brother's Navy and spoke knowledgeably to me of warfare and of strategies. He told me he had sired ten children upon his concubine, having not yet a wife.

I shall seek to ally myself to Mr King George as a true kinsman by marrying one of his nieces to Ha-Re-Shunghie, and he and I together can conquer Te Wai Pounamu, the South Island, that my friend the king may be styled thereafter Mr King George IV of Te Wai Pounamu, Great Britain and

Ireland. And I shall be Mr King Hongi I of Te Ika-a-Maui, the Fish of Maui.

I hear the king laugh, see his belly wobble. 'An alliance, Mr King Shunghie? You to live on the Fish and I on the Canoe of Mouwee. A capital idea, Sir, capital!'

I spoke of my intention to Turi-Ka-Tuku, expecting her admiration and assistance. But she was enraged.

'Allow Ha-Re-Shunghie to marry with the Pakeha! Are you mad, Husband? Has your mind been turned by this voyage you have made? Already you have "given" Tunga-Roa to that drunkard Keni, and now you wish to marry our son with a Pakeha.

'The Pakeha are our enemy, they will never be our kinsmen. Cease your dreams of domination, of conquering other Maori. Give up your battles against your own kind even if they are not of your iwi. Make alliances with the southern tribes; with the Arawa, the Tai-Nui, the Whanga-Nui, even with the Rangi-Ta-Ne and Muaupoko of the Head of the Fish. And together drive out these white men.

'Oust the Pakeha, rout him before it is too late. More will come and more. And all of them armed. And while you and the other chiefs are slaughtering one another, the Pakeha will stealthily, silently, steal our land. From beneath your warring noses. Fool that you are!

'To *marry* with the Pakeha! Never speak again to me of this madness.'

THOMAS KENDALL.

MISSIONARY.

BORN NORTH THORESBY,

LINCOLNSHIRE,

1778.

ORDAINED LONDON,

1820.

DIED NEW SOUTH WALES,

1837.

I am the happiest of men!

Shunghie has built me a little hut at Matau-Whi, across from Ko-Ra-Re-Reka, his summer pa near the River Kiddi-Kiddi. Tunga-Roa tends the nearby kumara patch and a slave pounds fern-root for our eating. Shellfish and hapuka and pork we dine upon, and steaming native cabbage. Not even the King's collation could taste as sweet to me as these.

And in the nights, Tunga-Roa comes to me and all my wildest depravities she accounts as mere pleasure. She has placed her mouth upon my privy member and sucked my juices from me just as did the stinking fisher lad of Grimsby, hidden behind the dunes on the Lincoln shore. She does not feel the sin and shame of this but takes it as a natural thing in her life and my own. I am resolved to cast aside the very sin of sin and become as she.

While I was in Cambridge, I revelled in the pleasure of water warm for shaving, the proliferation of soap and towel cloths, the shining blade itself, the pleasant ritual of my daily toilet in the house of Professor Lee. Yet now I am returned here to my true place in the universe and Tunga-Roa scrapes my face and renders me clean-shaven with a shell, and after, I smear with dust my face, then rinse it from me with a gourd of sea water and toss away the tapu shell in a place where no other may accidentally come upon it, I feel the want of civilization no more. Here is true freedom.

I burn daily, hourly, for Tunga-Roa. And she, in the free indulgence of my constant desires, has rendered me so vigorous I am constantly amazed at the strength and potency of my own virility.

I am resolved to shed my Englishman's apparel and to become as one with my brethren, with Shunghie and my congregation. I shall become a New Zealander.

HONGI HIKA.

PARAMOUNT CHIEF OF THE NGA-PUHI OF AO-TEA-ROA.

BORN *1772.*

DIED *1828.*

I fear that Keni's thoughts have been seized by evil goblins. Some malevolent spirit has invaded his heart and troubles him.

I think it may be the spirit in the rum he barters constantly from the crews of the ships which put in here to us at the Bay. He is drinking more and more. And, as a consequence, his mind is dulled, he speaks of monsters, raves at all about him, and I am pressed, indeed, to take the sense of what he tries to tell me.

I have, too many times now, returned him in my own canoe to Matau-Whi after he had become insensible and could not stand upon his own legs. Tunga-Roa, on the last occasion, refused to have him near her and ran away from the shore at our approach. Keni fell from my canoe into the water and, though I raised him up and supported him to the beach, once there, he staggered heavily against the rocks and cut his head and I was forced to sleep the night upon the sands with him.

And Turi-Ka-Tuku's wrath at me next day was very great.

THOMAS KENDALL.

MISSIONARY.

BORN NORTH THORESBY,

LINCOLNSHIRE,

1778.

ORDAINED LONDON,

1820.

DIED NEW SOUTH WALES,

1837.

I am powerless to command myself. Even as I lie with Tunga-Roa shuddering in ecstasy, the visions of Hell arise before me.

I can no longer pray. God is not mocked. He sees the hollowness of my heart. He knows my sins and weaknesses. As I am withdrawing from the body of my concubine, before me appear the faces of Reverend Wood, Reverend Pratt, Professor Lee and, behind them, the Awful Visage of my Maker. God will be revenged upon me that has not secured for Him a single Christian soul within this place.

It may be I am approaching Death. I feel a pain, a gnawing at my vitals. And now I may be damned. Condemned to wander everlastingly in a kingdom of ghosts and monsters or to suffer the torments of Hellfire.

And yet, if the Maori Heaven is as Shunghie has told me, I have naught to fear. I have come from the First State of union and perfection, that field of skulls wherein all Life and Death is held in timeless diffusion. The Supreme Deity, his powers unexercised, is and fills that universe. He is kai, a body of pure food. A self-existing Deity who, under the name of First and Last, eats only – or, more properly, preserves – his own dung. He is the pure food of his own food.

First I existed out of time unbounded. Then by the very action of my birth, I entered into time. I am alive, therefore I exist in the Second State in time. Man is a partly living and partly dead creature. He is dead as to time past, and lives only in time present. And now, to come to the Third and final State of perfect rest, where my bones and my spirit will be eternally, utterly as one, I must die. And then my soul, purified, will return to that Home from whence it came. And time shall be no more.

Here is my hand upon my head. I feel it, this repository of my ancestors, this temple of ideas and thought, this storehouse wherein is lodged my Maori grammar. Everything I have known and seen, my researches and my writings, all, lie only in my head. Which must decay. And should I die here, there will be no record, nothing of my theories, for posterity; only the worms and the wind moving through my empty skull.

My hand I place upon my chest where lives my breath, my warrior spirit, my nobleness of heart, my wai-rua. Within the cavity of my chest lies hid the invisible hand which ploughs my furrow through Life's field.

I touch my belly where reside my guts, my entrails, my sex. Seat of the emotions, all longing and desire. Corrupting me. Dragging me from the noble things of the spirit to vile baseness. Nga-rara, the lizard, is gnawing at my entrails, devouring me.

*

It was Maui-Po-Tiki brought Death into the world. He boasted he would conquer Death for ever by crawling through the womb of great Hi-Ne of the night, the moon. And as she slept he changed himself into a nga-rara and slipped into her intimate parts. But the little fantail bird, spying him, laughed at the ridiculous sight, and great Hi-Ne woke and closed her thighs upon him, killing him.

I too have been destroyed by Woman.

My soul is damned. I shall be condemned eternally to the Fire and the Pit. The Devil will claim me for his own. I feel already the torments of the flames, the agonies of the torture. Nightly, the monsters of Hell appear before my wakeful eyes.

To Rangi-Houa I travelled today to visit with Jane and my children and seek forgiveness. But Jane would not speak with me; and Sannah, upon a sight of me, ran weeping away. She has been turned against me, her own loving father, by her mother. And, at the contemplation of it, a bitter rage against Jane arose in my breast.

I have awoken fully to my shame. I have sent by the whaler *Deliverance* a letter of confession to Marsden in Parramatta, telling him of my state of affliction and disorder, that I have not considered the consequences of the wickednesses of my own heart. So aptly named was the vessel, I felt it an omen from the Lord.

Within a six week I have had reply from Marsden.

'Was you to ask me my opinion of you as a Christian and a man, I should say as a Christian you possessed many valuable qualifications as a missionary but these only shine forth occasionally, like the sun on a winter's day; but as a man I would say you were under the dominion of very strong angry passions and obstinately bent upon following your own opinions on all occasions, regardless of future consequences. You appear never to suspect your opinion may be erroneous. This has been the rock upon which you have often struck, and upon which I fear you will continue to strike, against all remonstrance, till you are involved in difficulties out of which you may never easily escape.'

Marsden is a most unChristian man and the most slovenly figure for a parson I almost ever saw.

Today I have suffered another blow from the hand of him who should be my succour and support. I boarded the *Transit of Venus* for barter and society when it put in at the Bay, and while sinking grog with the master heard from him that he had news for me and would have sought me had I not first found him. He told me that Marsden is sending from Parramatta to Kiddi-Kiddi a new missionary, Reverend Williams, and another, Mr King, to Rangi-Houa. From Marsden, he bore a letter suspending me from my ministry for drunkenness. I tore it into pieces and flung it over the side upon the waters of Tanga-Roa.

HONGI HIKA.

PARAMOUNT CHIEF OF THE NGA-PUHI OF AO-TEA-ROA.

BORN *1772*.

DIED *1828*.

Keni wishes me now to take up my kingi musket, to put on my armour and fight for him. Against *Matenga*!

I am engaged in battles already. I am preparing, once I have humbled all the southern tribes, to fight my great war of vengeance for the dead of Mo-Re-Mo-Nui, my own brothers. With this I am greatly occupied; my time is taken up in planning for this utu of all utu.

And I cannot rise up against Matenga. It is true, as Keni reminds me daily, that now I have a store of muskets. But I need powder for them; they must be mended; I need iron, a blacksmith. I cannot afford to antagonize Matenga. He will take the Mission elsewhere and cease my trade with him and the ships he sends here.

Keni is my friend, my hoa, but he has become a trouble to me. He can no longer reason clearly. His words are all of gods and stars and dung beetles. I shall send him to my kinsman Po-Ma-Re, far from here. Give him land and mana with it, send Tunga-Roa to him, appease and gratify all his earthly hungers.

But I do not believe anyone, not even I, his friend, can now assuage the hunger of his troubled spirit.

THOMAS KENDALL.

———

MISSIONARY.

———

BORN NORTH THORESBY,

LINCOLNSHIRE,

1778.

ORDAINED LONDON,

1820.

DIED NEW SOUTH WALES,

1837.

In the early evening I went down to the water to meet
Reverend Marsden, of whose arrival I had been apprised but
yesterday.

As the ship approached, I waded into the waves and stared
fixedly at him. He was standing on the deck, beside him Tuai,
returning from Botany Bay. Tuai's relatives pushed out their
canoes, indicating to me their offer of passage.

I declined and remained there, up to my knees, watching
the tableau as they paddled towards the ship, hacking at
themselves with sharks' teeth, sobbing and lamenting as if
they were lost souls.

Lost souls.

Like some frightful vision of the Damned putting out to

Hell in their barques and Marsden the cold-eyed minister of Satan. A black and fallen angel.

'But that fallen soul,' I whispered to myself in agitation, 'is not Marsden. It is I.'

The sky darkened. Thick grey cumulo-nimbus clouds, gathering, lowering. A scene of Purgatory before my eyes – the screaming, the bleeding, the wild frenzy of half-naked greeting, the lamentations and the gnashing of teeth. The ship rode up above the waves, tossed at anchor. The Damned seized her ropes.

I locked my gaze solely upon Marsden. His black frock coat and trailing breeches flapped in the wind and water rising from Tanga-Roa. His narrow mouth, the mouth of a repressed sensualist, I have always thought, pouted its dissatisfaction. He waved his stick, like the staff of Moses, at the land before him.

The screams from the canoes and the ship's deck redoubled in force as Tuai's relatives swarmed up the ropes, seized him and embraced him with cries and tears.

Of a sudden, I felt my own heart rise in an excess of lamentation and grief. I, too, wished to cast off my raiment, to race naked into the water, to cut at my sinful body in penitence, clamber aboard that ship of souls and be saved. To weep, confess my agony and guilt. And be shriven. Be washed in the Blood of the Lamb.

They were ferrying Marsden ashore in the leading canoe. I clasped my hat over my breeches and my sinful parts. The morning breeze, cold and bitter, flung the smell of Tunga-Roa in my face, mocked me. The swell of the sea rose like her belly, the seaweed fronds, her hair.

A thunderclap!

'Oh Lord God,' I prayed silently. 'Send me Thine Everlasting Grace. Let this be a sign unto me.'

Marsden stepped from the canoe and waded ashore through the water.

I strode towards him, my hand extended in Christian friendship, eyes fixed anxiously upon his parson's face.

With a wide sweep, he brushed aside my hand. 'Stand back,' he ordered.

I did so. Three paces.

Marsden examined me for several minutes in silence. Then he spoke. No light shone from his countenance. No charity bespoke his eye. 'Mr Kendall, I am here solely on your account. I am come to tell you you are no longer an ordained minister of the Church of England. These papers from the Church Missionary Society will confirm what I say. You have sinned before God and man and are no more worthy to be called God's minister. Do you hear me, sir? You have become as one with the Heathen whose souls you were sent to garner. You have lost your Faith, Mr Kendall.'

'Then restore it to me, I pray.'

'*I* restore it? Indeed I cannot. Only God may do that.'

Another thunderclap.

'See,' said Tuai, wading from behind us to the shore, 'the Sky-Father is angry.'

He and his family had ceased to wail. The blood dripped from their wounds, washing their sins away into the grey sand below their feet. Their gods are the gods of natural law, appeasable, each in his place. Their gods watch over them, do not desert them in their hour of need.

Last night, Tunga-Roa refused to join me within our hut, here at Matau-Whi. She sat, cloaked, sleeping upon the beach. She does not come so willingly nor so often to me now as formerly. And she no longer shaves me nor performs such little offices for me as were her wont.

And as I lay wakeful, my mind dwelling upon Jane and Tunga-Roa, I felt a melancholy sadness sweep my frame and, looking up, beheld in the corner of the hut my own dearest Mother, wringing her hands and weeping.

I awoke next morning with a throbbing in my temples, a sickness in my stomach. The sun glittered too bright.

I walked all the morning with leaden steps about my little chores but, by noon, the heaviness that lay on me burdened me so greatly I was driven to seek respite from it.

I knelt to say aloud the Lord's Prayer but, at my stumbled beginning, it came to me that I no longer knew nor understood its words or form.

Gathering my courage, I resolved to go for my succour to my other gods, the gods of Shunghie and Tunga-Roa. A native, for a nail, ferried me back to Rangi-Houa, depositing me, at my request, upon the deserted farther end of the shore, from whence I stole, unobserved, to the tapu burial place I had so long ago visited with Shunghie.

Through the clear and shining weather, I took my way with lighter steps, removing my coat against the heat of the sun. And made my way deep within that graveyard to the resting place of the bones.

The supplejack vines twisted and pulled about my ankles, the trees themselves seemed denser and more obstructive as I tried to push my way between them to find again that shelved cavern of the dead.

And then, of a sudden, sprang up a mighty wind, which whipped from me my hat and shook the branches that slashed against my face. A freezing cold descended. Shuddering, I went to put my coat about me, only to find it had gone and nowhere could I spy it.

The wind now increasing in force to a gale and I reduced to clinging to the trees to remain upright, I turned and retraced my steps, vowing to return when this freak of Nature should have passed, and slowly, drenched and icy-cold, I dragged myself back to my entry point and stepped from the forest into the clearing.

There, to my utter astonishment, I saw the sun shone still as bright as before, the ground was dry and had seen no trace of rain and not a breeze ruffled the air about me.

Bedraggled and sick to my soul, I staggered to the beach, where my waiting Charon assured me a flat calm had prevailed since my absence.

I was obliged to tell him I had fell from a rock into the sea and to endure his ribald comments until we landed once more at Matau-Whi. Where Tunga-Roa made known to me that her family has summoned her away. She does not know when she will return.

I wandered alone by the shore. Among the little crab-grass flowers, brave stars dotting the firmament of sand, I knelt down and tried again to pray. A moon pool of water glittered and shone before me. From the hills at my back the drying bones of the ancestors called, 'Stay with us, ch Keni. Stay,'

I raised my arms and railed at the skies. 'Give me back my Faith, O Lord. Give it back, I pray Thee.'

I waited for the clouds of glory, the shadow of my God upon the moon.

'Give it back to me, Lord. Do not abandon me now, in the hour of my need.'

At my side, Tanga-Roa's waves slapped and frothed the shore. Above me, in the heavens, the eyes of a thousand chiefs gazed into the hearts of their tangata whenua, their own people.

But of my God there shewed no sign.

JANE KENDALL.

MISSIONARY'S WIFE.

BORN BROCKLESBY,

LINCOLNSHIRE,

1784.

DIED NEW SOUTH WALES,

1866.

Me husband be mad. Crazed, like daft Matthew Grewn in Brocklesby, singing and cavorting and shaking of his head to and fro, to and fro, down by the river. A lunatic, Tom be now, in a Bedlam of the Heathen.

Even the Maori do seek to move theirselves when he approaches.

And I, with all me bairns to shift for, canna do nowt but wait. Wait and watch to see what might mebbee befall.

And him that wishes for me more than all this world, and I alike for him, canna now be nowt of salvation to me and mine.

He were come too late.

THOMAS KENDALL.

MISSIONARY.

BORN NORTH THORESBY,

LINCOLNSHIRE,

1778.

ORDAINED LONDON,

1820.

DIED NEW SOUTH WALES,

1837.

Jane has brought me to a bitter Calvary. Though I yearn with all my heart to remain here in Ao-Tea-Roa, she is set upon leaving for ever. She desires nothing more than to embark for Botany as soon as ever we may.

And on my telling her that I would give up Tunga-Roa and return to her at Rangi-Houa, that I would sacrifice my passion to my duty and that I had writ already to Marsden before his arrival here, assuring him of my repentance, confessing all my sins, she gave again that mad wild laugh which chills me so, and said the Lord and Marsden never would forgive me.

'Shunghie has given me his solemn word,' said I. 'He will build us a house, no hut but a proper Mission House.'

'I wants no Mission House and you be no longer a missionary.'

'I tell you that I am. Marsden speaks false. That paper from the Society was a forgery.'

'Oh aye, a forgery. Signed by Mr Basil Wood hisself. In Marylebone.'

'Marylebone is far from here. Were Mr Wood now to appear, the justice of my case would be revealed to him.'

'He niver will come here. And tha hast not justice on thy side. Adultery, says the paper. And all here do know it. No secret, you and Tunga-Roa. Ordained missionary and a Heathen. They will niver forgive thee.'

'Thou hast forgiven.'

She shrugged her shoulders. 'Desire be desire. Canna be bidden yea or nay.'

'It was thee that turned me to it. Hard thou hast been to me. And cold.'

'Oh aye, it were none of thy decision. The fault do lie only in me.'

'On all of the voyage back, I thought only of thee. Our children. It was thy face I wished to see, thy voice I longed to hear.'

'Be only God tha knows, Tom Kendall. Of man, tha knows nowt. And woman, mebbee less than nowt. Tha canst desire but tha canna love.'

'I have loved thee, Janey.'

'Not love. Nor niver were. Needed me, tha did. For that tha seemst, beside the likes of me, a great and clever man. Book learning tha hast and I none.'

'Shunghie has no book learning.'

'Now he do. Tha hast seen to that. But me? Tha willna give instruction to me. Be left to Stockwell to teach *me* the writing of me own name. What can us do that canna read nor write? How be it, dost think, I may write to Marsden, tell him what passes here, ask for what I needs to fill the bellies of me bairns? Nay, I must go to the whalers, pleading for a spoken message took on me own account and that of all thy children.'

'Why could not Sannah write for thee?'

'*Sannah* must set down the fear and trembling of her mither? Her mither that canna feed her? That lives in fear of all us being slaughtered like calves afore the butcher? Her that have already lived beyond her years? It be not a matter for bairns to sort nor fret over.'

'But Shungie's family has treated thee and thine as their own.'

At this, she rounded upon me with a look so mad, so crazed, she seemed like one demented. On instinct, I drew back. She laughed, a dreadful sound.

'Oh aye, flinch from me, Husband. Draw back. Let me not sully thy purity of heart. Beholden us be to the charity of savages and Heathen. But all be well. Though us here starve and struggle, me husband, ordained belike, have consorted with His Majesty the King. So what has I to fear?'

And weeping, she broke from me and ran, a wild witch, away towards the tapu burial grounds.

We leave within a seven day. In short, by her obduracy, Jane has forced me to return with her to Botany, abandoning the Maori and my scientific discoveries. She has, with Marsden, arranged already passage for us. How I am betrayed by my own.

Before me, the glittering waves spring to shore, the sunlight riding upon their backs. The po-hutu-kawa trees drip tears of blood to the earth below. The palisades of the pa, the dense tapu bush surrounding the graveyard on the hillside cry out, 'Eh-Keni, do not leave us!'

'I pray to Thee, my God, Whoever Thou mayest be, only to send me a sign. Thou canst not cast me off, banish me for ever from this place. Here is where Thou hast called me: here is where I must remain. Send me a sign if Thou hearest me, if Thou lovest me, I beseech Thee.'

And Jane again at my heels. 'Th'art drunk and raving, Tom Kendall. Dost still hold hope of God saving thee? Even yet? What must be sent? A lightning bolt? Or do it be the sea must cleave apart that us might mebbee walk from here to Botany?'

*

And now upon the shore, at the hour of our departure, she has around her all our children, five dark heads, one Viking-fair, and the infant Laurence a pate of feather down. Scattered beside are all our meagre possessions. In the wooden chest in which first it lay upon this shore is stored *Britannica*. Two trunks, a native kit apiece for the eldest children, and flaxen Samuel clasps a little casting net, a gift from Shunghie's eldest daughter. The Heathen love him dearly for the novelty and originality of his hair, and Turi-Ka-Tuku, for whom he is an especial pet, has, though she has never seen it, a tendril of it plaited into the feathers of her cloak, the colour being a marvel to all the Maori and frequently made comment of by Shunghie.

Who himself does now appear, his sons beside him, atop the brow of the hill.

'Eh-Keni.'

'Eh-Shunghie.'

He strides towards us and I sense Jane's agitation, observe how her face closes and she turns away at his approach.

RICHARD STOCKWELL.

CONVICT TRUSTY.

BORN NORFOLK,

1777.

DIED NORFOLK,

1859.

I hold, clear as dawn light, the vision of the last time that I saw her, the night before they would sail with Marsden for Botany.

I had all but abandoned my pleadings with her to come Home with me. Some stubborn misplaced nobleness in her character held her fast to Kendall and though she had told me already, and a more honest woman never lived, that all intimacy between them had passed since before the birth of Laurence, yet she planned to go with him, with their children, to New South Wales, Marsden to be their shepherd upon the voyage.

And my heart lay heavy in me at thought of what might be in store for her whom I loved so much and would have died to keep from the slights and injuries which surely must accompany their return.

'It will not be easy, Jane.'

'Aye, I knows it.'

'Kendall is daily more obsessed with all his theories.'

'Aye. But if we can leave Shunghie and his brethren set behind us here, belike he may come back to what he were afore.'

'For your sake, I would wish it but I do not think it likely. He is a man possessed. His mind has been taken utterly by these Heathen fancies. And Marsden will never forgive him.'

'At Kiama, us be far from Botany and Marsden.'

'But how will you live?'

'Better than here. Us has the right to claim a grant of land at Ulladulla. And the Governor will supply to Tom a little vessel for trading in supplies along the coast.'

'Tom Kendall a trader?'

'He were afore a draper. And no bad dealer with it neither. And I has give to Marsden me word upon us going. Be me only hope, Dick. All that be left now to me and mine.'

Into my hut before dusk she slipped. And with her a package, large and awkward-shaped, wrapped in layers and layers of linen flax cloth, then tied about with twine. So bulky was the bundle it was all that she might do to balance it in her grasp.

She placed the cumbersome thing carefully in my hands. My heart, so grieving, was touched. 'And what is this?' said I, thinking it a gift for me.

'Nowt for thee,' she said. 'Be for me brother, Sam. And nowt tha needs be knowing about. When tha be Home, wilt tha seek him out and give it him? From me, his sister. Please, Dick. I begs thee, take it. It matters very great tha does this for me. I has no other I might ask and I knows Sam be angry with me still. I wants to make it right with him.'

'But it may be I shall not see Sam these many years. Perhaps never again in all my life.'

'Many years it must be then. Not niver, I prays. Please, but promise tha wilt try.'

'I will, indeed,' said I, secretly cast down because the package was not for me. With all my heart, I wanted something of her. To hold as keepsake, clutch against my loss.

She had understood my longing before I knew of it myself. From within her ragged bodice, she drew another package, long, flat, thin. Handed it to me.

'And this one be for thee. Nay, nay,' as I made to unwrap it. 'Be for later. When that I be gone.'

I drew her to me and kissed her. Held her. Inhaled her own musk smell. Tie up my eyes even now and I would know her by the waft of her if she were come within a mile of me.

I tried for one last time to sway her will. 'Come with me,' I said. 'Be not so stubborn. Yield to me in this and you will never in your life again regret it. We shall live together always. I love you, Jane. You are all I wish for.'

She shook her soft dark hair. 'Seven children has I already,' said she, 'and more to come. For certain more if I lived with thee.' She looked at me directly as she said it. Her eyes gazed black and clear, sharp into my soul. I knew she loved me still.

'Three are almost grown,' I said. 'Four we can keep. And more.'

'Nay,' shaking her head again, 'I has told thee already. Be . . . other things. And I canna leave him now. He have like to lost his soul. And what of me own soul? And thine? If it be not for me and Thomas Surfleet, here Tom mebbee might have stayed. But Shunghie have disappointed him. Refuses to wage a war to put him back into the Mission.'

'He believes that Shunghie would fight on his account?'

'Aye. He does that.'

'But Shunghie would never, never agree to . . .'

'I knows it. Be Tom must be persuaded thus, not I. He thinks if Shunghie did but mount a force against the Kiddi-Kiddi natives, with all them muskets now at his command . . .'

'But those are Shunghie's cousins!'

'Aye. And, inside a week, says Tom, the missionaries newly landed there by Marsden would flee and he then have the Mission for hisself. And be the Reverend there and hold the services.'

'He is raving mad. Shunghie would never agree to such folly. What said he?'

'Mebbee this, mebbee that. He niver says direct to Tom what truly be within his thoughts.'

'He stalls him?'

'Aye. And Marsden have made it plain to Shunghie that if he do support Tom, no more trade be coming to him within the Bay of Islands.'

'A very powerful argument.'

'Aye. And Tom have seen the force of it. He have agreed to sail with all us to Botany.'

'Because he cannot have his Maori friend wage war on his behalf?'

'Aye. And ... because that we has insisted, I and Thomas Surfleet.'

'*You* insisted?' Still I remember how shocked I felt. 'I thought that he—'

'So does they all, them other brother missionaries come now to Kiddi-Kiddi, sent here by Marsden to feed upon his corpse.' She looked her contempt. 'Who wouldna raise a hand to lift him up. Whose tongues strike harder than greenstone clubs. Who hates him, Dick, and canna wait too eager for his downfall.'

'In which he is daily giving them his assistance.'

'Mebbee so, but what be it else I may do? Remain here I, meself? Never will Tom go then to Botany. And what of all me children? What has they here from them other new missionaries but poverty, calumny, whisperings behind their backs?'

'True,' I said. 'Very little.'

'Be worse than little, Dick. Sannah, but five days ago, have come to me, innocent that she be, to tell me Reporo, the son of Shunghie, will make to her a present. "And what be that?" I asks. "Ah," she says, "a lovely baby girl he will give me for my own. Marama will be her name. Daughter of the moon." She have no knowing of his deeper meaning. But she be growing now. And Lizzie too. And all they has here be natives.'

'I am certain Reporo would never harm her.'

'Aye. But she grows very pretty. I has seen often how the native boys regards her as she passes.'

'As I once did her mother.'

'And Shungie hisself have made a plan. He brung it to me, did Tom, raving with the rum but like to thinking still I mebbee might give ear to it.'

'What was the plan?'

'Because Shunghie have the blood-brothership with Tom, he—'

'*Shunghie* has *blood-brothership* with Tom?'

'Upon the voyage here from Home, they mingled both their blood and sware an oath of kinship.'

'Then your husband is more lunatic than I thought. Marsden is right. His mind is turned.'

'Aye, mebbee. But still he be me husband and father of me children.'

'*All?*'

For answer she clung to me a moment, pressed her face an instant to my chest. I felt her breathe deep, then she pulled herself back.

'Shunghie have had a notion that if Tom but married our Sannah with his son, Reporo, then—'

'Kendall cannot be serious in this contemplation!'

'Be thee calls all men equal! Tom have cited thee and thy beliefs in this. If Tom but marry them together, Shunghie will give to us good farming land and great mana. And us then be under his protection always.'

'So Tom will be the Duke of Farthing Gutter, Pisspot Lane,' said I aloud, unthinking.

She drew away. 'What be it you be saying?'

'Forgive me. It was a foolishness.'

'So I have spoke with Thomas Surfleet deep and long. He must be father to his sisters now.'

'He is but ten years old. Come away with me and I shall be their father. And this I solemnly swear to you.'

'Nothing I wishes for more than that. But it be too late for me. I canna niver now return to Lincoln. I canna be now an Englishwoman niver. I has been too long here.'

'This is not so.'

'Oh aye, it be so. If tha hadst asked me same when Tom be at first to Parramatta, mebbee then me answer had been different. But now, I canna be as wife to thee.'

I put my arms about her. 'Be not so unyielding, I beg you. Come Home.'

'Listen to me well. Shunghie willna fight with Marsden, seeing all his trade depends upon it, but he would lay siege to any ship that tries to leave with thee and I and all me bairns.'

'Not so.'

'Oh, aye. Utu he would have for Tom. And great would be his joy to wage a war with all his musket force. And claim it be but to steal back from the vessel the wife of his blood-brother. Thinks tha I hasna thought on it? And would I see thy head upon a native pike, severed from thy shoulders, smoked and laid within a chest, on me own account? Nay, Dick, we has no choice.'

'We can go on separate passages to Botany and from thence together to England.'

'Guns has I sold. Muskets. And if Marsden be to turn against me, in Botany for that I mebbee charged and tried. Nay. We canna be together, Dick. And there be an end to it.'

Tears fell copiously now upon her cheeks, proof if ever I had needed it. And I saw, so plainly, that her mind was firmly fixed upon her course.

'You see,' she said, 'how it do be with me.'

'I do,' said I, holding her the tighter.

'Nay, not here,' she said. 'Too easy for other folk to see.'

'You cannot leave me yet. Lie with me one last time. The natives are at the shore with the ship's company. We shall not be discovered. Just once more, Jane, I beg you. To say farewell.'

'Oh, aye,' she said. 'Be what I come for, Dick, when all be said and done. To say farewell.'

*

294

And the afternoon following, they embarked on the *Brampton*.

I stood in the rain upon the brow of the hill beside the pa and watched as they were paddled through the heaving waves to the vessel and handed aboard. The sails were set, the ship turned, caught the wind and raced for the open sea.

For the third time in my life, I had found her, then lost her again. I could scarce contain the heavy pain that lay upon my heart.

THOMAS KENDALL.

BORN NORTH THORESBY,

LINCOLNSHIRE,

1778.

DIED NEW SOUTH WALES,

1837.

A sign I prayed for from my true god. And a sign has been vouchsafed me. My god it was that drove the *Brampton* on to the bar, sank it below the waves, placed Shunghie and his people beside us in their canoes so that all have been saved. My heart is swollen in my breast with joy. It soars like a bird. My god has not forsaken me.

Tanga-Roa is his name and he has told me, 'Eh-Keni, stay.'

RICHARD STOCKWELL.

CONVICT TRUSTY.

BORN NORFOLK,
1777.
DIED NORFOLK,
1859.

My heart has been restored to me. In fewer than seven hours, Jane has returned. And all from the *Brampton* with her. Close-packed, contained in the canoes that accompanied them out across the Bay. Rowed by the natives who plucked them all from the waves into which they were hurled when the *Brampton* crashed against a hidden reef and sank in the space of forty minutes.

In Shunghie's own canoe sat Jane and Kendall and the children. And Reverend Marsden, his face aflame with rage. As he set his foot upon the shingly sand, he swallowed back his fury.

'The Lord is wise and kind and does not err, nor does he afflict willingly,' said he as I assisted him from the canoe. 'Yet this is a very dark dispensation. I feel an inclination to murmur and complain.'

'It is the Lord's will, Parson,' said I, secretly rejoicing in his discomfiture.

'No ship was ever lost in the Bay of Islands before. It is most mysterious. The harbours are so commodious and fine.'

'It was the shoal that wrecked us,' rejoined the captain tetchily.

'Then this is the first ship of which I ever heard wrecked upon that shoal.'

'I hope you do not impute to me, Parson, deficiencies of navigation. It was clear to myself and all my officers that sand bar took my vessel, and my navigator also, by surprise and stealth. It is not charted on our Admiralty maps.'

'It was the Divine Will she should be wrecked, for reasons which man cannot explain,' said Marsden, meagrely containing his fury at the actions of the deity. 'And though I may be detained for many days by reason of this stroke of fate, I cannot but accept my Maker's burden. Therefore, Thy Will be done, O Lord!'

But as the captain later held it, warmed and loosened of his tongue by grog, God's vicar had railed against his Creator with a mighty peevishness.

And Shunghie lost no time in claiming that the sea god, Tanga-Roa, had thrown up beneath the ship the bar of wrecking sand. It was the will of the Maori gods, he said, that Thomas Kendall never should desert his adopted land and brothers.

Not a man among them was lost. The captain held as a miracle the escape from Death of him and all his crew. None knew how to swim, as is the way with sailors in our navy, but all were saved because the natives who, according to their custom, had gone out in canoes to bid the Kendalls farewell, were at hand to effect their rescue as the ship went down. Shunghie, himself, lifted from the sea Tom Kendall and his family. And after, took them back to a dwelling made for them at Te Puna, promising to keep them under his protection and his cousin's, and to supply them with their food and all necessities.

My heart was sore for Jane and her predicament. But Shunghie was as pleased as Mr Punch. At the very moment when, to make the Kendalls greatest honour, all in his tribe were cutting at themselves with shells and flints – so that I, seduced and affected by their wailing, was weeping, too, upon the shore – his gods had sent a sign.

And Marsden and the Kendalls were returned upon the land of Ao-Tea-Roa.

Even I held deep within me some faint belief my desperate prayers had not gone all unheeded. That Jane had been returned to me by the workings of some well-disposed and gracious Divinity.

THOMAS KENDALL.

BORN NORTH THORESBY,

LINCOLNSHIRE,

1778.

DIED NEW SOUTH WALES,

1837.

'Stay if tha wishes, Tom Kendall,' she said, so quiet I could scarcely hear it, 'but within the month, with all us bairns, I leaves this place for iver. Whither tha comes or nay. And that be my final word to thee if tha stays in this Heathen Hell.'

And turned. And walked away.

'And Modder,' said Shunghie, 'will surely go. She has her whole heart in her words.'

Every moment of our final departure is engraved upon the stone that is my heart.

The skies opened as we were handed aboard the *Adventurer*. Sheets of battering rain lashed and tore at the vessel's sails.

Barely could we stand for the ferocity of its descent. The very heavens were weeping and lamenting our departure.

'I shall return . . . I shall return . . .' I cried aloud.

Shunghie shook his head so that his topknot swayed and the feathers adorning it dipped and fluttered. 'Eh-Keni. My hoa.'

Through blinding tears, I watched as he raised his shark's tooth and sliced its razor edge across his chest, so that red blood spurted over his old scars and weals. He too began to weep, louder and louder, until, throwing back his head, he let out a wail of such anguish I seized his parting gift, a shark's tooth ornament, sliced through my own jerkin and shirt and tore my flesh asunder in an excess of grief, wailing with him the while.

'Mr Kendall,' said Marsden, pulling roughly at my arm. 'Come below. You forget yourself. You are worse than a Heathen.'

I shook him away savagely. 'Yes, I am worse than they. I have not even the courage to cleave to my gods. I am a man entirely without Faith. And I am lost. Utterly lost.'

RICHARD STOCKWELL.

SMALLHOLDER.

BORN NORFOLK,
1777.
DIED NORFOLK,
1859.

Not a day has passed since I sailed from New Zealand that I have not thought of her, dreamed of her.

And I could not write to her nor she to me without another having the reading and the intelligence of it. So. Nothing.

It was from her brother, Sam, I next heard news of her. I knew already they had gone to New South Wales, to Kiama, a hundred miles north-east of Botany Bay where they had been granted land at Ulladulla on the coast.

Sam gave me the intelligence of something else too. I saw the tears well up into his eyes. 'Summat I must tell thee.'

And I fought shy of knowing what I most feared he might say. That Jane was dead. The hidden dream to which I hold so fast, that somehow I shall find her once again, shattered for ever. But it was a different blow he struck.

Little Lizzie had died two years after they left New Zealand. Fourteen years old.

'Were Captain Florance of the *St Patrick* told us when he were put in at Grimsby. Nearly killed our Jane, so he said. And tha'll be sad an' all, seeing as how tha knew little lass.'

I felt it like a mortal wound.

'Indeed I am sad,' I said when I had recovered myself.

I thought of Lizzie skipping along the shore at Rangi-Houa, laughing as she splashed Jane and Sannah with the boulder she had flung. Lizzie upon the deck with me on that first weary journey from Botany, her face alight at the sight of her mother again. Lizzie solemnly enjoining us to beware of Te Imu-Rangi and his power, clucking at Joseph and Samuel, sitting nestled in her mother's lap, sucking at her thumb. Lizzie with her merry hazel eyes, her childish chatter.

My heart burnt with pain for Jane who must live forever with the shadow of this lost child lying upon her heart. And I knew well how she would reproach herself, torment herself with the possibility that, had she but consented to come back with me, Lizzie might yet be living.

And, at this thought, my own heart was torn again with grief. And I asked myself once more why she had elected to stay behind with Kendall. Why she had not seized for herself, for all of us, the happiness which could so easily have been ours.

From here, where I sit at my casement, watching below me the bustle and the business of the street, a Norwich scene that for so long in my life I never thought to have again before my eyes, all that passed on those Antipodean shores seems no more than the madness and dislocation of a dream, out of time and place, that, if it ever truly were, passed only in the pages of a book, another man's phantasy. Not within the compass of my own life.

All men are not brothers nor ever will be. Nor equal either. And verity compels me say so. And yet, if no man tries to change the world about him for better and the common good, what value may we set upon life itself?

If I had never seen her walk upon Steep Hill, if she and I had never done the things we did, would our lives have fallen out so very differently? Would some other Richard have played my part upon that foreign shore?

It may be the native tapu touched us too. We lived on their land: justice dictates we should have been subject to the vagaries of their gods. Utu, they called it. The same thing we read of in the Scriptures. An eye for an eye.

And I remember still Sam's face as he told me Lizzie had died. The lines etched deep on either side of his mouth put me in mind of the Maori face carving. But no tears flowed and fell upon his cheeks, he merely sighed. 'The Lord giveth,' he said, 'and the Lord hath taken away.'

I recall how, as the *Brampton* turned her stern upon us and set her course to Botany, I drew from my shirt Jane's gift. It was all of her I then believed remained to me. And when I took out from the cloth what was inside, it was hard for me not to weep.

A pair of slippers lay before me, such as English ladies work for their lords, the uppers soft-coloured, patterned, finely wrought by her own hands in wools, and the soles of leather. An item of such delicious luxury, such fineness and such subtlety, my heart rose up, civilized again, within my breast.

She must have had one of the native women stitch the tops and soles together in their linen thread. Beautiful, they were. And are. I have them still, unused, upon my night chest, a memento of her love for me, of delicacy that yet holds fast below the coarse and brutal layers of inhumanity.

And beneath the slippers, wrapt in a light, thin cloth, lay a sheet of paper. Like a letter but thicker. And on it had been drawn the likenesses of herself and the child, Samuel, and Kendall's infant, Laurence, born just before he left for England. And I dwelt again in that far happy time when she and I were together at Rangi-Houa.

Laurence is but a suckling babe and she holds him in her

arms, head to her breast, but Samuel, my young Samuel, has his arm about his mother's neck and looks out from the page, smiling at me and his mother together. It is a likeness so remarkable it can be the work only of a true artist.

And gazing at it, I recalled how she had found for Mr Nicholas, who came on the *Dromedary* while Kendall was away, two fine hogs and a kit of kumara. And I remembered how I had railed at her folly in parting with food that was so scarce. And how she had merely turned her head from me.

It was payment for this likeness, now I saw it plainly. So she must have had it in her thinking, even then, that they would leave New Zealand after Tom Kendall's return.

After the sinking of the *Brampton*, Shunghie would not have them remain at Rangi-Houa. It was clear to him he could not afford to offend Marsden and jeopardize his trade. He moved them further down the coast, under the protection of his kinsman Po-Ma-Re.

So we never met alone again. Too many curious eyes were watching wherever we might go. I felt it more of an agony to have her there, almost within my reach, yet never to be with her, than to have her gone far away.

Many and many a night I woke and lay in my hut, willing myself be still, commanding myself I would not rise and leave my bed and go to her.

Within a two month came the *Dolphin* again to the Bay of Islands and Captain Fergusson renewed his offer of a passage home to Tilbury.

And so, it fell out, it was I left her behind me.

The afternoon before we sailed, aboard the vessel came a native, Hi-Ne-Moa, carrying a message written by Susannah at the dictation of her mother. A simple note, it wished me well, a long and happy life to come and begged me not forget to carry her fondest greetings, and the package, to her brother. And though it was Susannah who had penned the most part of the letter, the signature, in a hand hesitant but clearly formed, was Jane's own. I have it still, that note, and, when I unfold it and regard it, there rise before me visions of those times that she, with quill or charcoal, sat beside me, patiently learning her letters.

I sent her back, by Hi-Ne-Moa, my thanks, my warmest wishes and my gold fob watch, purchased for my skinning knife from Te Panau who, in turn, had had it of a sailor for a chunk of greenstone.

And with it went also my assurances that, were it within my power and God's will, I should fulfil my duty as she had charged me.

Nearly four years passed before I came to Sam. I carried that bulky lump halfway round the world and more, and, every time I thought to dispose of it, love for her held me back from the doing of it.

And when, finally, I brought it Home, to Norwich, and set my face to Lincoln, where I lodged at the Coach and Horses, and by skilful quizzing found Sam Quickfall had risen to bailiff now upon Lord Pelham's Brocklesby estate, I sent him word by a messenger to ask if I might come to meet with him. And he replied, by virtue of the tutor, that I should come and speak with him a three day hence and greatly honoured would he be to receive me in his cottage. And though I, being a gentleman, might find his dwelling rude and ill-equipped, yet would his hospitality be warm.

At this, I could not but feel the irony of my situation, that I, who had been shackled to my fellow man aboard a transport ship, be counselled that I might deem poor and mean a dwelling so superior in all respects to these it must be ranked a palace.

I travelled more than half my journey upon the Grimsby coach and there, to meet the stage, waited a horse and cart that transported me to Brocklesby, of which I already knew so much it seemed to me familiar at my approach, the huntsman's house as known to me as Master Abbott's works, the meadows and the kennels acquainted to my view. And Sam, his black eyes smouldering animated, stood by to hand me down himself and set me before his bachelor table where lay placed a supper of most acceptable proportions.

The present, my mandate, I had still in the cloth in which she had wrapt it. A flax mat, very fine and skilful in the weaving, precious for the fact her hands had touched and held it.

It was certain to me that Sam knew things had not gone well for her, but, as he did not quiz or speak, nor did I either.

'Tha writ to us of Isaac,' he said. 'Be kind of thee. But from me sister, niver no word. Nowt of he nor his grave at Botany, neither.'

'Hard,' said I, 'to find a man in all that heaving swamp.'

'Us be counting on her,' said Sam. 'Killed me Uncle Silas it did. Year after year and nowt from Isaac, nowt from Jane. Tom be made a Reverend, tha knows. Ordained. Musta been able then to find our Isaac.'

'It's a vast country, Sam,' said I. 'Nothing like here.'

'Died of grief, did Uncle Silas,' said Sam.

How might I explain to Sam the impossible things. Isaac, it is true, was hanged, and this I cannot tell him. But even suppose he had lived, a man flogged and beaten, humiliated before his own kind, has but little desire to return to those who sent him there.

From Home, each thing smells different. Right seems wrong; wrong, right. I know well why so many transports who survived never would return.

'Nowt of sense from our Jane,' said Sam. 'No news, niver. Nowt. Mither dies and she dinna send no message. Same for Hannah and Father.'

'It may be,' I suggested, 'she does not know how to say what it is she feels.'

'Nay,' said Sam. 'Be more than that. What, I canna know, but summat. I feels it in me bones.'

'But I have seen her. And I tell you nothing is wrong, I swear it. Just a different life, that's all. Her love she sent you. She longs, indeed, for Home. But how may she return with all her children and everything that she must do? God's work she is about now, Sam.'

'Man's, more like,' said Sam, grim and set.

I felt a shiver of worry. 'Look,' I said, conscious of my own clumsiness, how wrong I was with the timing of it. I held out the package. 'I have a gift for you. A present. Something particular of which she charged me with the deliverance. This she gave to me herself, begging me be sure it reached you by my own hands. Four years and more I have held this close and now I am come to discharge my duty and deliver it to you. Here.'

He took it reluctantly. 'Not a gift I be needing. News, more like.'

'But this is her way of giving you news,' said I. 'Take it. Open it.'

'What be inside?'

'I do not know. Unwrap it, man. The cloth about it, I may tell you, is of a very fine quality.'

Sam put the package upon the table. Sighed. Fingered the flaxen cloth.

'The natives make it from a plant,' said I. 'And it is much sought after by all the captains of the vessels which lay anchor at the North New Zealand coast. For this she will have bartered hard.'

Despite himself, I saw that he was pleased. But, 'More like some old piece she have a-lying about,' he said ungraciously.

'Listen,' I cried, in hot anger, 'and listen well, you daft booby. She has nothing lying about. *Nothing*. Keeping her children fed is hard enough for her.

'This cloth is precious. For this, I tell you, she could have had food for her family for six weeks and more. For *you* she bartered this and whatever may be inside it.'

He put his hand up to his head. 'Me,' he said. 'A temper like always. I dinna know what took I.'

I shook him by the shoulder. 'Come now, lay your anger by. Unwrap your gift.'

'I be sorry for speaking so,' he said. 'Be but because of all them ... Mither, Hannah, Father, Isaac, Silas ... Too much sometime it do seem.'

He unwound the linen cloth gently. Well-wrapt, it had been,

in several folds and layers, and, when they had been stripped away, inside there lay revealed a large flax kit tightly tied and bound with strands of rough-spun flax. Palm leaves covered the top and whatever object lay within. So strong was the flax, Sam's fingers could not snap nor stretch it. Fetching his knife he hacked the strands asunder, pulled apart the lips of the kit and lifted out the leaves.

'Wrapt it fine and good, she have.'

'Indeed she has. And those leaves there they call the nikau palm. The natives build and thatch their houses with it.'

'They has the craft of thatching?'

'Certainly,' said I. 'It is not so far from us as you may think.'

Which may have been an untruth but took his mind aside from his grievance towards her.

'Ah, now,' he cried. 'Nearly at it.'

Locks of long black weed shewed visible to us both.

Of a sudden, I felt my heart lurch. No, no. She could not have. She would not have.

'Seaweed, it looks,' said Sam. 'Or more of them native plants, belike.' He lifted the weed, pulled. Screamed and staggered back.

Out from the kit, crown downside to the table, upturned towards us, eyes closed and sewn in perfect sleep, lips barely parted, came a full-size tattooed Maori head. A chief's head. With full moko.

And I knew him.

I had bartered kumara from him, sat on the River Kiddi-Kiddi shore with him on a fine February evening watching the sun go down.

Te Maraunga. Sworn enemy of Shunghie who had murdered him in battle, eaten one missing eye and destroyed the other, I had no doubt, then smoked and preserved his head and served upon him the ultimate terrible fate: he had bartered him to Jane to send him on a voyage to the country of the missionaries, dividing him from his ancestors for ever, banishing him far from his tribe, who could never now recover his head and revere it.

'God Our Saviour,' whispered Sam. 'Be me sister mad?'

Te Maraunga! I staggered out of the doorway and lost my stomach in the yard. I had seen such trophies many times before. And worse and bloodier far than that. Mouths grimacing open, staring eye sockets, stuck on poles after battles, being sold for powder from the canoes, used as kicking balls, going forth on a spear to offer as a truce.

A truce!

I wiped my lips and went back in. Sam stood staring at the head like a man in a nightmare. 'I dinna believe it. Our Jane. To do to me summat so.'

'Listen,' I said, placing a hand upon his shoulder. A vision of her face rose for a moment before me. 'She is too far off from Lincolnshire. That is all. And you are not far enough away.'

He gazed at me, shocked, uncomprehending.

'If you had been where she and I have been, Sam, you would see at once the value of this thing. Captains of ships, Governor's men, traders, men of fashion on their voyages, all of them, all, fight for the chance of a trophy like this one. I have seen men give up gold watch chains and silver-chased muskets for plenty less well carved than this. Take it to London, Sam, and you may command any price you wish for such an object.'

I saw he was softening.

'You must send word to her, Sam, and tell her ... tell her ... what a fine remarkable thing she's sent you. How splendid a gift it is. Come, Sam, truce. This is her way of speaking to you. Call off your anger to her. By this she meant only to please you and enrich you. Have the Reverend write for you. Make your peace with her. Come. Give me your word on it.'

'Well, then,' he said, reluctant.

'I urge you now. Stop punishing her, man.'

He considered. Scrutinized the head again. Sighed. 'Be valuable, tha says?'

'It is indeed. Far more so than you may suppose. Come, Sam, put your anger by.'

He sighed. 'Suppose I might then, mebbee.'

Which in Lincolnshire stands for aye.

JANE KENDALL.

WIDOW.

BORN BROCKLESBY,

LINCOLNSHIRE,

1784.

DIED NEW SOUTH WALES,

1866.

It do seem to me now, old as I be, mebbee it be not me own life I remembers but some other Jane's. Some stranger from a dream, half-knowed, half-seen, that do float away wheniver I comes nearer. Hangs on the edges of remembrance but niver can come out into the light. I looks at meself in the glass in me room, the cruel Kiama sun cutting in behind me. And sees me, meself. But who be I? And who were she?

All that show in the glass be a little old lady, short as the Queen, plain, clad in her best black, hair grey, skin puffed up and down like dough, edges of her neck swollen over her collar like the Reverend Marsden's. Good clean white-lace cap. Rakes of wrinkles to the eyes and mouth.

Where have she gone, that soft wench that come so far, lost

so much, yearned so hard? For God. For love. For nowt. Inside I feels the same. Only the glass and the slowing of me limbs, the shallowness of me breath and the turkey-neck skin tells me different.

I recollects them all but only as they falls away. Sam, Isaac, Dick and Tom. Were that I so filled with lust and heat for two of them? And three of them for me? Me body still remembers. Sometimes gives a shudder like a hanged man, jerking whether he will or nay. The bum-fidgets, me mither called it.

I be still dreaming when Thomas Surfleet's little Lizzie calls me to me dinner.

In this bare and bitter country will Thomas Surfleet bury me. By Baby John, him that I loved least of all me bairns. And by Lizzie, me lost little Lizzie. Her that be allus laughing, chattering, so full of noise and life that when she were carried home to me, white and still, I couldna account it owt but an effigy they had brung. And days and days I waited for her dancing step upon the wide verandah, her shrill scolding of her brothers to sound again beside me. Where might mebbee such a lively joyful thing be vanished to in so little a space?

Me Sannah be married and gone. And me boys scattered. Joseph and Basil a-farming beyond Parramatta, Laurence to sit on a tall stool in the offices of the Crown Surveyor. Me flaxen Samuel travelling all the world, a captain in the navy.

All but Thomas Surfleet, who have carried home hisself the spars from off his father's vessel, sunk almost a thirty year since along this eastern coast. Tom's body niver found, the blackfellows plucking at the cargo from the wreck and making off with all that they might plunder. Laid the spars here, did Thomas Surfleet, in the orchard, all that stands now to touch me memories of that far land called Home.

Planted them apple trees, too. All and ivery one. Brung out on Captain Scribner's vessel, the *Mary Ann*. Ocean voyage done for them same as for the transports. Only them that was hardy be set down here in New South Wales. Transplanted same as I, they flowers and fruits in a strange new land. But does their roots cry out in the soil and burrow through this harsh, foreign earth searching, stretching, back towards the place from which they come?

I didna think to see another spring, yet here I stands under canopies of white, a bride, no longer old, blossom waterfalling over me in a shroud. It mebbee this be Death. This, not the blackness of the night nor the dark depths of the sea. The sea that God have parted for them Israelites. That Jesus have walked upon. The kingdom of Tanga-Roa, its gate the bleeding tree at Te Re-Inga, from where the spirits of them Maori dead leaps down upon the last voyage they might mebbee iver make.

All the creases, folds, the sags and jowls of me old, old skin, the hummocks of fat that swings on me thighs like me mither's old porker that she had nine years in the yard, all fallen off from me in a moment. The sky, white blossom-feathers, closes slowly about me head like to angels' wings folded about me, a-holding me tight within. And all me sins is washed and whitened away, bleached back to the bones, me clean dry bones.

Painted their bones with red earth after death, they did, them natives at Rangi-Houa. Left them in secret, tapu, till months after, then brung them back and laid them in sacred ground. Or mebbee, if they was enemies' bones, carved them into fish-hooks full of witchcraft.

She told me, Turi-Ka-Tuku, Mrs Shunghie, the blind one, that her own father were slaughtered and his bones turned into fish-hooks so. And for that insult, Shunghie vowed revenge and slew with his muskets more than a hundred men to lay her father's soul to rest in peace.

A lake of blood, there were, she said. But, at last, there comes from out a hut the nephew of one of them murdered, holding her father's head upon a long stick, to sue for peace. And this be ten years after that he were slain.

I feels a tweak of pity to me heart for her when I hears it. Her, that of all them, was the only one that iver looked direct at me.

*

313

Still sleeping on her own, far from them others on the shore, she were, when she told that tale to me. Waiting for her husband to come back with Tom from England, alone, same as I. But in the day she walked about like usual, to the kumara fields, the pa, always a-feeling with her feet, like she saw with them. And clear, too. In all us time in Ao-Tea-Roa, I niver seen her once to stumble.

She have beckoned me to follow her to the pa that day. To go into her hut. Small, theirs were. Same as all the others, not one better for him that was the chief. Liked this, did Dick.

'Tom Paine would be for that. Equality. The same for all.'

'Frenchie, be he?'

'American in thought. English by birth.'

'The natives be not equal all in other things.'

'Ah, I know. I have seen. But in this idea of property they are more advanced than any of us Pakeha.'

'Slaves, they has, and that be not equal.'

'We have slaves in England too. Men tied to their masters at the mills, in the fields.'

Sees him so clear, I does, yet. Furrows between his eyebrows, pale English white within the plough-lines, though the rest of his face be sun-browned to the colour of the Maori. His lion mane so fair it be near to white. And blue eyes blinking like birds' eyes when he were thinking deep upon an idea. Which were always. Or so it did seem. And a way to look at me that were so full of feeling for me, meself, times I couldna look back at him. And times I couldna look away.

If the ship by which he were carried to stay again with me at Rangi-Houa when Tom were gone Home did have put out from Botany two weeks afore ... If it have not been held by storms outside the Bay of Islands ... Niver would I of sunk to what I did, niver would it be I iver must bid farewell to him I loved so dear.

Home with him and me children, to live, us all, in Norwich where he have a house. So did he offer me. Money he have had enough for all us passage Home. Pardoned and a free man he were by then.

'Half my life have I been from Norwich,' says he. 'And now return. Come with me, Jane.'

But how do I who has forgot meself and now be as the Heathen, who has seen and done what niver can be washed away, how does I go Home? How be it I might mebbee live there now? I have ate of the Tree of Knowledge and canna be what I were afore.

'That Jane tha loves be gone,' I says.

'Nay.' Shakes his mane.

'Lost, she be.'

'She can be found.'

'Niver.'

'Listen to me, Jane. Tom Kendall will never take you Home. He is possessed by this place. Bound by his friendship with Shunghie.'

'Belike, when he be Home, he will bring Shunghie to God. He have told me.'

'You believe this?'

I shakes me head.

'If there is to be a convert on their voyage, it will be your husband, never Shunghie. In all my life I have known of but two men of fine intellect and great oratory who see the future and embrace it. Clever, both. And cunning. Tom Paine is one.'

'The other?'

'Shunghie. A man more intelligent and warlike does not live. Had he but led the French at Waterloo, they had been the victors, not we.'

'He canna be a warrior in England.'

'Nay. Strategy is his weapon there. And your husband is but his puppet.'

'Tha wrongs Shunghie. He have a true friendship with Tom.'

'I do not doubt it. But if the day dawns when he must make a choice between his own people and Thomas Kendall, it is his own he will choose.'

'Nowt more than any other.'

'There is no other like him. He has seen what lies ahead. Power he knows. And power lies in our English muskets.

With these he will reign supreme. Let Kendall stay with him at Rangi-Houa. Come with me, Jane. To Norwich. Lincoln, if you want. Anywhere you desire. In three months, I am a free man again.'

'I canna.'

He do draw back of a sudden. 'It is because I have been a transport. You are shamed by your association with me.'

And it comes to me now, sudden, clear, like it were but yesterday, that day that Tom were gone with Shunghie, the ship at last vanished utterly from sight of us that waved it farewell. And I feels again the terror and sinking of me heart as I looks around me and sees, to the other side of the bay, the alien pa, natives here, natives there, and no one other that be like to me.

And it comes to me mebbee Tom will niver return. And what do become of all us then? How may I shift for me own? How return all us Home? And to where? Seven children has I and no husband, he being gone to England on God and Mr Marsden's business. Nowt to put in me children's bellies but what Marsden takes it to his mind to send. No sail showing nowhere to the horizon. No way to send for nowt neither. And it be, at the least, a sixteen-day sail from here to Botany.

And at another week's end, of Marsden's vessel there be still no sign.

Marsden, that holy parson, that have niver lost a moment's sleep upon his pillow on account of us that must languish, starving and friendless, in this alien place of Heathen.

And I knowed right well, though niver has I said it to a living soul, not even Dick, that these Maori be not the simple Heathen Tom and I, and Mr Wood and them of the Church so far away in London, has spoke. These be proud and arrogant men. And niver will be brought to the love of us God. Being that they has gods of their own they loves already.

'Mither,' says Sannah, breaking in upon me thought, 'Joseph have the seat from his breeches and I have nowt with which to patch nor darn them.'

'Hush, missie. It be of no matter.'

'But he has but these breeches and no other. Basil's are worn too great to put upon Joseph.'

'I am hungry, Mother,' Basil whines.

And Joseph also. All us now be eating only fern-root and pippis, the little native shellfish, like to cockles. Fifty or sixty it will take to fill up me meself and a dozen only has I for all us.

Potato crop of English seed from Parramatta have failed again. Only them feeble poisonous green shoots remains and us with nowt to plant. Word has I sent now by three whalers to Reverend Marsden, who have not come and who, I sees plain, cares not whither us lives or dies.

And I sees again, though it be all them many years so long ago now, Thomas Surfleet appear by the entrance to our hut, wherein I be resting from the heat and pondering about and about within me mind what it be I might mebbee do to ease things with us.

'Reporo's modder gave me kumara.'

Unbidden, a little drool forms at me mouth.

'Roast in the fire. She will not go from the shore at night until Shunghie returns with Father.'

'Aye, I knows it.'

'Huia is feeding her with a long stick. Reporo told me she is tapu until Shunghie returns.'

'Reporo be tapu also?'

'No. He is not a man. He has not yet his moko. Nor have I.'

'Lincolnshire lads has no need of tattooing like savages.'

'But I am not a Lincolnshire lad, Mother. When I am a man, I shall be blood-brother to Reporo.'

'Tha talk'st the greatest nonsense.'

'No, indeed, I do not. Look, I have carved a fish-hook out of bone like the one Shunghie gave to Father.'

I snatches it rough from his hand. 'Give that here. Who shewed thee how to carve it? Whence came the bone for it?'

He stares at me, confounded. 'Reporo gave me the bone. From the great fish his brother caught. Do not put it away so in your pocket, Mother. It is magic. With that, I shall be like Maui and catch us all a great fish to fill our bellies.'

I looks at him, troubled. 'Then needs tha catch it soon, Thomas Surfleet. Me head be weak with hunger and the sun.'

'Reporo's mother bid me tell you go to her upon the sands as soon as you may.'

'When said she that?'

'As I came from her. It was for that she sent me. I am sorry, Mother, I had forgot.'

I sighs. He be but ten year old.

'Bring with you your kit, she says.'

Me heart do rise a little with hope, but only a little. Many weeks has we struggled with the fern-roots and the pippis, and no help from Shunghie's wife. Nor any other, neither.

And still I sees no sign of Marsden's ship. And nowt of any food has I now. Flour sacks empty, crocks bare, even the fern-roots be gone. It mebbee the ship might niver come. I sighs and picks up the large kit Ngaio have wove for me. She be gone, too. Back to her own people by night on a whaler. Swum out there and were gone clean away by morning. But for her I wouldna wish it any other wise. This kit she left behind inside the hut: a present, for me, wove by her own hand. Long and wide with strips of flax a-plaited through for handles. I puts it down, takes up a smaller one, a present from Shunghie's daughter to Sannah long ago, who, in return, have give her a scarlet ribbon from the bodice of her frock. Friends them two, always.

'Come then, Thomas Surfleet, tha must talk for me and tell me what she says.'

'She says that Shunghie came to her in a dream two nights ago. And in her dream, he told her he had met with the King of England.'

'A fine dream, indeed. And were your father there also? Consorting with His Majesty?'

'Aye. And Wai-Kato, too. In fine clothes all. And good spirits but that Shunghie had a fever upon his chest.'

I smiles, despite. 'What says she else?'

'The King of England waddles like a pukeko, a swamp hen.'

Down the steep hillside to the sea us goes, I trudging, me head mazy for that I have ate so little, he walking beside. Towards that great and mighty beehive pitched upon the shore that be Shunghie's wife, wrapt against the elements in her flax and feather cloak, blind eyes gazing to the other side of the world, waiting by the sea.

'Tena-ko-e, eh-Ranga-tira.'

'Tena-ko-e, eh-Modder.'

She waves her hand for me to sit upon the shingle, which I does, but careful not to come within her tapu space. Further down the shore do squat her new tohunga, Manu, him that reads the tokens and witchcraft signs of war. Bad luck to catch his eye. I gazes past him to the water.

She speaks to me, rapid-like.

'She says,' says Thomas Surfleet, 'the winds are fair set and all the omens good for their return.'

'Aye.'

'Soon they will depart.'

'Oh, aye.'

'In the night, the great sea god Tanga-Roa whispered to her from the waves. He swore he would bring them safe home. He will calm the waters for their voyage.'

'That be to the good, then.'

'She asks how we be.'

'Tell her . . . say . . . us waits for a vessel from Mr Marsden.'

He tells her in the native tongue. She answers very strong.

'She says Mr Marsden is not a good man.' He looks at me in surprise. 'But that is not true, Mother.'

'Hush, Thomas Surfleet. That be not for you to judge.'

Turi-Ka-Tuku swings her gaze towards me. I has seen milky eyes like so afore, on game poached and brung by Isaac and Sam. The film of death. Shivers, I do. And she knows it.

'She says her cough is bad again.'

319

'It be not good for her to sit so in the damp air.'

'She must. Lest Tanga-Roa take offence against her and her own.'

Turi-Ka-Tuku's chest heaves. She breathes deep but ragged.

'She says we smell hungry.'

'Us be very hungry.'

'She says your tribe does not look after you. But I look after you, Mother.'

'Aye, thou dost. Tell her so.'

At his speaking, she throws back her great ugly head and laughs from her belly.

'She says I have a great heart but I am still a sapling and I do not yet give shade enough for others.'

'Be a kind word she speaks to thee. Thank her.'

'Kia ora, eh-Ranga-tira.'

She answers him.

'She says I speak like a true warrior. And she has a gift for me and my family. Lay the kit upon the shore and she will tell Rerehu and Huia to fill it to the brim with good pork and kumara and they will carry it to us later.'

Hunger have took me. I wishes only that I has carried hence the larger kit.

'Tell the Ranga-tira,' I says, 'us has nowt to give in exchange for her food.'

'It will be a present. She does not want exchange for this. But it may be tomorrow, or the day after, when that food is gone, we will need more.'

'Tell her all that be left to us be three long iron blacksmith's nails.'

'She says those will do for the second kit. But what of the third? And the fourth?'

'Us has nowt to barter.'

'She says you have much.'

'And what be that?'

Again the Maori woman raises her head, seems to see me face. Be like the full moon shining cold upon me.

'Eh-Modder,' she says to me in English, 'eh-Modder. Musket.'

320

'Which Keni have left me to protect us by.'

'Two musket.'

'Aye.'

More native talk she have with Thomas Surfleet.

'She says you do not need two. One is enough.'

'Be forbidden to us to barter muskets with the natives.'

'The lower rank of natives, yes,' translates Thomas Surfleet, rapid-like, 'but she is a princess and the wife of a paramount chief. This is different.'

'Belike Parson Marsden will not think so.'

She spits contempt upon the shingle. 'Eh, Matenga.'

'She does not trust Reverend Marsden. She feels the trees draw back from him when the canoe lands him upon this shore. The shingle whines as he sets his feet upon it. Marsden will steal her land if she is not always awake. She will never tell *him* of this barter.'

'And she will give food to us?'

'She will give us pork such as we have never tasted. Fine, succulent, with crackling and juices. Oh, Mother,' he cries, 'say yes. The little ones are so hungry. And Sannah, too, and Lizzie. Say she may take our musket, Mother. Say.'

Turi-Ka-Tuku speaks again.

'You have muskets but no food. She has food but no muskets to protect herself and her children. This is a good and fair exchange.

'And, while Shunghie is away, when the whaler ships come next to the Bay of Islands, she will give you pig and kumara. Her native oarsmen will paddle you to the whaling vessel, you will trade these with the sailors for their muskets, then she will feed us all.'

From behind us rises the smell of steaming pork, its roasted flesh mingling with the soft, sweet bread-breath of kumara. Turning, I sees Huia with a bulging kit of fresh-cooked food.

'Aye,' says I, 'it be a bargain.'

And it be not till a ten day following that the ship do come from Marsden. And on it be a trusty sent – Dick, me own dear Dick. And all me heart can feel be that if he have but come a two week earlier, upon a favouring wind, it mebbee he had saved me from all me life that have followed.

Me cheeks, me neck, me belly, be stung and rubbed to red by his stubble growth. Wet be seeping out between me thighs, his and me own together. A great ease do wash over me, through me. I thinks to stroke his back, but so soft, like to dough, I feels, I canna find the strength to raise me arm. Me mouth be smiling but nowt to do with me.

Dick have his head and face pressed deep into me neck, which he have bit and sucked so greatly afore, and I feels how he have fallen into a great sleep, body still astride me, but little and wet his dangler nestles now against me thigh, where it have slipped from inside me. The reek of grass and his own seed and us sweat do ooze and drift from him, a smell of kindness, comfort, which wraps about me like to me Gamma's blanket. And so I falls asleep.

And when I wakes, the Southern Cross have risen and I sees through the doorway how it gazes in upon us. Dick have moved to beside me and I feels he be wakeful, though silent.

'It be for goodbye, that one?'

'Yes.'

I puts me hand to him. Hard he be again already, wanting me still. I knowed it as I woke.

He sighs for pleasure as I touches.

'Be a miracle tha can. All that afore and standing like a soldier of the regiment to fire again thy musket.'

He hesitates. 'I would not hurt you for the world, my Jane.'

'Nay, tha shalt not. Lay thy head here. On me breasts.'

There be silence between us. For a great space.

'I am begging you one last time. Jane, I pray you, relent. Come with me. Come Home.'

I shakes me head. 'I canna, Dick.'

'You do not love me enough.'

'Nay, I loves thee too well. I niver now can go to any place from here but Botany. I loves thee more than the world, Dick, but I be not fit for thee.'

'You think, because you are not my equal in Society,

because you are unlettered, I will take you Home and then abandon you. Never will I tire of you. I will not, for my life...'

'It be not that. Tha'rt a man of honour. That tha hast give thy word on, that tha would'st do. I knows it. I trusts thee.'

'Then is it loyalty that holds you back? To *Tom Kendall*? What has he ever done for you but bring you low?'

'Aye, I has been brought low. But that were not by Tom. Be me own doing.'

'Because I am your lover?'

'Nay. Niver. Thy love be all that have kept me from despair. But, Dick, I canna come with thee. And there be an end to it.' I takes his hand and lays it to me heart. 'Tha must believe it.'

And with me other hand I takes him and guides him where he wants to go. And I, too. And careful do he slide into me, so gentle that I winces but a little.

'Too painful for you?'

'Nay, no longer.'

And very slow and quiet do he move in me, until, sudden, I be stirred again by love for him and us be trotting together, like Milady's little mare. Then us be faster, cantering, galloping, racing. Until us leaps together at the great wall and falls both upon the other side.

Ah, niver in all me life has I knowed afore how well I loves it with a man that breathes and moves as I does.

And it takes me all me will that I doesna cry aloud that me thought have changed and I and me children will go Home with him and niver will depart from there again.

But that I loves him more than I loves meself so I catches back me breath, stays silent, until it do come about that he must go from me.

Be Dick that have gone back Home. And I left here, shallow-rooted.

And after I and all me bairns has been a year or more set down from Rangi-Houa in Kiama and has us little house and Tom be trading on the east Australian coast, us hears at last of all that passed with Shunghie. From the captain of the *St*

Patrick, his vessel being laid to port here direct from the Bay of Islands.

I hears it plain still, as if Captain Florance be speaking now afore me, not forty year since. And us set down within the parlour, Tom and the captain with their little glasses full of rum.

It be knowed in all New Zealand, said the captain, how Shunghie with his muskets, them from the king and them he have bought hisself in England and in Botany, have gone upon a reign of terror, like to any Frenchie mob's killing-frenzy, and all the tribes be cowering afore him and his guns, so mighty have he now become.

And greatly pleased I were to be not there no more. Safe from all that madness and destruction.

And Shunghie, so the captain have said, were, but a two month earlier, minded to go on one last great campaign for utu for his brothers. Against the Ngati Wha-Tua of Mo-Re-Mo-Nui, whose chief held to that day his brothers' heads, trophies of war, within his waka-chest in his own hut. And Shunghie being ready for his expedition and the war party like to leaving, to the beach at Rangi-Houa comes Turi-Ka-Tuku.

And, 'No,' she says. 'Enough. The omens are not good. You must not go. Last night, the more-pork, the night owl, flew within our wha-re as we slept upon the beach and there it perched this morning still. The gods say you have killed enough.'

But Shunghie would not heed her. Crazed with power, he were, by then and drunk upon his murdering and killing. Like to thought hisself almighty, and terrified the life from all his foes, appearing afore them in that suit of armour give him by King George when he were Home with Tom. Thought he were a ghost, they did, or evil spirit.

'This,' he tells Turi-Ka-Tuku, 'is my final battle. After this, I will fight no more. Everywhere I have conquered but Mo-Re-Mo-Nui. My honour rests upon this last campaign. Once I have regained my brothers' heads, I swear to you, before my warriors, upon my kingi musket, I will not go to war again.'

'You must not fight,' she says, standing, said the captain,

who have seen it, like to a Christian prophet on the shore at
Rangi-Houa, hand raised toward the heavens, wild blind eyes
rolling in her head.

But Manu, he that were the new tohunga, wishing the glory
of reading the omens in battle, denied her. So Shunghie,
promising he have the tohunga's word upon it he will win his
war, calls farewell to her from his great canoe and sets out.

Three days be all it took for him to rout them enemies with
his muskets, till, said the captain, they be crying out for mercy,
and all his brothers' heads returned in triumph in his war
canoe.

But nowt too much of triumph, neither. Shunghie, it be true,
were safe but Ha-Re-Shunghie, who us has known since
Parramatta, eldest and favourite son of Turi-Ka-Tuku and his
father, have fallen in the battle. Shunghie, seeing his enemy
aim a musket at his son, have flung hisself in front of Ha-Re-
Shunghie, belike that he might save him. But, in ivery battle,
he do wear his armour from the king. And the musket ball,
deflecting off the metal, have come to rest within the bosom
of Ha-Re-Shunghie, where it have lodged, killing him.

And Shunghie's shame and grief be so terrible he wouldna
return upon the Rangi-Houa shore to Turi-Ka-Tuku but
stayed in his canoe beyond the headland. And she have gone
out in a small canoe, alone, and ordered him come back to
her.

And Ha-Re-Shunghie be decaying now, upon a stage, like
all them Maori dead.

And Shunghie were tapu sitting on the shingly sand, away
from all his tribe, far down the shore. And one of his daughters
did sit there, too, and did feed him with a long stick. And he
have swore he niver would again put on his armour. And he
were grieving piteously.

Turi-Ka-Tuku were living in a tapu space farther off still
upon the selfsame shore and food brought for her, too, to be
give from off a long stick. And she were breathing rough and

coughing blood, like she have took upon herself the wound of
Ha-Re-Shunghie.

Then Shunghie, so the captain told us, took with him his
men and went to Whanga-Roa and on to Hoki-Anga for utu
for Ha-Re-Shunghie. And, as he have not wore his armour, he
were shot there, in that battle. And now he have a hole from
front to back within his chest, through which the daylight
mebbee seen, and a whistling sound do come from it. Like to
the whistle of an atua.

And when that Shunghie be carried home, wounded so,
Turi-Ka-Tuku were already dead for grief of Ha-Re-Shunghie.

And I be sick at heart to think on it.

Kind to me and mine, she were. No more than I, she wanted
only that she had need of. Me heart be full of pity for her
now. I thinks on how, a-passing us hut after us has made us
bargain, she have called me follow her to the pa. And Thomas
Surfleet making like to come, that he might answer for me,
she raises up her hand and stays him where he stands.

'No.' And shakes her head, then speaks with him.

'She wishes you will go alone with her, Mother. I may not
come. You only.'

Climbs us together to the pa and so into her wha-re. She do
amaze me as to how she stoops below the lintel, feels her way
about and niver once do knock herself nor stumble.

'Waka,' she says and points towards a carved chest hanging
from the rafters. It be almost the only thing within the hut
and beautiful with spirals and cuts across the wood made very
fine.

'Ataa-hua. Most worthy,' says I.

She opens the chest and lifts out a feather, glossy black.
'Huia,' she says. I nods. I seen afore them feathers on the
cloaks she wears. And in the hair of Shunghie and Ha-Re-
Shunghie also. Only the chiefs does wear them. So much for
Tom Paine and his equality.

She reaches within again, pulls out a little cloth of linen flax.
Unwraps it, showing powder for a musket.

'Ataa-hua. Most worthy,' she says.

326

She points for me to sit. Goes back to her waka box.

'Te matenga,' she says, most solemn. 'Fadder.'

And she lifts from within the chest the smoked, preserved head of her own father, which she holds like a holy thing gentle between her hands and presses her nose to his.

So quiet were his face, eyes closed, lips together, so peaceful his looks, be hard to believe he were dead. A head only she held, but it be like the whole of him be there. His chief's moko were covering all his face and I seen for the first time how beautiful be the patterns in the carving.

Long sticks of green jade and huia feathers together was poked through them holes in his ears. His hair, white as Samuel's, were twisted into the topknot and a feather stuck in. First time in all me life at Rangi-Houa I looks at one of them savages and be not afraid, sees him how he truly be.

And he be wondrous. Nothing to fear though dead. And nothing of rot nor decay to him neither. He have the face of an angel.

I struggles for words for what I longs to say. Gazes at him a long time. 'Eh-fadder kingi?'

'Kingi. Ranga-tira. Te ariki.'

Again she do press her nose to his, tears running on her cheeks, then lays him back in his holy box, his waka, his little canoe.

And I wishes with all me heart I had me mither's head to speak with and be comfort to me.

'I has no waka,' says I. 'No holy thing of mine for thee.'

She tries to say to me some thing I canna understand. Points to herself, to me, to the little box. But though I strives to take her meaning, I canna know what it be she do wish to tell me.

She stops her speaking, turns her dead eyes full towards me, raises a hand to her own head. Touches her hair. Nowt she says at all now and yet, of a sudden, it be plain to me what she desires.

I leaves her hut, goes back at speed to mine. Takes up a shell, cuts from Samuel's snow-white hair a little tress. And I be sure the hair be not touched by me hand, nor none of it do fall upon the ground. I catches it within a second shell, in which I carries it careful back to Turi-Ka-Tuku, where I lays it at a tapu distance. And next when I sees her she have wove it into the front of her flax and feather cloak.

In Marsden's house at Parramatta, Tom have read me from *Britannica* about them Persians that puts their dead ones out for birds to peck the flesh from off their bones.

'Poor, depraved Heathen,' said he.

I be Heathen too. Like said Reverend Marsden. Cool I saw them bones, like water, when Tom told it to me in the heat of Parramatta, that day so far off, long ago.

And now that I meself be near to Death, I fears that Heathen stain upon me soul. Be there a cross like to the mark of me name, writ in blood? Be me soul now black? Mebbee even Hell be closed to such as I and it be only to the Heaven of the Maori I may go, that Heaven of one-eyed chiefs.

And I recalls it sharp, harsh, like I be living it again – that day at Rangi-Houa on which I told to Tom the thing which marked me out from Christian souls. And me children also, even me little suckling Laurence. Tainted all. Like I be.

Hot, it had got, and hotter. Not heat like that in Botany but hot that stops the breath. Hot that holds back arms and legs from movement. All what I did that day went slow, slower, me limbs heavy through the air like I be fighting me way through water, dragging me legs over sand. In the hut, out of the hut, the same, the world a-winding down slow like the great grandfather clock I seen so often in the big hallway at Brocklesby, the one only Milady herself might wind, so old it were.

And I thinks how us little hut be but a cabinet to fit in Milady's great hall.

And what would me mither say now to Milady? Her being so proud and all of me that had married above me station and be off to London and have a husband going for the Church.

'Our Jane be the fine one. Clergyman's wife, our Jane. Be like our Jane, our Hannah, there's good for ye.'

And if she have seen me here at Rangi-Houa, me mither? Living like to a savage in a dirt hut, me children in rags, no food to their bellies and all us bitter and fighting fierce, and round us only wild men with wild gods, that eats each other and murders, and covers theirselves with mad prick-marked designs?

And Isaac. That me mither loved like to her own. Poor crazed Isaac. Were it the sun, mebbee, turned his mind? Were it I that done it? What if he have niver gone out poaching that night? Niver been taken by the keepers? He and I has been surely wed. And what might me life be then?

Sam no more me cruel enemy. All me life in Brocklesby, safe, hard by me mither's hand. Me and Isaac. And us Sannah.

I remembers still what Tom have said to me upon that day.

'It could be, Jane, we must stay here in Ao-Tea-Roa always.'

'Th'art in jest.'

'No, I do assure you. I have been this morning to Matau-Whi, to Po-Ma-Re.'

'And Tunga-Roa?'

He do not answer.

'Go back to her,' I says. 'Your Heathen jade. That native trollop. Fuck her. Lie in her stink. What cares I? She be but an evil greasy little c——'

And on me lips comes that ugly, most forbidden word. Bit back.

It be but a memory now, how I did look at Tom, hot rage rising in me, hatred burning at me heart.

And Tom, stung by the harshness of me speech, 'It is you, yourself, Jane, who have driven me to this. You have been cold to me. Refused me. Shamed me before Marsden and the Church Missionary Society. My own wife a trader in pigs and muskets.'

I looks at him, a nowt, a faded cur. Throws back me head, laughs at him. 'Traded pig, did I? And where were me husband? Traded muskets, did I? And thee thinks that evil?

How else might mebbee I provide for all thy children? Tell me that then, Thomas Kendall.'

'Consider the lilies of the field, Jane. Only have Faith.'

And 'Faith,' screams I. *'Faith!* In Marsden's God? Or thine?' And in me fury strikes the wall. Bruise on me hand for a three month after.

I flings down lid of useless churn. 'Show me God's butter!' Kicks over empty crock. 'Show me God's salt turnip! God's chitling hanging from the rafters! Where be He then, this God of Faith? One thing only be sure to me, God be not a woman. Not Him that leaves his children starving. Casts them into Darkness. Cares not for His own.'

'Jane,' he orders. 'Hush your mouth. Be silent. These are the words of the Devil.'

'Aye, indeed. The Devil! I knows right well the Devil. A pact I has made with the Devil! Fish the Devil do have. Kumara. And pork. Aye, salty, succulent, cracklinged pork. Be not thee, Tom Kendall, that fills thy children's bellies. Be the Devil.'

Hard by the doorway, Samuel watching me. Yet something in me canna stop me mouth. Like all them years of heat and loneliness be rising up in me and pouring out. Samuel in his breeches of sacking from the flour bag and growing out of them already. And me that were to be wife of a man of God. With me children matted, filthy, in flour sacks and rags. And all around us, Heathen savages, wild men and women with clay-smeared hair, stinking of fish worse than the wives of Grimsby. That clotting rotten smell, warm and bitter-salty, knots of blood on gutted flesh.

And it wafts to me again, that wondrous tang of pork that have floated to us from the pa when Tom were gone with Shunghie. Home to England. Brocklesby. Cambridge. London. Names to fall like honey off the tongue.

And the pig-drift so deep and rich it have made me mouth to drool with spit just to smell it. And I sees her again, blind Turi-Ka-Tuku, feeling her way to me door. And behind her, her two girls. And all them clutching flax kits with nikau leaves over the tops and steam seeping through. And me heart lurches with hope. Food, I prays. Let it be for us.

'Tena ko-e, eh-Modder,' says the girls. But she says nowt. Looks through me, past me, with them milky eyes that doesna see.

I knows she be waiting for me to speak. That being their way.

'Tena ko-e, eh-Ranga-tira,' says I. Polite. And hoping, hoping the pork smell that do fill the hut be truly for us. Not just that they be on a journey to somewhere carrying it.

And one by one slides in all me children, drawn by the scented steam, shy, hanging on the walls. Until little Samuel, hungry, makes bold, sidles up to Turi-Ka-Tuku, plucks at her flax mat. Puts a hand upon her thigh showing through the crossover.

'Nay, Samuel!' I cries. Snatches him to me. For that, one of their own would be killed. 'Please, please, forgive,' I babbles. 'He dinna know right from wrong. Too young. Still a baby.'

Silence. Me heart drops. Then she reaches out a hand, finds his arm, strokes it. Laughs. 'Eh-moko-puna,' she says to Samuel. 'Ma-te-kai? Hungry, eh?'

And now me heart be lurching again, with hope. Food, I were praying. The food she have promised us. And so it were.

And still I remembers the taste of that pork, like to nowt I have ate in all me life since Ao-Tea-Roa. Delicate, it were, the crackling crisp and full, the fat dripping down me chin and the sweet white soft flesh beneath so good in taste it would make me mither's best Lincoln pork to taste like swamp hen.

'Kood kai. Eat, eat,' says Mrs Shunghie. And all us falls upon that meat and devours it with hands and teeth and lips, laughing and weeping for the pleasure of its taste.

'Be meat to die for,' I babbles.

Turi-Ka-Tuku speaks to Thomas Surfleet in her own tongue.

'Slaughtered yesterday, on our account, Mother.'

She comes towards me, squats beside me but keeps her tapu space.

331

'She asks if you will keep your bargain.'

'Tell her I have give me word. When that the next ship comes, she must send for me.'

'When she brings us the next kits of meat and shellfish, you must give her girls the nails, then the first musket. The one you have here.'

'Aye, be a bargain.'

Turi-Ka-Tiku heaves up her great bulk to go with her girls. 'E noho ra, eh-Modder,' she says.

'Haere ra. Goodbye. And thanks to you, eh-Ranga-tira,' cries I as she stoops without seeing to duck below the lintel.

And when she be gone and all us eaten our fill and me children tired and sleepy now, I sees there be pork left still in one kit.

'And I knewed,' says I to Tom, in cold and bitter rage, 'when I looked proper at them pieces of meat, why it be so succulent and soft to chew upon. Flesh cart I seen many and many a time at Brocklesby. Piled with meat for the hounds which Milord doted upon like to his children. And I looks again at Mrs Shunghie's pork. The size of them shanks. The flesh tense and springy upon them bones.

'A child they had killed for us, special.

'Cannibal, be I, thy wife. *And* thy children. And it be thy doing, not mine. Thine and godly Reverend Marsden's who has left us here with the Heathen to fend for usselves alone and cared not whether us lived nor starved.

'Puts me hand into that kit, I did, when that I knewed what be in there, and takes another morsel. Eats. And still the taste falls sweet upon me tongue. No bar to me it were a human soul. And do it again I would, I swears, if it were that or perish.

'Be just as Shunghie have said. I be like to them now. A Heathen.'

'And I be going from this evil place,' says I to Tom, me husband, though what that be worth be but little. 'I and me children with me. All. Us leaves when the *Navigator* puts in at Rangi-Houa. And there be an end to it.

'And Sannah and Lizzie and Thomas Surfleet marries none of them Heathen. With me all me children goes, whither I lives or dies.'

'And how will you provide their passage, Mrs Kendall?'

I looks at him, full of scorn. 'Muskets I has, Mr Kendall. Six, and well concealed from thee. Six muskets buys us passage on any ship which puts in at New Zealand.'

'The ships' companies have no need of muskets.'

'Thinks thee *I* doesna know that? Pig and kumara they has need of. And she that will give them to me have need of muskets.'

'And who is this fine lady?'

'Her that have fed us, succoured us, when that tha were consorting with kings. Her that do give me fine pork to feed me starving children. Her that be wife to thy native brother, Shunghie ... Turi-Ka-Tuku.'

Little of passion has I in the recollection of it now. It be washed away by time. Thinks I only on this orchard canopy, a wave, apple-green and white, dense about me head.

Up, up, it rises, out of an ocean of blossom, curling at its top, and there it do hang, a spiral of swaying water. And I sees, drifting in its green wall, all them I has thought on, one by one. I reaches to them. Puts out me hand into, beyond, that pale green illusion. Me hand slides easy, empty, through the mocking water.

'What be Faith, Dick, dost think?'

'"Faith is the substance of things hoped for, the evidence of things unseen."'

I ponders it a little. 'Tha means tha thinks it be a good thing, Faith?'

'I judge it neither good nor bad. It is a form of sustenance.'

'Tom have Faith. And Marsden.'

'No, theirs is not Faith, it is but opinion. And conceit.'

'Dost have Faith thyself?'

'I lost it once, then regained it. And now I have lost it again.'

'How might I mebbee gain it?'

'Ah, that I do not know. Perhaps we should have Faith only in that which manifests itself to us. That which we see with our own eyes, of which we are certain.'

'But then it be not Faith.'

He laughs. 'That is the problem.'

And sudden, now, I sees that for all of me life it be Death have followed me, hard at me heels, wheriver I might mebbee go. His breath on me own breath, his face by mine. He have stalked me from the northern to the southernmost world. And when he hasna captured me meself he have claimed, as his, me own.

Isaac, Death have. Lizzie. And Baby John. Me mither, me father, Tom and Ha-Re-Shunghie. Death, it were, lay chained by Dick, in irons, upon the transport ship. Death that have foundered the *Brampton* on the reef but have seen us snatched, all, from his jaws by Shunghie and his people.

Death, the owl, the great hound, which Shunghie have thought to have defeated with his musket, have turned the chief's own weapon hard against him, to take again His victory. And I sees it now, too late, all she were trying to say to me that day within her hut. Her, Turi-Ka-Tuku. When that she shewed to me her father's head.

They knows, them Heathen, how it do truly be. They has no need for us Faith. In all their lives they knows that Death must come. That no man, nowhere, cheats him of his prize. That all us must be gone to dust and none has niver come again with nowt to say of that kingdom in the heavens where God and all his angels sings and lies upon the clouds.

For this the Heathen keeps them heads within their wakas. Reveres their dead and gazes long and often on them. And I meself must soon be but as they. Dry bones alone. Since none there be to smoke and keep me head.

It be long that I has been here, in this world. Yet it be but a little space.

The foam do toss and play about me head. Under its curl, I finds meself swaying and lifting, rocking like in the feathers of that great white angel. I that so hates the sea, soothed at the breast of the wave. Swallowed foriver in the vastness of that green-white tide.

Up into the swell floats Baby Kelly in her poor white burial frock. Above her, beaming through the curving water, do shine a star, bright and glittering as frost. And Shunghie be laughing at me from the water wall. One hole to his chest, another to his left eye socket. Beside him, Turi-Ka-Tuku stares at me with eyes that see.

'Eh-Modder,' she cries, 'eh-Modder!'

So far below do go the wave, the sand at its base be hid. And as I gazes on them shadows that swells and tosses within the water, of a sudden they has vanished all. And there do spread afore me now the soft green fields of Brocklesby and I finds I be walking, fixed upon me course, west into the setting sun, along a path both straight and wide. And far ahead there be a tree, a single tree, grey arms hanging, fingertips blossoms of blood. Touching to the ground of Te Re-Inga, the Leaping-Place.

I doesna slow me pace but, rapid-like, I walks across them meadows that I loves, a-glancing neither left nor right, a-staring only at that tree. Where I wishes most to go.

And as I stands beneath its falling boughs I sees how, in the sea beneath, that wide path do shine on plain afore me. And I gathers meself and springs from the great cliff, down to the path, into the water below.

Above, though I canna see it, I knows the wave be bridging. Over me head, me eyes, me limbs. It do rise to its peak, then tumble in on itself, a shell of water, sucking me into its inmost spiral, away to the place of ghosts and spirits, to that tapu realm where the Broad Path of Ta-Ne do lead me.

SELECT BIBLIOGRAPHY

Most of the principal characters in *Tapu* were real people but little is known of many of them. Thomas Kendall has been the subject of a biography by Dr Judith Binney and has left his journal and letters for posterity. Details of the life of Hongi Hika (Shunghie Ika) are recorded in oral and written histories. Almost nothing is known of Richard Stockwell and very little of Jane Kendall. To the best of my knowledge, Turi-Ka-Tuku's history is purely orally recorded. Samuel Marsden's life, however, has been widely studied and his journals and letters are freely available.

Historical events and biographies provided the very loosest of frameworks for this novel, which is a work of the imagination, but I drew information, where possible, from the following books:

Beaglehole, J. C., *The Discovery of New Zealand*, Oxford University Press, 1961
Best, Elsdon, *Some Aspects of Maori Myth and Religion*, Dominion Museum Monograph No. 1, Government Printer, Wellington
—, *Spiritual and Mental Concepts of the Maori*, Dominion Museum Monograph No. 2, Government Printer, Wellington
—, *The Lore of the Whanau Marama*, Dominion Museum Monograph No. 3, Government Printer, Wellington
—, *The Maori Division of Time*, Dominion Museum Monograph No. 4, Government Printer, Wellington
—, *Polynesian Voyagers*, Dominion Museum Monograph No. 5, Government Printer, Wellington

—, *The Maori School of Learning*, Dominion Museum
    Monograph No. 6, Government Printer, Wellington
Binney, Judith, *The Legacy of Guilt*, Oxford University Press,
    1968
Convicts of Lincolnshire, Lincolnshire County Council, 1988
Cruise, R. A., *Journal of a Ten Months' Residence in New
    Zealand*, Longman, Hurst, 1824
Easdale, Nola, *Missionary and Maori*, Te Waihora Press, 1991
Hiroa, Te Rangi (Sir Peter Buck), *The Coming of the Maori*,
    Whitcombe and Tombs, 1966
Howe, Ellic (ed.), *The Compositors' Handbook*, Biographical
    Society, 1947
Howes, Edith, *Maoriland Fairy Tales*, Ward, Lock and Co. Ltd.
Hughes, Robert, *The Fatal Shore: A History of the
    Transportation of Convicts to Australia 1787–1868*, Collins
    Harvill, 1987
Kendall, Thomas, unpublished journal and letters, Hocken
    Library, Dunedin
Lee, Jack, *I Have Named It the Bay of Islands*, Hodder &
    Stoughton, Auckland, 1983
Maning, F. E., *Old New Zealand*, Creighton and Scales, Queen
    Street, New Zealand, 1863.
Markham, Edward, *New Zealand or Recollections of It*,
    Alexander Turnbull Library Monograph, 1963
Murray-Oliver, Anthony, *Augustus Earle in New Zealand*,
    Whitcombe and Tombs, 1968
Myers, Robin (ed.), *The Auto-biography of Luke Hansard*,
    Printing Historical Society, 1991
Nicholas, J. L., *A Narrative of a Voyage to New Zealand,
    1814–1815*, vols 1 and 2, James Black and Son, 1817
Paine, Thomas, *The Rights of Man*, Everyman Edition, J. M.
    Dent
Rutherford, John, *The White Chief*, Whitcombe and Tombs, 1908
Sharp, Andrew (ed.), *Duperry's Visit to New Zealand in 1824*,
    Alexander Turnbull Library, 1971
Shortland, Edward, *Traditions and Superstitions of the New
    Zealanders*, Longman, Brown, 1856
Sinclair, Keith, *A History of New Zealand*, Penguin, 1988
Sissons, J., Wihongi, W., and Hohepa, P., *The Puriri Trees Are
    Laughing: A Political History of Nga Puhi in the Inland
    Bay of Islands*, Polynesian Society, Auckland, 1987

GLOSSARY

aata-hua	very fine, worthy
Ao-Tea-Roa	the Maori name for New Zealand
e noho ra	farewell, goodbye, stay in peace
haere-mai	greeting; *lit.* come this way
hei-tiki	carved greenstone, nephrite jade neck ornament
Hi-Ne	the goddess of the moon
hoa	friend
hongi	Maori greeting by placing noses together
ika	fish
iwi	tribal group
kaha-wai	native flying fish
kai	food
ka-inga	native hut
ka-re-tao	child's jumping jack
kia ora	Maori greeting or thanks; *lit.* good health
Kiwa	Pacific Ocean
kumara	sweet potato
kuri	small native dog
maku	wet
mana	prestige, status
marae	sacred area in front of a meeting-house
ma-te-kai	hungry; *lit.* in want of food
matenga	head
Matenga	Maori transliteration of Marsden
Maui	mythical demi-god ancestor
me-re	war club
moko	facial tattoo

moko-puna	grandchild, descendant
nga-rara	lizard
pa	settlement
Pakeha	white man, European
Papa	Earth Mother (*myth.*)
paua	native shellfish with iridescent inside shell
po-hutu-kawa	native red-blossomed tree which blooms at Christmas
Puanga	Rigel (*astron.*)
pu-hanga to-hora	spume of the whale
pukeko	swamp-hen
ranga-tira	high-born aristocrat
Rangi	Sky Father (*myth.*)
Rongo	the god of crops
rua-hi-ne	old woman
tai-aha	wooden spear
Ta-Ne	the god of forests
Tanga-Roa	the god of oceans
tangata	people
tangata whenua	local people, kinsmen; *lit.* people of the land
tangi	obsequies
tani-wha	mythical saurian river monster
tapu	sacred, set apart, forbidden
te ariki	chiefly leader (Jesus)
tena ko-e	hello (Maori greeting of welcome to one person)
pl. tena kou-rua	hello to you, too (more than one person)
Te Ika-a-Maui	the North Island of New Zealand; *lit.* the Fish of Maui
Te Wai Pounamu	the South Island of New Zealand, also known as the canoe of Maui; *lit.* the greenstone waters
tohunga	priest with powers of divination
Tu	the war god
tu-puna	ancestor
umu	earth oven
ure	penis, descendants
utu	revenge
wa-hi-ne	woman, wife

wai	water
wai-ata	song, usually sung on formal or ceremonial occasions
wai-rua	spirit, essence
waka	canoe
whanau	family group
whenua	the land
wha-re	house

'Tamoneekees' and 'coeteedos' (p. 103) represent Marsden's attempt to express the Maori words 'tamariki' (children) and 'kotiro' (girls).